Highly Satisfactory

Steve Schach

Wandering in the Words Press

Requests for permission should be sent to Wandering in the Words
Press: 2131 Burns St, Nashville, Tennessee, 37216
www.wanderinginthewordspress.com

PUBLISHED BY WANDERING IN THE WORDS PRESS

ISBN-10: 0991078756
ISBN-13: 978-0-9910787-5-2
First Edition

To Sharon

CHAPTER ONE
Siegfried and Brünnhilde
1939 to 1941

London
Monday, September 4th, 1939

Helga Ziegler approached the sergeant on duty at the front desk at Scotland Yard.

"I'm a German agent, and I'd like to turn myself in."

"Yes, miss," the police sergeant replied. "This morning we've had a quite a few German secret agents wanting to turn themselves in. Won't you please wait with them in that room over there?"

It was blatantly obvious to Helga from the sergeant's tone of voice that he did not believe her. The obvious reason was that she was a woman, and everyone knew that there were no female secret agents. In addition, the declaration of war the previous day could certainly have unhinged a number of individuals who were living close to the edge of reality, and she realized there might well be a crowd of people in the waiting room who were clearly suffering from the delusion that they were German spies.

But Helga was not going to allow a policeman to treat her that way. She placed her suitcase on the wooden desktop, opened it and said, "Sergeant, do the other people in the waiting room all have a German radio transmitter like this one?"

Near Carltonham, England
Monday, January 6th, 1941

Lieutenant Emil Ketelsohn flew his fully laden Heinkel He 111 bomber in a northerly direction through the darkness of the night toward its target in the English Midlands. The portion of England below him was blanketed in thick clouds at low altitude. Nevertheless, he knew that he was flying perfectly on course because in his earphones he could hear the tones of the German beam system, code-named *Knickebein* (knock knees), guiding him unerringly on the correct flight path.

The beam, transmitted from Sortosville-en-Beaumont in Normandy, in Nazi-occupied France, was pointed directly at the Spitfire factory in Carltonham. Listening to the tone that one of the two *Knickebein* receivers in his plane emitted, Ketelsohn was filled with pride at German creativity and inventiveness. There was no question, he thought, that Aryan superiority in all things would soon result in victory for the Third Reich over its effete and morally decrepit enemies.

As the bomber neared its target, the cloud cover cleared. This had no impact on the mission. Ketelsohn and his bombardier did not need to peer blindly from the fully glazed cockpit into the blackness to try to locate the Spitfire works. Instead, they began to listen for the tone from their second receiver. They had tuned this receiver to receive signals from another *Knickebein* transmitter, this one on Stollberg hill in Nordfriesland, just south of the German border with Denmark. The German broadcasters had aimed both transmitters directly at the Spitfire factory, that is, the beams crossed at the target. So, when the bombardier heard steady tones from both transmitters at the same time, he did not even try to visually locate the Carltonham Spitfire works through the darkness. After all, he knew with absolute certainty that he was in precisely the correct place to release his eight SC 250 bombs, each weighing about 550 pounds.

As the bombardier screamed out "Bombs away!" searchlights pinpointed the He 111. Almost immediately, a battery of QF 3.7-inch heavy anti-aircraft guns started pumping out shrapnel shells. Ketelsohn's attempt at evasive action was useless. With most of his training devoted to learning to fly along a *Knickebein* beam, his clumsy maneuvers to elude the shrapnel were futile. The bomber was soon hurtling toward the ground, with one engine out of action and the other burning fiercely. It was impossible for the crew to eject in time. Ketelsohn's last thought as his plane plowed into the ground and a wing fuel tank exploded was, "Why did they build a Spitfire factory right in the middle of an empty English meadow?"

The five British officers were clustered around the table in the basement room for their daily 9:15 a.m. meeting. Promptly on time, Air Commodore Archibald Pankhurst walked in. The others were pleasantly surprised to see that his craggy face held a smile, and that the scowl that usually lowered his bushy salt-and-pepper brows down to the level of his hooded eyes was gone, at least temporarily.

"You all know how the *Knickebein* system works," he said in his gruff voice. "If a German pilot flying north from France to England accidentally deviates even slightly to the west side of his predetermined course, he hears a series of short tones followed by long pauses and he immediately corrects his direction. If he flies fractionally to the east, his headphones are filled with long tones followed by short pauses. Only when he flies on exactly the correct route does he hear a continuous signal, consisting of the short and long tones precisely interspersed.

"The good news," the air commodore continued, "is that our new ASPIRIN device worked perfectly last night. As some of you know, we first tried to disrupt their system by broadcasting a beam signal of our own, so the German pilots would hear two signals and not know which one to follow. Sometimes they got lucky—they chose the *Knickebein* beam and dropped their bombs on their intended target. And sometimes we got lucky and they followed our beam and dropped the bombs where we wanted them to jettison them. Then our scientists became even smarter, and we broadcast interference signals in such a way that the pilots heard the continuous tone wherever they flew in the vicinity of the target. That is, we managed to widen the beam. As a result, the Germans often dropped their bombs in the wrong place."

Lieutenant Reginald Wallstead of the Corps of Royal Engineers raised his hand. The predominant feature of Wallstead's oval face was his high forehead, topped by wavy light-brown hair. His eyes were never still.

"But that sometimes resulted in terrible civilian casualties," he remarked.

"Precisely!" Pankhurst replied. "Instead of bombs falling on a factory, sometimes large numbers of men, women and children have been killed and injured when a German bombardier dropped his load onto a densely populated area, especially in the vicinity of the docks in the East End of London. So we need a way of tricking the Germans into dropping their bombs every single time onto an uninhabited area.

"Last night," he continued, "instead of widening the beam, for the first time we managed to 'bend the beam.' We knew that the German bombers were headed for the Spitfire works at Carltonham. Our scientists and engineers sent out a set of short tones precisely synchronized with the *Knickebein* long tones. So when their pilots flew exactly on the beam, they heard our spurious short tones and they thought that they were too far to the west. Accordingly, they turned east, away from the target—the effect of the new device was to bend the beam. So, instead of intersecting over the factory, the pilots were fooled into thinking that the *Knickebein* beams met over a meadow about six miles east of the Spitfire works. And we'd positioned our anti-aircraft batteries at that spot.

"The outcome of last night's air raid was most gratifying. Firstly, there's a series of large bomb craters in the middle of a pasture between Carltonham and Sheepspool. Secondly, there are three chickens on a neighboring farm that the noise of the exploding bombs frightened to death, or so the farmer claims. No, he's not going to get any compensation. Thirdly, our anti-aircraft batteries made good use of an unexpected large gap in the clouds and shot down three He 111s. Fourthly, our Spitfire pilots claim to have shot down another 13 bombers—four of the kills have been confirmed so far. But I've left the most interesting outcome for last."

Air Commodore Pankhurst paused for effect, then added, "I'm sure you're all wondering why I'm smiling so broadly this morning."

This remark triggered an insincere but voluble chorus of "No, sir" and "Not at all, sir."

"I don't pretend to fully understand what our scientists told me about their tricks," the air commodore continued. "However, I do know that our boffins were able to achieve their aim, which was to fool the German aircrew. In short, the main beam was fine until the pilots started to approach the vicinity of Carltonham. Then our new ASPIRIN device bent the beam and they dropped their bombs precisely where we'd intended. But no one considered what would happen to the *Knickebein* beam, as a result of our interference, beyond the new intersection point. And do you know what the result was?"

Once more he paused for effect. His audience of five officers knew better than to respond in any way to this rhetorical question, so they simply waited with expectant looks on their faces.

"The best answer that I could get from the scientists this morning is that the beam was 'messed up' in some way. Now as everyone around this table knows, the German pilots and navigators have been told to navigate exclusively with the aid of the beams. And we're all exceedingly aware of how methodically and rigorously the Germans instruct their aircrew. So what happened? After they dropped their bombs, the Heinkel pilots who had managed to evade both the heavy anti-aircraft guns and our Spitfires suddenly found themselves flying beyond the target in a world where the main beam was 'messed up.' They landed two of their planes on RAF bases in southern Scotland, because the pilots believed that they were somewhere in northern

France. Most scientists are shy and taciturn, but this morning our boffins are strutting around, boasting loudly that they were responsible for our receiving two Heinkel He 111s in perfect working order. The fact of the matter is that neither they nor anyone else had even remotely anticipated this outcome of their tinkering with the beams."

His audience first thought that Pankhurst was playing some sort of practical joke on them, but they quickly remembered that the air commodore had no sense of humor. So they smiled politely as they imagined the looks on the faces of the German aircrew as they climbed down from their planes after a "triumphant bombing run," suddenly realizing where they really were.

"However," Air Commodore Pankhurst went on, "I didn't bring you here today to laugh about the serendipitous by-product of beam bending. The purpose of this meeting is to decide where we go to from here. The Germans are soon going to learn from reconnaissance photographs that their bombers completely missed the Spitfire factory at Carltonham. At the same time, all the pilots who managed to return home are going to tell their commanders that they dropped their bombs in precisely the right place. Eventually the Germans are going to realize that their beams aren't working any more, so there are three issues for us to discuss today. The first is: How are we going to keep secret from the Germans the fact that we're bending their beams? Secondly: Once they do catch on, what's their next step going to be? And finally: What should *our* next step be in anticipation of what we think *their* next step will be?

"But before we discuss these three items, are there any questions?"

A Royal Navy lieutenant commander raised his hand.

"Yes, Chulmleigh?"

"Sir, I understood you to say that we were able to bend the main beam because we knew that they were headed for the Spitfire works at Carltonham. Does that mean that this method doesn't work unless we know in advance where they're going to direct the beams?"

"Correct. We need to know the location of the transmitter the *Luftwaffe* will use for the main beam along which their bombers are to fly for a given raid, and where they will aim that transmitter. Our people can then set up their new beam-bending device in the correct position relative to the intended target. But if we don't know in advance where the bombers are headed, the best we can do is to put the older ASPIRIN devices, the ones that widen the beam, near all expected targets of night bombing.

"Any other questions?"

This time it was Lieutenant Wallstead.

"Sir, how did we know that the German bombers were headed for Carltonham and which transmitter would carry the main beam?"

Even though Pankhurst took a long time before he replied, Wallstead realized almost instantaneously that he had committed a grave faux pas. During the silence that seemed to last for ever, Wallstead braced himself for the expected outburst. When it came, it was surprisingly mild and brief.

"Wallstead, if you want to continue to sit around this table, you're going to have to refrain from asking questions like that."

"Yes, sir. I'm sorry, sir," said Wallstead, grateful that the air commodore was in such an excellent mood that morning.

"Now, gentlemen, let's get back the agenda. Does anyone have any ideas regarding the three issues I raised?"

Reginald Wallstead realized that he needed to make up for his earlier gaffe. So he raised his hand.

"Sir, your agenda is essentially about a scientific arms race. The Germans invent a beam, our scientists invent a countermeasure, the Germans come up with a better beam, we come up with a better countermeasure, and so on. I'd like to suggest an additional approach."

"Go on."

"Well, sir, by bending the main beam last night, we created a phantom target, namely, the meadow that the Germans bombed in place of the Spitfire factory. Instead of bending the beam, wouldn't it have been easier to have convinced the Germans that the Spitfire factory was actually located on that meadow?"

"What are you saying, Wallstead?"

"We need to deceive the Germans as to the location of their targets. They can then use their highly sophisticated and accurate radio navigation systems to bomb mountains and meadows to smithereens, leaving untouched our factories, airfields, harbors, military bases and, in particular, our women and children."

He paused. He briefly considered making a further suggestion, decided against it, then quickly changed his mind again and blurted out: "And another thing, sir. We need to move London about 12 miles west from where it is at present."

London
Wednesday, January 4th, 1939
to Monday, September 4th, 1939

Helga Ziegler was one of tens of thousands of refugees who had poured into Great Britain early in 1939. Unlike almost all of the other refugees, however, Helga was actually a Nazi agent, code name BRÜNNHILDE, sent to lie low in London until the war broke out.

The *Abwehr*, the German military intelligence agency run by Admiral Wilhelm Canaris, had been placing undercover agents in Britain for several years, but Helga was unusual in two respects. First, she was the first female secret agent they had sent to Britain. Second, her instructions were that she was to do nothing until war broke out. She was too valuable to the Nazis to risk the possibility of MI5, the British counter-intelligence and security agency, catching her before hostilities began.

The *Abwehr* had equipped her with a radio transmitter; the probability that an officer of His

Majesty's Customs might ask her to open her luggage on her arrival in Harwich on a crowded cross-channel steamer was extremely small. Helga took the boat train from Harwich to London, and soon found a room to rent in Coldharbour Lane in south London.

The *Abwehr* had provided her with generous funds for living expenses. Nevertheless, she decided to take a job because she realized that no one knew when war would be declared and she was, therefore, concerned that the funds that they had given her might not last. Also, she was masquerading as a refugee, and it seemed that all the other refugees she had met were employed.

Directly after leaving school, Helga had worked as an assistant in a hat shop in Frankfurt, her hometown. When she left the milliner to start training as an *Abwehr* agent, the shop owner had provided her with a glowing reference. One morning soon after arriving in London, Helga was walking toward Brixton Station, virtually around the corner from Coldharbour Lane. She saw the owner of a newsagent and tobacconist shop near the station placing an "Assistant Wanted" notice in his shop window. Helga immediately walked in and applied for the job.

The swiftness of her response to his advertisement overwhelmed him, as did the outstanding reference that Helga translated into English for him. He hired her on the spot. One reason he thought that she would make a good assistant was the almost accent-free English that a team of capable *Abwehr* language instructors had taught her. The fact that she was extremely attractive, with long blonde hair framing her peaches-and-cream complexion, straight nose, tumid lips, and big blue eyes, was also a consideration in his instant decision to take her on, as was her perfect body.

Notwithstanding all the many factors in her favor, Helga was careful not to try to negotiate a higher wage than what he was offering, for fear of not getting the position.

The nature of her role as a Nazi agent forced Helga to live alone in a foreign country, with no family or friends. This had a profound effect on her. It was almost as if her rented room was a solitary confinement prison cell. She greatly missed living in Germany and longed to be back in Frankfurt with her loving family and her many friends.

One day after work, she walked past the local public library. She was feeling acutely homesick when the idea suddenly came to her that the library might carry the *Frankfurter Zeitung*, her hometown newspaper, for the many German refugees who lived in the area. She stopped in her tracks, turned and walked into the library.

As she entered, she smiled at the gray-haired librarian behind the desk to her left. Straight ahead was the shelf of new acquisitions. She noticed a book by a man whom Joseph Goebbels, the Nazi Minister of Public Enlightenment and Propaganda, had declared to be "a liar and a warmonger of the worst kind." She picked up Winston Churchill's

While England Slept, opened it, read the first paragraph, and became completely engrossed. She stood by the shelf, compulsively reading page after page, until the elderly librarian touched her on the shoulder and politely told her that the library was about to close.

Helga joined the public library on the spot and took the book back to her room. She was simply unable to put it down until she had finished it. The idea that utterly infallible German National Socialism might just possibly be wrong on one or two issues had shaken her to her very core, and that night she had the greatest difficulty falling asleep. The next day during her lunch break she returned the book to the library and took out the first two of many books on anthropology and sociology. Three weeks of constant reading in those areas led to her starting to question the scientific accuracy of Hitler's racial theories. Numerous books on the history of the Great War followed, by both Allied and Central Powers authors. After carefully weighing up their disparate opinions, she came to the conclusion that Hitler's repeated claims that the politicians and the Jews were responsible for Germany's surrender at the end of the First World War were equally false. The more extensively she read, the more she began to realize that, since 1933, the Nazi propaganda machine had fed her an unending diet of lies.

For the first time in her 27 years, she started to think about the meaning of life. She continued to read voraciously, immersing herself in innumerable nonfiction library books on a broad array of topics.

Fortunately for Helga, her employer had no objection to her reading a worthwhile book when the shop was empty, and she now spent her lonely evenings in the company of her books. At school she had read only the material required by the curriculum, but now she explored an expanding universe of knowledge that previously had not even existed for her. For six months Helga read scholarly works that, in her opinion, were largely objective and impartial. Her disillusionment slowly grew until finally she became unconditionally opposed to National Socialism and everything it stood for.

Although war now seemed inevitable, she was able to postpone dealing with the issue by convincing herself that, if and when hostilities actually broke out, she would come to a decision as to where her loyalties lay. In the meantime, Helga was able to ignore the turmoil going through her brain by focusing single-mindedly on the contents of book after book.

Britain declared war on Germany on Sunday, September 3rd, 1939. Helga immediately resolved her conflict. Early the next morning, she packed all her possessions in her suitcase, including her radio, and took a bus from Brixton to Victoria Station and a second bus from there to Whitehall. She alighted from the vehicle, then walked from the bus stop to Number 4, Whitehall Place, better known as Scotland Yard. She went up to the sergeant on duty standing behind the front desk.

"I'm a German agent, and I'd like to turn myself in."

The sergeant did not believe her. He courteously invited her to take a seat in a waiting room with the other implausible self-identified German agents who had come to Scotland Yard that morning. But when Helga showed him the German transceiver in her suitcase, he immediately summoned a constable to escort her to Inspector Fagan's office.

Instead of arresting her on the spot as an enemy agent, Fagan invited her to sit down and tell him all about it. After about five minutes, he realized that this was not a matter for the Metropolitan Police. He had to call in MI5 at once.

Leaving her suitcase with its precious radio in his office, Fagan escorted Helga to an interview room, locked her in, then phoned his contact at Wormwood Scrubs prison. Just before the war broke out, His Majesty's Prison Service had removed the prisoners from Wormwood Scrubs so that the War Department could use the building for secure storage. In addition to storing a set of its files there, MI5 moved its headquarters to "The Scrubs."

Half an hour later, Inspector Fagan unlocked the door of the interview room and two men joined Helga. They told her that their names were Johnson and Carlyle. It was clear from the way they introduced themselves that these were not their real names.

"Helga Ziegler?" Johnson asked. He was tall man with fair hair parted on the left, an elongated face with a pointed chin, and brown eyes with long fair lashes.

"Yes."

"Are you a German citizen?"

"I was born in Frankfurt in 1912 to German parents."

"Do you realize that, as an enemy agent, you are liable to be sentenced to a long term of imprisonment, and possibly the death penalty?"

"Yes, I do."

"Why did you turn yourself in this morning?"

"I have no wish to spy on Britain. I no longer believe in National Socialism."

Johnson nodded and then continued the questioning. "Do you appreciate that turning yourself in will in no way mitigate the fact that you entered Britain as an enemy agent, carrying a radio for transmitting information to your handlers in Berlin?"

"Yes, I understand that, too."

"What actions have you taken since arriving in Britain?" Johnson asked.

"I was told to lie low until war was declared. All I have done is to take a job as a shop assistant at a newsagent and tobacconist in Brixton. Other than entering Britain illegally, I have not broken any laws."

"Why did you enlist as a spy?" Johnson enquired.

"They recruited me. I met this handsome man at a party in Frankfurt and—oh, what's the use, you're not going to believe me."

"Oddly enough, Miss Ziegler, we do believe you. You'd be surprised how many secret agents have turned themselves in, either immediately on arrival here, or abroad at the nearest British consulate soon after they arrived there. And many of them told us the same story. They enlisted for a glamorous job, but when they actually set out on a genuine mission, they quickly realized that they didn't want to be spies. But your case seems to be different. You told us that you're disillusioned with the German government, rather than with spying."

At this point, Carlyle took over. He was a head shorter than Johnson, stockily built, with slicked-back black hair. The snub nose seemed too large for his round face. He could charm people with his ready smile and crinkly brown eyes.

Carlyle grinned briefly to reassure their prisoner. "Miss Ziegler, until last year Britain had an invariable policy. When we arrested a spy or if he turned himself in, we brought him to trial, usually a public hearing. At the end of the legal proceedings, the judge sentenced him to a long term of imprisonment. When the prospect of war loomed, things changed and we implemented a new policy. You fall under this new policy."

Carlyle paused to see Helga's reaction. Her face was a blank mask.

"We're now offering a choice to captured German agents. Option one is to become a double agent. You will work for us. You will transmit by radio to Berlin what we tell you to transmit."

"And option two?"

"Death by hanging under the newly passed Emergency Powers (Defence) Act. As a woman, you would be executed in Holloway Prison," Carlyle said.

"I am willing to work for you in any way you wish. I no longer consider myself to be a German citizen."

"I have to warn you that, if you choose to work for us, you will be carefully watched. The slightest attempt to escape or to warn your former controllers in Berlin that you are now a British double agent will result in your immediate transfer to Holloway for execution. There will be no trial; you've already confessed to us. Do you understand that?"

"Yes."

There was a long silence.

"What will happen to me now?"

"Our people will interrogate you at length. First and foremost, we need to know if you're telling us the truth. In addition, we want to learn as much as possible about your training and about the structure of the *Abwehr*. What you tell us will be compared with what we've already learned from the many other German agents we've arrested. Most of them turned themselves in, just like you. The rest made elementary mistakes and were arrested. So we've built up a large body of information about the *Abwehr*, its personnel and its methods. I'm telling you this now in case you're thinking of lying to us, or even attempting to mislead us in any way. Implicit in option one is that at all times you will tell us the truth, the whole truth, and nothing but the truth. So that means if you choose option one but lie to us or hold back information, that will be tantamount to your choosing option two."

"I understand."

"I hope you do," Carlyle said.

"Yes, I do understand. I will cooperate fully."

MI5 Headquarters, London
Tuesday, September 12th, 1939

"It's going very well," Johnson said to Carlyle. "During the past week of intense interrogation, Helga appears to have answered every question we've put to her as precisely and completely as she could."

"Yes, indeed. Many of her answers went far beyond what we asked her. When I asked her how many other individuals had trained with her in Berlin, she gave a physical description of all the other agents in her class and then proceeded to analyze their strengths and weaknesses as she saw them. Furthermore, she volunteered additional information that might help us capture those agents, such as their interests and hobbies. Of course, she had no way of knowing that every one of the *Abwehr* agents she described so carefully and in such detail was either already in our custody or dead."

"She's provided a mine of information that'll be of considerable value to MI5—if she's telling us the truth."

"Do you think that she realized what we really wanted to know from her?" Carlyle asked.

"You mean the instructions that the *Abwehr* gave her for sending radio messages?"

"Yes. We've been trained to elicit that information as if it were merely a minor detail, but Helga is certainly the cleverest spy I've ever encountered."

"I'm not sure if she caught on," Johnson said.

"And do you think she's told us the truth?"

"Again I'm not sure. Her answers were consistent. You'll remember that she informed us that the *Abwehr* instructed her to send her first message at 11 p.m. London time on the day that war was declared and thereafter every Thursday evening at 11 p.m. When you repeated the question the next day, not surprisingly she gave the same answer. But it could have been the same false answer. All week we haven't caught her in a lie, but that doesn't mean that she was telling the truth."

"Look. She seems to be cooperating fully and we've received permission to make her part of the Double Cross System. What do you think? Is she ready?" Carlyle asked.

"As ready as she'll ever be. Let's visit her."

Johnson phoned the car pool. They reached the main entrance of Wormwood Scrubs and found a black sedan waiting. "We're going to 73 Pavilion Road, Knightsbridge," Carlyle told the driver.

When they arrived at their destination, Johnson and Carlyle walked up to the top-floor flat. The armed guard outside the front door greeted them and unlocked the door. A second guard was on duty inside the flat. Johnson looked around and was pleased to see that there were heavy bars on the windows.

Helga was seated in an easy chair. Her hands were folded and she was staring into space. She looked up as she heard the two men entering but said nothing.

"Helga, you've told us that you're prepared to cooperate fully. Are you willing to transmit a radio message to Berlin?"

"Yes, of course."

"Here's the message. As you can see, it begins by your explaining that you were on holiday in the Orkney Islands in far northern Scotland when war broke out, so you were unable to transmit a message either on that day or on the first Thursday of the war. The rest of the message tells your handler that you've met a handsome young Army captain who works at the War Office, and describes what he's told you about the ways the government is preparing London for the coming conflict. Don't worry, you're not giving away any British secrets. All the information in your message was in *The Times* two days ago."

He smiled warmly to reassure her. Then he went on.

"You've told us that your messages to the *Abwehr* are to be written in German and encrypted using the Playfair code, with the name of the next month as the key. It's now September. Would you please encrypt the message?"

This was a subtle trap. Helga had told her interrogators that, even though all her messages were to be in German, the encryption key was the name of the next month *in English*, in this case OCTBER.

(The letters in a Playfair key have to be unique—a repeated letter is simply omitted.) Johnson wanted to see if she deliberately encrypted the message with the German key OKTBER, which would have alerted her handlers in Berlin that something was wrong. When she was finished, he compared the answer written in her neat handwriting with the encryption of the same message that an expert MI5 cryptologist had performed the previous day; the two were identical, letter for letter.

They heard a polite knock. The guard inside the flat unlocked the door. A compact man with reddish hair over a square face entered the flat. He was holding an attaché case. Helga immediately noticed the prominent band of freckles across his nose and cheeks.

"Helga, this is Eric Clerkwell," Carlyle said. "Let's all go into the kitchen and sit around the table. Eric, can we please have the telegraph key?"

Clerkwell reached into the case and handed it to him. Carlyle passed it on to Helga.

"Helga, please send the encrypted message."

"But it's not my transmission time yet," she protested. "And in any case, the key isn't connected to the transceiver. All that will happen is that you'll hear a series of short and long taps, the dots and the dashes."

"Just do as I asked, please," Carlyle said.

Helga was baffled by the request, but she complied. When she had finished, Eric asked her to do it again. It was clear that she was about to protest, but she tapped out the message a second time. Eric nodded his thanks.

Johnson explained. "Helga, Eric is an expert on Morse code. He now knows your 'fist,' that is, the characteristics of the way you send Morse. It's like your handwriting."

"But everyone sends Morse the same way," Helga insisted. "There are rules. A dash is three times as long as a dot. The gap between two letters is as long as three dots, and the gap between two words is as long as seven dots. And everyone has to obey the rules exactly, otherwise we wouldn't be able to communicate with one another."

"Correct, but in practice every operator has his or her own characteristics, such as slightly longer or shorter dashes or gaps, perhaps only before or after specific letters or numerals. Just as our own individual handwriting uniquely identifies each of us, each Morse code operator has his or her own recognizable fist. Right, Eric?"

"Yes, indeed. For example, miss, you tend to rush when a word begins with the letter 't—you don't wait long enough before sending the dash."

He paused and then added, "You seem surprised by what I just said."

"Well, I am. I thought that my Morse was perfect. What are my other individual characteristics?"

"Let's not go into that now," Carlyle said quickly before Clerkwell had an opportunity to answer.

Now Helga had another question. "Why did Eric come here to learn my Morse code characteristics?"

"Surely you know?" Johnson insisted.

"I have no idea," Helga said.

Johnson and Carlyle exchanged glances. Then Carlyle nodded to Johnson, who started to explain.

"Helga, didn't they teach you about duress words?"

"Yes. I already told you that," she said. "They instructed me that if I was captured and given the choice of death or transmitting a message that the enemy had written, I was to agree to send the message. But in order to secretly inform the *Abwehr* that I was a prisoner sending a message compiled by the British, I was told to include the German word *dennoch* (nevertheless) in the first paragraph."

"But didn't they warn you that we'd probably be watching you like a hawk while you transmitted in order to ensure that you were sending precisely what we'd ordered you to send, nothing more and nothing less?" Johnson asked.

"Yes, they did."

"And?"

"And the instructor told me that if I couldn't insert the duress word, I should increase the gap between successive words. They've heard me transmit dozens of times in training, so they would immediately realize that I was sending the message under duress. Oh, now I get it. Eric has learned my 'fist,' as you called it, so if I change it in any way…"

"Precisely," Johnson said. "Whenever you transmit a message to the *Abwehr*, Eric will be seated right next to you to check that you send every single letter of the message correctly. Furthermore, he'll be on the lookout for even the slightest change in your fist. And you know what will happen then."

"Don't worry," Helga insisted. "I've told you repeatedly that I no longer consider myself to be German and certainly not an agent of the *Abwehr*, and that I am cooperating fully."

When Carlyle and Johnson were back in their office, Johnson turned to Carlyle.

"Are they going to move her to another location?"

"I don't think so. The top-floor flat where they've put her, under continuous armed guard of course, is secure. We dare not let her escape, or she'll give away the secrets of the Double Cross System."

"By now there must be at least 20 MI5 officers creating messages filled with disinformation that captured Nazi spies are transmitting to Germany. The Germans know the fist of each of their agents, so there are no doubts in the minds of the *Abwehr* handlers as to who is sending them the messages they receive. But if an agent manages to escape and send a message to Germany, that would unravel the whole scheme."

"Don't worry," Carlyle said. "There are guards inside and outside every location where we're keeping an agent, and armed guards also patrol the streets around the building."

"But there's another problem. If the Germans start to suspect that an agent whom they had trusted is a British double agent, they'll immediately discredit every past, present and future message that that agent sent. Eventually, suspicion will fall on the messages that every other German agent in Britain has transmitted."

"How could that happen? Before sending, every message is checked and rechecked by a whole host of people to make sure that there are no inconsistencies or contradictions."

"Yes, I know. But even if we take every precaution, a sentence may slip through that raises a red flag in Berlin.

"And there's something else that concerns me," Johnson continued. "They keep telling us that every agent Germany has sent to Britain is either dead, in jail, or in the Double Cross System. That is, they claim that one hundred percent of the information being sent from Britain to Berlin is actually MI5 disinformation. But what if they're wrong? What if there's a loyal German agent out there who's sending factual information that contradicts the fictional messages that our double agents are transmitting to Germany? Won't that bring the whole Double Cross System crashing to the ground?"

"Stop worrying. Don't you remember what D told us at that meeting two weeks ago? The Head of MI5 stated categorically that all the evidence points to the conclusion that there aren't any German spies still at large—for example, we've not detected any unexplained radio transmissions. And we've deduced from the messages that the *Abwehr* has sent to our double agents that the Nazis don't suspect even the existence of the Double Cross System, let alone that we've turned their agents."

"But what if D is wrong?"

Knightsbridge, London
Thursday, September 14th, 1939

Ten days after agent BRÜNNHILDE had given herself up at Scotland Yard, Johnson came to the Knightsbridge flat just after 5 p.m. Each German agent in the Double Cross System had a handler who met with that agent on a regular basis and did what he could to keep him happy. This might mean playing chess with the German spy, or arriving with a box of chocolates. Helga Ziegler was the first female double agent. After a series of lengthy and sometimes contentious meetings at MI5 headquarters, they decided to assign a female handler to her. However, there were no women in the relevant department of MI5, and there was no quick way to find someone appropriate, train her and give her the necessary "Most Secret" clearance. Accordingly, they then agreed that Johnson would be her handler temporarily, but they would transfer her to a female handler just as soon as this could be organized.

When he arrived at the flat, Johnson explained to Helga that he was her handler. He gave her a pile of a dozen nonfiction books on a wide variety of topics. Helga was delighted and thanked him warmly. Then he told her that she was to transmit her first message that evening, the one she had tapped out for Eric Clerkwell two days before.

At 10 p.m. there was a knock at the door. Eric was standing there with Helga's radio transceiver. He had already run an aerial from a chimney of the apartment building, through a window and into the flat. Eric placed the set on the kitchen table, connected the aerial and checked that the apparatus, which he had tested earlier that week in his office at Wormwood Scrubs, was still working correctly. He set the transmission frequency to the wavelength Helga had specified during her lengthy questioning. Then they waited.

At exactly 11 p.m., Helga sent her first message to Germany. Seated next to her with a copy of the message in front of him, Eric listened intently to the dots and the dashes as she operated the telegraph key. Johnson stood by the wall switch, ready to turn off the apparatus at the slightest signal from Eric.

The *Abwehr* receiving station, a converted luxury villa in Wohldorf, a suburb in the north of Hamburg, picked up the message. On the basis of the header information, the Hamburg signals clerk immediately forwarded the message to Berlin. The *Abwehr* signals clerk on duty there that night, Corporal Kleibl, decrypted the message and immediately took it to Captain Busch, the duty officer. Busch was delighted to see that agent BRÜNNHILDE had transmitted her first message. He briefly wondered whether he should wake Colonel Siegfried Kupfer, the head of Section I of the *Abwehr,* to tell him the good news that his star secret agent was now active and transmitting. Then he remembered that Kupfer had left instructions that the duty officer was to disturb him only if Hitler himself wanted to speak to him. So Captain Busch took the message that agent BRÜNNHILDE had sent and laid it on Kupfer's desk.

He knew that Kupfer had appointed himself to be her controller, and he wondered what instructions he would send back to her. The protocol in place was that they would transmit a reply to London exactly 22 hours after receiving the original message.

MI5 Headquarters, London
Friday, September 15th, 1939

The following night, Johnson sat in his office, waiting for the MI5 signals clerk to decrypt the message that came in promptly at nine. While he waited, he studied Helga's thick file once more. He reread parts of the transcript of Helga's interrogation, looking yet again for inconsistencies, omissions and contradictions. Then he noticed that there was a new item in the file. Carlyle had written a report in which he stated that her answers were "too good"—it was inconceivable to him that anyone could answer questions all day and half the night for a week without making a single mistake. Johnson thought about this for a while, then put it down to the fact that Helga was terrified that her captors would execute her, and therefore had made a great effort to ensure that her answers would satisfy her inquisitors. And the best way to achieve that would have been to tell the absolute truth. But other spies had been equally terrified, particularly those who had been caught, rather than voluntarily turning themselves in, but their responses had certainly never been as consistent as Helga's. Johnson decided to reserve judgment on Helga Ziegler. In the meantime, he was curious to be told how the *Abwehr* would reply to her first message.

A few minutes later, a signals messenger arrived at his office. Johnson tore open the envelope and glanced rapidly at the contents. Kupfer had instructed Helga to determine military preparedness on the south coast of England. She was to report on gun emplacements, shore defenses, submarine nets, troop deployments and camps. In short, Johnson was holding in his hands the first proof that Hitler intended to invade England from the south. And that meant that he first had to invade and conquer France.

The initial thought in Johnson's head was that the French had to know about this. The second thought was that this radio message had vindicated the Double Cross System; the Head of MI5 could utilize the piece of paper Johnson was holding in the unlikely event of a bureaucrat claiming that the entire scheme was a waste of time and money. Then came the third thought: Carlyle had said that Helga was "too good." Was Kupfer's message to Helga as deceptive as her message to him?

Then he reread the message, this time word by word from the beginning.

Knightsbridge, London
Saturday, September 16th, 1939

The next morning, Johnson came to the flat at eight. The guard inside the flat opened the door.

"Is Helga still asleep?"

"Yes, I believe she is," the guard replied.

"No problem. I'll just wake her."

Johnson knocked on the bedroom door. There was a muffled reply. He opened the door, marched in and demanded, "Why didn't you tell us that you were having an affair with Kupfer?"

Helga was still half asleep. Instead of giving one of her usual crisp, clear and complete answers, she groggily replied, "How did you find out?"

"He replied to your message last night. Anyone with half a brain could tell from the way he worded his response that he's romantically involved with you. The message begins: 'My dearest darling Brünnhilde, I was ecstatic to receive your first message since you left Germany nine months and 12 days ago. I miss you so very much. I thought back to the last time we were together, at that romantic inn on the River Havel just outside Brandenburg. As I read your words, I could see you lying next to me, your glorious body lit by the moon shining into our room.' Sickening stuff, isn't it? And that's just the first paragraph. Why didn't you tell us?"

"No one asked me about it. And I didn't volunteer it because I was ashamed."

"Ashamed? Why?"

"Kupfer had let it be known via a subordinate that he was strongly opposed to a woman agent being sent to Britain. So I stupidly decided to seduce him in order to get posted here. Soon afterwards I realized he'd tricked me; his 'opposition' was simply a ploy to get me into bed with him. For the rest of my training, I did everything I could to keep out of his way. I slept with him exactly twice. And I certainly didn't enjoy it on either occasion."

"You told us that your disenchantment with the Nazi system began as a consequence of your reading. Isn't the real reason that Kupfer tricked you into sleeping with him?"

"Are you suggesting that my motivation was emotional rather than intellectual, and that my subconscious mind is playing tricks with me?"

"Let's keep Sigmund Freud completely out of this," Johnson said. "Just answer my question: When did you start to become disillusioned with Hitler and his minions?"

"After I began to read those books and started to think for the first time in my life."

Johnson left the flat and went to see Carlyle.

"You put a report in Helga Ziegler's file stating that, in your opinion, she was 'too good' to be genuine."

"Yes. Do you disagree with me?" Carlyle asked.

"Until last night I would've strongly disagreed with you. Now I'm not so sure. Two days ago Helga sent her first message to Colonel Kupfer, her handler. Here's his reply."

Carlyle read the message. "Two things. One, Hitler's about to invade France and we'd better warn the Frenchies. Two, Kupfer is sexually involved with her."

"And she never said anything to us. I asked her about it this morning."

"And?"

"She says she's 'too ashamed' about what happened. How do you feel about her honesty now?" Johnson asked.

"Let's think about Kupfer's message to Helga Ziegler for a minute. A copy must have been put in an *Abwehr* file somewhere. If Admiral Canaris were to read that message, he'd fire Kupfer on the spot. So, the message must have been sent to deceive us. And that means that Ziegler's a German agent who's going to tell Kupfer about Double Cross just as soon as she can find a way to escape from the Knightsbridge flat."

"Hold your horses for a minute," Johnson responded. "You're assuming that Kupfer knew about the Double Cross System when he sent Ziegler to Britain in January. And that's impossible; the system was started only later this year. Also, Kupfer would've had to know that we would read and decrypt his message to Ziegler. How could he possibly know that?"

"Suppose he'd instructed Ziegler to turn herself in when war broke out?"

"But how could he have known that we forced her to send out our message on Thursday night?" Johnson asked.

"There's no way he could've known. But wait a minute. What if clever *Fraulein* Ziegler somehow managed to send a duress signal two nights ago?" Carlyle asked. "In that case, Kupfer would've known that we've turned her and that we'd therefore read and decrypt his reply."

"Correct. But if he knows that we've turned Ziegler and that therefore we're going to read all his messages to her, he'll take every precaution not to make us suspicious in any way. In particular, he'll be careful not to let us know anything about his feelings toward Ziegler. So I think we can safely assume that Kupfer doesn't know we've turned Ziegler or that we're reading his message."

"I disagree. If he knows we're reading his messages, he's going to fill them with disinformation. One way to try to convince us that his messages are genuine is to decorate them with amorous remarks."

"Correct again," Johnson said. "So one possibility is that Ziegler has fooled everyone, and that Kupfer is extremely clever. But there's another possible explanation for his sending a compromising message like that, knowing that there's always at least one copy on file somewhere, and usually in more than one place."

"And that is?"

"Kupfer is a stupid fool," Johnson said.

"Some of the cleverest people in Germany serve in the *Abwehr*. No one in that organization could be that stupid, especially not a full colonel. But now that I come to think of it, there's a third possibility. Siegfried may be impregnable."

"Impregnable how?"

"We know that Kupfer is a confidante of Adolf Hitler. He was a Nazi even before the 1923 Beer Hall Putsch. Canaris can't touch him, and they both know it."

"That would explain the tenor of the message from Kupfer to Ziegler. So, the bottom line is: Can Helga Ziegler be trusted?"

"I really don't know," Carlyle replied. "Either we're the victims of an extremely clever German deception, or we have in place a beautiful former German agent who's now on our side, and Kupfer will implicitly believe her every report, because she's his former lover and he's still hopelessly besotted with her. At this stage, we've no way of knowing which of the two it is. But I would strongly advise you, as her handler for now, to take every precaution. I'd better be there with you whenever she sends our messages to Germany. You need to double the armed guard at her flat, and you have to personally warn all the armed guards that, even though she's a woman, she's a dangerous enemy agent. They mustn't allow her to communicate freely with Berlin under any circumstances whatsoever. And talking about communicating with Berlin, who's your Morse operator? Eric Clerkwell?"

"Yes."

"He's really good. You need to keep him on the job and get a second operator, as well. And make sure that they both know why."

"I agree."

"And you need to send a detailed report to D. This is either our biggest coup so far or the biggest mistake that the Double Cross team has ever made, and the Head of MI5 is the person who has to decide which it is."

MI5 Headquarters, London
Monday, September 18th, 1939

Two days later, a secretary summoned Johnson and Carlyle to a meeting with D.

"Carlyle, you and Johnson are responsible for creating the messages to be sent from Helga Ziegler to the *Abwehr*. Is that correct?"

"Yes, sir."

"We've been studying her file and the message that Colonel Kupfer sent her. We've come to a number of conclusions. First, we're convinced that Kupfer has no idea that we've turned Ziegler or that we're reading his messages to her.

"Then, we've detected what appears to be an inconsistency in Ziegler's story. Johnson, you've reported that she told you that Kupfer tricked her into seducing him. She then said that they slept together on only two occasions, and thereafter she avoided him as much as she could. In other words, he simply made use of her physically and that was that. However, this message from Kupfer to her seems to reveal that he's well and truly in love with her. And a man who has genuine feelings toward a woman doesn't use a subordinate to trick her into going to bed with him.

"Thirdly, we noted that Siegfried Kupfer assigned the code name BRÜNNHILDE to Helga Ziegler. Someone pointed out that, at the end of Hitler's favorite opera, Wagner's *Siegfried*, the eponymous hero, Siegfried, and the Valkyrie, Brünnhilde, fall passionately in love. This reinforced our view that Kupfer is beyond all doubt deeply emotionally involved with Ziegler, notwithstanding her statement to the contrary.

"Our conclusion is essentially the same as yours. That is, at this time we simply cannot tell if Helga Ziegler is on our side or on theirs.

"I strongly endorse your decisions to double the armed guard and to utilize the services of a second Morse operator. Furthermore, everyone involved has to be vigilant at all times until we've resolved this matter one way or the other. In particular, you are to order the guards to shoot to kill if Ziegler makes any attempt to escape.

"Finally, a word of warning, though probably superfluous. No matter how explicit the messages from Colonel Kupfer may become, the replies that *Fraulein* Ziegler sends to Berlin must always be businesslike in every respect. Any and all personal remarks in Kupfer's messages, amorous or otherwise, must be studiously ignored. Do you both appreciate why this is so essential?"

"Would it possibly be," Johnson asked, "that at some future time the Nazis may want to see the actual messages that Ziegler has transmitted, rather than Kupfer's reports about her messages? Kupfer's romantic remarks have made us highly suspicious. In the same way, the Germans are unlikely to believe the material we send to Germany via Ziegler if they realize that she and Kupfer are romantically involved, and that Kupfer might therefore be blind to disinformation in her messages."

"But surely they'll also want to see his messages to her," Carlyle said.

"Possibly. Possibly not," D replied. "And even if they do, once they see that her replies are businesslike and that she's purposely disregarding his amorous advances, it'll strengthen her credibility even more."

London
September 1939 to September 1940

Each week, Carlyle and Johnson put together a report for Helga to transmit to Germany in response to Colonel Kupfer's instructions. From his first message in September 1939 until Hitler called off Operation SEA LION in September 1940, Kupfer ordered agent BRÜNNHILDE to obtain information of various kinds to assist in Hitler's plan to invade Britain from France.

Initial messages asked for information on the battle readiness of the forces on the south coast of England but, as time went on, the requests became more specific. Kupfer's area of interest shrunk every few messages, until it finally became clear that, when the invasion started, the Germans would make landings between Portsmouth and Ramsgate. The British high command used Kupfer's messages to focus the defense of Britain on that area, with only a token force in position to the west of Portsmouth.

In his message of July 19th, 1940, Kupfer had instructed Helga to supply detailed information on coastal airfields, presaging Operation EAGLE ATTACK, the German air assault against the English airfields that protected the coast; the air attack began 25 days later. And on August 23rd, he sent her a lengthy list of questions regarding targets all over Britain. The Battle of Britain started 18 days later with 400 bombers protected by some 600 fighter planes bombing the East End of London day and night. But when Siegfried Kupfer's message of September 20th, 1940 contained nothing at all about southern England, the British government realized that Hitler had postponed his invasion plan until the *Luftwaffe* had destroyed the Royal Air Force.

From the start, Johnson and Carlyle realized that Kupfer had not thought through the practical implications of the instructions he sent to Helga; it would be physically impossible for one agent to gather information from the entire length of the southern coast of England, never mind being back in London every Thursday night to transmit her weekly message to Berlin and then stay there until Friday night to receive Kupfer's response. So they came up with the idea that Helga would recruit a set of subagents who would bring information to her on a regular basis. Helga soon would become the organizer of a vast spy ring, rather than an agent ferreting out secret information herself.

She recruited her first subagent when she "visited" Portsmouth. According to her report to Kupfer, she stopped for a cup of tea at a hotel near the Royal Naval Dockyards. The waiter who served her made disparaging remarks about the Royal Navy. During a return visit the next day, she obtained information from him about the morale of the sailors. Keeping to the Wagnerian theme, Johnson and Carlyle gave him the code name ALBERICH, leaving Siegfried Kupfer to deduce that the waiter was a short man.

In her message the following week, agent BRÜNNHILDE pointed out that the exigencies of wartime travel had made it impossible for her to get back to Portsmouth to meet with subagent ALBERICH. Instead, she said, in the future she would spend as much time as possible in London pubs, talking to people whose work required them to travel, especially to the south coast. Over the next two months, she befriended six individuals. One in particular provided her with endless details of what was happening in southern England. He was the owner of a fleet of some 20 fishing vessels, each based in a different harbor between Bognor Regis and Sandwich to maximize the chance of a good catch, and he tried to visit every one of his skippers once a fortnight. He was, she told Kupfer, a former member of the British Fascist Party, but had resigned in 1937 "for personal reasons." Accordingly, he had not been interned in 1939 when war broke out, nor did he think that he was on any list of Nazi sympathizers living in England. He had lost an eye fighting in World War I, so naturally Johnson and Carlyle assigned him the name WOTAN. Every Saturday night, Helga and subagent WOTAN would get together in the pub in Atlantic Road in southwest London where she had first met him, and in her radio transmission on the following Thursday she would report everything she had learned from him. Johnson and Carlyle hoped that Helga's regular meetings with her nonexistent subagent would make Siegfried jealous and, therefore, even more careless.

In March 1940, they decided to test the credibility of Helga's messages. Johnson constructed a report that included information from subagent WOTAN that the Royal Navy had installed a coastal artillery battery inside a cave just outside Yearville. Despite the fact that straightforward inquiries would quickly have revealed that there are no sufficiently large caves in the area, two weeks later a German radio message was intercepted that warned ships about the new battery. It was now obvious to the Double Cross team that the Nazis believed Helga's messages and trusted her and her subagents.

Toward the end of September 1940, when it became clear that Kupfer was no longer interested in the south coast of England, Carlyle decided that it was time to dispose of subagent WOTAN. In her next message, Helga told Kupfer that on Saturday night she had gone to the pub to meet with WOTAN as usual. As she turned the corner into Atlantic Road, she saw a police van parked on the side of the road.

Plainclothes men were hustling a man into the Black Maria. From his black eye patch there was no doubt that the man was subagent WOTAN. She kept walking at the same steady pace toward the bar, occasionally glancing mechanically at the Special Branch policemen but otherwise showing no interest in the proceedings. Helga assured Siegfried that she had not been compromised in any way. After all, subagent WOTAN had never visited her room and he had no idea where she lived. It was most unlikely, she stated, that MI5 could have found out about their regular weekly meetings. But, as a precaution, she would immediately find a room in another part of London, and she certainly would never return to that pub again. Kupfer's reply the next evening yet again revealed his true feelings toward her. He stressed the importance of her taking every precaution not to arouse the suspicions of the British authorities. Johnson and Carlyle realized that they had an almost foolproof mechanism for sending disinformation that Nazi Germany would treat as the gospel truth.

MI5 Headquarters, London
Tuesday, January 7th, 1941

Johnson was walking to his office when he bumped into Lieutenant Reginald Wallstead.

"I say, Wallstead, why so glum? Come and have a spot of lunch with me. I'll cheer you up."

"Oh, hello, Johnson. No lunch for me, I'm afraid. I've got a corker of a problem to solve, and I simply don't have the first idea where to start."

"Come to my office and let me solve it for you."

"I'm sorry to have to tell you that this problem is too hard even for you."

"Really? Then it must be unbelievably hard. Here we are, come in, sit down and tell me all about it."

"I need to move London by 12 miles to the west."

"Is that all? By the way, why on earth would you want to do that?"

"Our clever boffins have succeeded in bending a *Knickebein* beam, but only when we know the target in advance. Last night we persuaded the *Luftwaffe* that the Carltonham Spitfire works is situated some six miles to the east of where it actually is, and they dropped all their bombs in a field."

"That's excellent! Well done, old boy!"

"Yes, but the problem is that when we don't know where the bombers are headed, we can't bend the beams. What I need is a way of deceiving the Germans into believing that the main beam has been bent by 12 miles, without actually bending it."

Johnson thought for a moment. Then he turned to Wallstead and smiled beatifically. "Reggie, old chap, I know exactly how to do it. Here's the drill."

And Johnson outlined his solution.

Wallstead was delighted. "By George, you've got it! Let's go and tell the air commodore."

"Of course. But I think that we need to bring Carlyle into this, too."

A few minutes later, Wallstead brought Johnson and Carlyle to Air Commodore Pankhurst's office.

"Sir, may I introduce Johnson and Carlyle? I'm not yet cleared for Double Cross, so I'll leave you now."

When the door was closed, Pankhurst turned to Johnson, stared at him intensely and then asked, "When you opened the batting for Harrow against Eton at Lords, your name wasn't Johnson, was it?"

"No, sir. It wasn't."

Then looking Carlyle straight in the eye, Pankhurst went on. "You're the spitting image of your twin brother, who acquitted himself so valiantly at Dunkirk. Strange as it seems, even though you're identical twins, for some utterly inexplicable reason his name isn't Carlyle, is it?"

"No, sir, you're quite right. It isn't."

Grinning fiendishly, the air commodore continued, "Well, now that we've all been introduced to one other, what have you come here to tell me?"

Johnson spoke first. "Sir, we have an agent from the Double Cross System sending disinformation weekly to the *Abwehr*. They treat the contents of her messages as incontrovertible and irrefutable. We propose to use her to tell the Germans that the main beam is currently being bent by about six miles. Once they're convinced of that, I want her to inform them that we're going to double the bending to 12 miles.

"Why on earth do you want to give away a top secret? Are you both certifiably insane?"

"Sir, would you please look at these aerial reconnaissance photographs? They were taken this morning. They clearly show that the Carltonham Spitfire factory is completely untouched, whereas there's unmistakable evidence of bomb damage in an empty field exactly 6.13 miles east of the works. The Germans either have similar photographs already, or they will have very soon. All their pilots (or, at least, the pilots that got back to northern France) have no doubt told their intelligence officers that they dropped their bombs at the exact point where the two *Knickebein* beams crossed. They've known for weeks that we've been interfering with their beams, adding an additional beam, widening the beams, and so on. So, either they already know or they'll know very soon that we bent the main beam to the east. We made a bad mistake. Directly after the raid, we should've put a camouflage net on top of the Spitfire works that was painted to look as if the factory had been destroyed."

"Just a minute. Since the outbreak of war we've been painting factory roofs to look like fields and put dummy factories in meadows nearby. This has partly worked. The Germans have wasted thousands of tons of bombs on painted plywood and canvas structures standing in the open countryside. But it hasn't always worked. The location of many of our factories built before the war is common knowledge—you can find their addresses in a telephone directory—so the *Luftwaffe* has succeeded in destroying some factories that we carefully disguised. But it sounds to me that what you're suggesting is not as simple as disguising a factory as something else. If I've understood you correctly, you're saying four things.

"Firstly, you're saying that we should stop bending the beam on those occasions when we know in advance what the target will be, and instead deceive the Germans into believing that we are now bending every *Knickebein* beam to the east."

"Correct, sir." Johnson responded. "In fact, all attempts on our part to modify the beams must cease."

"Secondly, I think you're saying that we need to persuade the Germans to compensate for the fact that we're bending their main beam to the east. As I understand it, we've developed a device that currently bends the beam 6.13 miles to the east in the vicinity of a target. So, we want the Germans to direct their main beam at a point 6.13 miles west of a target, to cancel out our bending."

"Again correct, sir. But the cross beam that they transmit from just south of Denmark doesn't change, only their main beam."

"I understand," the air commodore replied. Then he continued.

"Thirdly, you're saying that, whenever the Germans drop bombs, we need to determine the precise location where they hit the ground. We then mark this point on a map. We can then identify their actual target as lying 6.13 miles to the east."

"Correct, sir," Johnson said once again.

"Fourthly, you're saying that immediately after we've identified the intended target, we need to put appropriately painted camouflage nets on top of the target they intended to hit, be it a port, a factory, a fuel depot, or a power station. In that way, when the Germans look at their reconnaissance photographs, they'll think that they successfully bombed the target, and they'll keep dropping their bombs to the west of the main beam, away from their targets."

"Yes, sir, that's what we're suggesting."

"Interesting. It may even work. Now, how do you propose to tell the Nazis to change the aim of their main beam?"

"Well, sir, two nights from now, our agent BRÜNNHILDE will be transmitting to the *Abwehr*, as she does every Thursday night. Her *modus operandi* is to visit various pubs looking for informants. It appears that tonight she'll go to a pub a little further afield than usual from where she lives. There she'll meet a scientist, slightly drunk—he'll be celebrating the fact that he managed to bend the beam. Despite being a shy, introverted researcher, he'll try to seduce her—as everyone knows from the cinema, that's the invariable effect of alcohol on lonely, bashful boffins when they meet beautiful women with perfect bodies. She'll ignore his clumsy attempts. So he'll try to impress her with science. He'll take a set of aerial reconnaissance photographs of last night's raid out of the inside pocket of his tweed jacket. He'll point out to her the Spitfire works, untouched. He'll proudly indicate the meadow where the *Luftwaffe* bombs landed. One photograph will have been annotated to show the *Knickebein* beams intersecting at the meadow, not the factory. Also the distance of

6.13 miles will be clearly marked on the photograph as the amount that the beam was bent to the east. Most important, he'll tell her that the distance of 6.13 miles is fixed, though we might increase it at some future stage, if necessary.

"Agent BRÜNNHILDE will get the boffin extremely drunk by telling him that she goes for men who can hold their liquor. Of course, she'd like to steal the photographs, but she won't dare, because if the scientist finds them missing in the morning, he may call in the police or MI5 or someone. So, when he passes out, she'll copy the key aspects of the photographs onto a piece of paper, then she'll replace the photographs in his jacket pocket and leave the bar."

"You're both completely out of your minds. No one is ever going to believe a story like that. What scientist, drunk or not, would try to seduce a woman using Most Secret aerial reconnaissance photographs? This is preposterous!"

"Sir," Johnson responded, "the radio message goes to Colonel Siegfried Kupfer at the *Abwehr*. Siegfried is head-over-heels in love with agent BRÜNNHILDE. He declares his undying devotion in every message he sends her. For example, two weeks ago he wrote to her, 'I love you. I will love you until the day I die. And I will love you when we are together forever in Valhalla.' He frequently states, 'I think of you all the time, day and night.' The man is besotted with her and, as a result, he believes anything and everything she tells him. We know this for a fact, because we've sometimes deliberately introduced far more preposterous items into a message, and he's swallowed them lock, stock and barrel, and then reported them to his good friend Adolf Hitler. Furthermore, we know that the idea of anyone trying to seduce the woman whom he loves enrages him—what little judgment he exhibits goes out the window whenever agent BRÜNNHILDE even hints at the possibility of another man in her life. So, we have ample evidence that Kupfer is going to believe every word of Thursday night's message and will pass on the entire message, as factual, to the *Luftwaffe*."

"But will the *Luftwaffe* believe it?" the air commodore asked.

"They already know—or very shortly will know—that last night every one of their bombers missed the target by 6.13 miles. The message from agent BRÜNNHILDE will confirm that exact distance and will carefully explain that the main beam was bent by 6.13 miles in the vicinity of the target. That should surely convince the German bomber command that our message is genuine. In any event, on Friday night, if the German bombers drop their munitions 6.13 miles to the west of their target, we'll know that they've fallen for it."

"I won't say that you've convinced me, but I'm not completely skeptical about your idea. Now tell me why your message to Germany will say that the amount of bending is about to be increased in the near future."

"There are two reasons. First, Lieutenant Wallstead feels that it's necessary to move London westward by 12 miles. That is, he thinks that if the Germans can be deceived into dropping their bombs a full 12 miles from their London targets, primarily the East End Docks, then the dockyards and the goods they contain will be spared, especially the military equipment and supplies. Also, the German bombs will fall in less built-up areas. Yes, there will be civilian casualties, but fewer than in the densely populated East End. When the target is in a city smaller than London, doubling the bending to 12.26 miles should be enough to ensure that the bombs will land in the countryside outside that city.

"The other reason," Johnson continued, "is that, if our deception on Thursday night goes wrong for some reason, agent BRÜNNHILDE can tell her Siegfried that the bending changed from 6.13 miles. That will adequately cover any discrepancies in her message."

"But what if the Germans bend their main beam 6.13 miles to the west of the target and this causes the bombs to fall into the sea?"

"In that case we may not be able to identify the target accurately. If we get it wrong, the German reconnaissance photographs will show that the wrong target was bombed—we'll have put the camouflage nets in an incorrect place. But at least the actual target will be spared."

Pankhurst thought for a moment.

"I still can't say that you've convinced me yet, but I'm prepared to take your proposed plan of deception one step further. Prepare a draft of the message you want agent BRÜNNHILDE to transmit on Thursday night. Bring it to me tomorrow afternoon at three. It will be a great help if you obtain Double Cross System approval before you bring the message here. Good day to you, gentlemen, whatever your names may be."

MI5 Headquarters, London
Wednesday, January 8th, 1941

When they returned to Air Commodore Pankhurst's office the following afternoon as he had ordered, Johnson and Carlyle were pleasantly surprised by the warm welcome he gave them. It seemed to them that Pankhurst had discussed the issue with other senior officers in MI5 and the Royal Air Force, and he had now decided that the proposed deception might actually work.

Carlyle handed him the draft of the message that Helga was to transmit. Pankhurst read it slowly, marked two changes in pen, signed the bottom of the last page and handed it back to them.

"Let me know what happens. In particular, we have to decide whether, when, and how to tell Kupfer that our bending has been doubled to 12.26 miles. Good luck!"

The two MI5 agents left, taking the corrected and signed copy of the message to the encryption specialists.

Knightsbridge, London
Thursday, January 9th, 1941

The following night they handed the typed message to Helga. Like all the encrypted messages she had sent, it consisted of groups of five letters, such as AUEHW or OEIEP. It was therefore incomprehensible unless she decrypted it, but they were always careful to take the message away with them directly after she had transmitted it.

She looked at the numerous five-letter groups and said, "It's a lot longer than usual."

"You've transmitted much longer messages in the past," Carlyle replied. "This one shouldn't be a problem."

"But why is it so long?" she asked.

Her remarks greatly disturbed Johnson. She had never commented about a message before. Now, however, at an absolutely crucial point in the war, with Britain facing almost unending bombing at the hands of the *Luftwaffe*, Helga was taking what he considered to be a most unhealthy interest in what she was about to transmit. On the one hand, he certainly did not want to upset her before the transmission, but on the other hand, he wanted to remind her what would happen if she tried anything.

Quickly making up his mind, he decided to say nothing. He assumed that she was aware of the price she would have to pay for anything short of full cooperation. Furthermore, there was no way she could know how important the current message was. So he relaxed his body, and hoped that this would result in Helga becoming calmer. Unfortunately for him, it did not work.

"I asked you, why is this week's message so long?" Her voice held a petulant tone he had never heard before. Also, she was speaking more loudly than usual.

Now he decided to be firm with her. "Helga, you've transmitted longer messages than this before, and you did so without any problems. Remember that, for your sake, it's important that you transmit this message as flawlessly as in the past. We insist on your fullest cooperation at all times, including now."

He could see the conflict within Helga. There was no question that she was getting close to her breaking point, possibly due to her confinement in the flat for more than a year now, or conceivably due to a build-up of guilt at turning traitor to Germany. But at the same time, it was clear that she was only too aware of the consequences of allowing her steely self-control to crack.

Finally, at 10:58 p.m., Helga managed to pull herself together. She sat at the table, carefully positioned the message and the telegraph key in front of her, and waited for the signal from Clerkwell to start transmitting. When he nodded, she started to send. To Johnson and Carlyle, it sounded just like her usual transmission, but the real arbiters were Eric Clerkwell and Alfred Hall, the other Morse expert. Alfred Hall was short and fat; at school the other boys called him "Albert Hall" for obvious reasons.

Clerkwell and Hall had witnessed Helga's tantrum, so they were as concerned as Johnson and Carlyle that she might break down in the middle of sending the message or, worse, send some sort of duress signal. When the transmission was about halfway through, Johnson looked at Clerkwell. Johnson raised his eyebrows, as if to ask, "Is everything satisfactory?" Clerkwell was unwilling to acknowledge that they were out of the woods yet, so he just pulled a face. Unfortunately, Johnson misunderstood what Clerkwell was trying to communicate—he thought that Eric was saying that something had gone wrong. But before turning off the switch and terminating this vital transmission, Johnson raised his eyebrows again, just to be sure that he had not misinterpreted the look that Clerkwell had given him. This time Clerkwell smiled, and the entire transmission was dispatched into the ionosphere without a hitch of any kind.

With the tension over, Johnson thanked Helga warmly and removed the encrypted message from the kitchen table. Clerkwell took the radio set, and they all left. Outside on the street, Johnson turned to Carlyle and said softly, "We have a problem."

"Yes, we have."

"So what are we going to do about it?" Johnson asked.

"I don't know. We certainly need to consult our colleagues to see if any of them have previously encountered this sort of difficulty with their double agents. But I suspect that we'd have been consulted if there'd been any other predicaments of this kind. I think we're on our own with our problem."

"We certainly need to talk to D about this."

"Yes, indeed. But we have a week to sort it out, so there's probably no cause to worry," Carlyle replied.

Unfortunately, Carlyle's reassuring words proved to be quite wrong.

MI5 Headquarters, London
Friday, January 10th, 1941

The following night, just after 9:15, the signals messenger on duty arrived at Johnson's office bearing Siegfried's decrypted reply. It was surprisingly brief, given the importance of the message that agent BRÜNNHILDE had sent him. The first part of his message was a warm sentence of congratulations, followed by an affectionate remark that was completely inappropriate in that context. Then Siegfried ordered BRÜNNHILDE to transmit at 11 p.m. whenever she had any more information from the scientist, not just every Thursday night. He ended by instructing her to acknowledge receipt of the message that evening.

This last part caused immense problems for Johnson. He had to locate Carlyle as well as Eric Clerkwell and his colleague Alfred Hall, order a car, and rush them all and the radio to Pavilion Road, Knightsbridge. On the way he had to compose a brief acknowledgement message in German and encrypt it using the Playfair code, remembering that it was now January and so the encryption key was FEBRUAY and not FEBRUA (from the German *Februar* with the repeated letter removed). When they arrived at the flat, he would have to rouse Helga if she was asleep, and somehow or other persuade her to send the message.

Fortunately for Johnson, Alfred was still in MI5 headquarters, vainly trying to repair a broken transceiver, a newer model than Helga's. The police had found it in the possession of an *Abwehr* agent arrested the previous week, immediately after landing from a U-boat on a remote island beach in northwest Scotland.

Alfred grabbed Helga's device from the shelf where it was stored and rushed to the waiting car. There was no sign of Eric Clerkwell anywhere in the building, and Carlyle had left for the night leaving a note saying he was going to the cinema—there would be no way of contacting him in time.

Johnson had had the sense to order a police car. With siren blaring, they raced to Knightsbridge. Luckily for them, there had been no air raids earlier that evening in that part of London, so all the roads were still open. When they arrived at the flat at 10:35, Johnson went to wake Helga, while Alfred neatly rewrote the hastily scribbled groups of five letters so that Helga would be able to read the encrypted message. Then he thought that he should encrypt the original message again, just as a check. After all, when encryption is performed in a police car speeding through the streets of London darkened for the blackout, mistakes are easy to make. Alfred corrected the one error he found and then waited for Helga to appear with Johnson.

He heard her screaming hysterically, followed almost immediately by a loud slap. A few minutes later, she appeared, wrapped in her dressing gown. She was sobbing quietly, but was apparently in a fit state to transmit. Alfred passed the brief handwritten message to her and pushed the telegraph key gently into her right hand. Johnson then entered the room and stood, as usual, by the switch, so that he could terminate the transmission if there were problems of any kind.

At precisely eleven, Alfred smiled gently at Helga and nodded the way Eric usually did. Helga stopped sobbing and sent the brief message. Afterwards Johnson escorted her back to her bedroom. He instructed the guards that one of them had to stay with her at all times; under no circumstances was she to be left alone in her current state. Then he and Alfred returned to the police car with the radio and the message. The driver took them back to MI5 headquarters, where Johnson wrote a report for Air Commodore Pankhurst and another for the head of the Double Cross System. He then decided there was no point in going home that late, so he took off his jacket and tie, and lay down for the night on a couch in an office near the radio room. Notwithstanding the tensions of the evening, he soon fell into a deep sleep. He awoke the next morning at eight, refreshed.

MI5 Headquarters, London
Saturday, January 11th, 1941

Lieutenant Reginald Wallstead and the other four British officers were seated around the table in the basement room for their daily 9:15 a.m. meeting. They were delighted to see that, when Air Commodore Archibald Pankhurst walked in, he was once again in a good mood.

"There were two German bombing raids last night," he announced. "The one target was the tire factory in Derbyshire. You will be delighted to know that all the bombs fell on top of a hill in a rural area, slightly more than six miles to the west of the works. Five sheep were killed, one was lightly injured. The elderly shepherd is in a severe state of shock but he should recover. We immediately put a camouflage net over the undamaged target. I haven't received an aerial photograph yet, but they tell me that the artists have excelled this time—the detail and realism of their depiction of the damage to the factory are apparently astounding. I look forward to seeing the aerial photographs later today.

"The other target was probably Bootle Docks, just to the north of Liverpool. Reports have been received of a large number of bombs falling into the sea north of Hoylake, narrowly missing both a fishing boat and a steamer from Belfast. We don't know where the bombs landed to the nearest inch, of course, but the area was roughly six miles west of Bootle Docks. Furthermore, you may recall that the *Luftwaffe* has already damaged more than half the houses in Bootle, so it's a good bet that the docks were their target. Our new nets have already been placed on the dock area, especially on the railway lines, which we know are a favorite German target.

"Any questions so far?"

"I have two questions, sir, if I may," Lieutenant-Commander Chulmleigh responded. "Last night was clear, I believe. Does that mean that the German pilots knowingly dropped their bombs into the sea?"

"Yes, that's what happened. The Jerries have been taught to obey orders implicitly. In particular, it's been drummed into their brains that they have to follow the beams. When they returned to northern France, they must have told their superiors that they thought that they dropped the bombs into the water, but our camouflage nets will show that the beams are still working correctly, provided that they continue to adjust for the 6.13 miles bending.

"And your other question, Chulmleigh?"

"Are the docks still operable with the nets in place, especially over the railway lines?" Chulmleigh asked.

"Yes, certainly. The nets have been placed on top of sections of wooden scaffolding that span the railway lines—it's something like a set of temporary tunnels—so the trains can pass freely through the docks. The only problem is: What will happen if the Jerries decide to photograph Bootle Docks at the exact moment when a train is passing under a net, with the train engine emerging from the front of the tunnel and the last few carriages about to enter it?

But I don't think we need worry too much about that."

"Any other questions?"

No one said anything, so Pankhurst continued. "The next issue is whether we should inform the Germans that we have doubled the bending from 6.13 miles to 12.26 miles and, if so, how."

"Surely the 'how' is obvious," commented Wallstead. "It should be done the same way the 6.13 miles was communicated to Berlin." He added hastily, "Whatever that was."

"No, Wallstead, we have a problem there. I have another meeting this afternoon to discuss that very point. In fact, in the interest of time, just tell me this: Do you think that there's much to be gained by doubling the bending to 12.26 miles?"

"Yes, sir, I really do," Lieutenant Wallstead said. "When I made my original proposal of moving London by 12 miles, I did so after carefully evaluating numerous targets both in London and elsewhere, including the Midlands, Wales, Scotland and Northern Ireland. On the basis of my figures, I consider that the potential benefit of doubling the bending far outweighs the risk of making the Germans suspicious. Even if we consider just London, I believe that increasing the distance to 12.26 miles will save many lives, as well as tons of vital military equipment and supplies, especially fuel."

"Let me have your calculations as soon as we're finished here," ordered Pankhurst. "I need to know all the facts before this afternoon's meeting, which may well prove to be extremely difficult."

That afternoon, Air Commodore Pankhurst convened the entire Double Cross System group, including all the Morse code specialists.

"I've called this meeting to help me decide an important question: Can agent BRÜNNHILDE be trusted to send a vital final message to Berlin? If we have to terminate her transmission midway through, the damage will be incalculable—they'll mistrust everything she's sent them up to now, and they may well start to doubt the messages they've received from the other double agents, also. I'd like Johnson to describe the situation regarding agent BRÜNNHILDE."

Johnson began by briefly summarizing what had happened regarding Helga from the day more than year previously when she gave her herself up. Finally he arrived at his conclusion.

"The obvious explanation for what has happened now," he said, "is that, unlike any of the other double agents, agent BRÜNNHILDE is a woman. I reject that explanation. Up to this point, agent BRÜNNHILDE has proved to be in a better psychological condition than almost all of our male double agents. She's never made a mistake in transmission. She has nerves of steel. Yes, she's locked in a prison, a luxurious prison, but then so are all the others. The only difference I can see is that agent BRÜNNHILDE is an undoubted thinker. She studies nonfiction books voraciously and she evaluates and assesses everything she reads—she accepts nothing without first thinking things through as carefully as she can. In my opinion, the problem is that agent BRÜNNHILDE is just too intelligent to make a good double agent. Give me an unthinking automaton who carries out orders instinctively any day, rather than a highly intelligent autodidact."

Carlyle was now asked to comment. He began by saying that he agreed with everything his colleague had said, with one exception.

"In my opinion," he declared, "the problem has been caused, or least exacerbated, by her unusual relationship with her handler, Colonel Siegfried Kupfer. There's no question whatsoever that he's head-over-heels in love with her. Innumerable radio messages from him to her have made this patently obvious. What's less clear is how she feels toward him. She's told us that he seduced her through trickery. Given the apparent genuine intensity of his feelings toward her, the sequence of events as she described them seems most unlikely. On the other hand, everything else she's told us appears to be absolutely truthful, without exception. To date, we haven't been able to resolve this issue, one way or the other. My opinion from the start has been that she didn't tell us the truth about her relationship with Kupfer and, after having worked with her for more than a year, my view hasn't changed. I think that she's probably in love with him, and that she now feels that she's betrayed him. I stress that this is a personal issue for her. I don't think that she feels the slightest guilt at her renunciation of the Fatherland."

Seated at the top of the table, the air commodore spoke again. "I would like to thank Johnson and Carlyle for their insightful remarks. But now we have to turn to the critical question: Can agent BRÜNNHILDE be trusted to make that vital final transmission?"

One of the other handlers raised his hand. "Sir, with the greatest respect, I think that the situation is far more complex and dangerous than that."

It was clear from the enthusiastic expression on Pankhurst's face that this was just the sort of challenging remark that he wanted to hear from his subordinates.

"Please go on," he urged.

"Sir, suppose that you decided not to allow her to make that final vital transmission. Expanding on what I understood you to say when you opened this meeting, the effect will be that the Germans will suspect that we've arrested her. Immediately, the *Abwehr* will ask pertinent questions, such as: Has she been transmitting under duress? Can any of her messages be trusted? Eventually they'll decide to reject all the information that agent BRÜNNHILDE has sent us, and months of work will be wasted. Worse, if the Germans conclude that they've been fed disinformation, they'll be able to deduce all sorts of facts from her messages that none of us would like them to conclude. After all, disinformation that's known to be disinformation can in itself be an excellent form of information.

"On the other hand, if you were to allow her to send that final message, the silence that will then follow will be as damaging to us as if you'd prevented her from making the transmission. What I'm saying is that it doesn't matter whether or not you allow her to send this vital message; the key point is that she has to keep transmitting week after week until we've finally won the war."

"But what if we give her a good reason for stopping?" another handler asked. "For example, what if she concluded her next transmission by saying that she's gone to live with the scientist?"

That remark triggered a widespread outburst of head shaking and muttering. "If we give that reason," another handler volunteered, "they'll instinctively mistrust every single thing she's sent from the very start." He added, "In fact, any reason for terminating will be equally damning."

There was a long silence. The air commodore waited expectantly for more suggestions. Nothing was forthcoming. Finally he spoke again. "Some of you may be wondering why I asked our Morse code experts to be here today. I was hoping that we could find another solution, but it seems that we need agent BRÜNNHILDE to keep broadcasting until the war is over. However, I think all of us can agree that she's headed for a breakdown of some kind, and that there's nothing we can do to prevent it."

Most of the handlers indicated their assent by nodding. Some had worried expressions on their faces; they realized that the agents they controlled might also have some sort of breakdown in the near future.

Air Commodore Pankhurst continued. "Clerkwell and Hall, you've both been present every time that agent BRÜNNHILDE has transmitted to Berlin."

The two Morse code specialists were seated together at the far end of the table. They both nodded their heads in agreement, even though Alfred had missed the first transmission, and Eric had not been present the last time that Helga had sent her message to Siegfried.

"Could either of you imitate her fist?"

There was a stunned silence as everyone suddenly realized what the air commodore was asking.

Alfred Hall responded first. "Sir, with all due respect, I really don't think I could do that. I can certainly detect even an extremely subtle change in her fist, but I just don't think I could replicate it." He leant forward over the table, his face red with embarrassment.

"What about you, Clerkwell?" Pankhurst asked.

There was a long silence. Then Eric rose slowly to his feet. It was obvious that he was thinking furiously. Then he suddenly came to a decision. "Sir," he said, "I don't know if I could, but I'd definitely like to give it a try. Hall here would be able to evaluate my performance and tell you how good a job I do. What I'm saying, sir, is that I'll do my best, and Hall will be able to judge if it's good enough to fool the Jerries."

"That's the spirit! Now, is there anything else we need to discuss?"

Another of the handlers raised his hand. "Sir, looking ahead, if someone can accurately mimic a double agent's fist, why would we need to keep him alive? If we execute him as a spy, we'd save an incredible amount of time, money and effort."

"What's the weakness in that otherwise excellent suggestion?" Pankhurst called out.

No one said anything for a while and then one of the Morse code experts spoke. "What if the Germans get suspicious and ask the agent a question that only he can answer? If we treat him nicely all the time, he may tell us the answer. But he can't help us if he's dead."

There was a stunned silence and then everyone around the table started grinning.

Then Carlyle chimed in, "And even if we just throw him into prison, he's not going to cooperate with us. It seems to me that we've got to continue to be courteous and pleasant at all times to our double agents, even if we can copy their fists perfectly."

"Meeting adjourned," Pankhurst said. "Johnson, Carlyle, Hall, Clerkwell, come with me now."

They followed him out. When they were all seated in his room, the air commodore announced, "I want to do a test immediately. Johnson, do you have any of the messages that agent BRÜNNHILDE has previously sent?"

"Yes, sir, I have all of them locked in my safe."

"Bring a typical one here right now. Clerkwell, go and fetch your telegraph key."

A few minutes later the test began. Eric sat at one end of the air commodore's wide desk with a page of five-letter groups in front of him and his key under his hand. Alfred sat at the other side. It was apparent that he still felt embarrassed by his public admission of failure at the meeting. At the same time, it was obvious from his posture that he was going to do his best to evaluate his colleague's imitation of Helga's fist.

Eric started to operate the key. Even Johnson and Carlyle could tell that, even though Eric was trying as hard as he could, he simply was unable to replicate Helga's characteristics. But suddenly, halfway through the message, the cadence of dots and dashes changed, and they realized that Johnson had picked up her rhythm. By the end, Alfred was grinning broadly, and so was Eric. It was clear to the air commodore that Eric's emulation was perfect.

But Pankhurst couldn't have risen to the heights of MI5 without being a perfectionist who dotted every "i" and crossed every "t" every single time. So he asked Eric to start again from the beginning, just to be sure. When Eric had finished, Alfred turned to the air commodore. "Sir, he's flawless. When I closed my eyes for a second or two, it was as if I was back in Helga's kitchen."

All five men were smiling, until Johnson said, "Sir, what's going to happen to Helga?"

And Eric Clerkwell added, "I hope you don't intend to hang her."

The air commodore made an impatient noise that sounded something like "P'tcha!" Then he went on. "No one has the slightest intention of hanging anyone. When we started the Double Cross System a year ago, we decided that we needed the threat of capital punishment to ensure full cooperation from the double agents. But that's all it was—a threat. In fact, we're not even going to put poor Helga in jail. As you heard at the end of the meeting, we may need her to respond to a question from Siegfried that only she can answer, so we want to keep her firmly on our side. She'll stay in that flat on Pavilion Road, under close guard of course, until the war is over. Then we'll probably grant her British nationality and send her to university. No doubt she'll be a model citizen.

"Johnson and Carlyle, I want you to prepare the next message from agent BRÜNNHILDE. Let's try and get it on the air tonight at eleven. It needs to say that she's just returned from meeting the scientist in the same pub and that he told her that, from tomorrow night, the beam bending will be 12.26 miles to the east. In other words, the main *Knickebein* transmitter must direct the bombers to fly 12.26 miles to the west of the target to compensate for our bending of their beam. She must promise to give him more details the following night. That will give us time to flesh out the story.

"And talking about flesh, we're going to need to decide in the next few days whether or not the scientist seduces her. On the one hand, it'll make Siegfried so furious that he'll lose what little judgment he has left. On the other hand, it might make him vengeful, and that might cause problems—for her and for us. We'll have to look at this issue extremely carefully from all angles. In the meantime, please draft the message, get the Double Cross people to approve it, and bring it to me for final signature."

"Is Johnson going to send it out from here?" Carlyle asked.

"Under no circumstances whatsoever," Pankhurst said. "The Germans may be using some sort of direction finder, and the radio has to be in the same place as always. It was bad enough when Helga sent the Jerries the message that she was going to find a new room somewhere else in London but the Double Cross team forgot to move her to a different location. I noticed that yesterday when I read her file from cover to cover. From now on, whenever Eric transmits, be careful to make sure that Helga is in her bedroom with a guard. We have to take precautions in case something snaps and she goes crazy during a transmission."

At eleven, Johnson and Carlyle watched as Eric Clerkwell, seated at the kitchen table, accurately imitated Helga's fist. Alfred Hall sat next to him, listening as intently as ever, but now to ensure quality control. At the end, the four of them were careful not to congratulate one another. Instead, they left the flat as quietly as they had entered. When they returned to MI5 headquarters, however, it was a different story. The air commodore was there to thank them all in person, and he produced a bottle of champagne that they all enjoyed immensely. The mood was one of noisy celebration, even in the presence of an air officer. In fact, Pankhurst seemed to be enjoying the informal party more than any of them. Carlyle wondered to himself how long it had been since the last time that the air commodore had celebrated anything.

Knightsbridge, London
Sunday, January 12th, 1941

The following evening, the team of four was back in the flat on Pavilion Road. That night's message from agent BRÜNNHILDE was somewhat apologetic in tone. On the unanimous advice of the psychologists working for MI5, she stated that, in order to obtain vital information about the beams for the Third Reich, the previous night she had had to sleep with the scientist, whose name turned out to be Clarence Westfield. Furthermore, she was about to move in with him, not—she stressed—because she had any feelings for him, but because it was the only way she could be assured of a continuous flow of information regarding the bending of the beams. She confirmed what she had said in her previous message, namely that the main *Knickebein* transmitter must now direct the bombers to fly 12.26 miles to the west of the target to compensate for the fact that the British were now bending all beams 12.26 miles to the east. Finally, she stated that she would transmit her future messages at 11 a.m. on weekdays, when Clarence would be safely away from home, at work in his laboratory.

After Eric Clerkwell had completed the transmission, the four men again left the flat in total silence. They all knew that this was the last message they would transmit from there, because they would send all future transmissions from Clarence Westfield's flat, which just happened to be located at MI5 headquarters. From then on, they could send messages to Berlin during their normal workday; there was no longer any need to travel to Knightsbridge for an 11 p.m. transmission.

Near London
Monday, January 13th, 1941

As he piloted his Heinkel He 111 bomber through the pitch-black night toward the Royal Albert Dock in the East End of London, Lieutenant Markus Krakauer kept thinking about the pre-flight briefing that the aircrews had received just before take-off. As best as he could understand the colonel's garbled and confused explanation, the British had somehow managed to bend the *Knickebein* main beam so that the point where the two beams crossed was now exactly 12.26 miles to the east of the actual target. However, the clever German scientists had managed to bend the main beam back to where it had been, so the bombardiers were instructed to drop their bombs in the usual way when they heard the steady note coming from both transmitters. Nazi science had triumphed once more, and the place where the two beams crossed was again precisely the location of the target.

However, it seemed that there was still one scientific problem that had not yet been solved. As a result of the interference signals that the British were transmitting, the beams were no longer reliable beyond the target point. Accordingly, if their course seemed to be wrong after they had dropped their bombs and were returning to their base in northern France, the navigators had orders to ignore the beam for once and instead navigate the old-fashioned way. Krakauer had little faith in the ability of his navigator/bombardier, Second Lieutenant Karl-Joachim Schmieder, to plot a course using dead reckoning or celestial navigation. The only reason that Schmieder had not been thrown out of the *Luftwaffe* aircrew-training school was that he understood better than anyone else in the class how the *Knickebein* beams worked. In fact, he knew far more about the navigation system than even their instructor. All the student navigators fully realized that theoretical knowledge of the principles behind the beam system was irrelevant when it came to actually navigating a plane with the aid of the beams, and even more irrelevant when other methods of aerial navigation were used. Nevertheless, solely on the basis of his deep understanding of how the beams worked, Schmieder had graduated top of his class of 35 navigators, and was therefore assigned to Krakauer, the top pilot in his class at flying school. Krakauer shuddered at the thought of what would happen if Schmieder had to calculate the route they would have to follow to return to northern France.

Krakauer continued to listen to the tones from the main *Knickebein* transmitter in Sortosville-en-Beaumont. Most of the time he heard the steady note, but every so often he accidentally allowed his bomber to veer slightly off course. When this happened, the resulting short tones or long tones assisted him to get back on the beam immediately. Now he started to hear a series of short tones from the receiver tuned to the crossbeam transmitter, the one situated in Nordfriesland. He alerted his bombardier.

At the instant that the steady tone that both receivers emitted informed them unequivocally that the Heinkel was precisely at the location of the target, the navigator/bombardier released all eight of the SC 250 bombs the plane carried. With the weight of the Heinkel reduced by nearly 4,500 pounds, the plane rose. Krakauer scanned the night sky for Spitfires. Seeing none, he headed for home, desperately hoping that he would not have to rely in any way at all on Karl-Joachim Schmieder's entirely inadequate navigational skills to get them back to base.

MI5 Headquarters, London
Tuesday, January 14th, 1941

When Johnson and Carlyle arrived at work, they found notes on their desks summoning them to the air commodore's daily 9:15 a.m. meeting. They both arrived a few minutes early and greeted the five officers already seated there, including Wallstead and Chulmleigh. On the stroke of the quarter hour, Pankhurst walked into the room. Everyone rose, and the military officers stood to attention. Pankhurst indicated that they should sit. As they did so, they all saw that he had a strange expression on his face. In fact, none of them had ever seen him looking that way before.

"Last night there was only one air raid," he said in a strange low voice. "Once more the Jerries targeted the East End of London and, more specifically, the Royal Docks in East Ham and West Ham. As you all know, there are three huge docks there: The Royal Victoria Dock, the Royal Albert Dock and the King George V Dock. Last night they chose as their target the Royal Albert Dock."

He stopped for a few seconds. It was clear that he was struggling to speak. He swallowed, blinked, and then blurted out: "The flat at 73 Pavilion Road, Knightsbridge, is located exactly 12.26 miles to the west of the Royal Albert Dock."

CHAPTER TWO
Two Cities: A Tale
1942

Abwehr Headquarters, Berlin
Monday, February 23rd, 1942

The sergeant ushered him into the office. One look at Lieutenant Colonel Emil von Krassheim was enough to make it abundantly clear that he was energetic, efficient and highly intelligent. His uniform was impeccable. His long thin face was perfectly shaved, and his black hair, recently cut, looked as if he had just combed it.

Behind the desk sat Colonel Siegfried Kupfer, head of Section I of the *Abwehr*. In contrast to his recently appointed second-in-command, Kupfer was fat, bald, lazy, inefficient and not particularly bright. His narrowly set eyes protruded. He had obtained his position because he had joined the Nazi Party in 1921 and had risen in the ranks due almost solely to his great skills as a street fighter and an enforcer. His appointment as head of Section I was made over the strongest possible objections of Admiral Wilhelm Canaris, the head of the *Abwehr*.

Von Krassheim marched smartly into the room, halted and gave a crisp *Heil Hitler* salute. In reply, Kupfer half raised his right hand, palm upward, then used the same hand to wave von Krassheim into a chair. The second-in-command sat down nimbly. He immediately opened his leather briefcase and took out three manila folders tied with red tape and marked *Streng Geheim* (Top Secret) in Gothic script.

"Krassheim," Kupfer said, "The sergeant said you wanted to see me."

"Yes, Colonel," von Krassheim said, his Prussian accent revealing his ancestry. "Our agent code-named PICKFORD in England has told us about three newspaper articles that are extremely puzzling and may have wide-ranging ramifications for the future conduct of the war."

Colonel Kupfer looked bored. British newspapers did not interest him. The only paper he read was the official Nazi newspaper, the *Völkischer Beobachter* (The People's Observer)—no other paper was worthy of his attention.

Von Krassheim persisted. He opened the top file and extracted a piece of paper. "The first article appeared in *The Times* of February 12th, 1942. It describes the capture of a German spy, one Fritz Gerber. It seems that we parachuted him into England but his parachute caught in a tree. He was trapped, unable to move. A Home Guard volunteer spotted him dangling from the branches and called the police. Gerber was easily captured. Two weeks later he faced a British firing squad."

"So. We've been losing a lot of spies lately. What's so special about Gerber?"

"Colonel, the newspaper article states that Gerber fell into a tree. There are very few trees in the Norfolk fen country, and certainly none in the area in which Gerber was dropped. Here's an aerial photograph of the target area. You can clearly see that there are no trees in the picture."

"So the pilot dropped Gerber in the wrong place. That also seems to be happening too often."

"With respect, Colonel, I have checked with both the pilot and the navigator. Gerber was dropped at precisely the correct place. Also, subagent MARTIN CHUZZLEWIT has disappeared. He was supposed to assist Gerber after he landed in the fen as arranged. Agent PICKFORD assumes that MARTIN CHUZZLEWIT was arrested at the same time as Gerber. It seems unlikely that Gerber was dropped in the wrong place and that MARTIN CHUZZLEWIT just happened to be in the same wrong place, too."

"What kind of code name is MARTIN CHUZZLEWIT?" Kupfer asked, completely oblivious to the main issue, which was that the British had known exactly when and where Gerber was going to be parachuted into Britain.

"He's the eponymous character from a book called *Martin Chuzzlewit* by the English author Charles Dickens. You'll remember that all the subagents that agent PICKFORD controls have been assigned names of Dickens characters."

"So the British newspaper got the story wrong. Do you expect an inferior race to have newspapers as good as the *Völkischer Beobachter*?"

Von Krassheim decided to treat the question as rhetorical and opened the next file.

"The second article appeared in *The Times* of February 14th, 1942. It described the arrest of a German spy named Hans Glocken. It states that he rowed ashore in a dinghy from a U-boat. However, once on land he tripped on a rock and fell and broke his leg. It was a severe compound fracture rendering him unable to move. A passerby out for an evening stroll found him lying on the rocks and called the police. Glocken was arrested and shot two weeks later."

"So?" Siegfried Kupfer asked, clearly still uninterested.

"Colonel, the U-boat dropped Glocken at a sandy beach. As you can see from this aerial photograph, there are no rocks anywhere near the area. There's no way that Glocken could've tripped and broken a leg."

"So the U-boat captain is as incompetent as the pilot who dropped Gerber. Obviously he was left on the wrong beach."

"Again with great respect, Colonel, the U-boat navigator is absolutely adamant that no mistake was made. Furthermore, subagent NICHOLAS NICKLEBY was supposed to be on the beach flashing a light to indicate to the sailors where to land. Members of the U-boat crew on watch have reported seeing the correct sequences of flashes at the pre-arranged time. And NICHOLAS NICKLEBY has also disappeared."

Slow as he was, Kupfer was starting to see a pattern. "So, we have two agents whom our armed forces delivered to the correct place. The British knew in advance exactly when and where both agents would arrive and they were waiting for them. They arrested both agents, as well as the subagents who were supposed to be on site to assist our agents when they landed. The British executed our agents. The two subagents have disappeared—they're probably dead, too. In both cases, an article appeared in the same newspaper describing a most unlikely accident that resulted in the capture of each of our agents. So?"

"Colonel, the third article was also in *The Times*," von Krassheim said as he untied the tape on the last file. "The article appeared on February 20th, 1942. It stated that an agent named Evan Williams-Davies landed from an E-boat. The torpedo boat dropped him on an isolated Welsh beach. From there he walked to the nearest railway station, where an alert policeman arrested him. It seems that Evan Williams-Davies was wearing clothing with a foreign cut and spoke English with a foreign accent. His papers were forged. Like our other two agents, the British executed him two weeks later."

"This story is not quite the same as the other two. What are the facts?" the colonel asked.

"Evan Williams-Davies was a Welsh nationalist, born and bred in Llandrindod Wells. An E-boat picked him up and brought him to Berlin for discussions. After two weeks, the same E-boat returned him to Wales, wearing the same British clothes as when he left his native shores and carrying the same valid identity papers. Furthermore, he spoke English with a Welsh accent, the same accent as hundreds of thousands of other Welshmen. Our subagent SYDNEY CARTON was supposed to be in the waiting room of the station to assist Williams-Davies and he's disappeared, too.

"Finally, as you pointed out, an unlikely and somewhat humorous account of each arrest appeared in the same newspaper. What's not so funny is that we've lost three more *Abwehr* agents, as well as the three subagents who were supposed to meet them."

"Who knew that our three agents were coming to Britain? And who knew when and where they were arriving?" Kupfer asked.

"The usual people here in the *Abwehr*, of course, plus agent PICKFORD and the subagents whom he told to retrieve the new agents."

"But each time a different subagent was involved. So it's not the subagents. I see two possibilities: Either PICKFORD is now working for the British, or the information he receives from us reaches the British without PICKFORD's knowledge. Which is it, Krassheim?"

"Colonel, in answering that question, the key issues seem to be: Why did the British tell us through *The Times*, not once but three times, that the information we send to PICKFORD goes straight to MI5? And why did PICKFORD tell us about the three newspaper articles that apparently conclusively prove that he's not to be trusted?"

Kupfer was not going to admit to von Krassheim that he had no idea whatsoever. So he gave his usual delicately nuanced reply to questions that he could not answer.

"You're so clever asking these stupid questions, so you answer them."

"I can certainly tell you why PICKFORD told us about the newspaper articles. Damning as they are to him, they're no worse than the three separate reports that PICKFORD radioed to us after each agent was captured. He's been completely open and honest in his messages; he didn't attempt to hide any fact, no matter how badly it appeared to reflect on him. I think that there were two reasons why he told us about the newspaper articles. He assumed that we'd eventually get to hear of them via a more circuitous route. But more importantly, he's trying to convince us that he's trustworthy in every respect."

"But how can he be trustworthy? It's clear that all the details of our instructions to him regarding the arrival of the three new agents were passed on to MI5."

"Colonel Kupfer, I think he's trying to tell us that someone else is the traitor."

"But how can that be? If I recall correctly, our station at Hamburg transmits the messages to PICKFORD and to no one else."

"But what if the British are intercepting the messages?"

"My dear Krassheim, the messages we send to PICKFORD are in code. How can the British possibly decrypt them?"

There was a pause while Emil von Krassheim tried to decide just how to respond. "Sir, the British may be an inferior race, but it's just possible that they've broken the code. After all, we gave the code to agent PICKFORD in September 1937. There've certainly been improvements in decryption techniques since then. So, I believe that PICKFORD told us about the newspaper articles to warn us that his code has been broken, and we need to send him a new code."

"But if that's the case, why didn't he just send a message saying something like, 'The British appear to have broken the old code you gave me four and half years ago. Send a courier with a new code.' Why is he playing games with us?"

"Colonel, if he knows that the British are intercepting our messages to him and can decrypt them, then he knows that the British are probably intercepting his messages to us and can certainly decrypt them, too—after all, it's the same code. So, he doesn't want the British to know that he's caught onto the fact that they're reading our messages."

"And why not?"

"Because once there's a new, stronger code in place, the old code can be used to send fictional messages to deceive the British."

There was a much longer silence as Kupfer thought about his second-in-command's last remark. "That's absolutely brilliant. And so appropriate. We punish the British for daring to break our code by tricking them with false information. Agent PICKFORD is a genius! Summon the head of our cryptographic department, get an unbreakable code from him, and send it to London by courier right away. The information that agent PICKFORD supplies us is absolutely invaluable to our war effort. We have to do everything in our power to ensure that he can resume sending secret messages to us as soon as possible."

Von Krassheim sat still for a second or two. Then he spoke. "Colonel, what of the other question?"

"What other question? When I give you an order, you carry it out right away. Why are you still sitting there? Didn't I just tell you that this matter is of the highest importance and extremely urgent?"

"But Colonel, why did the British put those three articles in *The Times*?"

"What? What do you mean? They put them there to tell PICKFORD that the code was broken, so he could tell us that the code was broken, so we could send him a new code, which is what I just ordered you to do."

"But Colonel, there was no need for the British to tell PICKFORD that the code was broken. He's a loyal servant of the Reich, he didn't tell anyone about the three agents whom we sent, so he knew at once that the only way that the British could possibly have known precisely when and where our agents were coming was if they'd intercepted our messages to him and had broken our code. I have to ask you again: Why did the British put those three articles in *The Times*? Until we know that, surely we should wait before sending confidential information like an unbreakable code?"

"*Go!*" yelled Kupfer.

Von Krassheim went.

Abwehr Headquarters, Berlin
Tuesday, February 24th, 1942

Otto Trumbauer was a most unlikely spy. Drafted into the German army in September 1939, the authorities found him to be medically unfit for active service because, like Kaiser Wilhelm II, he had a withered left arm due to Erb-Duchenne palsy. Instead, they appointed Otto to be a clerk in the *Abwehr*. Otto had a degree in English Literature from the Friedrich Schiller University of Jena. But because Otto was physically handicapped, his supervisor automatically assumed that Otto was not too bright, and at best would make a barely competent filing clerk in the personnel department, so Otto toiled away for two years in that position.

The other filing clerks in his department despised Otto. They were two middle-aged spinsters known to one and all as *Fraulein* Mecklenburg and *Fraulein* Rott—as far as anyone knew, neither of them had a first name. They had worked together in the personnel department for many years, and now they continually complained to one another that not just a male, but a male cripple, had invaded their private fiefdom. One day they decided to play a cruel joke on him. A selection committee had chosen a number of *Abwehr* personnel for training as secret agents. When *Fraulein* Mecklenburg pulled their files, she added Otto Trumbauer's dossier to the pile. *Fraulein* Rott then added Otto's name to the list of students, written in a passable imitation of Colonel Kupfer's unlettered handwriting.

The course instructors, who naturally assumed that Kupfer himself had selected Otto for the course, made every accommodation for his physical handicap. When the results of the final examination were handed to Kupfer, he was astounded to see that Otto was far ahead of all the others in almost every category. In short, Otto was the perfect spy, on paper at least. Furthermore, his handicap could be considered a strong advantage. After all, whoever heard of a secret agent with a withered left arm?

Colonel Kupfer summoned Otto, whose uniform revealed that he was still a private in the German Army. His face was squarish, with a straight nose and a receding chin. The skin surrounding his brown eyes was puffy.

"Trumbauer," Kupfer said, "you have been chosen to serve the Third Reich in a unique capacity. I firmly believe that you are not just the right person for this critical mission, you are the only person who could succeed."

"*Heil Hitler!*" Otto shouted, with true National Socialist zeal. Finally he could serve his *Volk*, his *Reich*, and his *Führer*.

"You are to travel to England with all haste to deliver a book to a senior agent."

"A book, sir?" Otto's reaction was first confusion, and then bitter disappointment. He was ready to give his life for Germany in the course of carrying out this secret mission for which he apparently was so ideally suited, and now it seemed he was nothing more than a courier. But even a courier could play a vital role by transporting highly confidential plans or the blueprints of a secret weapon of inconceivable destructive power across enemy lines. Instead, Otto was to carry a book.

Even Siegfried Kupfer was able to see the utter disappointment in Otto's face.

"No, my boy, you don't understand. This is one of the most important missions of the war. The British have broken a code for communicating with our brave agents in England. Your task is to bring a new, unbreakable code to London as quickly as you can. This will achieve two major objectives. Our agents in England will once again be able to send messages to Berlin that will be unintelligible to the British. And they will send messages to us in the old code to spread disinformation among the enemy."

Otto perked up a little on hearing this, but he was still somewhat surprised that he was to carry a book.

"But if I carry a codebook, Colonel Kupfer, and I'm captured, the new code will fall into the hands of the enemy."

"Trumbauer, you will not be carrying a codebook. You will be carrying a novel by an

English author called Charles Dickens. The name of the book is *A Tale of Two Cities*."

And Otto understood immediately. In the lectures on codes and ciphers, he had learned that almost every code can be broken. One of the few unbreakable codes is a book code. For example, *A Tale of Two Cities* begins with the words, "It was the best of times, it was the worst of times." The word "best" is the fourth word in the first line of the first page. The letter "e" is the second letter in that word, so in a code message the four numbers 1, 1, 4 and 2 would represent that letter. More generally, any letter in a *Tale of Two Cities* would be encrypted as four numbers: the page number, the line number on that page, the word number in that line, and the letter number in that word. And it would be impossible to decrypt the message unless one had an exact copy of the book that was used to encrypt the message, letter by letter—a different edition would be useless.

"But why do I have to travel to London?" Otto asked. "London has the greatest second-hand bookshops in the world. Even though our valiant *Luftwaffe* flattened most of London during the Blitz, there must be several still standing. Surely all we have to do is send a message by radio to our agent with precise details of the edition of a *Tale of Two Cities*?"

Kupfer smiled. It was a cruel smirk, a vicious grimace of triumph, a sneer that trumpeted aloud that he, Kupfer, was far more intelligent than Otto Trumbauer, notwithstanding Otto's remarkably high test scores, as well as his degree from one of Germany's top universities.

"Trumbauer, how would you inform our agent by radio without the British overhearing? I told you that they've broken the code that we're using at present."

With his withered left arm, Otto was so used to insults, disparagement and ridicule that he was impervious to the undisguised contempt in Kupfer's brutal answer.

"Here's the book you'll be carrying," Kupfer continued, oblivious as always to his sadistic streak. "You'll read it from cover to cover during the course of your journey—it must look like a well-read book, otherwise it may stick out like a sore thumb during a customs inspection. It's absolutely vital that the book appears to be an integral part of your luggage, not something special that you're carrying from Berlin to London."

Kupfer handed Trumbauer a paperback edition of *A Tale of Two Cities*. "Guard this book with your life. It is absolutely essential for us to be able to continue to communicate privately with our agents in London—the outcome of the war depends on it. Keep it in the inside pocket of your jacket. Take it out and read it whenever appropriate. It must seem that the book is in your inside pocket for your convenience, not as a hiding place.

"When you leave this room Captain Bernhardt Fasch will brief you. You remember him from the course—he taught you how to travel in enemy countries. You'll be taking a circuitous route, so you'll need to leave early tomorrow morning so that you can deliver the book as soon as possible. Good luck, Trumbauer!"

Otto left Kupfer's office and went to see Captain Fasch. His former instructor looked extremely worried. His whole face seemed to be frowning, with lines on his forehead, over the bridge of his nose and on his cheeks. He did not smile when Otto walked in, but kept his lips pursed.

"Otto, as I'm sure you've been told, this is a vital mission. The book has to be delivered to London without fail and as soon as humanly possible. We've recently lost agents whom we parachuted into Britain or who rowed ashore from a U-boat or an E-boat to a deserted beach at the dead of night. So, we need a different way to get you to England. We've decided that you'll take a train from here to neutral Portugal. From there, you'll travel as a passenger on a cargo vessel to the neutral Republic of Ireland. The only tricky part of your journey will be when you clandestinely cross the border from the Republic of Ireland into Northern Ireland, part of the United Kingdom. You'll then take a boat to Heysham and a train from there to London—the last part of your trip should be straightforward.

"Regarding your cover story: The Republic of Ireland is short of wheat, so the Irish Mercantile Marine is importing grain from South America. We have no objection to that, because Ireland is doing its utmost to maintain true neutrality. Our U-boat captains know that the ships of the merchant navy of the Republic of Ireland fly large Irish flags and that they have the word "EIRE" (that's the name of their country in the Irish language) painted in huge uppercase letters on the sides and decks of their ships. So grain shipments for the people of the Republic of Ireland are arriving safely in Cork, Limerick and Dublin. The problem is our allies in the Republic of Ireland, the Irish Republican Army."

"I didn't know we had allies in Ireland," Otto said.

"Surely you're familiar with the Arab proverb, 'The enemy of my enemy is my friend'?" Fasch asked. "The IRA has been fighting the British since the First World War and their leaders are hoping for help from us to strike against Britain in Northern Ireland. They're helping us with information for air raids against industrial targets there, especially aircraft factories.

"However, the IRA is critically short of money," he continued. "So, even though their leadership has strictly forbidden this, many IRA members earn funds for the organization by smuggling goods across the border from the Republic of Ireland into Northern Ireland. We've learned that many tons of South American wheat have crossed into Northern Ireland and from there into England. In other words, our U-boats sink British grain carriers headed for England, but allow Irish ships to break the blockade."

"Can't you stop the wheat coming into Ireland from South America?" Otto asked.

"Not without sinking Irish ships, which we very definitely don't want to do. For strategic reasons, we have to remain on excellent terms with the Republic of Ireland at all times. So, we're sending a senior *Abwehr* officer to Dublin to meet with IRA leaders and determine how to stop the smuggling. We'll probably have to agree to give them weapons and ammunition, explosives, and, above all, lots of money."

"What about radio equipment? Don't they need that?"

"Yes, of course, but a radio could be traced back to us, and cause a diplomatic incident or worse. As I said, we need to keep the Republic of Ireland neutral at all costs."

Captain Fasch explained further. "So, you and Major Georg Strauss will travel to Dublin disguised as Irish grain buyers. You'll travel by train from Berlin to Lisbon. To ensure that you get to Lisbon quickly and with minimum interference, you'll be wearing the uniforms of SS-officers until you reach Madrid. You'll find that you'll have every compartment to yourselves, no matter how full the train may be, so there won't be problems with inquisitive fellow passengers. And the Spanish border guards and customs officers will just wave you through.

"At the German embassy in Madrid you'll be equipped for your onward journey as Irish citizens who emigrated from Germany in 1936, including money and papers. After we're finished here, we'll go to the photographic department—you'll need to take with you a photograph that our representative at the embassy will paste into the Irish passport he'll give you.

"Both you and Major Strauss speak excellent English but with a heavy German accent, so no one would expect you to have acquired any sort of Irish lilt when speaking English. Once you get to Dublin, you'll both make contact with the IRA. Strauss will then negotiate with them, while you'll pay them to smuggle you across the border into Northern Ireland. After that, it should all be plain sailing for you."

"How do I make contact with our agent in London?"

"That's the whole problem."

"What do you mean?"

"Agent PICKFORD has evaded capture by MI5 for nearly five years by staying hidden. He has a large team of subagents who carry out his orders and report back to him. Even they never interact with him. Communication is always via dead-letter drops and accommodation addresses. The problem is that we can't get in touch with him without the British finding out because, as you know, they've broken our code, the one we gave him in 1937."

"So what am I to do when I get to London?"

"You'll contact agent MISS HAVISHAM. She's a subagent of PICKFORD. And the reason you'll contact her is that, unlike any of the other subagents, we know where she's staying. For the sake of security, we've gone to a lot of trouble to ensure that no subagent knows enough about any of the other subagents to be able to give them away if the British capture that subagent. But the weakness in our scheme is that we've assumed that we could always communicate with PICKFORD by radio and, through him, with all the subagents. So, now we have a web of agents in London communicating with PICKFORD, but that's as far as it goes. His team is gathering vital information, but we've no way of laying our hands on it."

"And how do I contact MISS HAVISHAM?"

"Her address is Flat 12, 22 Howland Street, Camden. It's just off Tottenham Court Road."

"What are the sign and the countersign?"

"When she opens the door, you say, 'I'm here to sign the papers.' The countersign is, 'I hope you brought a fountain pen with black ink.'"

"And do I give the book to her?"

"Under no circumstances whatsoever. You must ask her to arrange a meeting with PICKFORD and you will hand the book to him personally."

"How do I identify myself to PICKFORD?"

"You say 'Charles Darcy sent me.'"

"Don't you mean 'Charles Darnay'? Fitzwilliam Darcy is a character from Jane Austen's *Pride and Prejudice,* and Charles Darnay is a key figure in a *Tale of Two Cities* by Charles Dickens."

"No. That's the whole point. The sign is a first name of a Dickens character with the last name of a Jane Austen character."

"And what is the countersign?"

"He should reply, 'Ah, yes, Fitzwilliam Darnay introduced me to him.' Do you see the pattern?"

"Yes, that's clear. But anyone who's reasonably well read in English literature who heard the 'Charles Darcy' sign would easily be able to come up with the 'Fitzwilliam Darnay' countersign. How will I know that the person MISS HAVISHAM takes me to is actually PICKFORD?" Otto asked.

"Excellent question! You're worried that PICKFORD might have been arrested and that the person you're taken to meet is actually an imposter from MI5, aren't you?"

"Yes, quite right."

"That's going to be hard to solve," Captain Fasch said. "The only contact we've had with PICKFORD for the last five years has been radio messages back and forth."

"Don't you have a photograph in his personal file?"

"We don't even have a personal file. In mid-1937, agent PICKFORD sent a package to the German consul in Edinburgh enclosing the plans for the Muir bombsight. Everything he's given us subsequently has also been of superlative quality. Just before the war broke out, he sent us a radio message asking us to send him an assistant. Someone in the *Abwehr* got confused and, in his reply, referred to the agent as 'Pickwick.' That gave PICKFORD an idea—he insisted that his new assistant's code name had to be a character from the works of Charles Dickens. The network has grown and all the subagents have names of that kind."

"Isn't that dangerous?" Otto asked. "Once the British find the pattern, it could result in the whole network being exposed."

"I don't think so. We know nothing at all about PICKFORD. He transmits from somewhere in North London, but he could live anywhere. None of his subagents know anything about him, either. As I said, they use accommodation addresses and drop boxes to communicate with him. And I doubt that he personally picks up the messages. He surely sends intermediaries, and he's probably told them he's working for the British secret service. So, no, we don't have a photograph of PICKFORD. We don't have an address, we don't have a telephone number, we don't even have a description of him. And I know what you're going to ask next—we don't even know if PICKFORD is a 'he.' Up to now we've assumed that PICKFORD is a man, but for all we know, he's a she.

"Now, what was your question again? Oh, yes, you were wondering how you could tell if the person you meet is actually PICKFORD. Let me think about it."

Captain Fasch pondered for a while, then his face lit up. "I know. When they take you to PICKFORD, ask him to tell you what his last message was. If he tells you about three articles in *The Times* regarding three *Abwehr* agents who were captured right after they arrived in Britain then he's PICKFORD."

Fasch had blundered. When Otto heard the words "three *Abwehr* agents who were captured right after they arrived in Britain," he suddenly realized that the mission for which he had been selected would be anything but straightforward. He knew that the *Abwehr* had not bothered to upgrade the code for five years. He was aware that MI5 had intercepted and decrypted radio messages between London and Berlin. Was he heading straight for the lions' den?

"What have you told London about my arrival?" Otto asked, trying to hide any nervousness in his voice.

"Nothing, of course."

"Who knows about my mission?"

"Only the relevant personnel in the *Abwehr* and one person in the German embassy in Madrid. That's all."

"Are you sure about that?"

"Of course I'm sure."

"But you've lost three agents on their arrival in Britain. MI5 must have known all about them."

"But that was because they broke our code, and we've not used that code subsequently. I assure you, we've sent nothing whatsoever to London."

Otto Trumbauer believed Fasch, but he nevertheless was extremely concerned. Now his biggest worry was what would happen when he arrived in London.

"What am I to do if MISS HAVISHAM turns out to be an imposter?" Otto asked. "Or if she's been turned, and the person she takes me to isn't PICKFORD?"

"Both of those eventualities are most unlikely. But if something like that should happen, get back to the Republic of Ireland as quickly as you can."

"And then?"

"Go straight to the German legation in Dublin. They'll help you to return to Berlin."

Otto recalled that Fasch had informed him that German policy was to ensure that the Republic of Ireland stayed neutral "at all costs." So, there was no way that any German diplomat in the Republic of Ireland would help him under any circumstances. It was now unambiguously clear to him that, if anything went wrong on this mission, Otto would be up the river without a paddle. The question in his mind was whether the river in question was the River Spree in Berlin or the River Thames in London.

Berlin
Wednesday, February 25th, 1942

As he boarded the Paris express at the Berlin Central Station early the next morning, he wondered if *Fraulein* Mecklenburg and *Fraulein* Rott would have realized that SS-Captain Vogel, wearing a smart black SS-uniform, was none other than their erstwhile colleague, Otto Trumbauer. He eased his way into Compartment Seven, where he found SS-Colonel Maximilian von Krammländer equally smartly attired. Otto took a careful look at von Krammländer and realized that his handsome

98

traveling companion was Major Strauss, from Section II of the *Abwehr*. Like Otto, von Krammländer worked at *Abwehr* headquarters at 76/78 Tirpitzufer, a shady street next to the Landwehr Canal. Otto saluted his senior officer smartly, then asked permission to take a seat opposite him.

"Of course, SS-Captain. Make yourself comfortable. We have a 15-hour journey ahead of us, assuming that there are no 'interruptions' between here and Paris." Otto realized that his companion was referring obliquely to Allied bombing raids, which were starting to hamper German rail traffic quite severely. Otto took his lead from von Krammländer, and resolved that, until they reached Madrid, he would invariably address his traveling companion by his SS-rank and treat him with due deference.

A minute after Otto had entered the compartment, an obese German civilian dressed in a tweed suit flung open the door and marched in. He was about to toss his suitcase onto the rack when he suddenly noticed the two SS-officers seated in the compartment in which he had reserved a seat. He somehow managed to apologize abjectly for the intrusion and simultaneously leave the compartment, closing the door considerably more politely than the way he had opened it. The train was full, but the fat man preferred to stand in the corridor all the way to Paris. Otto now appreciated why Captain Fasch had told him that he and Major Strauss would have their compartment to themselves the entire journey to Madrid.

The train pulled out of the Central Station precisely on time. Otto took *A Tale of Two Cities* out of his uniform pocket, and using the formal third person, asked if the SS-Colonel would mind if Otto read. The SS-Colonel nodded nonchalantly, and Otto opened the paperback.

As a requirement of his degree in English, Otto had taken a course on Victorian literature. As a result, he had read a number of novels by Charles Dickens but, for some reason, the list of prescribed books had not included *A Tale of Two Cities*. So, Otto looked forward eagerly to reading the famous story set in London and Paris before and during the French Revolution.

They arrived at the East Station in Paris only a few minutes later than scheduled. The train had had to slow down when it reached tracks that had recently been repaired after a bombing raid, but the driver managed to make up some of the lost time.

"Captain, we have just under two hours to get to Austerlitz Station to catch the night train to Madrid. I'd have liked to invite you to join me for a dinner of French food and French champagne, but I don't think we can enjoy a leisurely meal and still make the train. So, let's take a taxi to Austerlitz Station and eat at the brasserie there."

The two men strolled out of the station to the taxi rank. There was a long line of people waiting but, as SS-officers, they simply walked to the head of the queue and took the first cab that arrived.

They ate dinner at Austerlitz Station. The food was far superior to what was available in most restaurants in Berlin at that time, and the champagne they drank was excellent. Both men kept a careful eye on the clock, and made sure to leave the brasserie in good time.

They boarded the train and entered their sleeper compartment. Two Frenchmen were already there. Their reaction was the same as that of the fat man in Berlin that morning—they fled. Von Krammländer and Vogel settled down for the night, each in a lower bunk.

Vogel woke up when the train had just pulled out of Poitiers. He sat up and stretched. Von Krammländer woke a few minutes later. They washed, dressed and went to the dining car for breakfast. The dining car was the last car in the train so that, after the meal service, it could easily be uncoupled at the next stop and prepared for another train.

The next halt on their route was Bordeaux, some two hours away; Bordeaux was the site of a major base for U-boats. Hardly had they started to eat their meal when a flight of RAF planes, returning to England after bombing the submarine pens, flew overhead. One Avro Lancaster had not managed to drop all its bombs, so the bombardier jettisoned the final bomb as the plane overflew the Paris–Madrid train; for safety reasons, it was strictly forbidden to land a plane with munitions still in the bomb bay.

The bomb exploded in front of the train, destroying the rails. There was an ear-shattering noise. The dining car rocked dangerously on its bogies, but after a few seconds fell heavily back onto the track. And then there was silence, broken by a high-pitched scream.

Vogel turned to von Krammländer. "Colonel, am I to assist with the rescue operation?" he whispered.

Von Krammländer hissed back, "You are an SS-officer. You will sit here and enjoy your breakfast. The conductor will come here and report to us, you can be sure of that."

Five minutes later the French conductor ran into the dining car and stopped at their table. He addressed them in pidgin German, interspersed with long stretches of excited French.

"Gentlemen, the track ahead of us was destroyed. It seems that the engineer tried to stop the train, but there wasn't time, so the engine and the coal tender were derailed and they overturned. All the crew are dead. The front wheels of the first carriage left the track, but the carriage stayed upright. All the other carriages appear to be undamaged."

"Have you radioed for help?" demanded von Krammländer.

"Yes, Colonel."

"Fine. Then we will wait until they get here. In the meantime, bring us fresh coffee."

It took several hours before the track repair could be completed. Then a crane had to lift the first carriage back onto the rails. Finally, the railway men coupled a new engine and tender to the train. During that time, Vogel finished reading his book. He immediately started again from the beginning.

Abwehr Headquarters, Berlin
Thursday, February 26th, 1942

"Krassheim, have Strauss and Trumbauer arrived in Madrid?" Kupfer asked.

"Not yet, Colonel."

"But didn't I impress upon you the extreme urgency of Trumbauer's mission? Didn't I explain to you that the book has to get into the hands of agent PICKFORD as soon as humanly possible?"

"Yes, Colonel, you did. But the British bombed the railway line between Poitiers and Bordeaux. A track crew from the French National Railway Company rushed to the scene. They've completed the repairs, so our men are on their way again."

"But they're late."

"Yes, they were held up for several hours. However, Captain Fasch designed his plan to be flexible enough to cope with delays caused by factors beyond our control. I assure you that Trumbauer will deliver the book in London on schedule."

"Krassheim, I am not in the least interested in your assurances. From now I want you to keep me informed of Trumbauer's location at least twice a day. The fate of the war may well depend on that book."

"Yes, Colonel."

"And another thing. Contact our representative at the embassy in Madrid and impress on him the extreme urgency of the mission. And instruct him to pass that message on to Strauss and Trumbauer without fail."

Madrid
Thursday, February 26th, 1942

SS-Colonel von Krammländer and SS-Captain Vogel arrived at Atocha Station in Madrid more than 24 hours after they had left Paris. The two men immediately took a taxi to the German embassy. The guards in front of the building inspected their papers carefully. Then the sergeant escorted them inside.

"We need to see the Cultural Attaché," von Krammländer barked.

The guard did not bat an eyelid, even though it was now the middle of the night. He was well aware that the Cultural Attaché, Baron Heinz Ludwig zu Baden, was the *Abwehr* representative in Madrid. The sergeant invited the two SS-officers to take a seat while he went upstairs to wake Baron zu Baden.

A few minutes later, a tall, thin aristocratic-looking man in a double-breasted suit descended the staircase. He was prematurely bald. A monocle sat in the orbit of his right eye. Otto took one look at him and immediately thought of the Planter's advertising logo, Mr. Peanut.

Zu Baden greeted the two men by asking to see their papers, which he scrutinized even more closely than the guards. Then he requested their *Abwehr* papers. These, too, he examined meticulously. Finally satisfied, he smiled broadly—without letting his monocle drop—and extended his hand to each man in turn.

"My dear Trumbauer, welcome to Madrid! How nice to meet you, Major Strauss! Please come to my office—you'll be so much more comfortable there. I gather from the lateness of your arrival that you encountered some problems?"

Georg Strauss explained what happened.

"I'm so sorry to hear that. But you are now safe and sound in Madrid. With your permission, let's get to work."

He offered them cigarettes from a silver filigree box on his desk, which they both declined. He took one, lit it, and inserted it into a long ivory cigarette holder.

"You'll be traveling from now on under your own names."

"Why?" Otto spluttered.

"Well, your cover is that you emigrated from Germany to the Republic of Ireland in 1936. That means we can use German records up to that date, and you don't need to memorize any of our fabricated information before then."

Otto was impressed with this answer. He nodded his head appreciatively.

"You're both grain buyers who have come to Portugal and Spain to buy wheat for Ireland. The Irish people are deeply religious Roman Catholics who know their Bibles well, so you're working for a firm of grain merchants called Joseph's Brothers."

Major Strauss looked at him blankly, but Otto caught the reference. "In the Book of Genesis, Joseph's brothers go to Egypt to buy grain."

"Exactly!" Baron zu Baden beamed.

He went on. "While you were in transit we prepared papers for you, including Irish passports—

you both became citizens as soon as you could. If you would be so kind as to let me have the photographs that Captain Fasch gave you, I'll paste them in. Sign here, please, Trumbauer. Major Strauss, your signature goes there. Please let the glue dry for a few minutes. Now, this folder contains correspondence with Spanish and Portuguese grain sellers."

Georg glanced through the letters sent to and from Ireland and remarked, "A lot of work has gone into this. You've prepared carbon copies of letters that Joseph's Brothers sent and originals from Iberian grain sellers on what seems to be authentic letterhead paper."

"We made the first set a while ago. We've used this cover documentation before. Each time we reuse it, we merely revise the dates. And we'll continue to use it in the future unless you tell us that it's fallen into the hands of Irish or English officials."

"I assume that, when we get back to Germany, you'll want us to destroy these letters."

"Of course. We'll prepare a new set from our originals for the next users, dated appropriately."

"That's all clear," Otto said.

"The other folder contains your cover information," zu Baden said. "Obviously you know your names, but you'll need to memorize your home address in Dublin and so on. You'll study this material on the train and continually review the contents of the folder there. Make sure you destroy it before you arrive in Lisbon. There's also an envelope for each of you containing Portuguese money, a second envelope with Irish money and a third envelope with British money. Don't worry, it's all the real thing—we don't give the counterfeit stuff to our agents.

"Now, as to your clothes, I've assembled a set of Irish-made clothing and personal effects for each of you. Would you please come with me?"

A few minutes later, two Irish grain buyers, resplendent in Irish tweed suits and overcoats, re-entered the Cultural Attaché's office. The only item that they had kept from their previous identities was Otto's copy of *A Tale of Two Cities*, now nestling in the inside pocket of the jacket of his well-worn suit.

"That's so much better!" zu Baden insisted, once again smiling broadly. "By the way, this afternoon I received a rather stern message from Berlin stressing that your mission is vitally important and that you're to travel as fast as you possibly can. There's an express train leaving for Lisbon in 90 minutes. I suggest you walk to the hotel on the next block and take a taxi from there. We don't want you to be linked to the embassy in any way. Here are some Spanish pesetas you'll use to tip the doorman and pay the taxi, and to buy your tickets to Lisbon. I know that you've used Reichsmarks to pay your travel expenses up to now, but you're no longer SS officers.

"On the train, I want you both to memorize not just your cover information but also all the details of the correspondence I've given you so that, if necessary, you can answer questions about your activities in Spain and Portugal. I'm sure there's no need to remind you to be sure to sit and read the material in such a way that your fellow travelers don't get a glimpse of what you're studying.

"When your train arrives in Lisbon, take a taxi to the harbor. This envelope here contains Portuguese escudos for the taxi and any incidental expenses. Obviously, we can't put you onto an Irish ship— you'd be exposed as German agents almost immediately—but there's a Portuguese freighter in port, the *Coimbra*, loading goods for Cork. I've arranged for a cabin for the two of you. You won't have any difficulties on board because the captain, João Torga, is a good friend of Germany. He'll arrange for you to take your meals in your cabin to keep you away from inquisitive crewmembers or other passengers, if there are any. By the way, there's no need to pay for your passage; Captain Torga has recently received a large sum for his services, present and future, which include keeping the ship in port until you arrive.

"Also, you're probably wondering how you're going to get back after you've completed your respective missions. Well, the *Coimbra* plies back and forth between Lisbon and Cork, so all you have to do is return to Cork and wait for the *Coimbra* to arrive, and that's it. Stay away from the German legation in Dublin, please—I believe you both know why. And I don't want to seem inhospitable, but I think you should leave now if you want to catch the Lisbon express."

Georg and Otto took the small suitcases that Heinz Ludwig had given them and walked into the lobby of the hotel near the German embassy. Two minutes later they emerged and, in English, asked the doorman to call them a taxi. They arrived back at Atocha Station with plenty of time in hand to buy their tickets.

As they entered their compartment, they saw that a middle-aged Spanish couple had already taken the other two seats. This time, of course, their fellow passengers did not flee into the corridor when Georg and Otto walked in. Instead, they politely greeted the two grain buyers.

They settled themselves down for the 14-hour trip: Georg started reading the folder containing the Joseph's Brothers correspondence while Otto studied the cover material. An hour later they exchanged folders and kept memorizing. Over the course of the long day, they both napped briefly once or twice, but they repeatedly went over the contents of the folders so that, if officials en route interrogated them, they could answer without thinking. And as they neared Lisbon, Georg went to the washroom in their carriage where he disposed of their cover material.

Lisbon
Thursday, February 26th, 1942

The train arrived in Lisbon in the early evening. The wind was blowing strongly, the sky was black with heavy clouds, and gusts of rain drummed on the roof of Rossio Station. There was a lengthy line of taxis outside, so Otto and Georg did not have to wait in the foul weather to get a ride to the docks. The taxi driver asked the customs officer at the harbor entrance where the *Coimbra* was moored, and they soon found themselves standing at the bottom of the gangway. In front of them was a small cargo vessel, badly in need of a new coat of paint. In addition to looking worn, the ship seemed dirty, and the plethora of rust made it clear that the *Coimbra* had not been properly maintained for years.

An armed guard stood at the foot of the gangway.

"We'd like to see Captain Torga," Georg said.

The guard shouted something in Portuguese in the direction of the ship; Otto assumed he was saying something like "visitors for the captain."

There was a long wait. Fortunately the rain had stopped, but the cold wind continued to buffet them. Eventually a disheveled looking man appeared on deck and indicated to the guard that he was to let Otto and Georg on board. As they climbed up the gangway, the man at the top suddenly doubled over in pain. He was still in apparent agony when they stepped onto the deck. But neither grain buyer knew what to do, so they just waited patiently. Finally, the man next to them at the top of the stairs straightened up. From the look on his face the pain seemed to have lessened a little, but it was obvious that he was still in considerable discomfort. He took out a large dirty handkerchief that had been white in the far distant past, mopped the copious sweat from his brow and then, with the same perspiration-laden hand, shook hands with Otto and Georg.

"Welcome aboard, *senhores*! *Capitão* Torga at your service." The captain reeked of alcohol and his speech was heavily slurred. João Torga was drunk.

Otto took a good look at the ship's master. He was grossly overweight, with a big round face. He clearly did not care about his appearance. His clothes were filthy, and stained with food and oil. His straggly hair was tousled and tangled. In fact, Otto wondered when he had last combed his hair, let alone washed his greasy locks. He had not shaved for many days.

Otto was about to respond to the captain's greeting when Torga grabbed his abdomen and once again bent over as the pain intensified again. Then he vomited all over the deck. Otto and Georg looked at one another; Georg shrugged his shoulders. Finally the captain straightened up again, mopped his brow and shouted for a deckhand to come and clean the mess.

"Gentlemen, I apologize. You are in *Cabine Uma*— Cabin One. Find your own way there. And stay there. I'll tell the steward to bring you your meals. We sail at midnight. And you need to know—"

Again the inebriated captain doubled over as his agony increased once more. He grasped his ample stomach and groaned. Then he straightened up and slowly walked away from Otto and Georg, presumably in the direction of his own cabin.

"What do you think is wrong with the captain?" Georg asked, as they attempted to find Cabin One.

"I hope it isn't appendicitis," Otto said. "These cargo ships with fewer than 12 passengers don't carry a doctor. The steward is the nominal medical officer. I, for one, wouldn't want an amateur to operate on me, especially with the ship tossing and turning in the Bay of Biscay—and that's when it's calm. If the wind continues to blow like this, not even the world's leading surgeon would be able to perform an operation."

"Let's hope that it's not appendicitis then. But what else could it be?"

"Could it be pancreatitis?" Otto asked.

"What's that?"

"Inflammation of the pancreas. It's common in alcoholics. And, yes, it can be fatal—an uncle of mine died from it. So let's hope it's not that, either. Maybe he has gallstones. But whatever it is, it doesn't look too good. I'm counting on him to get us safely to Cork."

"And he's got to get us back to Portugal afterwards."

"Yes, indeed," Otto said. "So let's hope he recovers soon. Why doesn't he go on shore and see a doctor, I wonder? If he can't leave the *Coimbra*, I assume he could arrange with the shipping company to have a doctor come and examine him aboard."

"I don't know. There are some men who consider it unmanly to ask for help of any kind, be it directions or medical assistance. I certainly don't like the idea of being at sea with a captain who's drunk and in agony. But what choice do we have?"

At that juncture, a member of the crew, realizing that Otto and Georg were lost, directed them up to the boat deck, where they found Cabin One easily. They were too tired to unpack the few possessions they had.

"Shall we turn in?" Otto asked. "We haven't slept much for days. I'm asleep on my feet."

"Let's watch the ship leave port—it'll only be a few more minutes. It's probably the small child in me, but I love to see what's happening when a ship I'm on enters or leaves port."

So they lay on their bunks until just after midnight when they heard the sound of the engines throbbing through the ship. Then they went outside. The boat deck was deserted. Below them they saw the deckhands busy at work, and on the deck above they could see the helmsman at the wheel in the bridgehouse. As they stood on the boat deck the wind ceaselessly buffeted them. They had difficulty keeping their balance when an occasional gale-force blast assailed them.

Even though the *Coimbra* was relatively small, the strong wind meant that two tugs were needed to extract her from her berth and guide her through the harbor opening. As the ship left the shelter of the port, the *Coimbra* started to pitch and roll in the heavy seas. Then the rain started to pelt down.

"Let's go to bed," suggested Georg. "Yes, I love to watch a ship leave port, but not under these conditions."

They opened the cabin door, levered themselves inside, then closed the door with difficulty as the wind increased in power again. Exhausted as they were, they fell asleep almost at once.

Abwehr Headquarters, Berlin
Friday, February 27th, 1942

"Where are they?" Colonel Kupfer asked.

"I assume that they're both safely on board the *Coimbra*," von Krassheim said.

"Krassheim, I've had enough of your assumptions. Here in the *Abwehr* we deal with facts. Do you know where they are?"

"No, Colonel."

"What did Captain Torga say yesterday in his daily radio message to the Lisbon embassy?"

"I contacted Lisbon a few minutes ago. They've heard nothing from Torga since the *Coimbra* docked in Lisbon Harbor four days ago."

Kupfer glared at von Krassheim. "If that book is not delivered to agent PICKFORD on schedule, I will personally transfer you to a punishment battalion on the Eastern Front. Now get out!"

Off the Portuguese Coast
Friday, February 27th, 1942

Georg and Otto had expected the steward bringing their breakfast to Cabin One to awaken them the next morning. Instead, an angry, red-faced man with a long scar on his left cheek accompanied by a tall man with a handgun burst into their cabin. The gun was pointing at the direction of the bunks.

"Who are you?" asked the angry man in English with a heavy accent.

"Who are *you*?" Georg asked.

"Pereira. First mate, now acting captain. Again: Who are you?"

"Why are you the acting captain?" Otto asked. "What's happened to Captain Torga?"

"Died last night. We'll bury him at sea. For the third and last time: Who are you?" As he said the words "last time" he glanced meaningfully at the gun the tall man brandished.

Georg and Otto looked at one another. Otto spoke up.

"We're grain buyers from Dublin. My name is Trumbauer and my colleague here is Strauss."

"No, you're not. You're German agents. You're violating the neutrality of Portugal."

"Why do you say that we're German agents? Yes, we were both born in Germany, but we came to the Republic of Ireland in 1936 and we're now citizens. Here, I'll show you our passports," Trumbauer said.

"Don't bother. You're German agents. Captain Torga has been ferrying German agents back and forth for months. Everyone in the crew knows about it, but there's been nothing we could do about it— until now."

"Look, I don't know how you got the crazy idea that we're German agents. As I told you, we're grain buyers. We work for Joseph's Brothers in Dublin. If your armed friend would let me, I can show you papers that will convince you beyond all doubt that we are who we say we are," Georg replied.

"Don't bother. The papers are forged. I know. I've been seeing those papers for months, too."

"I tell you, we live in Dublin."

"Where in Dublin?"

"I live at Number 17, Emmett Street."

"And how can a man who works as a grain buyer afford to live in a house that's a block or two from the City Hall?"

"Emmett Street is nowhere near the City Hall," Trumbauer said.

"Really? Where's Dublin City Hall?"

Trumbauer was silent.

"And Saint Patrick's Cathedral? And Nelson's Pillar? And Dublin Castle?"

Trumbauer remained silent.

"What about you?" Pereira asked, pointing to Strauss. "Your friend says you've lived in Eire for six years. Where are those Dublin landmarks?"

Strauss also said nothing.

"Get dressed."

Both men quickly put on their clothes and took their suitcases.

"I'm going to toss you both in the chain locker. You'll stay there until we get back to Lisbon, when I'll hand you over to the authorities. They know exactly how to deal with people who break our country's neutrality."

Pereira and the armed crewmember marched Otto and Georg down to a small compartment in the bow of the ship. The space contained the anchor chain, a bucket—and that was all. For five days, Otto and Georg were confined to the chain locker. When Pereira remembered, food and water were brought to them. Even less frequently, the bucket was emptied. Otto passed the time reading and rereading *A Tale of Two Cities*; Georg just sat on the metal deck.

Abwehr Headquarters, Berlin
Monday, March 2nd, 1942

"Krassheim, what have you heard regarding Trumbauer?" Kupfer asked.

"Nothing, Colonel."

"And Captain Torga?"

"Still nothing. There's been no reply to any of the radio messages sent to the *Coimbra* from our embassy in Lisbon."

"Krassheim, Otto is scheduled to deliver the book on Thursday, in three days' time. The *Führer* doesn't tolerate failure, and neither do I. So, unless PICKFORD starts sending us messages encrypted using the new book code by the end of this week, you're on your way to the Eastern Front."

Cobh, Republic of Ireland
Tuesday, March 3rd, 1942

The engines of the *Coimbra* stopped.

"I think we're in Cork," Otto said.

"Should we try and overpower the next man who brings us food?" Georg asked.

"What good will that do? Other members of the crew are sure to see us as we try to get off the ship, and then we're done for."

"Not necessarily. If I recall correctly, international law says that they're supposed to hand us over to the Irish authorities, not take us back to Portugal. If I'm right, they won't lay a finger on us."

"How certain are you?" Otto asked.

"I'm not certain at all, but it's our only hope. So, when we next hear someone coming, I'll stand on this side of the door with the bucket in my hand. You stand on the far side of the locker opposite the door. He'll open the door, he'll come into the locker and see only you—the open door will hide me. He'll advance toward you. Then I'll slam the door shut and hit him with the bucket."

An hour or so later they heard stealthy footsteps. Georg positioned himself at the side of the door, bucket in hand. The door slowly opened and a heavily bearded head looked in.

"*Schweig!* (Silence!)" The visitor spoke in German. "I've come to rescue you."

"Who are you?" Otto asked.

"A friend. Come quickly. We can talk later."

The two grain buyers grabbed their suitcases and accompanied their rescuer, who wore a white boiler suit. The three of them walked swiftly. An Irish policeman stood at the foot of the gangway. Being careful not to run, they descended the stairs rapidly. Otto looked at his watch—it was nearly noon.

Their liberator led them to the harbor gate—the customs officer ignored them. Directly opposite the gate was a pub. By unspoken agreement the three of them crossed the road together and entered. They walked past a noisy crowd of sailors standing at the bar to a quiet corner table.

"Can I buy you a beer?" he asked, now speaking English.

"That would be wonderful!" Georg said. Otto just smiled.

The man in the white boiler suit brought their drinks to the table. They were all extremely careful to say "Cheers!" and not "*Prosit!*" as a toast. They sat in companionable silence for a minute or two, and then the man started speaking. Notwithstanding the raucous shouting at the bar, he kept his voice low. In fact, he spoke so softly that there were times when the two grain buyers couldn't quite catch what he said. They tried to read his lips, but were severely hampered by the thick brown beard and mustache.

"My name is Kemper. I work for the same people as you do, or rather, I used to. About three months ago I was sent to Ireland to talk to our allies there about wheat. My cover story was that I was a representative of Joseph's Brothers—do you know the company?"

Both men nodded.

"They told me to report to the *Coimbra* in Lisbon Harbor. They said that, after I'd completed the negotiations in Dublin, I was to return to Cork and wait for the *Coimbra* to return and take me back to Lisbon.

"I arrived at the ship, and a drunken Captain Torga met me. He told me to go to Cabin One and stay there for the whole voyage—the steward would bring me my meals. The first 24 hours at sea passed quietly. Then suddenly the ship stopped. I rushed onto the deck to see what was happening, and I heard a loud splash that came from the other side of the ship from where I was standing. Then members of the crew started running onto the deck and shouting. I didn't know a word of Portuguese, so I'd no idea what was happening. I crossed to the other side of the ship. Below me about a dozen men were standing at the rails, pointing and peering into the water. I still didn't understand the situation.

"I stood there until about 15 minutes later the captain came up the ladder from the deck below. He was drunk, of course—he was always drunk. He asked me, 'Do you know anything about marine engines?' I told him that before the war I'd been a mechanical engineer.

"It seems that the engineering officer of the *Coimbra* had turned off the engines, climbed from the engine room to the deck, and then jumped into the sea. Captain Torga didn't launch a lifeboat to try to find him or make any other sort of rescue effort. Instead, he immediately ordered the two engine room hands to restart the engines. But they're both essentially unskilled laborers and they told Torga that they had no idea what to do. In desperation, Torga came to me.

"I somehow managed to start the two engines, despite the fact that I'd never seen a marine engine before. Torga asked me to act as engineering officer until we reached Cork. During the course of the short voyage, I realized that the captain was a hopeless drunk. The ship was actually under the control of the mate, Pereira, the red-faced man with a long scar on his cheek who locked you up. Pereira is an impassioned patriot, pathologically obsessed with Portuguese neutrality in this war. I'm convinced that he's an agent of PIDE, the Portuguese secret police.

"There was no doubt in my mind that, when I stepped ashore in Cork, Pereira would immediately inform the Irish authorities that I was a German agent. At best, they'd arrest me and I'd go to jail for the duration of the war, if not longer; at worst they'd hang me as a spy. In any event, I was certain that, thanks to Pereira, my mission for our employer was hopelessly doomed. So, one day before we arrived in Cork I came to Torga and offered him my services as engineering officer on a permanent basis. He accepted with alacrity, and I've been on the *Coimbra* ever since."

"You mean you've stayed on the ship?" Otto asked.

"Precisely. I couldn't leave the *Coimbra* at either Lisbon or Cork for fear that Pereira would have me arrested. In fact, once we were in Portuguese territorial waters he could easily have summoned his PIDE colleagues to throw me into jail, but he took no action so long as I remained on board. I've learned that there's a real shortage of engineering officers in Portugal at the moment—something to do with the war. I assume that his masters at PIDE want the *Coimbra* to continue to ply between Lisbon and Cork, and for that to happen I have to stay on as engineering officer. My plan today was to let you out of the chain locker, escort you to the gangway, and leave you there. But there was no sign of Pereira or anyone else around, so I took a chance and escaped."

"Are you going to go back to ship?" Otto asked.

"Definitely not. I've got my Irish passport in my pocket, and I keep my key papers on me at all times."

"Including Joseph's Brothers correspondence?"

"Just two letters. Otherwise it would be far too bulky."

"We've got Joseph's Brothers letters, too," Georg said.

"I'm sure you have, but with different dates to mine. We're going to have to separate—we dare not be questioned together, of course."

"What are you going to do?" Georg asked.

"I'm not sure, but at least I'm off that cursed ship. I think I'll stay somewhere in the Republic of Ireland for the duration of the war—it's a neutral country, after all. And you two?"

"My guess is that I'm your successor," Georg said. "Your aborted mission sounds a lot like what I'm supposed to do. But even if I were to make contact with our allies in this country, I've no way of getting back, let alone telling our masters what happened."

"What about the German legation in Dublin?"

"Lieutenant Colonel von Krassheim told me in no uncertain terms to stay away from there, for fear of damaging neutrality. In fact, both of us have received unambiguous instructions to respect Irish neutrality."

"You could send a letter to the legation," Kemper suggested.

"Yes," Georg agreed, "but the Irish postal people are sure to open it, and I don't have a code I can use. And the same problem arises if I were to telephone the legation, not that they would take my call. And in any event, the Irish authorities have confiscated the radio belonging to the German Minister in Dublin to prevent him or anyone else at the legation from passing information on to Berlin."

"So what are you going to do?" Kemper asked.

"I don't know. I haven't thought about it. Until you released us less than an hour ago, I was certain that we were going back to Portugal," Georg said.

Turning to Otto, Kemper asked, "And what are your plans?"

Otto decided to be extremely circumspect. He didn't know if he could trust Kemper—did the engineer still view himself as a loyal *Abwehr* agent, or had he simply opted out as a neutral for the duration of the war? Or was he now working for the other side? Or, worse, was he playing for both sides at the same time?

"My assignment is different from yours," Otto said. "I'm going to complete my mission, no matter what. Yes, I've come to a similar conclusion—there's probably no way for me to get back to Germany after I've successfully carried it out. But I'm going to do what I've been ordered to do, then I'll just do my best to find some means of returning to Berlin somehow or other."

"Well, whatever each of us decides to do," Kemper said, "one thing is absolutely certain: We all need to get out of Cork, and quickly. And now that I come to think of it, coming to this pub was unwise—a member of the crew of the *Coimbra* could easily have decided to have a drink here while we were talking.

"From what I've learned on previous trips, I can tell you that we're currently in Cobh, the main port of Cork—you know that Cobh was the last port that the *Titanic* left. My shipmates have mentioned that the train from Cork to Dublin actually starts from here. So the question is: Do we go to Cobh station in order to get to Dublin quickly but with the risk that someone from the *Coimbra* might spot us? Or would it be safer to take a bus from Cobh to, say, Waterford, and take a train from there to Dublin? In my case, I first have to buy some clothes. I can't travel in my boiler suit. Fortunately Captain Torga paid the crew at the end of each trip, alternately in Portuguese escudos and Irish pounds."

"I'm in a hurry," Otto said, "so I'll go straight to the station here."

"I'll come with you," Georg said. "Our cover documentation is for two grain buyers."

"I think I'll avoid trains until the *Coimbra* sails," was Kemper's response. "It's the bus for me until then. I hope I bump into you in Dublin. So, farewell for now."

"I haven't had a chance to thank you," Otto said. "But there's no way I can put my gratitude into words. If it weren't for you, we'd still be in that chain locker, and who knows what would've happened to us when we returned to Lisbon. If there's ever anything I can do for you in the future, you only have to ask."

"Same for me," Georg chimed in. "I cannot thank you enough."

"I understand," Kemper said. "Look after yourselves."

And with that he stood and left the bar.

"Let's give him two minutes, then make for the railway station," Georg said.

"Do you know where it is?"

"No, but any passerby should be able to direct us."

Sure enough, 20 minutes later the two grain salesmen found themselves seated in a train traveling to Dublin. As Georg had predicted, the first person they stopped told them exactly how to find the station. Fortunately for them, they did not encounter anyone from the Portuguese ship. Their biggest fear had been the possibility of bumping into Pereira and, as they walked to the train, they kept glancing from side to side to see if the mate of the *Coimbra* was watching them. But they reached the Dublin train unobserved.

Dublin
Tuesday, March 3rd, 1942

After a quick evening meal of potatoes, bacon and cabbage at the buffet at Kingsbridge station in Dublin, the two men left the building and started walking along the south bank of the River Liffey. Otto looked round. They were alone. He stopped walking and turned to his colleague.

"How are we going to make contact with our IRA comrades?" he asked.

"Find a public telephone not too close to the station. I have a contact number."

"More to the point, *why* are you making contact with our allies?"

"Meaning what exactly?"

"Well," Otto said, "suppose you meet with the IRA leadership and everything goes according to plan: You promise them arms and money, they promise to stop the grain smuggling. What then?"

"Just what are you getting at?"

"How are you going to tell the *Abwehr* the details of the agreement? The IRA people don't have a radio that can reach Germany, and you're not allowed to approach the German legation. So what point is there negotiating with the IRA?"

"Otto, the IRA people approached us, and we've responded to their messages. So there must be some kind of communications channel between the Republic of Ireland and Germany. Once we've settled the grain smuggling issue, I'll rely on the IRA to put me in touch with the right people. And then the *Abwehr* will get me back to Berlin."

"I'm glad you didn't say all this when we discussed our plans with Kemper in that pub in Cobh."

"With Kemper? Are you crazy? I don't trust that man farther than I can throw him."

"Me, too. But if he's not on our side, why did he let us out of the chain locker?"

"My concern is that he's playing some sort of double game. So, he let us out supposedly because he's working for Germany, but as soon as he left the pub he probably went straight to the Irish authorities and gave them a detailed report about us."

"You may be right. The main thing is that neither of us trusts him, and neither of us told him anything important. I was careful not even to tell him my name, and I noticed that you did the same. Let's walk on."

A few minutes later they found a green phone booth. Georg had paid for their meal in the station with a pound note, so he had coins for the public telephone. He dialed. The phone was picked up right away.

"Yes?"

"Is William Garland there?" Georg asked.

"Who is this?"

"It's Peter Gotham from Bantry Bay."

"Where are you now?"

"We're in a phone booth on Victoria Quay."

"Near the station end?"

"Yes."

"Walk along the river away from the station until you reach St. Augustine Street. It's a one-way street just after Usher Street. Near the corner you'll find a taxi waiting. Tell the driver your name and where you come from."

There was a click and the call ended. Otto and his companion walked in the direction indicated until they reached St. Augustine Street. They turned right. Not far from the corner they found a black taxi waiting.

"I'm Peter Gotham," Georg said.

"From where?" the driver asked.

"Bantry Bay."

"Jump in."

The driver hardly waited for Georg to close the door before he sped off. They drove for about half an hour. It seemed to Otto that the driver was taking a circuitous route to disguise the fact that they were heading north, in the direction of Belfast. Eventually the car stopped at a cottage on the side of a country road. A man in a tweed cap emerged from the cottage carrying pieces of cloth. The taxi driver turned to the two grain salesmen.

"Even though it's nighttime and there are heavy clouds, it's blindfolds from now on, me boyos," he said in a matter-of-fact voice. The man in the cap opened the back door, entered the car, and proceeded to cover their eyes and most of their faces with the cloths. They heard the taxi start up again. They felt the car turning this way and that.

Finally the car stopped, and the man in the cloth cap removed the blindfolds. An oil lamp burned faintly in a window some 50 yards in front of them, and they could see that they were on a farm. The taxi driver led the way to the farmhouse, with the man in the tweed cap bringing up the rear. Otto turned around to look at him as they walked, and noticed a bulge in his jacket pocket. He was holding his right hand close to the bulge.

The driver gave a series of raps on the door of the farmhouse. There was a longish wait and then a tall man, so thin that Otto thought of him as skeletal, unlocked the door. He escorted Otto and Georg into a plainly furnished sitting room and invited them to sit down. The chairs did not look too comfortable. The taxi driver, the exceedingly thin man and the man in the tweed cap all remained standing.

"I'm William Garland. Who are you and where are you from?" the thin man asked, turning to Otto.

Georg replied. "I'm Peter Gotham from Bantry Bay."

"And who's your companion?"

"He wants to pay someone to take him across the border into Northern Ireland as soon as possible."

William Garland turned to Otto. "For the sum of 10 punt, the driver here will take you across the border."

Otto stood up, reached into his pocket and took out the envelope containing the Irish money he had been given at the embassy in Madrid. He extracted two five-pound notes and started to hand them to the taxi driver, who shook his head and pointed to Garland.

"The money's for our cause, not for me," the driver said.

"I'm sorry," Otto said.

"No matter. But you must leave now," Garland said.

Otto shook hands with Georg, nodded to Garland, ignored the man in the tweed cap and followed the driver out of the farmhouse. The taxi driver indicated that Otto was to sit in front with him.

"And you don't need a blindfold any more. Garland cleared you."

He started the car and drove off with tires squealing. "We're not that far from the border here but I have to take you to the official crossing place."

"No, no," Otto said. "I have to cross secretly."

"Precisely, boyo. That's why I'm taking you to the official crossing place."

Otto was on the verge of panic. He thought of jumping out of the car, but the driver was speeding along country lanes with abandon. Finally he drove to another farm and stopped the car.

"Seamus, I'm taking the tractor," he yelled.

They walked over to a barn; the doors were wide open. The driver climbed onto a tractor and indicated to Otto that he was to get into the large open trailer attached to the back of the tractor.

"Why take along such a big vehicle for one person?" Otto asked, pointing to the trailer. "Surely I can ride up front with you?"

"That's so that the British will know it's me."

"What?"

"The British patrol the border ceaselessly. There are 'unofficial' goods that they desperately must have. Those goods must pass through the border. So, we have an arrangement with the British. When we bring goods across the border that they need, like the grain, we use this tractor and trailer combination, and they turn a blind eye."

"But what if enemy agents try to get through that way?" Otto asked.

"Don't you worry your head about that, me boyo. I've no idea how, but I'm sure that the British have all that stuff under control."

Otto did not ask any more questions. He tossed his small suitcase into the trailer, clambered in after it, and lay down. The base of the trailer was wood, with a sparse covering of ears of wheat.

"You don't have to lie down," yelled the driver over the roar of the badly tuned engine. "Even if you stand up and wave the bloody Union Jack they won't see you. That's the beauty of this tractor and trailer—they're invisible at all times, and so are their contents."

Otto was not going to take any chances, so he stayed prone during the seven-minute ride from Seamus's farm in the Republic of Ireland to a farm in Northern Ireland on the other side of the border.

Eventually the tractor stopped. The driver shouted to Otto to climb down.

"I know it's really dark tonight, but do you see that clump of trees up ahead?" he asked. "Walk to those trees, and you'll find a road in front of you. Turn right, walk about a mile, and you'll be at Cavertown station. The first train from there to Belfast leaves at 5:30 a.m.—if the stationmaster manages to wake up on time.

"My advice to you is to spend what's left of tonight in the barn here—Patrick Fitzpatrick knows better than to visit his own barn at night after hearing Seamus's tractor. In the morning, take the train to Belfast. From Belfast, you can take the boat train to London."

"And what makes you think that I'm headed for London?" Otto asked.

"All you boyos go there. Why, I must have transported at least 20 of you across the border in the last year or so."

Otto thought for a minute. "How do they contact you when they want to get back into the Republic of Ireland?"

"They don't. They go to London and stay there."

"All of them?"

"All of them."

A light bulb lit up in Otto's head. "Very interesting. Thank you for the information. Good night!" And he headed for the barn.

As soon as he could no longer hear the roar of the tractor on its way across the border back into the Republic of Ireland, Otto left the barn and headed for the trees. He walked as quietly as he could. He had worked out how the British had solved the problem of enemy agents crossing into Northern Ireland with the help of the IRA. The unmistakable racket from the tractor alerted the troops that a German spy might be crossing in the trailer, and they would then converge on the farm and arrest the enemy agent. In Otto's case, they had heard the tractor coming and they had surely seen him alighting from the trailer—he was certain that they had night glasses. Perhaps they would be waiting for him at the station or, more likely, a cordon was already closing in on Patrick Fitzpatrick's barn.

Otto wondered just how near the British were. He decided to avoid the road beyond the clump of trees. Instead, before he reached the trees he turned left, away from the station, and cut through what he thought was Farmer Fitzpatrick's cabbage patch. He came to a low fence, which he straddled without too much difficulty. He continued through the neighboring farm, stopping from time to time to listen for pursuers. He heard nothing. But it was only a matter of time before a larger number of soldiers would be brought to bear to search the area, probably at first light. So he had to get out of the area quickly. But how?

He remembered that Kemper had mentioned buses. Taking a train was clearly out of the question—every station in the area was undoubtedly under the strictest possible surveillance—but surely there were too many local buses for the British to be able to keep a watch on all of them. So, he needed to be on a bus by daybreak. And that meant being at a bus stop at that time.

Standing at a bus stop miles from anywhere in the middle of the night waiting for a bus was a recipe for disaster. No, at dawn he had to be in a town, or at least a village, and he had to stay undetected until then. The next question was: Where was the nearest town? When he slipped out of Fitzpatrick's barn, if he had continued to the road beyond the trees and turned right, he would have arrived at the station. Instead, he had turned left before reaching the clump of trees. Consequently, he thought, he needed to try to find the road that led to the station but he had to turn left again when he reached it. It seemed reasonable to assume that there was a built-up area at the other end of that road.

However, he was much more likely to be caught walking in the open along a road in the middle of the night than if he stayed hidden in the fields. So, Otto decided to compromise. He would turn right and try to locate the road. When he saw it, he would turn left and continue to skulk through the fields, but always keeping the road in sight on his right. In that way, there was much less of a chance that the British might detect him. At the same time, if his hypothesis was correct and there was some sort of village at the end of the road, he would find it there.

Otto was delighted to find the road quite close by. He stuck to his plan, walking slowly and carefully through the fields, hoping that his progress would not rouse a farmer's dog. But luck was on his side as he made his way through the pitch-black night.

Eventually, as the sky behind him started to lighten, he saw a cluster of houses ahead. He decided that now was the time to take a risk. He was dressed in Irish-made clothes, so he hoped that no one would suspect that he was an *Abwehr* agent. On the other hand, all of the 20 or so other agents who, he assumed, had crossed the border straight into the arms of the British, were probably also wearing typical Irish clothing. But there was no question in his mind that he had to be on the first bus out of there, before they widened the search.

Otto walked to the road and started strolling through the village. He encountered a milkman with horse and cart. The milkman greeted him warmly, but Otto just smiled back and waved—his German accent was a major liability now. Otto kept on walking and came upon a bus shelter. A timetable was affixed to the wall. He was extremely pleased to see that the first bus was due in five minutes.

Half an hour later a hungry and extremely sleepy Otto was still seated at the bus stop. Now he recalled what the driver had said about the stationmaster—it seemed that, in this part of Northern Ireland at least, time was relative, just as Einstein had claimed. As he was about to lose hope, a rather ramshackle looking double-decker red bus drew up. To Otto's utter delight, the sign in front read "Belfast."

He clambered aboard and took a seat right by the entrance at the rear of the bus. The conductor came up to him. Otto reached into his jacket pocket, found his money and handed him a pound note.

"That's a Republican punt," the conductor said and looked sharply at him.

Otto quickly found the envelope containing sterling that Baron Heinz Ludwig zu Baden, the Cultural Attaché and *Abwehr* representative in Madrid, had given him. He reached into the envelope and handed the conductor a British pound note.

"Are you going to Belfast?" the conductor asked.

Otto just nodded. He was horrified at the elementary blunder he had made with the currency. He had to get off this bus as soon as he could—if soldiers stopped them at a roadblock and asked the conductor about any suspicious passengers, he would finger Otto at once. He took his change and the ticket that the conductor handed him. Otto continued to say nothing. Instead he just smiled.

The bus started filling up as it made its way toward Belfast. As far as he could make out, most of his fellow passengers were also headed for the capital of Northern Ireland. Looking at the suits and ties that they were wearing, he deduced that they lived in country towns but worked in Belfast. The seats downstairs were now taken, so new passengers went upstairs, followed by the conductor so that he could take their money and issue them with tickets. About 15 people were waiting at a stop in what seemed to be a relatively large town. They all climbed upstairs. Otto realized that the conductor would be out of the way for a while so, as soon as the bus was under way, he pulled the rope to alert the driver that he wanted to get off at the next stop.

The vehicle drew up at a bus shelter. The elderly man standing there waited for Otto to alight and then took the seat Otto had occupied downstairs. The bus pulled away, and Otto was safely out of sight of the conductor. With any luck, it would be a while before he had issued tickets to all 15 new passengers, and by then he might even have forgotten about Otto. On the other hand, Otto had made a significant negative impression on the conductor, who might realize that Otto had bought a ticket all the way to Belfast but had got off early. Well, there was nothing he could do about that now. His current objective was to get to Belfast as soon as possible, without falling asleep, fainting from lack of food or, most important of all, getting caught before he could successfully complete his mission, so critical for the Nazi cause.

Near Belfast
Wednesday, March 4th, 1942

The sound of a train roused Otto from his thoughts, and he realized that he had the solution to his problems. He would ask the first pedestrian he encountered how to get to the station, walk there, grab a cup of tea and a bun at the station buffet, and then take a train into Belfast. Yes, he would have to ask the buffet attendant for the food, but he felt that he was now far enough from the border for his German accent not to cause significant consequences for him. He also took the trouble to buy a newspaper to hide behind in the train.

Soon after he finished his breakfast a suburban train drew in and he clambered aboard, arriving at Great Victoria Street railway station in Belfast half an hour later. Otto was exhausted, far more tired than he had ever been in his entire life. Drawing on some hidden inner strength he had not known that he had, he managed to make his way to the boat train. He slept on the steamer to Heysham, waking just before he had to transfer to the train to London. No food was available on the train, so he had a good breakfast in Euston Station on his arrival in London. He was now rested and fed, and ready to meet MISS HAVISHAM.

He walked from the station building into the chilly spring air and hailed one of the many taxis waiting outside the station. Being careful not to give away his actual destination, he asked to be taken to the corner of Tottenham Court Road and Howland Street. The driver was taciturn to the point of sullenness and dropped Otto at the requested location without saying a word, not even thanking him for the tip.

Otto started walking down Howland Street looking for number 22. He found number 16 and then number 18. To his utter dismay, where numbers 20 and 22 should have been there was now a huge pile of rubble—the *Luftwaffe* had bombed the two buildings to smithereens during the Blitz. Otto immediately realized that his mission, too, was now in ruins. Not only was there no way for him to make contact with PICKFORD, but there was also no conceivable mechanism by which he could return to Berlin. He was trapped in enemy territory, his vital task inexorably aborted.

He was about to hail a taxi and surrender himself at the nearest police station when a voice behind him said, "Are you looking for someone?"

Otto spun round. He saw an attractive woman of about 40 wearing a dark brown beret perched on her light-brown hair. She wore a russet brown woolen twinset with a chestnut brown tweed skirt, brown stockings and reddish-brown leather brogues. She was carrying a brown leather briefcase, somewhat worn. The overall effect was somehow reassuring. This woman was clearly conservative and trustworthy.

"I was looking for a woman living at Number 22."

"I'm Mrs. Framingham, the local housing warden, responsible for helping bombed-out families find a place to live. I was just passing this way when I saw you standing here and looking puzzled. Which flat at Number 22 did she live in?"

Otto was too stunned to think clearly. Also, the woman's solid and sensible appearance overwhelmed him. Finally, he could not think of a good reason for not telling her the actual address. So he blurted out, "Flat 12."

The woman in brown opened her briefcase and took out a thick ledger. She paged through it for a few seconds, then said, "Ah, yes, Miss Harper. She's living in a room not far from here. Come on, I'll take you there."

Otto had no choice. He followed the housing warden as she briskly led the way to a shabby looking building in Whitfield Street. At the entrance, she checked the entry in her ledger.

"She's in Room 8, on the second floor. Go on up, the front door is always unlocked."

And she turned and walked away so swiftly that Otto did not have a chance to thank her. Standing alone in front of the building, he felt rather like a feather blown by the wind—his life seemed completely out of his control. The external forces that now impelled him pushed him up the stairs to the second floor. He found Room 8 in front of him. He knocked on the door.

"Yes?"

The woman standing there was quite pretty, with long dark hair that curled below her shoulder. She smiled shyly. She looked about 30, perhaps 35 at most. She was wearing a dress that did not fit her properly and was at least a decade old. Over her shoulders she had draped a blanket. Otto realized that she had lost her clothes in the bombing of Howland Street.

"I'm here to sign the papers."

She pulled him inside and shut the door firmly.

"I hope you have a fountain pen with black ink," she responded.

"Are you MISS HAVISHAM?" Otto asked in German.

"Sh! I'm Miss Harper. And here we speak English and only English."

"Can you put me in touch with PICKFORD?" Otto asked.

"Don't you dare ever say that name out loud! The best I can do is to leave a message for him. Then it's up to him. What do you want me to tell him?"

Otto thought long and hard. On the one hand, PICKFORD needed to know that Otto had brought the new code, so he had to make Miss Harper aware of the relevant details of his mission. On the other hand, the fact that Miss Harper knew the countersign meant very little. For all he knew, she was an MI5 agent masquerading as MISS HAVISHAM, so the less she knew of his mission, the better.

Otto eventually made up his mind. "Please tell him that I need to see him urgently to solve the communications problem."

"Fine, I'll pass that on to him. Now, where can I find you after I get his reply?"

"I've no idea. Where should I stay?"

"We're close to London University here, so there are lots of places in the vicinity with rooms to let. The landlady two houses from here is a Mrs. Goodge. People never seem to stay long at her place for some reason, so she may have a room for you. Mind you, with the housing shortage, even she may be full. Go out of this building, turn left and you'll find it. If you get a room there, put a piece of paper with your room number in my pigeonhole downstairs—just the number, nothing else. I'll come to your room at Mrs. Goodge's with the answer."

"And if she's full?"

"She probably is. In that case, you're going to have to walk the streets around here looking for a 'Room to Let' sign. Take whatever you can get and come back here this evening at 7 p.m. to tell me your new address."

"Would you have a reply from him by then?"

"Possibly, possibly not. Now go, please. The longer you stay here, the greater the risk for both of us."

Otto said goodbye to MISS HAVISHAM and left the building. He turned left and walked to the house two doors down. This proved to be even shabbier than the one where MISS HAVISHAM lived. There was a crude handwritten sign in the ground floor window that read "Room to Let."

This time the front door was locked. Otto raised the heavy metal doorknocker and rapped twice. There was a long wait. Finally he heard dragging footsteps. The door flung open, and an angry-looking gray-haired woman barked, "Yes?"

"Mrs. Goodge?"

"Yes."

"I understand you have a room to let."

"That's what the sign says."

"Can I see the room?"

"Please yourself. It's Room 12, up two flights."

Otto had to ask Mrs. Goodge to move aside so that he could walk past her up the stairs. He found Room 12 and entered. He quickly realized that the reason that no one stayed too long with Mrs. Goodge was not just her sparkling, delightful personality. The room was small and barely furnished. It certainly did not look too clean. The bed was most uncomfortable and the room smelled of urine. On the other hand, it was two doors away from where MISS HAVISHAM lived, and, even if PICKFORD proved to be elusive, Otto knew he wouldn't have to stay there for more than two or three days. So he decided to take the room.

He left his small suitcase on the bed and went downstairs. Mrs. Goodge was nowhere to be found. Otto waited for a few minutes. Then he knocked loudly on the front door. Finally Mrs. Goodge reappeared.

"I'd like to take the room."

"Suit yourself. It's two pounds a week, payable in advance."

This was a surprisingly high price for a single room, but Otto meekly handed over the money. Mrs. Goodge took a ring with two keys from a rack in the entrance hall and handed it to him without a word. Otto went back upstairs. He went through his jacket pocket to find the bus ticket that the conductor had given him. He scrutinized it carefully. As far as he could determine, there was nothing on the face of the ticket that identified the bus line—it was just a small piece of buff-colored paper with numbers on it. He turned it over. It was blank. Taking his pen, he wrote "12" on the back. He left his room, carefully locked the door, and went back to the building where MISS HAVISHAM was staying. He found her pigeonhole without any difficulty and left the ticket there.

Otto Trumbauer decided to return to his room to await a response from MISS HAVISHAM, but as he started walking back along Whitfield Street he recalled the smell of urine and nearly retched on the spot. He decided to go for a stroll. After all, it would be at least an hour or two before MISS HAVISHAM could get back to him with a reply to his message for PICKFORD, at worst considerably longer.

He walked to Tottenham Street, and from there he turned right into Tottenham Court Road. Diagonally across the street was the Goodge Street Tube Station. The name "Goodge" naturally rang a bell—it was the name of his enchanting and captivating landlady.

He walked on. The next street was Goodge Street. The coincidences were simply too strong. Something was wrong; the pieces just did not add up correctly. First, there was the fortuitous appearance of Mrs. Framingham, the housing warden dressed in different shades of brown, who just happened to know exactly where Miss Harper was living, down to the room number. The next coincidence was that, even though there was a grave accommodation shortage in London, there also just happened to be a vacant room two doors away from Miss Harper. Yes, the room was dirty, smelly and uncomfortable—factors that would explain why it was available—but even that was not enough to explain everything. And the third coincidence was Mrs. Goodge. She was overplaying her role. She was just too rude, too unfriendly, and she charged far too much for the room. No, this was a British trap.

What was he to do? Turning himself in at the nearest police station would achieve nothing. They already knew that he was a German agent. After all, he had said to Miss Harper, "I'm here to sign the papers." And Miss Harper was either an MI5 stand-in for MISS HAVISHAM, or she was the real MISS HAVISHAM who was now a double agent.

Trying to return to Berlin would be futile. In any event, he knew no one he could contact who could help him to escape from Britain. But what would he do when he met PICKFORD? Clearly the man was also an MI5 imposter or a double agent. There was no point in giving him the book. In fact, handing over *A Tale of Two Cities* would be an act of treason—Otto would be supplying the British with a perfect way of sending disinformation to his unsuspecting *Abwehr* colleagues back in Nazi Germany.

But Otto's message to PICKFORD had been that he had come to solve the communications problem. How could he do that without handing over the paperback edition of *A Tale of Two Cities* he had been given? As he walked through the Borough of Camden, Otto desperately tried to think of a way by which he could alert the *Abwehr* that the mission had gone dreadfully wrong, without the British finding out that he had done so.

Suddenly he had an idea. He started examining the shops on both sides of the road as he passed them. He soon found what he was looking for, a second-hand bookstore. He opened the door. As he did so, a bell on a spring attached to the top of the door rang clearly. The proprietor came forward, an elderly man with wire-rimmed spectacles, wearing a shabby suit.

"Can I help you, sir?"

"The print in my copy of *A Tale of Two Cities* is a little small. Do you have a paperback edition set in a larger type?"

"Let me see, sir."

Taking Otto's book, the owner ambled to the back of his shop, climbed a wooden ladder resting against a tall bookshelf and pulled a book from his crowded shelves. Releasing his grip on the ladder, he used both hands to open the two paperback books and compare the size of the letters. Otto feared that the old man might lose his balance. Satisfied with the edition he had chosen, the book merchant returned to Otto.

"Will this do, sir?"

Otto compared the two paperback editions. Page two of the book he had brought with him from Germany began with the words "the earthly order of events." The same page in the book printed in the larger font started "Mrs. Southcott had recently attained." If PICKFORD were to use the second book to encrypt a message, the result would be incomprehensible when the *Abwehr* tried to decrypt it using a copy of the paperback edition they had given to Otto.

Otto expressed his pleasure with the book that the proprietor had found for him. The price of the book was marked as sixpence, which Otto gladly paid. As he opened the door to leave the bookshop he stopped and turned toward the owner.

"Here, take my copy. I've no use for it. Perhaps you can sell it to someone else."

And before the second-hand book dealer could protest, Otto placed the book that Captain Fasch had given him on top of a pile of books lying on the floor by the door, and stepped nimbly out of the shop, closing the door behind him. Then he returned to his room on the second floor of Mrs. Goodge's domain.

He tried out the chair and the bed. Both felt like instruments of torture, but the bed was fractionally less uncomfortable, so he lay down there and started reading his newly acquired edition of *A Tale of Two Cities*. He was just starting the second chapter when he heard a light tap on his door. He got up, put the book in his inside pocket, and unlocked and gingerly opened the door.

Miss Harper stood there. She had taken off the blanket and now wore a somewhat threadbare coat.

"Come with me," she said in a low voice.

They turned into Whitfield Street and from there proceeded to the Goodge Street tube station. This was the route along which he had strolled earlier. As they walked together, he thought about what was going to happen as a consequence of his clever switching of the two books without the British being able to detect that he had done so. PICKFORD would now send messages to Berlin using the incorrect book code, but they would be unintelligible. This would alert the *Abwehr* that something had gone wrong and, hopefully, warn them that PICKFORD was a British agent.

They entered the underground station. She bought two tickets, and they walked down to the trains. "We may have been followed," she said. "We're going to take evasive action."

For the next hour and a half they kept changing trains. Otto was fully aware that Miss Harper was performing a farce for his sole benefit, but he passively played along, entering and leaving trains with her just as the doors were closing. Finally they returned to the Northern Line and got off at Hampstead Station.

Miss Harper led him to a tobacconist's shop on Hampstead High Street. She signaled to the tobacconist, who handed her a large envelope. Miss Harper took the envelope and gave it to Otto.

Otto opened the envelope and found a piece of paper and a smaller envelope inside. There was a one-line message typed on the paper. It read: "When you are ALONE, open the enclosed envelope."

Otto showed the note to Miss Harper who nodded and started walking back to the tube station. When she was out of sight, Otto opened the envelope. It contained a map of the area. A route was marked in red ink, culminating in a large red X on the east side of Well Walk. For some reason, the number of the house did not appear on the map. Instead, there was a pencil sketch of the front of the building, which seemed to be enormous.

Otto followed the route marked on the map, and soon arrived at Well Walk. Large homes lined the street on both sides. He walked to the location of the large red X, but the house there did not look anything like the sketch. He kept walking, and two houses down he found a building that closely matched the drawing. Otto rang the bell. Within seconds an imposing butler opened the door.

"Can I help you, sir?"

"Charles Darcy sent me here."

"Ah, yes, sir. Sir Percival is expecting you."

The house was furnished with gleaming antiques. The oriental carpets on the floor looked as if they belonged in a museum, and the paintings on the wall appeared to Otto to have been taken from the walls of a major art gallery. He passed a table covered in dozens of snuffboxes and then a large display cabinet filled with china. Finally he was ushered into a book-lined study. As he walked in, the man behind the desk stood up. Otto heard the butler close the door firmly behind him.

Sir Percival was white haired. Thick white eyebrows hovered over his piercing blue eyes. His face was strongly asymmetric—his pugnacious jaw stuck out firmly to the left. His nose appeared to have been broken and badly set; it, too, leaned to the left. Below the nose was a walrus mustache. The overall effect was one of power, enhanced by the magnificent furnishings of the house.

"You were sent here by—?"

"Charles Darcy."

"Ah, yes. Fitzwilliam Darnay introduced me to him. Won't you take a seat? Whisky?"

And without waiting for an answer to his second question, Sir Percival walked over to a table. A cut glass decanter and glasses stood on a silver tray. He poured two generous drinks, handed one to Otto and returned to his seat behind the desk.

"Your very good health!" He raised his glass.

"And yours!" Otto took a doubtful sip, waiting to see Sir Percival actually swallow some of the scotch in his glass. Reassured that the drink had not been drugged or poisoned, Otto took a large draft of the most wonderful whisky he had ever tasted.

Sir Percival got down to business. "I understand you've come here with a solution to our urgent communications problem."

"Yes, sir. But I'm instructed to first ask you: What was the subject of your last message?"

Sir Percival responded immediately. "Three articles in *The Times*. They dealt with agents who were captured right after they arrived here."

"Thank you, sir."

And Otto reached into the inside pocket of his jacket and handed Sir Percival the copy of *A Tale of Two Cities* he had just bought.

"Ah, clever. A book code. Unbreakable."

Sir Percival flipped through the paperback. "Have you read this?"

"Yes."

"Did you enjoy it?"

"Very much indeed."

"Yes, Dickens certainly has universal appeal."

Sir Percival, seeing that Otto had finished his drink, leaned forward and pressed a bell.

"Thank you for coming and bringing me this book. My man will show you out."

Otto followed the butler to the front door, which he deftly opened. As Otto walked through the magnificent carved marble doorframe, he saw that the police were waiting outside. He realized with a sense of relief that within a few days it would all be over—the British would kill the messenger.

Hampstead, London
Friday, March 6th, 1942

"When I reluctantly agreed to play the role of PICKFORD in 1937, I never realized the ramifications of the job. How many of their agents have we captured or have turned themselves in since 1939? Forty? Fifty? More? The *Abwehr* is going to find out that the supply of Dickens characters isn't inexhaustible. And as soon as you arrest a new agent, you have to get yet another creative writer at MI5 to make up those detailed fabricated reports. Every week you put the reports together and send a lengthy radio message to Germany, ostensibly from me. Each transmission is crammed with information that my myriad hard-working Dickens subagents have harvested. MI5 is going run out of inventive writers soon, I shouldn't wonder."

"Percival," D said, "you're having so much fun, it should be illegal."

"That's perfectly true. At the same time, I fully appreciate that for you, as the head of MI5, dealing with German spies in Britain is no joke. For me, however, it's a game. No, that's not quite fair. Catching these agents is like shooting sitting ducks, and that's certainly not cricket. More whisky? Yes? By the way, I forgot to ask you: What prompted you to plant those articles in *The Times*?"

"Well, ever since you sent them the plans for the Muir bomb sight—which we knew that they already had, of course—the *Abwehr* has been treating the contents of your reports as incontrovertible facts," D said. "Message after message has fooled them all, especially that lazy pompous fool Siegfried Kupfer—they tell me he's fatter than ever. But things changed after Admiral Canaris appointed Emil von Krassheim to be Kupfer's second-in-command. We learned from the new Dickens subagents we arrested recently that, for some reason, von Krassheim is suspicious of your reports. So, we needed a stunt to convince him that you're a genuine German agent."

"But even someone only one-tenth as clever as von Krassheim would've realized immediately that there was no need to put that crudely concocted material in *The Times*," Sir Percival said. "All it did was muddy the waters."

"Of course it did," D replied. "But we needed something really spectacular to attract Kupfer's attention, to get through that thick Kraut skull of his that we had broken the code they gave me in September 1937."

"So Kupfer sent his agent, Otto Trumbauer, to me with a book code. Obviously Kupfer and I are now going to send messages back and forth in the new code. I've no doubt whatsoever that von Krassheim has suggested to Kupfer that they should use the old code for fictional messages from them to us. So, we now have two sources of information from Germany: First-class information in the book code, and disinformation in the old code. And similarly, we now have two channels for fooling the Germans. Your creative writers will use the book code to send false information that even von Krassheim will be certain is genuine, and the old code to send disinformation ostensibly from PICKFORD. Your crowd is going to have as much fun as I'm having," Sir Percival said with a deep chuckle.

Then he stopped laughing and added, "But wasn't it fortunate that you ordered your men to follow Trumbauer from the time they saw him cross the border, instead of arresting him like the others? What made you take that risk?"

"I knew that Kupfer would be sending a book by courier, and I simply had to lay my hands on it. The problem was that I had no way of knowing whether Trumbauer was actually carrying the book with him when he crossed over from the Republic of Ireland. I needed him to come to your home to hand it to you."

"Well, your plan nearly went awry at the end. It's a good thing that your watchers were really on the ball, especially the one who saw what Trumbauer did as he left the second-hand bookshop."

CHAPTER THREE
Highly Satisfactory
1943

Los Alamos, New Mexico
Tuesday, June 30th, 1943

The sergeant ushered Ulrich zu Westerheimer into General Grove's office in Los Alamos. For three months, the Allies' top nuclear scientists had been hard at work in "Site Y," the vast secret location chosen for the group that would design and build the atomic bomb.

"Dr. zu Westerheimer, this is General Silas Comptine," General Groves said. "Dr. Robert Oppenheimer told me that you were the best person to explain to General Comptine certain aspects of our atomic bomb project here at Los Alamos."

"General Groves, you flatter me," zu Westerheimer said, with a heavy German accent. "There are hundreds of scientists here who are far more knowledgeable than I am."

"As you know, I'm in no way qualified to judge your scientific knowledge." General Leslie Groves smiled broadly. "But Oppy has repeatedly assured me that you're the only physicist in the whole group who can explain advanced nuclear physics in layman's terms, so you're the best person to explain to General Comptine what he needs to know."

General Comptine was a bulky man, tall and heavily built. His grey hair was short, even shorter than a crew cut. His squarish face was large and somewhat florid, with eyes of an unusual shade of grey-green. Incongruously, a pair of small rimless glasses perched on the bridge of his large nose.

Comptine had grown up in the mountains of West Virginia, the seventh son (and eleventh child) of a coal miner. Miss Perkins, the teacher in the one-roomed schoolhouse in his village, had quickly realized that Silas was a child prodigy, and she did everything in her power to ensure that he received an education worthy of his talents, culminating in an engineering degree from the United States Military Academy at West Point. Notwithstanding his best efforts, General Comptine had never managed to lose his redneck accent. However, he turned this to his benefit; he quickly realized that it was to his advantage if an opponent incorrectly assumed that he was an uneducated lout.

"Dr. zu Westerheimer," General Comptine said, "I'm here to learn from you. I studied physics at West Point, but that was quite a time ago—I know that there've been startling discoveries since then, including the theory of relativity, but especially in nuclear physics.

"Let me tell you why I'm here. It's a long story, I'm afraid. On August 2nd, 1939, Albert Einstein wrote a letter to President Franklin D. Roosevelt in which he made four major points. First, he stated that, on the basis of recent scientific discoveries, it was now possible to build a bomb of previously unimagined destructive power, an atomic bomb. Second, it was essential that the United States do all the research needed to be able to build such a bomb. Third, the United States needed to acquire the necessary uranium from other countries—there's far too little uranium mined here. And fourth, the United States had to develop the atomic bomb before Nazi Germany did.

"I'm involved with the last point. The effort to beat the Nazis to the bomb is proceeding in two directions. General Groves heads the drive to design and construct an atomic bomb as quickly as possible. You're part of the scientific component of that drive here in Los Alamos and, as you know, there are major ongoing engineering projects elsewhere in the United States to purify the nuclear fuel for the bomb.

"My role is somewhat more indirect. The President has entrusted me to mislead the Germans, so that they'll follow research routes that we already know will lead nowhere, wasting valuable time and resources, and allowing us to build the bomb first. I'd like you to be part of that effort."

In contrast to General Comptine, Ulrich zu Westerheimer had been born into an aristocratic Prussian family. He was tall and thin, with an elongated face. His hair was blond, almost white, and he wore it longer than the current military fashion. The right ear stuck out much more than the left, giving his face a curious unbalanced look.

In 1930, Albert Einstein, then director of the Kaiser Wilhelm Institute for Physics in Berlin, had appointed Ulrich zu Westerheimer to the position of professor of theoretical nuclear physics at the age of only 28. Three years later, when the Nazis barred Jews from holding any official positions, including teaching at universities, zu Westerheimer resigned in protest and followed Einstein to the United States.

Unlike Comptine, Ulrich zu Westerheimer was one of only two children. His younger brother, Carl Friedrich, was also an outstanding physicist. But unlike Ulrich, Carl Friedrich was a fanatical Nazi, so much so that he became an early proponent of "Aryan Physics," a nationalistic movement that was formed to oppose "Jewish Physics," and especially the work of Albert Einstein. Because Ulrich's research depended critically on the theory of relativity, this meant that Carl Friedrich strongly opposed the scientific work of his brother purely on ideological grounds—the scientific facts were irrelevant.

Dr. Ulrich zu Westerheimer was no fool, and he quickly realized that the reason that he had been chosen to assist General Comptine had nothing to do with his ability to explain physics to laymen. He cudgeled his brain to try to understand why General Comptine had selected him, but to no avail.

As if reading his mind, the general spoke up. "You're probably wondering why I've picked you to work for me rather than for General Groves here. The reason is: your brother, Carl Friedrich."

"But I've had no contact whatsoever with my brother since I left Germany in 1933. He considers me a traitor to Nazi Germany; I consider him a traitor to humanity. The last I heard of him was just before the war, when he was working for Manfred von Ardenne in his private research laboratory. The Reich Postal Ministry financed the research in nuclear physics."

"Yes, that was the source of the ridiculous story doing the rounds that the Post Office controlled all the uranium in Nazi Germany," Comptine said. "Even more ridiculous, when war broke out Adolf Hitler called up every able-bodied citizen, including physicists. And this despite the fact that nuclear fission was first observed in Germany—in December 1938.

"So, your brother became an infantry officer. He was actively involved in the invasion of France, and was posted to Paris for about a year. When Operation BARBAROSSA commenced in June 1941, your brother was transferred to the Eastern Front so that he could participate in the invasion of Russia. Soviet troops captured him at Stalingrad toward the end of January 1943. At the staging point for German officer prisoners of war, the Russian intelligence officers found his name on a list of Nazis wanted by the NKGB—that's the current name for the Soviet Secret Police.

"They took your brother to Moscow and imprisoned him in Lubyanka Prison. Under interrogation, all he could describe to his captors was the work he'd done with von Ardenne up to the outbreak of war. He did let slip, however, that he had a brother who's a nuclear physicist. And this gave General Vladimir Fomarenko, a Soviet intelligence officer, an interesting idea.

"Let's move to my office to allow General Groves to get on with his work, and I'll tell you all about it."

The two men moved to a smaller office at the end of the hall. When they were both seated, General Comptine asked, "How much do you know about intelligence and counterintelligence?"

"Very little," zu Westerheimer admitted.

"Do you know about General Allenby's activities in Palestine in 1917 and his Haversack Ruse?"

"No. I've heard the name 'Allenby,' but that's about it."

"Well, during the First World War," Comptine said, "the British controlled Egypt. To protect the Suez Canal, in early 1917 an Allied army consisting mainly of British, Australian and New Zealand troops advanced from the Sinai Peninsula into Turkish-controlled Palestine. After two disastrous attacks at the Gaza end of the Gaza–Beersheba line, General Edmund Allenby was appointed commander-in-chief. Unlike his predecessor, he decided to use guile. His goal was to convince the Turks that he was preparing for a third onslaught against Gaza, while his actual plan was an attack on

Beersheba, at the other end of the 30-mile long front."

"Go on."

"The most famous of the many tricks Allenby used was the Haversack Ruse. A British officer rode up to the Turkish lines. The Turks fired at him, as he'd expected. He pretended to be wounded and galloped away, dropping his bloodstained haversack as he did so—he'd earlier stained it with blood. The haversack contained fictional plans for an attack on Gaza, together with genuine personal effects designed to convince the Turks that the plans were real, too. To further deceive the Turks, Allenby arranged for radio messages to be sent out asking troops to search for the 'missing' haversack. Also, his staff prepared a set of daily orders that included sending a patrol to scour the area where the haversack had been 'lost.' They then wrapped a sandwich in those daily orders and left it near the Turkish lines! As a result of Allenby's numerous deceptive ruses, the Turks continued to concentrate their forces in the Gaza area.

"The Battle of Beersheba took place on October 29th, 1917. Even after the assault began, the Turks still believed that it was just a feint and that Allenby would make the real attack in Gaza. The battle culminated at twilight in a four-mile charge by the Australian 4th Light Horse Brigade, the last and greatest cavalry charge in history. As a result, Allenby took not only Beersheba but swept on to Jerusalem, eventually conquering the whole of Palestine."

"That's a fascinating piece of history," zu Westerheimer said, "but what does it have to do with me? Or with my brother, for that matter?"

"Hold your horses for a moment. Let's briefly discuss atomic weapons, and then I'll answer those questions.

"I think you'll agree," General Comptine said, "that there are two kinds of atomic bombs. First, there's the plutonium bomb. Plutonium is a by-product of nuclear fission. You build a nuclear reactor, you put in uranium fuel, you run it for a while, and then you extract the plutonium from the remaining uranium in the reactor. You then fashion two pieces of plutonium, each too small on its own to sustain a chain reaction, but together large enough to cause a nuclear explosion—the critical mass is about 22 pounds. Inside the bomb casing, you fire the one piece of plutonium into the other, and the atomic bomb explodes.

"And then there's the uranium bomb. About 99 percent of natural uranium consists of uranium-238, which is inert. The remaining one percent is uranium-235, which can be used to build a nuclear weapon. You need to construct a huge plant to remove most of the inert uranium-238, leaving you with highly enriched uranium consisting of at least 90 percent uranium-235. This is a very slow and expensive process, and you need about 110 pounds of highly enriched uranium for the bomb to explode. Once again, you make two pieces, each of which on its own is below critical mass in size but together are large enough. As with the plutonium bomb, you use conventional explosives to slam the two pieces into one another, and the bomb explodes.

"Have I got the physics right?"

"Yes, indeed," zu Westerheimer said. General Comptine's grasp of the scientific facts had considerably impressed the physicist. The general's ability to clearly present just the key points and ignore the details was equally remarkable, but zu Westerheimer did not say anything about that.

"Now," Comptine continued, "we want to convince the Germans that they need to build a uranium bomb, not a plutonium bomb. I'm sure you understand why."

"I'm afraid I don't."

"Well, to build a plutonium bomb all you need is a nuclear reactor, and the Germans can construct one in a large cavern far enough underground to be impervious to Allied bombing. But a uranium bomb requires a truly gigantic factory to remove most of the uranium-238, a factory that would be far too large to be built below ground. If the Germans were to build such a plant, it would consume vast quantities of raw materials that otherwise could be used for conventional weapons. Also, it would eat up huge amounts of electricity. Best of all, once they've built the factory, we can quickly bomb it into oblivion. Currently British bombers are carrying out strategic bombing by night and our boys are pursuing daylight precision bombing. A plant that size would be an easy target, no matter how hard the Germans try to defend it with their 88 mm flak guns and other anti-aircraft defenses.

"So, we want to convince the Germans not to build a plutonium bomb, but rather a uranium bomb. And we think we know how to do it.

"At the end of 1942," General Comptine continued, "Dr. James Chadwick wrote a research report in which he concluded that plutonium would be unsuitable for nuclear weapons because impurities in the plutonium would cause pre-detonation—the bomb would blow itself apart before it reached critical mass, and there would be no nuclear explosion. However, we've found a way around that problem, and Chadwick himself agrees that our approach will work.

"As you know, Chadwick won the Nobel Prize for Physics in 1935 for his discovery of the neutron, so his report on the unfeasibility of using plutonium for nuclear weapons carries considerable weight in the scientific community. We want to deliver a copy of his report to the Germans. We believe that it'll convince them not to build a plutonium bomb.

"Our challenge is this: How do we ensure that a copy of Chadwick's report is delivered to Hitler without the Germans suspecting that it's a piece of disinformation, designed to deceive the Germans into building a uranium bomb?

"Direct approaches clearly won't work. Putting a copy of the report into an envelope and mailing it to Germany marked 'Personal—for the attention of Adolf Hitler' will have the opposite effect to what we want. There's no question that the Nazis would treat it as disinformation.

"We know of couriers working for the German government. For example, there's a steward on a Portuguese liner that sails from New York to Lisbon and back. Portugal is a neutral country, so the steward is free to sail from the United States to Portugal, his home country, and back. When he arrives in Lisbon, he goes straight to the German embassy and hands over materials to Count Georg von Ottostorff, the German Military Attaché in Lisbon who, in turn, puts what he receives into a diplomatic bag to be flown to Berlin."

"So that would be a good way to get the report to Hitler," zu Westerheimer suggested.

"Probably not," the general said. "Spies and couriers are, by nature, dishonest. A spy pretends to be what he or she is not, and a courier has to find devious ways to smuggle materials across borders. So, as a matter of course, intelligence agencies mistrust all material that their spies and couriers provide. And, of course, each side does its best to try to discredit enemy agents in the eyes of their spymasters.

"All in all, intelligence agencies have to evaluate every single message from an agent on its individual merits. Even if an agent has transmitted a hundred messages, all of which have proved to contain correct information, the next message may contain disinformation that has been subtly fed to the agent. So, if the Portuguese steward were to hand over the Chadwick report, unless he had irrefutable evidence of how it fell into his hands, and also had absolute proof that what he was handing over was in precisely the form in which Chadwick originally wrote it, the Germans would probably treat it as disinformation, no matter how high the quality of the steward's previous messages may have been."

"So," zu Westerheimer said, "how do you propose to send the Chadwick report to Hitler?"

"Simple," General Comptine said. "You and your brother are going to deliver it."

Zu Westerheimer turned white as a sheet. General Comptine had to revive him with a shot of Kentucky Bourbon from the bottle that he kept in his second desk drawer on the right.

"Are you telling me that you want me to go back to Nazi Germany, so that the Gestapo can torture me until I reveal all of our nuclear secrets, after which they'll kill me?"

"Of course not," Comptine said. "You'll safely stay at least 2,000 miles from the nearest German soldier. Your brother will travel to Germany with the Chadwick report. We're going to fly you to Novosibirsk, the capital of Siberia. Military personnel will accompany you all the way, for your protection.

"The NKGB will bring your brother to Novosibirsk. You'll meet with him there and hand over the Chadwick report. Then Carl Friedrich will be flown to Germany, and you'll return here to resume your scientific work."

There was a long pause. Then the physicist responded. "This whole plan seems nonsensical to me. You're telling me that I'm to be flown to Novosibirsk to meet with my brother and give him a document. Then the Soviets are to fly Carl Friedrich to Germany. That's even more fantastic—the moment the Germans detect a Soviet plane over their territory they're going to shoot it down, never mind allowing it to land."

General Comptine's smile seemed to fill his whole face and flow infectiously into the office. "The plot is just a little more complex than that. Here's the deal: We've told the Russians that we want to deliver a fictional document to Adolf Hitler. You know how obsessed Hitler is about superweapons, or *Wunderwaffen*, and particularly rockets. The German people have been told so much about them that they even have a contemptuous abbreviation for them: *Wuwa*. The acronym sounds better in German—as you know, it's pronounced 'Voo-vah.'

"We're fully aware," he continued, "that the Germans have been developing rockets and flying bombs. In 1940, Ludwig Roth und Graupe designed the A10, a rocket that the Germans will launch from Western Europe to strike targets in the United States. However, they aren't going to build that rocket until 1946. We want to convince Hitler that America has already successfully built an equally powerful rocket that we'll launch from the east coast of America and that can reach Berlin and other German targets, under guidance from a control station in Britain."

"But why?" zu Westerheimer asked.

"So that Hitler will instruct his intelligence agencies to throw every spy they have in America and Britain into a futile endeavor to obtain details of this nonexistent rocket, code named 'Preparation 38.'"

"Why Preparation 38?"

"Germany's stock of uranium is in the form of yellowcake, a mixture of different uranium oxides. We've found out that the German code name for yellowcake is Preparation 38. By giving the rocket that name, we're sending the message that the rocket is nuclear powered. This will propel Hitler even more strongly to order his entire intelligence-gathering apparatus to obtain details of the rocket."

"General, I'm sorry to be so stupid, but I still don't see the point of the plan. Why would you want Hitler to do this?"

"The report we've prepared states that the rocket factory is located about 100 miles from anywhere, in the middle of the Mojave Desert in Arizona. More precisely, it's located at the end of a 10-mile long track that branches off the only road in the vicinity. Any stranger who travels to that area will immediately be arrested and interrogated. Of course, we've erected a large building that looks like a factory, together with worker housing, a recreation hall, two churches, and more. Naturally, we've made the factory and all the other buildings out of plywood and canvas and the like, but no one is going to get close enough to find that out. From the air, however, the factory and the other buildings all look like the real thing.

"Similarly," General Comptine went on, "we've located the 'rocket control station' in a remote area of the Scottish Highlands. Again, if the British find anyone coming into that area, he'll be arrested as a potential spy. In fact, the Brits have already constructed the control station, with interesting-looking aerials and dishes. Our scientists have told us that the building looks just like a rocket control station. If a spy should penetrate close enough to photograph the building from a distance, it will definitely fool the Germans."

"So this whole endeavor is an exercise to capture German spies in America and Britain?" zu Westerheimer asked.

"Wait. That's only part of it. There's much more to come. Do you remember," Comptine continued, "that in May 1941, Deputy *Führer* Rudolf Hess, third in line after Hitler and Göring, flew solo to Scotland to try to make peace with the British? He crash-landed and the British arrested him. He's currently locked up in the Tower of London.

"Now, we propose to do the same sort of thing with your brother. We'll fly him into Germany on a peace mission. The Red Army captured numerous German planes on the ground when they cut off the German 6th Army during the Battle of Stalingrad, and there are many German pilots in the prisoner of war camps."

"I think there's a fatal weakness in your plan. Let's suppose, just for the sake of argument, that a German pilot agrees to fly my brother back to Germany in a German plane with the help of the Russians. When they arrive, the Germans will immediately learn that the Russians are behind the whole endeavor, and the document Carl Friedrich carries will be suspect. No one will believe that Preparation 38 is real."

"As I said, it's a little more involved than that," General Comptine assured him. "We're going to fly your brother into Germany on a peace mission that Molotov, the Soviet Foreign Minister, has initiated. When Carl Friedrich arrives in Germany, he'll hand over the peace proposal, together with the Preparation 38 report. The cover letter from the Soviets will explain, in a diplomatic way of course, that the Americans are about to start deploying the rockets, so it would definitely be in the interests of the German government to make peace with the Soviet Union in order to be able to concentrate their war effort on the American rocket threat.

"Your brother," he continued, "will carry a briefcase we'll supply. In the lining, we'll have hidden a copy of Chadwick's report. Your brother will tell Hitler that you personally gave him the briefcase containing the Chadwick report, which will add authenticity to the entire endeavor."

"But why do you have to hide the Chadwick report?"

"Well, we don't exactly trust our Russian allies with our nuclear secrets. They don't have a nuclear program of their own, and we certainly don't want them to start one. After this war is over, America must be the sole possessor of the atomic bomb."

"Wait a minute," zu Westerheimer said. "I see another problem. I thought you said that this was a Soviet peace mission. My presence in Novosibirsk to meet my brother will imply that the Americans are involved. Why on earth would the American government voluntarily hand over Chadwick's report to the Germans?"

"Well, you won't be in Novosibirsk on behalf of the American government. You'll be there as the head of 'Scientists against Nuclear Terror' or SANT."

"What's SANT? I've never heard of it."

"Not every expert in nuclear technology is in favor of nuclear weapons," Comptine explained. "Some nuclear physicists are pacifists and are therefore opposed to all weapons of any kind. Others are philosophically opposed to the idea of using nuclear technology to kill people. They feel it should be used solely for the benefit of mankind. The good news is that no one who's opposed to our developing atomic bombs is actually doing anything about it. What I'm saying is that all the opponents of nuclear weapons are loyal Americans who personally disapprove of what we're doing, but their opposition stops there.

"Turning now from the real world to the fictional, we've come up with the story that a group of scientists who are opposed to the use of nuclear weapons formed SANT. They can't prevent us from developing the atomic bomb, of course, but they've come up with a way of stopping us from using it: mutually assured destruction, or MAD. The idea is that if we have atomic weapons and the Germans have atomic weapons, neither side will dare to use them for fear that the other side will retaliate by annihilating them.

"It's an ironic quirk of history that the scientific paper that showed that atomic weapons were feasible, also first put forward the idea of MAD. In March 1940, Otto Frisch and Rudolf Peierls, two German nuclear physicists who fled to Britain in 1933 when Hitler barred Jews from working in universities, calculated the critical mass needed for an atomic bomb to explode. Previously scientists had thought that several tons of fissionable material would be needed, making a bomb impractical, but the so-called Frisch–Peierls memorandum showed that only a few pounds would be needed. Consequently, we can build an atomic bomb that we can drop from an airplane. Anyhow, the first part of their memorandum outlined the consequences of their calculations. They stated that deterrence was the best means of combating an enemy with nuclear weapons.

"Taking the deterrence argument in the Frisch–Peierls memorandum to its logical conclusion, the fictitious members of SANT are actively engaged in stealing our nuclear secrets and trying to hand them over to the Nazis. You were a well-known pacifist when you lived in Germany. Consequently, many in the German intelligence service will believe the contents of the cover letter from SANT that you, amongst others, will have signed. The Chadwick report is intended to add weight to your cause, by supplying a guide to the Germans on how to avoid getting bogged down in a dead-end nuclear effort.

"Hold on, hold on, my head is spinning," zu Westerheimer said. "You're telling me that there are three separate plots.

"Correct."

"First, there's the anti-nuclear weapons plot, in which SANT, an imaginary organization, hands over the Chadwick report (which is real) to the Nazis, ostensibly in order to prevent us from deploying atomic weapons. The real reason, however, is to mislead the Germans into making a uranium bomb, not a plutonium bomb. Furthermore, the Chadwick report must be delivered clandestinely, in the lining of a briefcase—the Soviets are not even to know of its existence."

"Correct."

"Second, there's the Preparation 38 plot. You've made up the whole scheme—there's no rocket; the factory in the middle of the Mojave Desert is just canvas and plywood; the control station in an isolated area of the Scottish Highlands is just a building with aerials. In fact, the more people who know about the Preparation 38 plot, the more information (or rather, disinformation) the German intelligence services will acquire, and the more likely it will be that Hitler will believe the Preparation 38 report. The real aim of the report is to catch German spies here and in Britain, though the cover story is that the Soviets are including this report with their peace proposal in order to convince the Germans to sign the document."

"Again, correct."

"Third, there's the fictional Soviet peace proposal. Why on earth have the Soviets agreed to do this?"

"Because we asked them to."

"That isn't really an answer, is it?" zu Westerheimer said.

"Actually, it is. For the last year or so, we've been supplying the Red Army under the Lend-Lease program. We've sent them trucks, jeeps, steel, explosives and millions of pairs of boots. We've even provided huge quantities of aviation fuel. All of these supplies have been sent in arctic convoys via North Cape to Archangel, despite relentless German U-boats attacks. One of our convoys lost two-thirds of its ships. So, when we ask the Soviets for a favor, they now almost always agree, unless it isn't in their interests to do so. In this case, they've nothing to lose—so they've agreed."

"What do you mean by saying, 'they've nothing to lose?'" You said that Vyacheslav Molotov would be making the peace overture. But when Stalin learns about it, there's no question that he'll have Molotov killed. So why would Molotov agree to commit suicide by signing the peace proposal?"

"Who said anything about Molotov signing anything? There's a top official in the Soviet Ministry of Foreign Affairs named Osip Abramovich. Stalin is currently engaged in 'unmasking' Jews as Nazi collaborators. Yes, it's unbelievable, but it's happening right now. Abramovich is organizing the peace proposal. He'll sign the document on behalf of the Soviet Union, just as Molotov signed the

Molotov–Ribbentrop Pact. And once your brother has arrived on German soil with the peace proposal, Abramovich will be taken to Lubyanka Prison and shot."

Zu Westerheimer gasped. "Are you serious?"

"Oh, yes," the general said. "And there's nothing we can do to save his life. Uncle Joe has decided to murder Abramovich, and that's that. Of course, the execution of Abramovich will be leaked to the Germans, and that will have three direct results: They will instantly terminate the peace negotiations, which will suit the Commies—like us, they're not prepared to accept anything short of the Nazis surrendering unconditionally. Also, as a result of the Soviets murdering Abramovich, the Germans will in all probability view the peace proposal as a genuine document. Finally, as a result of the killing, they will also view the other materials that Carl Friedrich will be carrying as genuine, including the Preparation 38 document and the Chadwick report."

"I can't take part in a plan that will result in the killing of an innocent man," zu Westerheimer said.

"But you're prepared to build an atomic weapon."

Ulrich zu Westerheimer was silent.

Chukotka Autonomous Region, Siberia
Tuesday, July 6th, 1943

The C-47 Skytrain, the military version of the Douglas DC-3, was approaching Soviet airspace. It had taken off nearly seven hours earlier from Elmendorf Field, the United States Army Air Force base just outside Anchorage, Alaska. During the previous week, radio messages in a top-secret code had gone back and forth between Moscow and Washington to ensure that the Red Air Force would not shoot the plane down as it crossed the Bering Sea, which separates Western Alaska from the Chukotka Autonomous Region, the northeasterly corner of the Soviet Far East. The Soviet government had instructed them to land at the small town of Anadyr, and it had been made clear that under no circumstances was the C-47 to deviate from the agreed flight path.

In addition to the two military pilots and the steward, there were 18 passengers on the C-47. A variety of military personnel accompanied General Comptine and Dr. zu Westerheimer, including high-ranking officers from the Office of Strategic Services, translators and bodyguards. There was also one other civilian, a representative of the Department of State. When the team assembled in Anchorage, he had introduced himself to zu Westerheimer as Herbert Creekworthy, but he had said virtually nothing to the physicist (or anyone else) from then on.

Everyone aboard the plane was fully aware that this was not going to be an easy mission, even those who did not know the finer details of what lay ahead, so the passengers had been apprehensive from the time the C-47 had taken off early that morning. But as they neared Soviet air space, the tension aboard the aircraft grew measurably. Nearly everyone expected MiG-3 fighter aircraft to challenge the plane, and they hoped that the Soviet pilots would not open fire on them. At their final briefing the previous evening, a United States Army Air Force colonel had assured them that the gun sights of the MiG-3 were inaccurate, and a series of weapons failures had plagued the plane. Until the colonel made the statement, most of the team members had not even realized that there was a possibility of Soviet fighter planes attacking them. As a consequence of the "reassuring" statement, no one had slept much the previous evening. Zu Westerheimer, for one, had tossed and turned all night.

The cloud cover cleared for a short time, allowing them to see the rocky seashore ahead of them, with barren tundra behind it. The water in the Bering Sea was dark. They looked for icebergs but they could not see any.

Suddenly there was a cry from an air force officer seated near the front on the port side of the plane: "Five bandits at ten o'clock!"

The passengers crowded to the left side of the C-47. Five MiG-3 planes were flying toward them. They overflew the C-47, turned and took up positions around it: one in front, one on each side, and two behind the American plane.

The pilot's voice came over the intercom. "Gentlemen, as you can see, five hostile MiG-3 aircraft have surrounded our plane. Fasten your seatbelts and extinguish all cigarettes right away."

The lead MiG-3 rocked its wings up and down to indicate that the C-47 was to follow it. The American pilot had no choice. He took up position behind the lead Soviet fighter. They flew in formation for about 45 minutes. Finally, the pilot could see in front of him an airfield, situated close to the Bering Sea, that did not appear on the map that he had received in Anchorage. As they neared the airfield, the pilots in the two flanking MiG-3s gave hand signals, pointing downward to instruct the pilot of the C-47 to land.

The voice of the pilot, Captain Sean Fergusson, came over the intercom. "Gentlemen, we are about to land at an unknown airbase. As you can see, if I refuse to comply with the order to land, we will surely be blown to kingdom come. Make sure your seatbelts are tightly fastened—this may be a bumpy ride."

He lowered the landing gear and prepared to put the plane on the ground. Notwithstanding his announcement, the airstrip below him seemed to be in good repair. As he was about to touch down, the MiG-3s overflew the C-47 but circled over the unknown airfield, just in case Fergusson tried to take off again.

Captain Fergusson brought the C-47 to a halt near the end of the runway. An American-built Jeep bearing Red Army insignia sped toward the plane and stopped opposite the "barn door" on the left side of the aircraft. The steward opened the door, the steps were lowered, and the senior officer,

General Comptine, climbed down from the plane; one of the two interpreters followed him.

A Soviet general with a big smile on his face stepped out of the Jeep. General Comptine was a large, powerful man, but his Soviet counterpart was even taller and more heavily built. General Comptine saluted him smartly. The Soviet general returned the salute, and addressed Comptine in Russian. The American interpreter provided a simultaneous translation.

"Welcome to Meynypilgyno! I'm so sorry that I had to bring you here in this way. The obvious solution was to send you a radio message, but none of my men can speak English, and I didn't know if you had a translator. Also, I was sure that you didn't have a map showing this airport—it's top secret. So I thought that a MiG escort would be the best way to ensure that you arrived here safely."

"Thank you, General, but we were supposed to land at Anadyr. Why did you divert us here?"

"Unfortunately, we had to temporarily close the runway at Anadyr. In any case, the runway here is longer. While we refuel your aircraft for Yakutsk, the next stop on your journey to Novosibirsk, I invite you and your party for refreshments. Please assemble your men and follow me."

General Comptine returned to the plane and announced what had happened.

"They probably had a crash landing that's blocking the Anadyr runway, that's why we've been sent here," suggested Colonel Johanssen, Comptine's aide.

"I don't believe the story about the radio," another officer said. "They must've known that we had an interpreter on board. And it would've been nice to have been told about our MiG escort before they arrived and frightened the bejesus out of us."

"Wait a minute," General Comptine said, "take a good look at that general's uniform—he's NKGB, the Soviet secret police. This secret airfield is NKGB territory, and our diversion here is an NKGB plot. They didn't radio us for fear that the military, who are in control at Anadyr, might overhear the transmission. I'll bet there's no reason at all why we couldn't have landed in Anadyr. Men, be very, very careful. Take all your luggage with you—nothing is to be left on the plane that the NKGB might examine."

They trooped out of the C-47. The NKGB general was waiting, the big smile still on his face. He introduced himself as General Dmitri Gribowski, and presented his aide, Colonel Nikolai Pavlovich. General Comptine, in turn, introduced the members of his team.

"Let's go and have some refreshments," suggested General Gribowski. "Please follow me."

He led the party to a large hut on the edge of the runway. In the middle of the hut they found a long table covered with a white cloth. On the side of the table nearest to the door of the hut were 21 lead crystal vodka glasses; two more glasses had been placed in the center of the other side. Two stewards in white jackets now entered, and filled all 23 glasses to the very brim with vodka, then stood with their backs against the far wall. General Gribowski and his aide positioned themselves in front of the two glasses on the far side of the table. The Soviet general then motioned to the Americans to take their places on the other side, indicating that General Comptine should stand opposite him.

As zu Westerheimer moved next to General Comptine, he hissed, "Watch out, *in vino veritas.*"

Comptine nodded.

General Gribowski raised his glass of vodka to make a toast. Colonel Pavlovich did the same. He motioned to the Americans to do the same.

General Comptine spoke up. "General, I'm afraid that we're forbidden to consume any alcohol while on a mission."

General Gribowski's eyebrows rose. "General, in 1937 I visited Washington. Your military men consumed more alcohol there in just one evening than the whole population of the Soviet Motherland can drink in a year!"

"Yes, General," Comptine said, "but that was 1937. A lot of things have changed since we declared war on Japan on December 8th, 1941. And one of them is the new regulation that no alcohol may be consumed on missions."

General Gribowski knew that General Comptine was lying. And General Comptine knew that General Gribowski knew that he was lying. But General Comptine also knew that General Gribowski could not afford to pick a fight with him. After all, the Politburo had approved their mission, but authorization for the deviation to Meynypilgyno had certainly not been granted at that level.

General Gribowski tried again. "General, here in the Soviet Union, refusing to drink a toast is considered to be an insult, a deadly insult. And I was proposing to drink a toast to American–Soviet friendship. Surely you will allow your men one drink of vodka to cement our friendship?"

General Comptine smiled politely. "General," he said, "I would never dream of insulting you or our glorious allies, the people of the Soviet Union. But, like you, I'm a military man. And if I were to deliberately break an order of my commander-in-chief, it would be a greater insult to him, to you, and the people of the Soviet Union than refusing to drink your toast. General Gribowski, my men and I thank you for your hospitality. But we must respectfully decline." Turning to his men, General Comptine said, "Gentlemen, let us return to our plane. I'm sure that they've refueled it by now. We need to take off as soon as possible for Yakutsk."

Their plane had indeed been refueled, so Comptine ordered the pilots to take off immediately. Once they were at cruising altitude, Comptine gathered the team together.

"What do you think all that was about?" he asked.

"Clearly the NKGB's nose is out of joint," Colonel Johanssen said. "They weren't included in the loop, and they want to know what's going on. So, Gribowski arranged for us to be diverted to an

NKGB airfield where he hoped to ply us with alcohol and find out what we're up to."

Von Westerheimer spoke up. "But what about getting the MiGs? And why the NKGB uniform?"

This time it was the physicist's turn to puzzle Comptine. "Just what are you getting at?"

"Well, I don't know much about the NKGB. I do know that it's responsible for internal security (like our FBI) and intelligence abroad (like our Office of Strategic Services), but I doubt that they have their own air force. Getting those five MiGs must have involved high-level cooperation between the NKGB and the military. But the Soviet military are intimately involved with our mission. So, instead of supplying MiGs and agreeing to divert the plane, all the military needed to do was give the NKGB the information they wanted—there was no need for the diversion.

"And," von Westerheimer continued, "there was also no need for Gribowski to wear an NKGB uniform. All he had to do was to wear a regular air force uniform and tell us that the Anadyr airfield was temporarily closed. The purpose of the uniform was to mislead us into thinking that the NKGB is behind this.

"What I'm saying is this wasn't an NKGB operation at all. The Soviets don't trust us. They suspect that we're up to something. So their regular air force diverted us to their secret airfield at the place with the unpronounceable name…"

"You mean Meynypilgyno?" Colonel Johanssen said.

"Yes. And I'm not even going to try to say it. Anyhow, they diverted us there to extract information from us. They failed. But I'm sure they're going to keep trying."

General Comptine spoke up. "Two orders. First, none of you is to touch a drop of alcohol until we're back on U.S. soil. And that's not just to conform to what I told General Gribowski (if that's his real name). Alcohol loosens tongues, and there will be no loose tongues on this mission. Do you all understand?"

Everyone nodded.

"Second. I may be paranoid, but I'm certain that there'll be listening devices in every room they give us. That includes bedrooms, bathrooms, dining rooms, whatever. So, when indoors, the only topic of conversation will be baseball. That will drive the listeners crazy. In addition, they'll suspect that we're talking in code, and trying to break our nonexistent code will drive their code breakers crazy. Any questions?"

One of the bodyguards put up his hand. "Sir, I used to play professional football for the Pittsburgh Steelers. Are we allowed to talk about football, too?"

"Positively not. The Russkie listeners will just think that we're sports mad. If we stick exclusively to baseball, they'll assume it's a code, and that's what we want them to believe. Other questions?"

Von Westerheimer raised his hand rather tentatively. "General, I know nothing about baseball."

"Excellent!" General Comptine boomed. "In that case, you can make up names of players and teams. That'll keep the listeners guessing. But don't get too smart and come up with joke names. They'll catch on that we're pulling their legs."

Then von Westerheimer raised his hand again, equally tentatively. "General, you said that you were certain that the Soviets will have listening devices in every room?"

"I did."

"So, should we search the plane?"

Five seconds of total silence followed this question. Then General Comptine shouted, "Start searching every inch of this plane! And if you find anything, just leave it in place. And don't say anything anywhere near the listening device."

During the next hour they found two listening devices. While the C-47 was on the ground in Meynypilgyno, the Soviets had placed two AEG Magnetophone reel-to-reel tape recorders inside the ceiling of the plane, one near the front of the passenger compartment, one near the rear. But General Comptine was not satisfied, and ordered every member of the team to search again. This time a third recorder was found in the cockpit, hidden behind an instrument rack.

He called his team together. "We have a problem. Those three machines have certainly recorded everything we said just after takeoff about being overheard, as well as our planned baseball 'code.' If we leave the tape recorders there, the Reds will know that we've cottoned onto them. If we remove them, they'll also know that we realize what they're doing. Any ideas?"

"I'm pretty sure that those tapes can hold only one hour of recording," Colonel Johanssen said. "Why don't we rewind the tapes and record on them for an hour? If we all keep quiet for an hour, the Russians won't hear anything at all from us, just the noise from the propellers."

"Wouldn't that be somewhat unnatural? Observing an hour's total silence would also give the game away," the general said.

"Sir, I've had an idea," the former football player said. "Why don't we organize a sing-along? It's the kind of stupid thing that the Reds would expect from us."

"Great idea! Rewind those tapes, press the 'record' button and let's start singing."

A few minutes later the pilots were surprised to hear a dozen voices singing *Yankee Doodle* in half a dozen different keys. General Comptine appeared in the cockpit with a note that read: "Don't say anything, just sing along," which they did.

Unfortunately, the next song turned out to be "The Army Goes Rolling Along." The pilots naturally refused to join in with the army personnel. Instead, as soon as the refrain was finished, they started singing, "Off we go, into the wild blue yonder." The army officers equally naturally refused to sing "The Army Air Corps," so that song started and ended as a duet. The fourth song was "Home on the Range," which resulted in a truce.

An hour later they had filled the tapes with off-key renditions of patriotic songs, the fight songs of the two military academies (but no one aboard the aircraft seemed to know the words to "Anchors Aweigh," so they all just hummed along), followed by "Eskimo Nell" (which they sang twice), and all 26 verses of "The Mayor of Bayswater." Everyone was hoarse, with the exception of zu Westerheimer, who seemed to be in a state of total shock induced by the words of the two bawdy songs and said nothing until the plane landed in Yakutsk some nine hours after it had taken off from the secret airfield at Meynypilgyno.

It did not occur to anyone on the C-47 that General Gribowski's men had started the tape recorders running while the Americans were still in the hut, so the tapes should have had several minutes of silence at the beginning, followed by the sounds of the Americans returning to their plane.

Yakutsk, Siberia
Tuesday, July 6th, 1943

They landed at Yakutsk without incident. Yakutsk is the coldest city on earth, but they received a warm welcome. A military band was enthusiastically playing *Polyushko Polye* as they descended from the C-47. A ceremonial honor guard was drawn up and the commander invited General Comptine to inspect it. The band then played the two national anthems, after which the party traveled in a bus to the Lena Hotel.

Their hosts appeared to have emptied the hotel for their American visitors—they encountered no other guests during their stay. When they arrived, smartly attired waitresses escorted them to the hotel dining room. A large table groaned under the weight of a lavish buffet, which included caviar but no alcohol, much to everyone's relief. When they were not talking to their hosts through the interpreters, their sole topic of discussion over dinner was baseball.

Then their hosts took them to their rooms. They all strictly obeyed General Comptine's orders and again discussed only baseball, though some of the party, it has to be said, had great difficulty keeping a straight face. Most of them had problems falling asleep because Yakutsk is only 270 miles south of the Arctic Circle and this was midsummer, so the sun was below the horizon for only about two hours. The fact that it never became really dark outside had a deleterious effect on their sleep patterns.

Breakfast early the next morning was as lavish as their dinner had been: hot buckwheat porridge, omelets, open sandwiches, and blini served with sour cream. During the meal, everyone remembered to talk about baseball. The discussion became quite heated. In the 1942 World Series, the Yankees had lost four games to one to the St. Louis Cardinals, their first loss in the World Series since 1926. Passionate Yankees supporters at the table grew indignant at the very thought of their team losing again, so the Cardinals supporters teased them a little more than they should have. General Comptine deliberately allowed the discussion to get somewhat out of hand to perplex the Soviet eavesdroppers he was sure were listening, but fortunately he was able to restore order before physical violence broke out.

After breakfast they went back to their C-47 in the bus. They sat in the same seats on the plane as on the previous day, and promptly resumed discussing baseball, just in case the listening devices were still in place. After an hour, the general ordered them to search the plane again, but this time there were no tape recorders to be found. Much to everyone's relief, but especially to von Westerheimer, baseball was no longer the required topic for all conversations.

Their extra fuel tanks enabled them to fly directly to Novosibirsk, the largest city in Siberia. As they approached, they marveled at the wide River Ob gleaming below them in the late afternoon sunshine. In order to land into the wind, the pilots had to overfly Novosibirsk and then turn and come in from the west, offering the passengers an excellent view of the numerous factories and industrial enterprises. The plane landed at Severny Airport, located about five miles north of the city center.

Unlike at Yakutsk, their arrival in Novosibirsk was discreet. When the plane came to a halt, two militia women armed with PPSh-41 submachine guns escorted the party to the huge ornate sandstone terminal building that seemed so out of place at the somewhat small airport. They were taken upstairs to a reception room, where General Vladimir Fomarenko, General Comptine's Soviet contact, greeted them. Fomarenko looked more like a watchmaker than the deputy director of the GRU, the Red Army foreign military intelligence directorate. He was short and thin, with balding grey hair carefully arranged on his egg-shaped head. Beneath his long and narrow nose, his thin lips were tightly pursed. Thick glasses hid his eyes.

Through a Soviet interpreter, Fomarenko welcomed the team. He offered refreshments (again there was no alcohol), and informed them that they would be housed at a nearby military base. General Comptine thanked General Fomarenko for his help in arranging the mission and said that he looked forward to its successful completion. The formalities completed, a military bus took the team to the headquarters of the 52nd Rifle Corps just outside Novosibirsk.

Security at the military base was extremely tight. Notwithstanding the presence of General Fomarenko on the bus, GRU personnel scrutinized and re-scrutinized the identity papers of all the Americans on the team. They checked names off on lists, then un-checked and later re-checked them. They inspected and re-inspected the contents of all the baggage. They carefully examined the weapons of the American bodyguards and then returned them. And then they examined the weapons a second time. It was unclear to the Americans why the Soviets were behaving this way, but finally the visitors were allowed to leave the bus.

The GRU had requisitioned an entire building for the mission. The Americans and their Soviet counterparts were housed in separate wings, two to a room, but they shared the dining room and a large common room. There was a communications room and an operations room where the two teams could work during the day. Finally, three smaller rooms that they could use for private meetings were at the disposal of the participants.

The next morning the two teams met for breakfast in the dining room. Most of the Americans had slept relatively better than the previous night in Yakutsk—in Novosibirsk the sun was below the horizon for seven hours. But a few members of the party were still suffering from insomnia as a consequence of the extended daylight hours.

After another lavish breakfast they all moved to the operations room. The meeting opened with General Fomarenko reporting on his interview with the pilot chosen to fly Carl Friedrich zu Westerheimer to Germany. First Lieutenant Hans-Peter Schneider had been selected from the other captured pilots because he had considerable combat experience flying the Messerschmitt Bf 110 fighter, the aircraft the Soviet team had selected to transport Carl Friedrich to Germany. They had selected the Bf 110 for the made-up SANT peace mission because it was a two-seater aircraft with a range of 1,500 miles. This range was more than enough to fly the approximately 600 miles from Rzhev in the Soviet Union to Rastenburg in East Prussia, the town nearest the *Wolfsschanze* (Wolf's Lair), Hitler's headquarters, where the peace proposal from Osip Abramovich was to be delivered. Ironically, for his peace mission to Britain, Rudolf Hess had also flown a Messerschmitt Bf 110, but his had been equipped with drop tanks to increase its range.

"First Lieutenant Schneider was not particularly cooperative," General Fomarenko reported. "He made it overwhelmingly clear that he would rather die than do anything against the Thousand-Year Reich. I repeatedly pointed out that there was nothing disloyal, let alone treasonous, in bringing a document to Hitler that could bring the war to an early close and allow the captured Germans to come home to their families. Eventually Schneider insisted on seeing a copy of the peace proposal. I realized that, unless I did so, he would insist on seeing the document in the air on the way to Germany and, if he didn't like it for some reason, he would deliberately crash the plane.

"He read the document from cover to cover, then announced that there was no point whatsoever in his delivering it—Hitler would turn the proposal down because Germany is on the verge of glorious victory on all fronts. In response, I provided him with photographs of the surrender after the Battle of Stalingrad, starting with the picture of Field Marshal Paulus surrendering and then the aerial shots of some of the 100,000 captured German soldiers, including the 20 or so generals. I then showed him documents relating to the deaths by frostbite, malnutrition and disease during the winter before the surrender on January 31st, 1943; the translator assisted me.

"Schneider turned white as a sheet. Recovering, he went into denial and started shouting that the documents I had shown him were forgeries. Finally I said that he had a choice: He had seen confidential documents, so he could either fly the plane to Germany or face immediate execution. He calmed down, came to his senses and is now prepared to fly Colonel Carl Friedrich zu Westerheimer to Germany on a moment's notice.

"First Lieutenant Schneider has been moved to Rzhev. A captured Messerschmitt Bf 110 fighter is waiting in a hangar at the airfield there. We've serviced it; all it needs now is fuel. For obvious reasons we will not be providing him with ammunition of any kind. Our intelligence officers have assembled a set of captured German air force maps and they will give them to Schneider at the final flight briefing. At the last minute we will indicate on one of the maps where the current German front line actually is—it won't do them any harm in Rastenburg to learn just how badly their Army is really doing, as opposed to what Hitler is telling his people.

"Are there any questions about the pilot or the plane?"

There were none, so Fomarenko moved onto the next item on the agenda. "We now turn to Colonel Carl Friedrich zu Westerheimer. We've brought him here from Moscow—he's being held in the guardroom cells. My suggestion is that the colonel meets his brother in private, with two armed guards waiting outside. Is that acceptable to all?"

Again, no one said anything. So Fomarenko escorted Ulrich von Westerheimer and a Russian translator to one of the three smaller rooms. In the middle of the room was a table, with two uncomfortable-looking wooden chairs arranged on each side. He suggested that they sit, but the physicist was too tense to do that. He just stood and waited with Fomarenko.

After a few minutes there was a knock. Fomarenko opened the door. Standing there were three men. The two guards, armed with PPS-43 submachine guns, were wearing spotless NKGB uniforms; there was no separate military police unit in the Red Army. Carl Friedrich was dressed in shapeless Soviet civilian clothes—General Fomarenko had refused to allow anyone to wear a Nazi uniform on the military base.

The two brothers just stared at one another. The Soviet general motioned the translator and guards to leave the room. He followed, closing the door behind him.

Ulrich and Carl Friedrich continued to stare at one another. Ulrich noticed how thin his brother had become. In fact, Carl Friedrich had been even thinner. Before the surrender at Stalingrad, the German 6th Army was literally starving. And the rations his captors had given Carl Friedrich after the Soviet 62nd Army had taken him prisoner and during his imprisonment in the Lubyanka had been anything but generous. It was only after General

Fomarenko had come up with the plan of Carl Friedrich delivering the documents to Hitler that the Soviets provided him with adequate food.

Carl Friedrich noticed how well dressed Ulrich was. For the past six months, the civilians he had seen were all dressed in Soviet-made clothing. Ulrich was wearing the usual sort of clothes that an American college professor wore in 1943, but compared to Soviet citizens, he looked like a model in a high-fashion magazine.

The silence was palpable. Then Ulrich spoke. "How are you, Carl Friedrich?"

"As you see me."

"You look thin."

"I've been fatter."

And the silence resumed.

Finally Carl Friedrich asked the obvious question, "Ulrich, what are you doing here?"

"I've come here to save your life."

"But I'm not in any danger. Yes, I'm a prisoner now, but once we've conquered the Bolsheviks, I'll be free to go home."

"Carl Friedrich, Germany is losing the war. Total casualties at Stalingrad amounted to 750,000 soldiers killed, captured and wounded; the Soviets captured Field Marshal Paulus and 22 generals, with about 100,000 men. North Africa is lost. Sicily is about to fall, then comes Italy and finally Germany.

"And are you aware that the numerous German prisoners here in Russia are dying like flies? In March, the Reds buried 40,000 Germans in a mass grave, after a typhus epidemic. And, believe it or not, you were lucky to be sent to the Lubyanka—most of the prisoners have been sent to forced labor camps all over the Soviet Union, where tens of thousands of them are dying of cold, disease, overwork and starvation. They say that half the captives died on the forced march to Siberia.

"Yes, I've come to save you. The reason I'm here in the Soviet Union is that I'm heading a peace mission. A German soldier was needed to fly a peace proposal to Hitler at the *Wolfsschanze*, and I chose you."

"But you hate me and everything I stand for."

"I hate everything you stand for. But you're my brother, and that's why you and I are here."

"I cannot believe for one minute that Germany is losing the war. We've conquered most of Europe and are about to destroy the Bolsheviks. The *Führer* has repeatedly told us that we'll be victorious."

Ulrich looked his brother straight in the eye. "Carl Friedrich, please think carefully. If Germany were winning the war, would I be here? You know how I feel about your beliefs. Would I be in this room with you now unless I knew with one hundred percent certainty that this is your only chance for survival?"

But Carl Friedrich, fanatical Nazi that he was, could not comprehend the concept of Germany losing the war. Hitler had promised his people that he would build an empire that would last a thousand years. There was no way that the Nazis could lose battles to the "subhuman" Slavs. If Carl Friedrich were to die in Soviet captivity, so be it. He would die for a cause worth dying for, and through his death the Master Race would emerge victorious.

Ulrich realized that the mission was about to fail. He left the conference room abruptly and walked back to the operations room. It was almost deserted—only General Fomarenko and his aide, Colonel Bulgakov, were there.

"General Fomarenko, do you by any chance have the photographs and reports you showed First Lieutenant Schneider?" he asked in English.

Fomarenko stared at him blankly.

Colonel Bulgakov replied, "*Bitte sprechen Sie Deutsch.*"

So Ulrich tried again in German, addressing his request to the aide, who translated the question into Russian for the unilingual general.

General Fomarenko nodded, smiled and told his aide to tell von Westerheimer to wait. The general left the operations room. Ulrich von Westerheimer and Bulgakov were alone in the room. Bulgakov was about to make polite small talk when he saw that the physicist was in no mood for chitchat. On the contrary, it was clear that the meeting with his brother had greatly upset him. Some problem must have arisen that caused him to ask Fomarenko for the materials, so Bulgakov tactfully said nothing as they waited patiently for the general to return.

After about five minutes General Fomarenko came back to the operations room. He carried a cardboard folder tied shut with cloth tape. He handed the folder to von Westerheimer, who thanked him and returned to the small room. The two guards were standing stiffly outside, weapons at the ready, but they allowed him to re-enter the room.

Carl Friedrich was standing where his brother had left him with a blank look on his face, as if in a sort of catatonic trance.

"Let's sit down." Ulrich had to grab his brother with one hand, pull out a chair with the other and then push him into the seat.

Ulrich sat next to his brother. He opened the file. Even though all the documents and the captions of the photographs were in Russian, the scale of the Stalingrad defeat was obvious. The unending wide columns of German prisoners stretching to the horizon spoke for themselves, as did the photograph of Field Marshal Paulus and his aides after their surrender.

Carl Friedrich finally spoke. "No German field marshal has ever surrendered. This is not possible." And then he returned to his trance-like state.

They sat in an uncomfortable silence. Then Carl Friedrich spoke again. In a halting voice, half choking, he managed to croak, "You say that Germany will be defeated."

"Yes, it's inevitable."

"Is there no chance?"

"No chance at all."

"Will this peace proposal of yours lead to an honorable peace?"

Ulrich knew that the proposal was phony. Furthermore, even if it were real, there was no possibility whatsoever that Hitler would agree to any sort of peace. Nevertheless, he gave the only answer that could save his brother's life.

"Yes, Carl Friedrich, an honorable peace."

"What do I have to do?"

"You have to fly to the *Wolfsschanze*, to give the Soviet proposal to Hitler. And you'll take with you an American secret report that will strongly encourage Hitler to sign the peace treaty with the Soviet Union, just as Germany signed a peace treaty in 1917 with Russia."

"Can I see the report?"

"Yes. I'll fetch a copy for you."

Ulrich placed the photographs and the various documents back in the folder and tied the tape. He put the folder under his arm and left the room for a second time. It seemed to him that the two guards outside had not moved a muscle since he last saw them. He went to his room to get copies of the American rocket report. Then he returned to the operations room, where he was not surprised to find Fomarenko and Bulgakov waiting for him. He returned the cardboard folder to General Fomarenko, politely bowing slightly as he did so to show his thanks. Then, again speaking in German through Colonel Bulgakov, he asked Fomarenko for a copy of the peace proposal—there was no need to explain the reason for his request.

The guards had still not moved when he returned. He handed Carl Friedrich copies of the two documents: the peace treaty with its cover letter, and the Preparation 38 rocket paper.

Carl Friedrich started to read the peace treaty slowly, mouthing each word in an undertone as he read it. He seemed to be in a state of shock. The realization that Hitler's promises of German glory had been lies and that National Socialism had failed dominated his thought processes to the exclusion of all else. As a consequence, Carl Friedrich's brain could not comprehend the peace treaty before him.

After reading three clauses, he gave up. "I'll read the rest later," he said. "May I take these papers back with me to my cell?"

"I'm afraid not. But I'm sure that you'll have an opportunity to read them at a later stage."

It was clear to Ulrich that Carl Friedrich needed some time to digest what he had learned about the failure of Hitler and his Nazi dreams. Ulrich put his arm around his brother for just a moment—he had not forgiven Carl Friedrich for embracing Nazism. Then he rose and went out.

Ulrich returned to the operations room. Fomarenko had left, but Bulgakov was sitting in the otherwise deserted room. They spoke in German.

"General Fomarenko has asked me to apologize for his absence, but something urgent has come up that needs his immediate attention."

"I understand," Ulrich said.

"I assume that your brother is still in a state of shock," Bulgakov said. "Their leaders have so indoctrinated the German people that they simply cannot accept that they're losing the war. Could I suggest that you meet with your brother again tomorrow? A good night's sleep may help him to come to his senses."

The next morning the two brothers met again, once more seated next to one another at the table in the small meeting room with two armed guards standing stiffly outside the door. Carl Friedrich was deeply depressed. But it was obvious to Ulrich that his brother now fully understood the situation in which he found himself.

The meeting began with small talk. Carl Friedrich asked Ulrich what he had been doing. Ulrich was careful to talk only about his work at Princeton University where he had been a faculty member from 1933. He chose his words cautiously to ensure that Carl Friedrich would not realize that, less than six months before, Ulrich had moved from New Jersey to New Mexico, and was no longer a professor.

Ulrich then asked Carl Friedrich what had happened to him since 1933. Carl Friedrich similarly restricted his reply to his work before the German Army had drafted him. Unlike his brother's move to Los Alamos, Carl Friedrich's life since the start of the war was not secret in any way. But he was too embarrassed to tell Ulrich about the German victories in which he had participated—the crushing defeat at Stalingrad had made the inevitable downfall of the Third Reich all too clear.

Finally, Ulrich realized that it was time to show the papers to his brother. He opened his briefcase and took out the copies of the two documents again, placing them in a neat pile in front of his brother.

Carl Friedrich started with the top item, the peace proposal with its cover letter. He read it from start to finish, saying nothing. Next he read the Preparation 38 paper, again saying not a word.

Then Carl Friedrich turned to Ulrich. "What do you want me to do?" he asked, with a note of resignation in his voice.

"You will be flown from here to Rzhev, where you will change into the uniform of a German infantry colonel. A German pilot is standing by with a captured Messerschmitt Bf 110, ready to fly you from Rzhev to Rastenburg, to the *Wolfsschanze*. When you get there, you'll hand the documents to Hitler."

"Why should he meet with me?"

"Carl Friedrich, when a German officer, previously held as a prisoner in the Soviet Union and bearing an official Soviet peace proposal and an important secret American report, flies from the Soviet Union to East Prussia in a captured German plane, Hitler will see him."

"Are you sure? What if he tells an aide to handle everything?"

"You'll pass through many aides before you reach Hitler himself, but eventually he'll see you. He'll need to decide for himself whether the documents are genuine, and the only way he can do that is to speak to you personally."

At first Carl Friedrich seemed dubious, but Ulrich was able to persuade him. Ulrich took back the copies of the documents, embraced his brother somewhat more warmly than on the previous day, and left the room.

The leaders of both teams were waiting in the operations room with their interpreters. Ulrich reported on his meeting with Carl Friedrich. He concluded by saying, "In short, my brother is willing to fly to the Wolf's Lair and to hand Hitler the peace proposal and the Preparation 38 report."

General Comptine spoke next. Addressing General Fomarenko, he said, "Here is an official United States Army Officer's briefcase. Inside is a copy of the Preparation 38 paper. Please place the signed peace proposal inside, lock it, and seal the locks with your official seal."

Fomarenko motioned to Colonel Bulgakov, who produced a large envelope bearing a number of red seals. The Soviet general placed the envelope in the American briefcase. Bulgakov went out to fetch sealing wax and a seal, and the briefcase was locked and sealed the way that Comptine had requested.

Fomarenko turned to Ulrich von Westerheimer. "Would you like to say goodbye to your brother?"

Ulrich nodded his thanks, rose, and went to the small room for the final time. Carl Friedrich got up from the chair on which he had been sitting, staring blankly into space. Ulrich walked up to him and put his arms around his brother. As he did so, he whispered into his brother's ear, "Show the papers in the lining of the briefcase to Hitler."

Carl Friedrich nodded to show he had heard.

Ulrich released his brother, looked him in the eye and said, "*Auf wiedersehen.*"

There were tears in both brothers' eyes.

Rzhev, Soviet Union
Sunday, July 11th, 1943

The Messerschmitt Bf 110 fighter stood on the runway of the Rzhev air base. First Lieutenant Hans-Peter Schneider was in the pilot's seat. He had just received a detailed flight briefing for the 600-mile path he was about to fly. In particular, he was shown the location of the current German front line as well as German airfields along his route. A major Soviet concern was that German aircraft or flak crews, suspicious at seeing a plane coming from Soviet territory toward East Prussia and particularly in the direction of the highly sensitive area around Rastenburg, might shoot the German plane down.

Colonel zu Westerheimer now clambered clumsily into the rear gunner/radio operator seat. He had never been in a fighter plane before, and appeared bewildered.

General Gribowski climbed up the ladder and spoke to Carl Friedrich through the interpreter who had followed him. "Take this briefcase and keep it on your lap for the entire flight. It contains the documents you are to give to Hitler. You can see from the swastika on the outside that it is an authentic German Army briefcase. The locks have been sealed with Soviet Army seals. You are not to open the briefcase yourself—you must hand it to one of Hitler's aides for opening."

The general and his interpreter climbed down. The pilot retracted the ladder and closed the canopy. The control tower instructed First Lieutenant Schneider to start the two engines. The plane taxied, sped along the runway and took off.

As the plane reached cruising height, five MiG-3s joined it. One took position in front of the Bf 110, one on each side, and two flew behind, their wing tips nearly touching. The front MiG rocked its wings to instruct Schneider to follow it. Realizing that he had no choice, he obeyed. After all, the MiG-3 was a faster plane than the Bf 110. More importantly, Schneider had no ammunition in his guns. In any event, zu Westerheimer had never fired an airplane cannon. So Schneider followed the lead MiG-3.

As they crossed the German front line just east of Vitebsk, two Messerschmitt Bf 109 fighters rose to meet them. Immediately, the two MiG-3s on the port side of the Bf 110 peeled off and attacked the Bf 109 on the left, and the two on the starboard side dived toward the Bf 109 on the right. The fifth MiG-3 stayed where it was, and the Bf 110, with Lieutenant Schneider at the helm, followed it as before.

The dogfights were over in seconds. The Soviet pilots hit the two German fighters from above, before they had a chance to reach a height at which they could maneuver. All five MiG-3s immediately returned to the Soviet Union, in the hope that the Germans would not notice the Messerschmitt Bf 110 continuing into East Prussia.

Schneider and zu Westerheimer were now on their own. Schneider was a fine pilot and was able to navigate with ease to the Rastenburg Airfield about five miles southwest of the Wolf's Lair. To his delight, the fighter squadron that was stationed there to protect Hitler did not challenge him; on the contrary, the controller in the tower seemed to think that this was a routine flight. Schneider landed the plane without a hitch and taxied up to the control tower.

Schneider switched off the engines and opened the canopy. The two former prisoners of war climbed down the built-in retractable ladder. They stripped off their flying suits to reveal the pristine uniforms that they wore underneath. As they started walking toward the tower, there was a sudden command from two guards, members of the *Führer* Grenadier Brigade, the guard unit on the outer perimeter of the *Wolfsschanze*.

"Halt!" they shouted.

Schneider and zu Westerheimer immediately halted.

"Papers, please!" yelled the guards.

This posed a problem, because the GRU had confiscated both men's military identity papers when they imprisoned them.

"We've just escaped from the Soviet Union," explained zu Westerheimer. "We have secret documents for the *Führer*." And he held up the briefcase decorated with a swastika.

The guards could not have been more disbelieving if the two officers had claimed to have just flown in from Mars. They immediately drew their weapons and blew their whistles to summon an officer and additional troops. Soon some 25 soldiers surrounded Schneider and zu Westerheimer, their MP 40 submachine guns pointed at the two German officers.

An efficient-looking Lieutenant Schröder arrived, most surprised to see so many of his men belligerently surrounding an unarmed colonel and lieutenant. He turned to his senior NCO.

"Sergeant, what's all this about?"

"These two men claim to have escaped from the Bolsheviks in this plane here with secret documents for the *Führer.*"

"Impossible!" the Lieutenant said.

Turning to the aviators, he barked, "Show me your papers."

"They were confiscated when we were incarcerated in Lubyanka Prison in Moscow," zu Westerheimer said.

Lieutenant Schröder quickly realized that there were only two possibilities. Either these two officers were telling the truth, in which case they needed to be escorted to the Wolf's Lair right away, or they were lying, in which case he had to arrest them equally promptly. And then he realized that, if he guessed wrongly, he would be in awful trouble. So he did what all good junior officers do—he passed the buck up to a superior officer.

Major von Karlbach was perusing a summary of the day's events when his telephone rang. Annoyed at being disturbed, he yelled "*Ja!*" into the telephone.

Bearing in mind the number of generals at the Wolf's Lair, this was a somewhat foolhardy response.

The duty sergeant said, "Sir, Lieutenant Schröder at the airfield needs to talk to you urgently."

The first reaction of von Karlbach, still annoyed at being disturbed, was to tell the sergeant to inform Schröder that German officers are capable of solving their own problems. But something made him decide to take the call, perhaps the fact that Schröder had never bothered him before.

"What's seems to be the problem, Schröder?"

"Major, there are two men at the airport, dressed as German officers, who claim to have flown from the Soviet Union in a captured Bf 110 with secret documents for the *Führer*. They say they have no papers of any kind. Shall I arrest them?"

Von Karlbach re-read the item he had been reading when Schröder had interrupted him.

"Not yet," he said. "Ask them what the five MiG-3s did over Vitebsk."

Schröder naturally assumed that the major had gone insane. Nevertheless, as a sixth generation Prussian officer, military discipline was an intrinsic component of his very being, so he dutifully put von Karlbach's question to Schneider and zu Westerheimer.

Schneider replied, "Two MiG-3s peeled off and shot down one Bf 109, another two MiG-3s peeled off and shot down the other Bf 109, and the fifth one stayed in front of my Bf 110."

On hearing this bizarre response to the major's equally bizarre question, Schröder felt that he had gone crazy. Nevertheless, he repeated Schneider's words verbatim.

"Bring them to the *Führer* right away. But search them first."

"We've already searched them, Major, and they're unarmed. But the one wearing the uniform of an infantry colonel is carrying a leather Army briefcase. He insists only the *Führer* himself or one of his aides can break the seals on the locks. We've no idea what's inside the briefcase."

"Don't worry, I'll arrange for someone to be waiting with the security police outside the Reich Security Service building opposite the briefing room. He'll take the briefcase from the colonel, open it, and check the contents. He'll then escort the two men to the briefing room to meet the *Führer*."

Rastenburg, East Prussia
Sunday, July 11th, 1943

Adolf Hitler was in a fury. The Battle of Kursk had gone exceedingly badly for the Third Reich. Months before, the Red Army had found out exactly where the Germans were going to attack. Using this information, they had constructed eight lines of defense stretching eastward into Russia to a depth of nearly 200 miles. They had laid minefields to force the German tanks to advance along predetermined fire zones, and ensured that they had sufficient antitank guns to destroy the vehicles proceeding toward them along those zones. This defensive strategy had brought the German onslaught to a total halt and Hitler had been forced to order Field Marshal von Mannstein to withdraw. Now the German forces opposite Kursk were facing what seemed like the start of full-scale Soviet counterattacks.

To make matters worse, the Allies had just started their amphibious invasion of Sicily. The tanks that Germany needed to repel that invasion, units of the SS Panzer Corps, were stranded at Kursk. Not only would it take three months to transport them to Sicily, but transferring them from the Eastern Front would weaken the German forces there immeasurably. After all, the Battle of Kursk was the largest tank battle ever, with some 6,000 tanks involved. Moving any German tanks to Sicily in the face of overwhelming Soviet armor would probably result in defeat on the Eastern front. On the other hand, not having sufficient German tanks in Sicily would surely result in the fall of not just Sicily but, ultimately, the whole of Italy, which bordered the Greater German Reich to its northeast. So, unless Hitler could adequately defend Sicily, the Allies would sooner or later invade the sacred soil of Nazi Germany itself.

While trying to solve this problem, there was a knock on the door of the briefing room. Two strange officers entered, accompanied by SS-General Johann Rattenhuber—the general was the head of Hitler's personal bodyguard. All three men greeted the Führer with a resounding *"Heil Hitler!"*

Hitler noticed that Rattenhuber was carrying what seemed to be the remains of a briefcase. One of the officers seemed to be trembling with fear.

"My *Führer*," Rattenhuber said, "these two officers have no papers. They claim to have flown here from the Soviet Union in a Bf 110 that the Bolsheviks had captured. They have intimate knowledge of a dogfight that took place earlier today between five MiG-3s and the Bf 110 on the one hand, and two of our Bf 109s on the other.

"The Colonel claims that he was captured at Stalingrad. The Bolsheviks had him on their 'wanted list,' so he was interrogated in Lubyanka Prison. He says he told them nothing about our nuclear program—he claims he worked for von Ardenne before the war."

"What's your name?" Hitler snarled.

"Zu Westerheimer, my *Führer*," Carl Friedrich said.

"I know you," Hitler said. "You were a trailblazer of Aryan Physics. You certainly showed up that filthy Jew Einstein as a charlatan. What happened in Russia?"

"As the SS-General said, I was captured at Stalingrad and then imprisoned in Lubyanka Prison. They brought me to Novosibirsk, where my brother showed me two documents, a peace proposal from the Reds and an American report about their new secret weapon. It's an intercontinental rocket fired from the east coast of America, with a rocket control station in Scotland, that can reach Germany. As he said goodbye, my brother whispered in my ear that there was a document in the lining of the briefcase that I had to give to you. But when the SS-General broke the seals, the only document he found in the briefcase was the rocket report. The peace proposal (which I had read) was missing, and he found nothing in the lining."

"You mentioned your brother," Hitler said. "How does he feature in this?"

"He emigrated to America in 1933. He told me that he worked at Princeton University and had done research with Einstein. He said that he had come to the Soviet Union to save my life. That's all I know."

Hitler grew red in the face. "This is a Jewish Bolshevik plot," he screamed. "Why would the Bolsheviks show you a peace proposal to give to me and then not deliver it? And what is this rocket? And what is this story of papers in the lining that aren't there? And how dare you mention your Jewish-Physics-loving brother in my presence?

"Rattenhuber," he yelled, "have these two traitors flown to Berlin and turned over to the Gestapo. I want to know what really happened."

SS-General Rattenhuber opened the door of the briefing room and motioned to the guards standing outside to enter. He pointed to zu Westerheimer and Schneider. He said nothing—the guards knew precisely what to do.

Hitler turned to Julius Schaub, his chief aide. "I need to know in detail what's going on here. Admiral Canaris is always boasting about the vast network of spies in Britain and America that the *Abwehr* controls. I want him to investigate the rocket. After all, the *Abwehr* is responsible for intelligence and counterintelligence. Fly the briefcase and document to Berlin, and tell Canaris he has two weeks to find out the truth.

"In two weeks' time I want a conference here, with Canaris himself representing the *Abwehr*, together with representatives from all the other security services. I have to know if the Americans really have a secret weapon that we need to counter. And if they've built such a rocket, we can build a better one.

"More importantly, what's this peace proposal? Does this mean that the Bolsheviks are about to surrender? If that peace proposal is genuine, that tells me more about our success on the Eastern Front than all the communiqués from all my generals put together. Where is it? Why wasn't it in the briefcase?"

Rastenburg, East Prussia
Monday, July 26th, 1943

"This is highly satisfactory," Adolf Hitler said to Julius Schaub, rubbing his hands together with glee.

"Thanks to the Gestapo, we now know with almost total certainty that the Soviet peace proposal is genuine. So I can safely ignore my cowardly generals. They are advising me that I need to pull back to a defensive line in the face of the Bolshevik counterattacks to the north and south of Kursk, or else our glorious army will be annihilated—or so they claim. On the contrary, we're winning in the East, and we'll soon have total victory over the Slavs. My answer to Keitel and Jodl and all those other spineless generals is: Attack, attack, attack! The Reds are ready to make peace.

"Then, Canaris showed me nearly 20 reports from his spy rings in America and Britain regarding the American secret weapon. They all say the same thing: The weapon is still under development and isn't yet ready to be deployed. So there's no need for us to bomb the rocket control station in the Scottish Highlands yet—that would tell the Allies that we know all about their rocket. The moment that Canaris's spies tell us that the rocket is actually ready, we'll send in *Abwehr* saboteurs to destroy the launch site in Pennsylvania and the *Luftwaffe* will pound the Scottish control station to smithereens. Thanks to Canaris, we now know exactly where the installations are. And our engineers are now going ahead and building an even more powerful intercontinental rocket that can destroy the cities of America.

"But most important of all, we now know that Canaris really has highly-placed spy rings in place in America and Britain that can quickly respond to our questions. Furthermore, we can unconditionally rely on the information they send us. Up to now I've been somewhat suspicious of the material they've been transmitting to us. But the fact that all the reports he showed me are so consistent is absolute proof that the material we've been receiving from the *Abwehr* spies in both America and Britain is pure gold."

MI5 Headquarters, London
Monday, July 26th, 1943

"This is highly satisfactory," D, the Head of MI5, said to his deputy, rubbing his hands together with glee.

"We now know with almost total certainty that there are no *Abwehr* spies at large in Britain. All the German double agents received urgent radio messages, apparently from Canaris himself, ordering them to investigate the rocket control station in the Scottish Highlands. So we can conclude that he transmitted messages to every *Abwehr* agent here. The fact that not one person approached within miles of the 'control station' to investigate it reassures me that we have arrested every spy that Canaris has sent here.

"Furthermore, the fact that all the former German agents in the Double Cross System were sent messages is pretty convincing evidence that the Nazis don't have the slightest suspicion that their agents are in fact under our command.

"The other good news is that we haven't yet detected any messages sent to those agents whom we jailed or hanged. Canaris seems to have written off his failures. This is a further indication that the remaining agents, our double agents, are all credible.

"My one fear has always been that some of the spies we turned have deliberately tried to change their 'fists.' After all, every individual Morse key operator has his own unique way of sending signals, as unique as handwriting. I've lain awake at nights worrying about the possibility that, by making a slight change to his fist, one of our double agents may have tried to convey to his handlers in Berlin that we've turned him. But either they're all too scared to try that, knowing precisely what'll happen if they're caught, or else it's just as hard to make subtle changes to one's fist as it is to make equivalent changes to one's handwriting."

"Or possibly the listeners in Hamburg detected a minor change of some kind, but put it down to stress or illness or something," his deputy responded.

Both men puffed contentedly on their cigars for a while. Then the head of MI5 resumed.

"D'you know, I would've loved to be a fly on the wall when the handlers of those 12 double agents sat around a large table to create reports about our Scottish 'control station' that were alike but different! Those men deserve a medal. Working against the clock, they had to concoct reports that were similar in content but so distinct in outward appearance that no German counterintelligence agent could possibly guess that they were all written around the same table. And each messages had to be consistent with all the earlier messages that that agent had sent. We really need to send personal letters to each of the handlers to thank them for their impressive achievements.

"But most important of all, the fact that Canaris has received 12 essentially identical reports surely means that, from now on, Hitler will treat the reports from our double agents as pure gold."

NKGB Headquarters, Moscow
Monday, July 26th, 1943

"This is highly satisfactory," General Vladimir Fomarenko said to General Dmitri Gribowski, rubbing his hands together with glee.

"We've kept the Yanks happy by cooperating fully with them—at least, that's what they think. Also, that potentially embarrassing peace proposal that the NKGB concocted never left the Motherland. And we even managed to shoot down two Messerschmitts over Vitebsk.

"But most important of all, we obtained a copy of the Chadwick report in the lining of the briefcase. Comrade Stalin wants to build an atom bomb just as soon as we've won the Great Patriotic War. Professor Gordin and his team of nuclear physicists tell us that the information in that report is pure gold.

Los Alamos, New Mexico
Monday, July 26th, 1943

"This is highly satisfactory," General Silas Comptine said to General Leslie Groves, rubbing his hands together with glee.

"We now know with almost total certainty that we've captured all the *Abwehr* agents that Canaris and his team have sent here. The FBI spread the story that two convicted murderers who escaped from death row at the Arizona State Prison at

Florence had been seen in the area of the rocket factory. So they set up roadblocks, and for two weeks they stopped every car traveling in both directions within 50 miles of the factory. Not one stranger was detected—not a single solitary one.

"We received urgent radio messages sent from Canaris himself to his active *Abwehr* spies here, all of whom are now double agents, as you know. We immediately started crafting replies to be sent to the Nazis. As you also know, it isn't always possible for German agents to transmit messages across the Atlantic to Hamburg—it all depends on the current atmospheric conditions. So the *Abwehr* agents are instructed to transmit day after day at the same time until they can establish contact. We were lucky. Conditions were perfect on the second day that we tried, and we received acknowledgment of receipt of all five messages that were sent to Hamburg.

"Two of the agents that we've turned have been here since long before the war, and the radios that they were given when they left Germany aren't strong enough to generate signals that can be picked up across the Atlantic. The route they were told to use, sending radio messages to Mexico for forwarding to Hamburg, was shut down years ago, thanks to the cooperation of the Mexican government, so those agents were given replacement routes. We've been using those routes for a couple of years now. The Portuguese liner was fortunately in New York Harbor at just the right time, so we left a message for the steward at the usual dead-letter drop. A passenger on the Pan-American clipper to

China carried one of the messages. When she arrived in Shanghai, she took it to the Argentinian consul in Shanghai, who arranged for it to be radioed from there to Berlin. Our Russian friends picked up the transmission and forwarded it to us. All in all, the Reds have been most cooperative, I must say, especially the way they fell for our version of the Haversack Ruse."

"I agree," General Groves said. "But aren't you at all concerned that, after the Soviets found the Chadwick report in the lining of the briefcase, they might have sewed up the lining again with the report inside, and allowed Carl Friedrich to take the report to Hitler?"

"Not at all! Just after the European War started in 1939, Heisenberg told Hitler that he could build an atomic weapon for Germany. Hitler asked how long it would take him. When Heisenberg said two years, Hitler laughed. The war would be over before then, he declared. No, the Nazis aren't building an atomic bomb, and the Chadwick report would have been of no interest to them, in the unlikely event that the Russkies had sent it on.

"The key thing is that we've succeeded in passing the Chadwick report to the Russians via a mechanism that must have convinced them that the item is genuine. Once we start to use our atomic weapons, the secret will be out, and Stalin will surely start building his own nuclear arsenal. At that time, the Chadwick report will send them off in the wrong direction.

"But most important of all, five of the seven messages that their double agents sent to the *Abwehr* give the precise position of the rocket launch site in Pennsylvania. I just can't wait for the *Abwehr* to send teams of saboteurs to blow it up."

"Why?"

"Because the location happens to be a 100-acre horse farm in Bucks County that Hans-Heinrich Dieckhoff, the last Nazi ambassador to the United States, still owns."

CHAPTER FOUR
Operation KANGAROO
1944

Supreme Headquarters Allied Expeditionary Force, London
Friday, January 7th, 1944

The sergeant led Colonel Warren Foxgrove into General Comptine's office, then closed the door behind him. Foxgrove was a man of average height, but with broad shoulders and a physique to match. His black hair waved in all directions, defying anyone to attempt to comb it.

"Warren, welcome to Camp Griffiss, the only American military base in London," General Comptine said. "I'm so glad to have you on board again! If I had 10 times more men working here than the Army has given me, we still couldn't do everything that has to be done. There's an invasion coming up, and my job is to convince Hitler that it's going to take place in Pas-de-Calais and Norway. But I don't have enough people to do an adequate deception job for one nonexistent destination, never mind two."

"General, I had a great idea flying over here from St. Louis," Foxgrove said. "You know, of course, that Hitler is crazy."

"What makes you say that?"

"Well, for one thing, he relies on astrologers to decide what to do and when to do it."

"So does my wife, and she's not crazy."

Foxgrove realized he had made a bad mistake. He tried to recover.

"General, your wife comes from Omaha, Nebraska, doesn't she?"

"Yes, she was born and bred in the 'Gateway to the West.' That's something she's very proud of."

"Yes, sir, I know that. And what would you consider to be the most important product of her home city?"

"Why, Omaha Steaks, of course. Everyone knows that. Finest steaks in the world, if not the entire universe. Nothing like them—juicy, thick, succulent, flavorful. Food doesn't get any better than that."

"I fully agree, sir. You know, of course, General, that Hitler is a vegetarian?"

"A vegetarian? The man must be crazy."

"My point exactly, sir. And that's why I suggest we try to persuade Hitler that the invasion is going to come through Austria."

"Austria? Now it's you who's crazy. Give me just one reason for your ridiculous suggestion. Why should Hitler fall for it?"

"Sir, I can give you two reasons. Hitler was born in Austria. More precisely, he was born in Ranshofen in the municipality of Braunau am Inn, but he views Linz as his hometown. So, if he learns that the Allies are about to invade Austria, he'll view it as a personal insult, rather than the ridiculous idea that it actually is."

"And your other reason?"

"Since the *Anschluss* of 1938, Austria has been part of the Third Reich. Invading France in the region of Calais or attacking Norway in no way affects the territorial integrity of Nazi Germany. But he would consider an invasion of Austria to be a knife to the throat."

"Are you serious? It's January 1944. The Germans are still holding the Winter Line across Italy south of Rome. How are we supposed to reach Austria? Are you perhaps confusing Austria with Australia? Australia is that great big island in the southern hemisphere. We can easily land troops anywhere we like on the coast of Australia. It wouldn't be a problem at all—the only difficulty there is dealing with aggressive kangaroos. But Austria doesn't have a coast. In order to invade Austria, we'd have to land troops in northern Italy. And in case you didn't know it, the Nazis have controlled most of Italy since the Italian armistice of September 1943.

"Furthermore, we can't even get past the Winter Line, which runs across Italy somewhere south of Rome, but you want us to land millions of men near Venice or Trieste or some place, hundreds of miles behind the Winter Line. They'd have to fight their way through German troops, and then they'd have to cross the Alps. Are you maybe going to provide them with elephants, like Hannibal had? Foxgrove, Adolf Hitler may be mad as a hatter, but he's perfectly sane compared to you."

"Sir, this is as unreal as your plans to land troops near Calais or Oslo. I'm not suggesting for one moment that we should actually invade Austria. What I'm proposing is that you authorize me to come up with a plan for invading Austria that's sufficiently credible for Hitler to divert troops and tanks and airplanes away from northern France to guard against a nonexistent invasion of Austria."

General Comptine calmed down just enough to comprehend what his subordinate was saying.

"You're saying that we can improve our chances when we land in France if we weaken the Nazi forces there?"

"Yes, sir. Fewer of our men will be killed and injured in the forthcoming battle."

Comptine thought for a few seconds.

"Okay, Foxgrove, I'm going to give you 72 hours to come up with a plan. If it looks as if it might convince Hitler, we'll take it further. But I'm making no promises. Dismissed!"

Supreme Headquarters Allied Expeditionary Force, London
Monday, January 10th, 1944

"General Comptine, I've prepared an outline of the plan to invade Austria in July."

"I can hardly wait to hear this." Comptine's tone was pure sarcasm. "I've been on tenterhooks every waking minute. In fact, I haven't slept for three nights in a row in anxious anticipation." Then in his usual business-like tenor, he snapped, "You have exactly five minutes before I have to see General Eisenhower. Begin!"

"Agent PICKFORD will send a series of messages saying that he's been receiving confusing intelligence, that he has information from sources he regards as wholly reliable about three different sites for the invasion of Europe, but he'll try to separate the wheat from the chaff. A week or so later he'll say that he's been receiving more conflicting and inconsistent information, and that he's assigned his Dickens subagents the task of finding which of the three sites is the real site. Finally, he'll send a message saying that all three sites will be simultaneously invaded, and that he's assigned his subagents to get fullest details on all three."

"And just why would we invade in three places all at the same time?"

"Because if we invade in just one location, our forces may be wiped out. Also, Hitler won't be able to move sufficient reinforcements to all three sites simultaneously."

There was silence.

"That's either the best or the worst idea I've heard in ages. I'll see what Eisenhower thinks. Stay here—I'll be back in 15 minutes, 20 minutes tops."

Five hours later, after Foxglove had consumed innumerable cups of coffee that a sympathetic sergeant had brought him, General Comptine returned. Foxgrove jumped to his feet, snapped to attention and saluted his commanding officer.

"At ease! Sit down. Well, Warren, it looks like you may have just changed the course of the war. At least, that was what some of the 30 or so generals who heard your crazy plan said."

"What?"

"Here's how Eisenhower sees it. Hitler was defeated at Stalingrad, with about a quarter of a million troops killed, another half a million injured, and probably 100,000 captured. He fell back to the Kursk line. We've learned from German senior officers taken prisoner there that Field Marshal Keitel and Colonel General Jodl warned Hitler to defend the line where it bulged westward in the vicinity of Kursk. Instead, he fell for the fabricated Soviet peace proposal we sent him with zu Westerheimer, and Hitler attacked when he should have defended. The result: Total casualties amounting to another quarter of a million men, plus nearly a thousand tanks and a thousand aircraft destroyed. Even Hitler is starting to appreciate that the Eastern Front is now lost, and that it's only a question of time before the Red Army reaches Berlin.

"Also, at the end of 1942, Montgomery defeated Rommel in the Second Battle of El Alamein. As a direct consequence of that one loss, the Allies have completely swept the Nazis out of North Africa.

"The result is that Hitler is now acutely aware of the fact that defeat in just one battle can result in irreversible losses in both men and supplies. General Eisenhower is therefore sure that the idea of invading in three places at once, in the hope that the Nazis won't wipe out at least one of the three onslaughts, will sound sensible to Hitler."

Warren Foxgrove just smiled.

"But there's more. Hitler has gone over from an offensive war to a defensive war. Notwithstanding his continual calls to attack the Bolsheviks, his forces are falling back in Russia. They're currently holding the Winter Line in Italy, but they know that when spring arrives, our forces are going to try to push to Rome and beyond. We're bombing Germany by day and the British are pounding the Third Reich by night. Together we've rained destruction on Hamburg, much of the Ruhr, and even Berlin itself. Hitler is expecting an Allied invasion of Europe, so reliable information regarding this coming onslaught is going to fall on extremely receptive ears. Our good friend and certified moron Colonel Siegfried Kupfer in the *Abwehr* is a sycophant, and he makes sure that he tells Adolf only what Adolf wants to hear. So, if we use the British PICKFORD ring of Dickens subagents to tell Kupfer all the details of the coming invasion or, rather, three invasions, this will ensure that our disinformation will arrive promptly on Hitler's desk, accompanied by enthusiastic affirmations of its validity that Kupfer will pen."

"But won't Admiral Canaris urge caution?"

"We've been told that Canaris is largely out of the loop these days. It seems that he blocked Hitler's plot to kidnap Pope Pius XII and that Hitler found out about it. People who claim to know such things told me earlier today that any advice from Canaris will simply be ignored. Anyhow, thanks to you and your crazy ideas, I now have two more major assignments but no additional personnel to help me."

"Two assignments, general?"

"Yes, two. The first is to spread disinformation regarding our invasion of Austria. The second is organize a commando raid on Austria to obtain the information that we're going to need for our invasion."

"But the invasion is a figment of my imagination. We're not going to invade Austria. Why would we send men on a suicide mission for a nonexistent invasion?"

"General Eisenhower is worried that there might just be one sane man who has Hitler's ear. We know that if Admiral Canaris were to tell him that our plan to take Austria is nonsensical, that sage advice would be ignored. All that Canaris would achieve would be to strengthen Hitler's certainty that we're on our merry way to Austria to listen to the Vienna Boys' Choir and watch the Lipizzaner horses perform. But there might just be someone whom Hitler trusts who'll point out that any sort of invasion of Austria is nonsensical. So, once your invasion plan for Austria has been set in concrete, you'll be put in charge of organizing the commando raid.

"By the way, to save both of us time, let me tell you right now: Eisenhower has forbidden anyone with any knowledge of any of the details of the coming invasion, real or fictional, from leaving London. The risk is too great. If you or anyone else with your knowledge were to fall into the hands of the Gestapo, we may lose the war. So, don't bother coming to me to ask if you can lead the raid. The answer is no."

*Supreme Headquarters Allied Expeditionary Force, London
Monday, January 17th, 1944*

Colonel Foxgrove chaired the meetings of his Austrian invasion-planning group. For the first time, General Comptine was present at a meeting of the group. Three other Army officers sat around the table, two British, one American.

"Gentlemen," he began, "The purpose of this meeting is to finalize the Austrian mountainhead."

"The what?" Comptine asked.

"The mountainhead, sir."

"What's a mountainhead?"

"Well, sir," Captain Reginald Wallstead of the Corps of Royal Engineers replied, "when we land troops on a beach and they clamber ashore and set up a defensible perimeter that allows the rest of the invasion force to land, that's called establishing a beachhead. Unlike Australia, Austria doesn't have any beaches. Instead, sir, it has mountains, lots and lots of mountains. Accordingly, we're going to land paratroopers, antitank guns and anti-aircraft weapons by parachute, and they'll establish a defensible perimeter with their backs to a mountain.

We've decided to call that a 'mountainhead,' sir. Just as the sea behind it protects a beachhead, the mountain behind it protects a mountainhead.

"Best of all, sir, I was told that you were worried about aggressive kangaroos if we were to establish a beachhead in Australia. There is no such danger with a mountainhead, sir."

"Just who mentioned Australia to you?" Comptine demanded to know, looking straight at Warren Foxgrove. The colonel had known what was going to happen as soon as he heard Wallstead mention Australia, and he immediately began to stare at the far corner of the ceiling, an innocent expression on his face. He continued to gaze vacantly upward, ignoring Comptine's question and taking great care to avoid the general's eye.

"I'm not too sure, sir," Wallstead said, looking for support from Foxgrove, who disregarded the silent plea and went on staring at the ceiling.

"There'll be no more talk about Australia or kangaroos. Is that understood?"

"I'm afraid it's rather too late, sir," Wallstead answered, rather nervously.

"And what exactly do you mean by that?"

"Well, sir, a PICKFORD message went out yesterday to the *Abwehr*. It contained, among other items, a summary of a report from subagent OLIVER TWIST. It seems that OLIVER TWIST went to The White Stallion, a pub near an American Marine Corps base in Norfolk that's popular with their non-commissioned officers. He bought beer for a table of Marine Corps sergeants and sat with them. It seems that the marines were talking about an invasion, and they were worried about kangaroos attacking them. Bearing in mind that Australia is safely in Allied hands, OLIVER TWIST assumed that the Marines had misheard that there was going to be an invasion of Austria, and PICKFORD concurred. So, the kangaroo story has already been sent to *Abwehr* headquarters. Actually, sir, the PICKFORD team seems to think that sending the OLIVER TWIST message about the kangaroos was an excellent ploy. That sort of silly thing sticks in peoples' minds. The team members believe that the next time a PICKFORD transmission mentions Austria, the Germans will remember the report from OLIVER TWIST, thereby strengthening the deception."

General Comptine decided not to explode immediately, but rather to keep his powder dry for the next time Australia came up at a meeting of the group. Also, he wanted to get the planning group to stop using the term mountainhead.

"Let's get back to that stupid term you mentioned a while ago, before we got sidetracked."

"Did you mean mountainhead, sir?" the ever-helpful Captain Wallstead asked.

"Yes, that was the stupid term I meant. Why are we using it?"

"Well, sir, that term has also been sent in a PICKFORD message. It seems that subagent WACKFORD SQUEERS has a girlfriend, a cipher clerk in the Admiralty (or was it Royal Air Force Headquarters—I can't quite recall), and she'd asked him what a mountainhead was. WACKFORD

SQUEERS suggested to her that she'd misheard the word fountainhead. His girlfriend insisted that she had seen the word mountainhead go back and forth a dozen times that day in messages, and each time the word was definitely mountainhead. When WACKFORD SQUEERS asked her the context of the messages, she said communications with a U.S. Marine Base in Norfolk had repeatedly used the word. When he pressed her for more details, she realized she'd said too much, and clammed up. Then, in his message to Kupfer, PICKFORD asked if any of Kupfer's other agents had heard the word."

"And what did Kupfer say?" Comptine asked.

"He said that the word was new to him, too, but that he would ask about it. I'm sorry, sir, but the word mountainhead now seems to be part and parcel of this operation."

Like every good soldier, General Comptine knew when he was fighting a losing battle. "Let's turn to the operation itself. Foxgrove, what have you thrashed out so far?"

"Our plan specifies that United States Air Force engineers are to build air bases in three places: not far from Messina in Sicily; near Bari; and just outside Salerno. It turns out that there's no need to construct air bases out of plywood that'll be visible from the air to back up the plan, because those are going to be real air bases that they've already started building. Now that winter is nearly over, they're going to be used for the very real forthcoming resumption of the invasion of German-controlled Italy, not for our fabricated invasion of Austria.

"Similarly, the former Italian naval bases at Taranto and Brindisi will undergo major refurbishment, ostensibly for the invasion of Austria, but in actuality that work has already been started, again in preparation for the recommencement of the invasion of Italy. Finally, I won't bore you with the details, but in our plan a variety of camps are going to be prepared for the huge number of paratroopers from various Allied armies who are going to be dropped on Austria. Yet again, in reality the work has already started. In short, in our plan we reveal nothing to the enemy—all the proposed construction is already underway."

"What about the troops taking part in the phony invasion?"

"Again, we're piggybacking on the plans for the invasion of Italy. Of course, the corps and the regiments involved are completely different, because the invasion of Austria will be airborne, and also because we certainly don't want to give away who's involved in the invasion of German-controlled Italy. But the overall idea of both invasions is obviously the same. Our task is easy because Allied forces have already started implementation of the plans that they showed us for the invasion of Italy. All we have to do in our plan is to specify that Allied paratroop battalions from all over the world are to be sent to Austria, rather than to Pas-de-Calais and Norway."

"Has anyone checked that, when we leak details of the Austrian invasion to the Germans, we're not giving away details of the resumption of the invasion of Italy at the same time?" General Comptine asked.

"Our plan's been checked and rechecked, sir," Captain Wallstead said. "All the parties involved are understandably as concerned as you are that no secret information should be leaked to the Huns. In fact, not only is everyone satisfied that our plan gives nothing away, they're all looking forward eagerly to our sending it to Germany."

"Why?" Comptine asked.

"If Siegfried Kupfer can persuade Hitler that the plans for our Austrian invasion are real, that means that they'll believe that the ceaseless building activities going on in the south of Italy, the part we control, are for our summer invasion of Austria, not for our spring offensive against Italy. So they're less likely to try to attack our military installations there until it's too late."

"Well, I for one am delighted that our activities are so widely appreciated. Is the plan ready for PICKFORD to 'leak' it to Colonel Kupfer?"

"Yes, sir, we believe it is," Colonel Foxgrove said.

Supreme Headquarters Allied Expeditionary Force, London
Tuesday, January 25th, 1944

"They tell me that Kupfer has managed to persuade Hitler that the Allies are going to invade in all three places, including Austria," General Comptine said to Colonel Foxgrove. "I have to confess that I'm truly surprised. That Austrian plan of yours is so ridiculous, so implausible, so truly stupid that I thought that including it in the

PICKFORD radio messages would immediately tell the Krauts that the other two places where we're supposedly invading, Pas-de-Calais and Norway, are equally unbelievable. But no. They've bought all three locations, hook, line and sinker."

"If you were so unsure about Austria, General, why did you allow my plan to advance?"

"Because everyone said that you were right and I was wrong, including General Eisenhower and especially the whole PICKFORD team. They're the ones who convinced me, you know."

"Why them?"

"They've been playing with Hitler's mind since 1937. What convinced me is that the British have arrested every single Dickens subagent sent from Berlin to London, and yet the *Abwehr* still hasn't caught onto the fact that PICKFORD is a British ploy. The Germans keep telling him when and where the next subagent is going to arrive, and the cleverly constructed reports that PICKFORD sends that are supposedly coming via the new subagents keep fooling their intelligence officers. It's strange, because most of the *Abwehr* people are absolutely first rate, and we've found it almost impossible to fool them, no matter what stratagem or subterfuge we've employed. But for some reason they seem to have a blind spot regarding disinformation from PICKFORD—they pass everything on to Hitler as verified facts. So, as far as I'm concerned, whatever those PICKFORD guys say in regard to the minds of the Germans is gospel truth for me.

"However, I didn't ask you to come to my office to tell you that your plot has fooled the Nazis, notwithstanding my strongest possible reservations about it. The time has come to organize some sort of raid into Austria as further proof that your plan is genuine."

"But I thought you said we've fooled them completely."

"That was a slight exaggeration. Yes, we've fooled Hitler and his inner circle. But we haven't fooled Lieutenant Colonel Emil von Krassheim, Colonel Kupfer's second-in-command. We've discovered that he's almost convinced about Pas-de-Calais and Norway—they both make sense to him. But he's absolutely certain that the Austrian invasion is nonsensical."

"That's no problem. We'll convince him otherwise by sending a few commando teams into Austria. They can blow up some stuff. That'll convince even von Krassheim that we mean business in Austria."

"How will they get in?"

"That's no problem. We'll drop them by parachute. It's only about 500 miles from our air bases in Italy to Vienna. A B-29 Superfortress could easily manage that."

"And what about all their equipment?"

"That's no problem. A B-29 can carry 20,000 pounds of bombs. Everything a commando team could possibly need will weigh just a fraction of that."

"And what about getting them out afterwards?"

There was a long silence. Finally, Foxgrove said, "That *is* a problem."

"Get back to me when you've solved it."

Two days later, Warren Foxgrove was back.

"So, Colonel, have you solved the problem of getting the commandos back?"

"Yes, sir!"

"And?"

"Well, sir, you agree that we're not actually going to invade Austria? It's an imaginary invasion, right?"

"Right."

"The solution is to send imaginary commandos."

"What are you talking about? Are you out of your mind?"

"No, sir."

"Then what do you mean?"

"It's very simple, sir. We contact the Devil's Brigade, known officially as the 1st Special Service Force. They're a joint American-Canadian commando unit organized in 1942. They operate out of Fort William Henry Harrison just outside of Helena, Montana."

"Yes, I know all about them. I was at West Point with Robert Frederick, who raised the force. He's now a general, too. What this about the Devil's Brigade?"

"We tell them that we want them to do a training exercise. They're to choose a target in the middle of nowhere in Austria, perhaps a large dam like Mittelwald Dam with a hydroelectric power station, and then draw up a plan for sending 40 men to the target and destroying it. The plan has to be complete in every detail, especially the supplies to be parachuted in with the men. A key aspect of the plan is that a colonel will command the raiding party, with a major as his second-in-command.

"Then, under the highest level of secrecy, we assemble everything specified in the plan at an airfield within 500 miles of the target. Everything specified, that is, with the exception of the 40 men. We then take two corpses—"

"Did you say 'two corpses,' Foxgrove?"

"Yes, sir, two stiffs. We dress the one dead body in the uniform of a Special Service colonel, with the equipment he's supposed to carry as listed in the detailed plan, and the other dead body is dressed as a major. We then load everything into a B-29 Superfortress. The plane drops all the equipment plus the two corpses at the place specified in the plan. The Germans will see that we've tried to destroy the target—all the explosives and fuses and stuff will be lying there on the ground. They'll also find the bodies of the officers in charge of the plan. Oh, I forgot to mention, the officers will be carrying details of the plan in their pockets."

"Isn't that going too far, Foxgrove? Surely they would've memorized the whole thing? What if they were captured?"

"Sir, if this were an actual raid everyone would have rehearsed every step of the plan over and over again until it was so automatic that they could do it in their sleep. But this is not a real operation. As you've told me more than once, the Germans aren't particularly subtle. In fact, they're not subtle at all. If the leaders of the raiding party were alive, they could tell the Germans about the objectives of the operation. But the leaders of the raiding party are going to be dead, extremely dead. If the Germans see two dead U.S. Army officers and lots of explosives lying on the ground right next to an important dam, it's possible that someone will put two and two together and work out that we've sent a raiding party of commandos to destroy the dam and the power station. But it's also possible that they won't. So, the pockets of the two officers will contain pieces of paper headed 'Plan to blow up the Mittelwald Dam and the power station' so that the Germans will know why our men were dropped into Austria."

"But won't the plan specify 40 men in all? The Germans may not be subtle, but they are quite good at mathematics. Very good, in fact. And they'll realize after a short while that approximately 38 men are missing."

"Quite right, sir, quite right. Hopefully they'll assume that, with the loss of their commanders, the men decided that they couldn't carry out the mission, and they've fled. To back this up, in addition to what's specified in the plan we get from Fort William Henry Harrison, the B-29 will drop 38 opened parachutes. And that's the plan, sir."

There was absolute silence for nearly two minutes. Then General Comptine spoke.

"Foxgrove, do you recall my telling you that your original idea, a deceptive invasion of Austria, was either the best or the worst idea I'd heard in ages?"

"Yes, sir."

"Well, this latest suggestion is positively the very worst idea I have ever heard in my whole life. However, I'm going to have to put it to General Eisenhower, whether I like it or not, and I don't. Not a bit. The reason I have to tell him about this garbage of yours is that, clearly, we have to remove Austria as one of the three spurious targets because, as you have just so brilliantly demonstrated, it's simply impossible to come up with a reasonable plan for invading Austria at this point in the war. Austria is landlocked—you can't invade it by sea. And Nazi Germany controls the countries that surround it on all sides. Except on one side. And I can tell you now that we're not going to enter neutral Switzerland by force and occupy it just in order to invade Austria. And when I present your cockamamie plan to Eisenhower, the first question he's going to ask me is: Where are you getting the two dead bodies from?"

"Well, sir, sadly, soldiers here in England are dying of impact injuries every day, in car accidents, training accidents, and the like. Regrettably, it shouldn't be too difficult to come up with two dead American or Canadian bodies that look like they died from a parachute accident. Instead of returning them Stateside for burial, like we usually do, we'll tell their families that they died in action somewhere on a secret mission. We can then put the bodies on ice, dress them appropriately, and then drop them from the B-29. General, I know that there are some excellent German pathologists who would be able to see through our deception in a second, but they are unlikely to be in the wilds of Austria guarding a dam."

"And what about the troops guarding the dam? Surely they're going to rush after the 38 missing Special Services soldiers?"

"Not necessarily, sir. The soldiers guarding the dam are not going to be front-line troops. After all, as you said, Axis countries surround all sides of Austria. Plus neutral Switzerland on the one side, just like you mentioned. And other than my plan, no one has even remotely proposed invading Austria. So why are those soldiers guarding the dam in the first place? The answer is that, during wartime, all critical installations like dams and power stations are guarded against possible sabotage, but second- or third-rate soldiers do the guarding. I would guess that they'll have a force of no more than 15 men there, half of whom are on guard duty at any one time, to protect the dam and the power station. So, when they finally find 38 empty parachutes, 2 dead bodies and lots of explosives, all they'll be able to do will be to send a radio message to headquarters for assistance. Now, as far as I can determine, Mittelwald Dam is plumb in the middle of nowhere. It's going to be hours before anyone at all can get there, let alone enough crack troops who can take on the 38 remaining Special Services soldiers sent in to blow up the dam. By the time they start searching, our troops will be long gone, and no one will be surprised that the hunters can't find them. It's unlikely that the dead bodies of the two commanding officers will receive anything more than a cursory glance from a country doctor, if that. The bottom line is that headquarters in Berlin will learn that there's been an abortive commando raid in Austria. Two senior officers died, and they left lots of explosives behind. But the news will get through to Lieutenant Colonel Emil von Krassheim that we're seriously interested in Austria."

"Enough! Write all this nonsense up and I'll take it to General Eisenhower. One of two things is going to happen. The more likely outcome is that they'll reduce you and me to the ranks and send us to do guard duty in Greenland."

Supreme Headquarters Allied Expeditionary Force, London Wednesday, January 26th, 1944

"It's worse than I thought," General Comptine said.

"Worse than reducing us to the ranks and sending us to Greenland?" Colonel Foxgrove asked.

"Much, much worse. General Eisenhower loved your idea, especially the bit about 40 highly trained commandos taking on 15 incompetent elderly soldiers and blowing up the dam and the power station."

"And?"

"And it seems that there's some dam on the southern side of Austria, not too far from the Italian border. General Eisenhower wants you to send 10 or 12 commandos to blow up the dam and the power station, and then escape into northern Italy, which the Nazis still control. There are apparently bands of partisans who are quite active in that area, and he claims that they'll be able to shepherd the commandos to the coast, where a submarine will whisk them to safety."

This time Colonel Foxgrove was rendered speechless. After spluttering for a while, he finally said, "Sir, does General Eisenhower realize that the planned invasion of Austria isn't actually going to happen?"

"Yes, he does, believe it or not. But he's understandably concerned that the Germans may start to realize that, too, unless you successfully pull off the raid on that dam."

Supreme Headquarters Allied Expeditionary Force, London
Tuesday, February 8th, 1944

Two weeks later, a sergeant in the Royal Engineers escorted an elderly man into Captain Reginald Wallstead's office. The visitor was wearing an old-fashioned suit that showed signs of darning and other repairs.

"Dr. Eckstein, please sit down. Before asking you to come here, the relevant authorities gave you Most Secret security clearance. Nevertheless, they instructed me that, before we go any further, you are required to sign this document. It states that, in terms of the Official Secrets Act, 1939, anything you may hear or see in this building is Most Secret. Read the paper and sign at the bottom, please."

Eckstein read the two-page document carefully, and then signed where indicated in a meticulous hand.

"Doctor, I am also required to warn you that, in this country, we take the Official Secrets Act, 1939 extremely seriously, and any infringement, no matter how slight, can be severely punished by a long period of imprisonment."

"Captain Wallstead, I realize that you were instructed to tell me what you just said. But I want you to know that my wife and I fled Austria in 1937 and were given refuge in this country. We're both extremely grateful to the British people for literally saving our lives, and I can assure you that neither of us would do anything that might remotely have a negative effect on the war effort, which we both back as strongly as we can. I'm an old man, way past retirement age. Of course, we have no British pension, so I have to teach mathematics in a school in the East End of London, where we now live. But in addition, I spend every available hour volunteering as an Air Raid Warden. I signed the document because I had to, but I assure you that it was unnecessary."

"Yes, I understand that, Dr. Eckstein. Would you please come this way?"

Captain Wallstead led Eckstein to a large room in the basement. A cloth that looked like a number of rough bed sheets sewn together covered a vast table that filled most of the room.

"Dr. Eckstein, I fully appreciate what you said earlier. Nevertheless, I'm certain that you won't be offended if I tell you that I'm required to say once again before removing this cover that everything you see or hear in this building is Most Secret."

"Yes, that is understood." For some reason Dr. Eckstein's already heavy foreign accent had thickened; it was hard for Wallstead to work out what the Austrian refugee had just said.

"I'm sure you're wondering why you're here. Your name was given to my superiors as someone who might be able to assist us in a military operation."

"In Austria I was a civil engineer. I'm afraid that I have no military knowledge at all."

"Nevertheless, I was told that you've had some experience of hydroelectric plants, and you might have specialized information of some kind that could assist us."

"Of course I'll do my best, Captain. But I do not think that, even with the best will in the world, I can possibly be of any help to you."

"Well, we'll see."

And with that, Captain Wallstead folded up and removed the cover, revealing a model of a dam set in a mountain range. A long, narrow body of water with a large Alpine meadow at one end dominated the center of the model. The other end of the blue painted area turned sharply to the right. There a dark gray dam wall almost immediately terminated it. At the bottom of the wall on each side were exit pipes from turbine rooms. They extended beyond the dam wall.

"This is a typical Austrian hydroelectric power station."

"No, Captain, it's not typical at all. It's unique. It's the Spinnental Dam and hydroelectric power station in the Tyrol. The dam wall is 47 meters high, that's about 155 feet. The two turbines can each generate 48 Megawatts of power."

"And how on earth do you know all that?" the astonished captain asked.

"Because I was the chief engineer—I built that dam."

"Good heavens, sir, are you Heinrich Eckstein? When they instructed me to meet with you, they told me nothing about you. I'm delighted to tell you that I used two of your textbooks when I read Civil Engineering. It's an honor for me to meet you!"

"Thank you, Captain," Eckstein said, "but those days are over. Now I'm an elderly mathematics teacher and an Air Raid Warden. But looking at your model certainly brings back memories. Do you see the road? It starts here at the edge of the model and ends on the eastern side of the dam wall. The actual roadway starts at Spinnentaldorf, by the railway station. We had to bring everything that we needed to build the dam to Spinnentaldorf by rail. There we loaded the materials onto trucks and drove them to the site. And at the end of the working day, we all piled into the trucks to go back to Spinnentaldorf to eat and sleep—there was hardly enough room at the dam site for us to build it properly, never mind for accommodation for the hundreds of workers. I must have traveled that access route thousands of times, and what a road it was, up and down, round and round, potholes everywhere. If the engineers who constructed that track had built the dam, it wouldn't have lasted six months. But enough of the recollections of an old man. The past is the past. How can I help you?"

"Dr. Eckstein, I'm not permitted to answer that. Instead I'll ask you a question, and I have no doubt whatsoever that from my question you'll be able to deduce everything that you want to know."

"And what is your question?"

"Dr. Eckstein, how would you blow up that dam?"

Eckstein smiled. It was the smile of a man who had gone from a respected position at the very top of his profession in his native land to the humiliating depths of religious persecution there, followed by sanctuary and unending financial struggle in England, but who instantly realized that vengeance was about to be executed on his Teutonic tormentors.

"Captain Wallstead," Eckstein said, "all you need to do is blow up the turbines. If the explosion in the confined space of the turbine room is sufficiently powerful, it will separate the dam wall from its anchors in the rocks on each side of the wall, and the wall will come tumbling down."

"Go on, sir, please."

"In more detail, water flows from the lake into the turbine room through inlet pipes with openings exactly 36 meters below the level of the top of the dam wall. A team of frogmen would have to remove the gratings that keep debris from entering the inlet pipes or 'penstocks' as you and I call them, and then drop explosives down the penstocks. The penstocks suck in an exceedingly large quantity of water from the dam and rush it down to the turbines, and this strong flow of water will quickly wash the explosives down to the entrance to the turbines. If the right quantities of the right explosives are detonated, the shock waves will bring down the dam wall.

"Now that I come to think of it, I've a better idea. It's going to be hard for the frogmen to remove the gratings and drop the explosives into the penstocks without getting washed down the pipe to the turbine. The control room is here, on the eastern end of the dam wall, at the end of the road from Spinnentaldorf station. Your men need to go into the control room and turn on the switches to activate the motors that close the sluice gates at the entrance to the turbine room. That will stop water flowing down the penstocks and make it much safer to remove the gratings. You will have to weight the explosives, so that they descend to the sluice gates by gravity. Yes, I think that would be much safer and easier to accomplish.

"One final remark, if I may. Last year, the Royal Air Force breached the Möhne Dam in Germany— the 'Dam Busters' bounced a bomb on the surface of the lake behind the dam wall that hit the wall and exploded there. They destroyed the Edersee Dam the same way. But because of the way that the

Spinnental Dam lake suddenly turns to the right just before the dam wall, that approach cannot work. As far as I can see, what I'm suggesting is not just the best way of destroying the Spinnental Dam, it's probably the only way.

"Sir, you've been extremely helpful. But one final question: Can you estimate the explosive power needed?"

"No, I cannot. That question goes way beyond the scope of my expertise. But I'd be delighted to sit down with your colleagues in the Royal Engineers and try to reconstruct the drawings of the dam and plant from memory. I worked on that dam for five years, and most of the details are still imprinted on my mind—that was how I could tell you the exact depth below the dam wall of the tops of the inlet pipes."

"Dr. Eckstein, I'll certainly take you up on your generous offer. In fact, let's go over to headquarters now. We told your headmaster that you'd be away for two hours, but it's going to be a whole day or possibly more. For example, we're going to have to learn enough about the layout of the control room so that we'll know how to close those sluice gates. I'll ask my sergeant to phone the school, and then we'll leave for Regimental Headquarters at Chatham. Better still, let's go to your home first where you can pack a suitcase for a stay of a few days. We're going to learn from you everything about that dam that we possibly can."

Within days of the Royal Engineers finalizing the detailed diagrams of the dam, the hydroelectric plant and the control room, 12 men had flown from Fort Bragg in North Carolina to Fort Victoria on the Isle of Wight. All of them were Operational Swimmers from the Office of Strategic Services. Their training was in Special Operations, with particular emphasis on underwater operations, as well as in guerrilla warfare.

A committee assembled from various branches of the Allied armed forces had drawn up the plan for the operation. General Eisenhower himself had insisted on being briefed on every detail, because it was a component of the invasion that he was leading.

Training for the mission started as soon as they arrived at Fort Victoria. A major concern of the planners was what would happen if the demolition team could not close the sluice gates. Accordingly, a hydrodynamic device had been constructed that would enable them to practice removing the grating from a penstock and dropping down explosives while huge volumes of water were sucked into the penstock. The team practiced this maneuver repeatedly. But the force of the water flow was just too strong. In fact, three of the men had been seriously injured while attempting the procedure. Unless the remaining team members could close the sluice gates, it would be all but impossible for them to blow up the dam.

Tyrol, Austria
Monday, April 17th, 1944

One late spring day, an elderly army truck coughed and spluttered its way up the mountain road from Spinnentaldorf to the Spinnental Dam. In the back of the truck were two technicians who would alternate eight-hour shifts while running the control room of the hydroelectric plant for the next week, and 12 elderly *Volkssturm* (Home Guard) soldiers. They, too, were coughing and spluttering when they were not complaining about being separated from their families for a week. However, the military had called up all able-bodied men for active service soon after the start of the war, so only the elderly and the infirm were available for guard duties at insignificant outposts like the Spinnental Dam. The *Volkssturm* soldiers, too, would work eight-hour shifts, guarding the dam and the hydroelectric plant. But no one had ever bothered to explain to the men the nature of the possible threats to the dam. Consequently, the soldiers did not take their task too seriously.

That night, a B-29 Superfortress took off from Bari. It carried a nine-man demolition unit under Commander Wilson Austin, together with the equipment that the crew of the plane would drop by parachute onto the Alpine meadow adjoining the Spinnental Dam. The pilot flew over the Adriatic Sea and made landfall near Venice. He overflew the Dolomite Mountains without being challenged and then started descending as the plane neared

Spinnental for the low-altitude drop over the meadow.

The jumpmaster turned to Commander Austin. "We've been very lucky this trip—no one has fired anything at us. Let's hope that the trip back is equally uneventful."

"We chose a moonless evening for this operation. That should help."

"Ten minutes!" shouted the jumpmaster. Each team member repeated this command to the man to his right, to his left, and in front of him. "Get ready!" yelled the jumpmaster. The noise in the plane was so great that only the men nearest the jumpmaster could hear him, so after he gave the verbal command he followed it by the corresponding hand signal. As command followed command, the soldiers lined up and hooked their static lines to the appropriate cable. They checked their static lines and the rest of their equipment, and then waited for the "One minute!" and "Thirty seconds!" warnings. As the plane reached the drop zone, the light changed from red to green and the jumpmaster screamed out, "Go!"

Seven paratroopers were able to jump out of the plane before the light turned red again. The pilot of the B-29 came round in a big circle, then the light changed to green again and the remaining two men dropped into the target area, followed by the supplies. The B-29 turned south and began to climb as it headed back to Bari.

The men gathered their equipment and checked that everything had landed safely, especially their rubber boats, which they promptly inflated and launched. There was still no opposition of any kind to their arrival.

Aerial reconnaissance by the Allies had revealed that the Austrian Army had constructed a small wooden camp a few yards from the dam wall on the western side. However, the only places from which soldiers on guard duty could observe the lake behind the dam were on the dam wall itself, inside the camp, and in the area around the control room. Everywhere else the mountains rose vertically from the water's edge. Dr. Heinrich Eckstein certainly had not deliberately positioned the dam wall in a location where it would be hard to protect it against saboteurs. Nevertheless, that was the outcome of his design.

The initial task of the raiders was to put all the defenders out of action, and to do it quickly, before they could send a message by telephone or radio. The demolition team had the advantage of surprise for a number of reasons. Even though the Austrian soldiers would surely hear the B-29 flying low over the area, it was unlikely that they had the slightest idea that its role was to launch an attack against the dam. Then, the lake behind the dam wall was long and straight, but it turned sharply to the right just before the dam wall. That meant that the high mountains rimming the lake would block the defenders from seeing parachutes floating down to the Alpine meadow at the other end of the lake. Finally, if the demolition team stayed close to the right hand side of the lake as they paddled their boats from the meadow end of the dam to the dam wall, the guards would not be able to see them until they rounded the corner of the lake, which was close to the wall. In short, everyone involved in the operation generally agreed that neutralizing the defenders would be an easy task.

However, there was a serious dilemma. On the one hand, Dr. Eckstein had cautioned the commandos to take every precaution to avoid damaging the control room in any way, or it might be impossible to lower the sluice gates. But on the other hand, not attacking the control room might give the staff there enough time before the commandos burst in to alert regional military headquarters that an invasion was taking place.

The three boats rounded the corner and advanced on the dam wall. The commandos were equipped with night glasses, and they quickly saw that the elderly guard seated at the anti-aircraft weapon in the camp was fast asleep; the fat soldier leaning against the guard post in front of the camp buildings was staring into space; and the two guards patrolling the dam wall had lit cigarettes and were standing with their backs to the lake with their rifles lying on the ground. The two soldiers guarding the control room were talking to one another, so they did not see the commandos approaching.

As they had practiced so many times, the three boats fanned out into a line parallel to the dam wall. Using hand signals, Commander Austin ordered one commando in the rightmost boat to train his weapon on the fat soldier at the guard post, and another aimed at the guard manning the anti-aircraft gun. The third readied hand grenades to destroy the camp and its occupants. Two commandos in the middle boat aimed at the backs of the two guards on the dam wall. Two commandos in the boat on the left aimed at one of the two soldiers in front of the control room, while the third took aim at the other soldier.

At the signal, everyone fired their MP 43 German assault rifles or tossed their grenades. The initial barrage was well executed—the silence that followed the explosions seemed to imply that they had wiped out the defenders. But suddenly the door of the control room was thrown open and the technician on duty rushed out to see what was happening. One commando fired his automatic weapon instinctively. His first bullet narrowly missed the head of the technician and hit the control panel, generating a continuous set of sparks. Subsequent bullets killed the technician but did no further damage to the control room.

The annual spring thaw had started to melt the snows of winter, so the surface of the water on the lake was almost level with the top of the dam wall. It was therefore easy for the men to paddle swiftly up to the wall and clamber onto it. Some of the commandos rushed to check that all the off-duty soldiers who had been sleeping in the camp were dead. They dragged the bodies onto the dam wall, next to the corpses of the two defenders who had been smoking when they were killed. Commander Austin, in the leftmost boat, raced to the control room in order to flip the switches that would lower the sluice gates. Much to his surprise, the switches were already in the closed position.

And then he realized what had happened. When the technician heard the gunshots and the grenades, he had no idea what was going on—the idea of an airborne invasion was the last thing on his mind. So, his first reaction had been to protect his beloved turbines by closing the sluice gates. Then he had rushed outside to see what was happening.

Austin immediately gave the signal to his men to remove the grills on the openings to the penstocks. They attached 20-minute fuses to the explosives and dropped them down the wide pipes. The saboteurs quickly swam back to the dam wall, grabbed their knapsacks and weapons, and raced to the road. They ran at full tilt until they were behind a high bluff that sheltered them from the dam. There they hastily took off their frogman suits and put on the uniforms they had brought with them in their knapsacks. Then they waited expectantly.

Less than five minutes later there was a muffled explosion. A second muffled explosion, this one slightly louder, followed shortly after. Then came a brief rumbling noise as the dam wall started to crumble. Next the dam burst with an exceedingly loud crack. Finally they heard a sound like a thousand rivers as the water that had been pent up in the lake rushed into the gap, carrying away huge lumps of concrete loosened by the explosion.

The commandos were far too well disciplined to waste time celebrating the success of the first part of their mission. Instead, they grabbed their equipment and started marching along the access road in the direction of Spinnentaldorf. They halted in the middle of a steep downward slope. To their right, a mountain rose to the black sky. To their left was a vertical drop—they could not see the bottom of the inky valley below.

"Commander, how long do you estimate it'll be before they arrive?" one of the commandos asked.

"Dr. Eckstein said that the trucks take about 30 minutes to drive from the station in the village to the dam. But first the locals have to realize that the electricity is off, which may take some time in the early hours of the morning. Then they need to round up a squad of soldiers. I reckon it's going to be an hour or more before we have visitors."

It was closer to two hours before the six sentries watching from above the road heard the noise of an approaching truck. They stayed in place. Two of the other commandos moved to the middle of the road where they stood with their MP 43 assault rifles at the ready. In front of them stood an officer. All three wore SS-uniforms, the black uniforms of the *Leibstandarte SS Adolf Hitler*. It was well known in the Tyrol that the *Leibstandarte* were active just across the border in northern Italy, disarming Italian military units after the armistice and murdering partisans and Jewish refugees.

The Austrian sergeant driving the Henschel Type 33D1 covered personnel carrier turned the corner, slowing the vehicle down even further. The laden vehicle, with lowest gear engaged, struggled up the steep incline. Through the darkness of night the driver saw in the glare of his headlights that three men in *Leibstandarte* uniforms stood in the middle of the road ahead of him. Then he saw that the leading man held the rank of SS-Colonel, so he did not think twice before slamming on the brakes and bringing the army truck to a shuddering halt.

Wilhelm Ostenmann was born in Hamburg in 1911. He lived there until 1924 when his family emigrated to the United States. His parents proudly Americanized their son's name to Wilson Austin. Austin did everything he could to become an American in every possible respect, including wearing his blond hair in a crew cut. But one thing he could not control—his parents insisted on speaking their native language in the home to the total exclusion of English. Accordingly, Commander Austin had no trouble addressing the sergeant driving the truck in fluent, idiomatic German. Austin ordered the driver to form up his 12 passengers in a single line on the far side of the road, leaving their weapons in the back of the personnel carrier. The driver looked around, saw that he was in the middle of nowhere, and was somewhat mystified that an SS-colonel, no less, wanted his men to line up, unarmed, in the darkness with their backs to the steep drop.

When the sergeant had formed the men up, the lanky SS-Colonel with a chiseled face ordered the sergeant to take his place in the line. Despite being even more mystified, he instantly obeyed without question.

"Right about turn!" yelled the SS-Colonel. The men obediently executed the order. Immediately the six sentries descended and joined their three colleagues. Austin nodded, and two of them went to their knapsacks and took out old laddered nylon stockings.

Commander Austin and his commandos never found out why it happened, but before the two American commandos could approach the *Volkssturm* soldiers to tie their hands behind their backs, something took the Austrian sergeant from his previous state of mystification to outright suspicion. He suddenly shouted, "Enemy soldiers!" As the unarmed Austrian soldiers spun round, three of the commandos mowed them all down.

In the ensuing silence, not one of the Americans moved. They all appreciated that no alternative action had been possible, but nevertheless their shooting of 13 unarmed men revulsed them. After a few seconds, one of the commandos approached his officer.

"Commander, sir, I think that we can increase our chances of getting back safely if we drop the bodies over the cliff."

Wilson Austin thought for a few moments and then agreed. Once more the members of his team felt disgusted—there was no question in anyone's mind that the elderly Austrians they had killed deserved a decent burial—but they all realized that the disappearance of both the demolition party and the squad of Austrian soldiers would tend to center the forthcoming investigation on the dam site, rather than the stretch of Italian coastline to which they were headed. Accordingly, with visible extreme reluctance, they rolled the bodies over the edge of the cliff.

The commandos piled into the truck. The two SS-officers rode in the cab: SS-Colonel Wilson Austin in the passenger seat and SS-Major Fred Stone, who drove the truck. Both had been born in Germany, and both spoke perfect German. The seven enlisted SS-men sat in the back of the covered personnel carrier. Of them, only SS-Sergeant Al Greenwald spoke German, so he sat next to the opening to be able to handle any issues that might arise if the truck were stopped. Like the two men in the cab, Greenwald had been born in Germany. He had a large round face with broad forehead and a large chin. While playing the role of an SS-Sergeant, he was forced to consciously suppress his ready smile.

Austin turned to Stone. "Make a U-turn. No, wait! The road is too narrow here, and I don't like the look of the drop, particularly at night. It's only about a mile to the dam, and it'll be safe to turn there. Drive back to the dam."

When they reached the site, they were stunned to find that the explosion and its aftermath had carried away the entire dam wall as well as the control room. The five years of work under the direction of Dr. Heinrich Eckstein had vanished. The destruction of the dam had damaged even the approach road, so much so that it was almost as hard to turn near where dam had formerly been located as at the scene of the ambush.

Once they were under way, Wilson Austin asked his driver, "Fred, how much fuel do we have?"

"If this gauge is accurate, enough to get us to the border, but not much farther."

"Let's get us some gas when we get to Spinnentaldorf."

They arrived at the village at 3:30 a.m. As they reached the first houses, Commander Austin spied a gasoline station. He instructed Fred Stone to drive in.

"The place looks deserted," Fred said.

"No problem. We're SS-men; we just take whatever we need."

Wilson went to the back of the truck and ordered his sergeant to start operating the manual gasoline pump. It was fortunate that he chose a German-speaking commando to carry out this task, because hardly had Al Greenwald started to pump when a thin freckle-faced blond-haired boy of about 11 or 12 suddenly appeared on the scene.

He walked up to the NCO and asked, "Sergeant, where's my father?"

Greenwald was a kindly man, so instead of chasing the lad away, he asked, "What do you mean?"

"I know this truck," the boy said. "My father and the rest of the men in the other *Volkssturm* squad drove off in this truck about an hour ago. Where are they now? My uncle is in the other squad, the ones guarding the dam now. And you and the other SS-men in the truck—where have you come from? When my father came back home today after a week at the dam, he didn't say anything about any SS-men being at the dam. What's going on?"

Al Greenwald thought quickly.

"What's your name?" he asked.

"Eberhard Schweinfuss."

"Eberhard, can you keep a secret?"

The lad nodded his head vigorously.

"You mustn't tell anyone, not even your parents or your best friend."

Again the boy nodded with enthusiasm.

"Eberhard, I really shouldn't tell you, but I think I can trust you. The *Führer* has ordered us to test a new secret superweapon at the dam—didn't you hear the explosion earlier?"

The youngster shook his head, wide-eyed.

"Well, that's why there's no electricity—all the power is being used for the incredible *Wuwa*."

The boy nodded, still wide-eyed.

"The whole area is off limits. Both *Volkssturm* squads are there, guarding the environs of the dam."

Eberhard smiled, reassured that his beloved father was fine.

During this conversation, Greenwald had been keeping one eye on the fuel as he pumped it in, and he noticed that the gas tank was now full. Next, he wanted to fill the two jerrycans that he had found in the back of the truck. The problem was that, with the youngster standing there, he could not shout to his colleagues to bring the jerrycans. After all, if he asked them to bring the *Wehrmacht-Einheitskanister* they would have no idea what he meant. On the other hand, no SS-sergeant would fetch jerrycans himself. But he could not ask the lad to fetch them, because when Eberhard got to the back of the personnel carrier he would ask the other commandos where the jerrycans were, and that would be that.

He thought for a moment. Then he yelled, in German, "Fetch the jerrycans!"

Naturally there was no response, so he told the boy that the men must be sleeping. He walked to the back of the truck, muttered softly to the others to pretend to be asleep, fetched the two jerrycans himself and filled them.

"Can I carry them back to the truck?" Eberhard asked.

Again Greenwald thought quickly. Under no circumstances was the youngster to be allowed anywhere near the truck. But again he wanted to be kind, especially since he had just helped roll the dead body of the boy's father off the cliff and killed his uncle at the dam site an hour or two before. So he said, "Thank you, but that's strictly forbidden. Go home now!"

As the boy ran off, much to Greenwald's relief, he suddenly realized that if the lad had cottoned on to the fact that the men were American soldiers, they would have had to kill him, too. A biblical verse came into his mind, a Deuteronomic prohibition, against "killing a mother animal and her young on the same day." He had learned it as a boy from the rabbi in his local synagogue where he grew up in

Berlin, and he wondered if it applied to human fathers and sons, as well.

Speaking in German just in case other youngsters were around, the SS-Sergeant informed the two SS-officers that the truck was fully fueled, and that the two jerrycans in the back were full, too. He saluted, the two officers returned the salute, and he climbed into the back of the personnel carrier. The SS-Major, who had been carefully studying the map yet again with the aid of a shielded flashlight while the truck was being refueled, drove off in the direction of the Italian border.

It was just less than 250 miles from Spinnentaldorf to the pickup point in Italy via the shortest route, namely, through the Brenner Pass. But the American demolition squad had no intention of driving through the Brenner. Instead, they stuck to little-used side roads. However, this had two disadvantages: The route was considerably longer and the quality of the roads was such that they could not travel as fast. Nevertheless, the planners had stressed that the risk of being stopped on a major route was too great. So, the demolition squad drove along byways instead of highways. Their goal was an Italian village near the coast where a partisan band would shelter them until the following night.

As they started off, Fred Stone said to Wilson Austin, "As I understand the plan, the partisans are expecting us."

"Of course."

"But are they expecting us wearing SS-uniforms?"

"I don't know," Wilson said. "But I see your point. If Giuseppe Locatelli and his men see nine SS-men descending on their hideout, there'll probably be a shootout that'll end in bloodshed. But these are the only clothes we have. Let me think. Where can we get civilian clothes?"

"How about a clothing store in the next village?"

"At four in the morning?"

"What's the problem? We're SS-men. We can get whatever we want, wherever we want, whenever we want it. And it won't cost us a cent."

When they reached the next village, Fred slowed down. On the second block they spotted what looked like a clothing shop. The SS-Major parked the truck, and he and the SS-Colonel banged loudly on the glass door. Opening a window above the shop, the angry shopkeeper yelled, "Who's making all that noise in the middle of the night, when good citizens are trying to sleep?"

Then he saw the uniforms of the two *Leibstandarte SS Adolf Hitler* officers. He muttered a quick apology and rushed downstairs in his nightclothes to let the men in. He unlocked the door with shaking hands.

The SS-Colonel took command. "We're here on a secret mission and we need civilian clothes. Show me what you have," he ordered the terrified shopkeeper.

The owner of the clothing store stuttered, "Colonel, in my shop I sell only *Tracht* (traditional Alpine clothing)."

"Then provide us with *Tracht*!" yelled the SS-colonel.

He opened the door of the shop and shouted in German to the men in the back of the truck, "Come inside."

The shopkeeper realized he had exactly two choices: He could outfit all the men in *Tracht*, and thereby bankrupt himself, or he could refuse and end up in a concentration camp, probably with his whole family. And once they had arrested him, they would take the clothes anyway. So he wisely decided to be as cooperative as possible.

The SS-Sergeant, the only man in the back of the truck who had understood the barked order of the SS-Colonel, led the rest of the men into the clothing shop. They filed in somewhat sheepishly. Fifteen minutes later they filed out considerably more sheepishly. On their feet they wore rustic leather shoes with embroidered woolen socks that reached just below their knees. Next came *Lederhosen*, decorated shorts made of dark green or dark brown leather. Embossed leather suspenders with a wide decorated leather breastplate across the chest kept their *Lederhosen* from falling down. Over their ornamented white shirts they sported the *Steireranzug*, a grey jacket made from loden with green embroidery and contrasting lapels. But what embarrassed them the most were the shapeless grey felt hats with what looked like a shaving brush stuck vertically into each hatband. Adding to their discomfort, the shopkeeper insisted that the hats had to be worn on the top of the head, rather than over it. As a result, as far as they were concerned, the hats they were wearing were at least two sizes too small for them. Having given away a large proportion of his stock, the owner decided to go the whole hog and gave each man two metal hat badges to pin onto his hat. Nine speechless American soldiers dressed in *Tracht* filed out of the shop, carrying their SS-uniforms and weapons, and filed into the truck. The six unilingual soldiers had been speechless from the start, of course, but the three German speakers were now also mute from embarrassment.

When they were back in the truck, Fred managed to find his voice. He asked Wilson, "Don't we have to kill the shopkeeper to make sure he doesn't report us?"

"Don't be stupid. Who would have the courage to report an SS-Colonel? And who would he report us to, anyway? The police? They wouldn't dare challenge the authority of the SS. The SS itself? If the shopkeeper were stupid enough to file a report with them, they'd just throw him into one of their concentration camps. No, there's absolutely no need to do anything about that Austrian shopkeeper. By the way, we're going to have to put on our SS-uniforms right away—we're driving in a military vehicle."

Soon after they left the village, Fred spied a wide stopping place on the side of the road. The men quickly changed in the back of the truck, and then resumed their journey dressed once again as members of the SS.

An hour later they reached the border with Italy. The sleepy German guard took one look at the SS-colonel in the front seat of the vehicle and raised the barrier to let the truck through without checking anyone's papers.

Fred drove until sunrise when they took a break at a roadside café. The owner provided them with coffee and rolls, and they ate and drank their fill. Then they poured the gasoline from the two jerrycans into the gas tank of the truck.

Now Wilson took over the driving. As they neared the village of Santa Clementina, he stopped the truck in the parking area of an abandoned roadhouse, and they all changed back into their *Tracht*. Under normal circumstances, the men would have laughed uproariously at one another's appearance, especially the stag brush in each hatband. But the saboteurs still felt guilty about the unavoidable murder of the unarmed *Volkssturm* soldiers and the way that they had disposed of the bodies. It was almost as if the nine men felt that they had to wear those outfits as punishment for what they had done.

Fred drove the truck into Santa Clementina, and then continued through the village to a farm on a hill just outside the village. As previously instructed, they drove past the farmhouse into a fruit orchard. The men got out of the truck, carrying all their equipment and their recently removed SS-uniforms. Giuseppe Locatelli and his sons Pasquale and Gianmarco met them. None of the three Locatelli men could speak a word of English, but the village priest, Father Sebastiano, was on hand to translate for them.

Giuseppe Locatelli welcomed the American soldiers warmly but briefly. He did not ask any questions about their mission. Then he immediately got down to business.

"Tonight we will take you to the coast as arranged. We know the signals. There will be no problems. My sons know where to leave the truck. Is the package with the goods and the papers in the back, as we arranged?"

"Yes, it's there. By the way, we have SS uniforms with us. Would the truck driver like to wear one?"

"No, Pasquale can't speak German, and that could lead to problems. It would be bad enough for him to be caught driving a German army truck. But if he were in an SS-uniform, it would be even worse, if that were possible."

Pasquale got into the truck. Gianmarco produced a motorcycle that had been leaning against a tree. The two left immediately, with the truck ahead of the motorcycle.

Giuseppe now led the men to a wine cellar. The walls were lined with barrels, stacked three high. The partisan leader moved a stack of three barrels aside, revealing a low hole in the wall leading to a subterranean vault. He motioned the nine men to enter the hidden room. Father Sebastiano joined them.

"You will stay here until nightfall, then we will take you to the shore. In the meantime, my daughter will bring you food and wine."

Giuseppe now disappeared through the hole, which he immediately covered up. A few minutes later his daughter, Agostina, appeared with their provisions. The men ate and drank sparingly, still too tense to relax.

Three hours later the barrels were removed again. This time it was Pasquale and Gianmarco. Through Father Sebastiano, they excitedly told Commander Austin what had happened.

"I drove to the farm, as I was told," Pasquale said, "and Gianmarco drove behind me. We left the truck at the agreed place. I took the package out of the back, and left the goods and the papers in the disused wine cellar there. Someone had left a desk for us in the cellar, so I put the goods on the desk and the papers in the drawer."

"Then Pasquale got on the back of my motorcycle and we rode back here," added Gianmarco.

"Were you stopped on the way?" Austin asked.

"Luckily there were no roadblocks today. But I would imagine that, when the Allied advance reaches northern Italy, things are going to get even hotter for us partisans.

"In the meantime, we have to get you all to the coast before 1 a.m. I suggest you get some rest. My father will come here this evening and take command." The two brothers left.

The men tried to sleep, generally with little success. Later Father Sebastiano heard confessions from the four Catholic members of the squad, and then led the whole squad in prayer.

Giuseppe and his sons arrived at dinnertime. They ate with the American commandos. After the meal, Wilson took Giuseppe Locatelli and Father Sebastiano aside.

"We have two choices, as I see it. We can wear our SS-uniforms and march you to the beach at rifle point, as if you were under arrest. If we encounter any German troops, we just chase them away and keep going. Or, we can wear our Austrian *Tracht* and we all carry our weapons of choice. If we meet any Germans, we shoot them."

"Me and my men refuse to be marched at gunpoint by SS-men, even Americans pretending to be SS-men."

"That's what I thought you'd say. So, we'll wear our *Tracht*, and leave behind the SS-uniforms for you to utilize at some future time, even though you can't speak German."

"Don't you need them?"

"The Allies have far more German uniforms of all kinds, as well as German equipment, than we can possibly use. At the Battle of Kursk, the Red Army killed, wounded or captured over a quarter of a million German troops. The Russians have shared some of the spoils with us, including the uniforms that the nine of us were wearing on this mission. Keep everything we've given you, it may be useful to you someday for fooling the Nazis. We found a pile of Schmeissers in the back of the truck, together with lots of ammunition; I'm sure you can use those submachine guns. We'll keep our MP 43s with us until the last minute, because we may be attacked on the way to the coast. But once we're about to get into the dinghies, we'll hand them over to you and your men."

An hour later five other partisans joined them. The men left the vault; the three barrels were replaced. The commandos thanked Father Sebastiano and said goodbye to him. Then they all started off in single file. Giuseppe led the party, Pasquale brought up the rear. Interspersed among the partisans were nine Americans carrying MP 43s. They were dressed in *Tracht*, their grey felt hats perched on the tops of their heads, metal hat badges and all.

The 17 men reached the beach without incident. Giuseppe stood on a rock with a powerful flashlight and a piece of red cellophane. He watched the sea, waiting for the submarine that would take the demolition squad to safety. Finally a boat surfaced. Giuseppe flashed short white–short red–long red–short white. Back came the correct countersign. Then two inflatable dinghies were dropped overboard. Members of the crew of the submarine clambered into the dinghies and paddled toward the shore.

The nine commandos handed their MP 43s to the partisans, then plunged into the surf wearing their *Tracht* and swam to the dinghies. They climbed aboard and were taken to the boat. Within minutes the submarine had dived. The partisans, laden with automatic weapons, made their way back to the underground vault. They met no opposition on the way.

Reichssicherheitshauptamt Headquarters, Berlin
Monday, April 24th, 1944

SS-General Walter Schellenberg called the meeting to order.

"Let me remind you that the *Führer* abolished the *Abwehr* more than two months ago and that the *Reichssicherheitshauptamt* (Reich Main Security Office) has taken over its function. We will have no more of the incompetence that manifested itself under Admiral Canaris.

"The *Führer* wants a full report on the Spinnental incident. The purpose of this meeting is to record the facts as we know them, and then determine what happened. Colonel Kupfer, will you begin?"

"Thank you, SS-General. Two teams of 12 *Volkssturm* soldiers each, Squad A and Squad B, say, protected the Spinnental Dam. They guarded the dam one week on, one week off. A truck brought the members of Squad A to the dam on Monday, April 17th. When the truck arrived at the dam site, the members of Squad A climbed down and the members of Squad B, who had been guarding the dam for the previous week, climbed aboard. So we know that at about 9 a.m. on April 17th, the dam wall was still standing.

"At about 1 a.m. on Tuesday, April 18th, Elfreide Hagen, an elderly widow who lives in Spinnentaldorf, walked to the mayor's home to complain that the electricity was off not just in her home but all over the village. It seems that she suffers from insomnia, and while she was trying to read, her lights had failed. She went outside and found that the whole village had been plunged into darkness.

"The mayor, Meinhard Schweinfuss, decided that this was the work of saboteurs. He has been extensively interrogated on this point. It seems that he was fast asleep. He was dreaming about sabotage when Elfreide Hagen banged on his front door and woke him. He is old and somewhat confused, and somehow his dream became part of the actual situation. I repeat, we have found no rational reason why Schweinfuss decided that the hydroelectric plant had been sabotaged.

"Schweinfuss proceeded to round up the truck driver and the members of Squad B, and ordered them to return to the dam that they'd left nearly 24 hours before. When asked why he didn't summon the two technicians as well, he replied that he knew that it was sabotage, so what were needed were soldiers, not technicians.

"Meinhard Schweinfuss has been mayor of Spinnentaldorf for at least 30 years, so when he ordered Squad B to go back to the dam, they obeyed him without question. At about 2:15 a.m., the truck left for the dam with the members of Squad B. They haven't been seen since.

"The next morning, Meinhard Schweinfuss bumped into one of his grandsons, Eberhard Schweinfuss, who told him a confusing story. It seems that, even though the members of Squad B had disappeared, the truck came back about an hour or so later, waking the boy, who lives next door to the gasoline station.

"At that time, members of the SS, or more precisely, the *Leibstandarte SS Adolf Hitler*, manned the truck. Eberhard is certain that the driver of the truck was an SS-Major; the man sitting next to him was an SS-Colonel; and the person who pumped the gasoline into the truck held the rank of SS-Sergeant. Even though Eberhard is only 11, he turned out to be an excellent witness. In particular, he was able to draw the insignia that the three SS-men were wearing, and they accorded with the ranks that he reported. He was also certain that the truck he saw was the truck that took the men to and from the dam each week. He was able to recite from memory the number stenciled on the back of the truck, and the number he gave corresponded to the number of the truck listed in the military records for the region.

"It is possible that Eberhard, being only a boy, might have made the whole story up. However, a shopkeeper at the next village has given evidence under oath that, a little later that night, nine SS-men demanded full sets of *Tracht* from him. He has described what the men were wearing when they entered his shop. Being in the clothing business, he was able to provide detailed descriptions of all the uniforms they wore. He declared emphatically that the leader was an SS-Colonel, the second-in-command was an SS-Major, and the senior non-commissioned officer was an SS-Sergeant. The other six men were just troopers, and he noticed that none of them said a single word during the proceedings, even when the sergeant or the officers directly addressed them. He has also provided us with detailed descriptions of all the men.

"That evening, when the mayor noticed that the electricity was still not on, he tried to contact the dam by radio. He received no response. He tried again the next morning, after which he contacted military headquarters for the region.

"The duty officer dispatched a squad of regular soldiers to the dam. They arrived about noon on April 19th. They found the dam wall and the hydroelectric power station in ruins. There was a wooden camp for the *Volkssturm* soldiers on one side of the dam wall, but all they found there was a pile of ash and burnt-out embers. On the other side, the side with the access road, was the control room, which sat on the dam wall itself. The control room ceased to exist when the wall was destroyed. Also, they found no trace of any of the *Volkssturm* soldiers, either from Squad A or Squad B, or either of the two technicians from Squad A who were responsible for the running of the power station that night.

"The regular soldiers investigating the situation radioed their headquarters, and this resulted in an area-wide search for the nine SS-men and the truck. Then someone delivered an anonymous letter to military headquarters at Trento stating that the truck missing from Spinnental was in a particular place on a farm near Udine. A squad raced to the farm, and they found the truck in the specified location. The squad immediately searched the rest of the farm. In what looked from the outside like an abandoned wine cellar, they found black market goods. The items in question were made in the United States of America, and it appeared that someone had smuggled them to Udine from Sicily; regrettably, that island is currently under American control. The soldiers searched the wine cellar and found correspondence and ledgers that proved, beyond all doubt, that the owner of the farm, Basilio del Monte, was the leader of the black market in that area of Italy.

"The soldiers arrested del Monte on the spot, and the local Gestapo and Italian secret police quickly rounded up all the other individuals named in the correspondence. A court operating under German law summarily tried them. When the judge allowed him to address the court, del Monte declared that he knew nothing about any of the goods found on his farm and that he had had no involvement whatsoever in any black market of any kind. However, he was unable to explain the damning evidence, especially the detailed ledger that was clearly in his handwriting. Then he declared that he'd been a member of the Nazi Party since 1931 and gave his membership number. The judge chose to ignore his remarks, and del Monte and his co-accused were sentenced to death for black marketeering and consorting with the enemy. A firing squad carried out the sentence at once.

"Two days later it was discovered that del Monte had lived in Germany before the war, and had indeed been a member of the Nazi party since 1931. More significantly, he and the others named in the correspondence had not just been cooperating with the German administration in the area since the armistice, but had been leading the fight against the partisans in the region. An expert closely examined the letters. He came to the conclusion that the entire correspondence was an excellent forgery, as were the ledgers detailing the black market dealings.

"The military now conducted a house-to-house search of the area, but they found nothing else that was relevant. They increased the radius of the search area, but again they found nothing suspicious. In particular, they found no trace of the SS-men.

"Are there any questions so far? Does anyone disagree with anything I've said?"

No one seated around the table responded. Kupfer took a drink of water, and then continued.

"I turn now to the results of our investigations. The investigators we've sent to the site are certain that someone introduced explosives into the bases of the penstocks. Because the dam wall collapsed on top of the turbines, they've not yet been able to determine the type of explosive that was used or how it was detonated. It would take many weeks of excavation to remove enough of the debris to reach the area where the explosions took place, with no guarantee that any evidence will be found.

"Then, as I mentioned, they've found no trace of the SS-men. No soldiers from the *Leibstandarte SS Adolf Hitler* stationed in Germany, Austria or Italy are missing. Furthermore, the guards in the Brenner Pass state categorically that no truckload of SS-men drove through the pass that night. So, my conclusion is that that night the SS-men went back to their base, probably in Austria, and someone else drove the truck to the area of Udine in northern Italy.

"Now I return to Eberhard Schweinfuss. His grandfather, a shrewd man, realized quickly that his grandson was holding something back. It turned out that the SS-Sergeant had sworn Eberhard to secrecy, then told him that the SS-men had been involved in testing a superweapon, and that they had diverted all the electricity that the hydroelectric power station was capable of generating to the superweapon test. I fully appreciate that, by its very nature, a superweapon is top secret. Nevertheless, we contacted every possible agency and asked if they knew anything about testing a superweapon in the Spinnental area. All replies were negative. My conclusion is that the story the SS-Sergeant told the boy was nonsense. However, we've not yet been able to determine what the SS-men were doing in the area if they weren't involved in testing a superweapon.

"There are a number of open issues: Why was the dam destroyed? How did the SS-men get to the dam? And where are the SS-men? I assure you, SS-General, that my division is working night and day to answer these questions." And Colonel Kupfer shut the thick folder in front of him and sat back with a self-satisfied look on his face.

Lieutenant Colonel Emil von Krassheim waited for a few seconds. Then he spoke in a soft but clear voice.

"Colonel, let's return to the SS-men that the boy, Eberhard Schweinfuss, and the shopkeeper who supplied them with the *Tracht* observed. Are you sure that they were indeed members of the *Leibstandarte SS Adolf Hitler?*"

"Both the boy and the shopkeeper unhesitatingly identified the uniforms. They did so independently. As far as I'm concerned, there is no doubt whatsoever that the nine men were members of the *Leibstandarte SS Adolf Hitler.*"

"I understand. And if I were to put on the uniform of the *Leibstandarte SS Adolf Hitler,* would that make me a member of that august body of men?" von Krassheim asked.

Kupfer was utterly flabbergasted. He tried to find a reply. "So who were the SS-men?"

"I think they were enemy agents sent to blow up the dam."

"But where did they get the uniforms?"

"Colonel, total German casualties at Kursk amounted to about 250,000 men, including members of the *Leibstandarte SS Adolf Hitler.* I have no doubt that the Allies have acquired numerous sets of different uniforms of our forces, and have no hesitation about using them to deceive us."

"And where are the enemy agents now?" Kupfer demanded to know.

"Colonel, my initial hypothesis was that they crossed from Austria into Italy wearing their newly acquired *Tracht.* But they were riding in the army truck, so then I realized that they had to be in uniform. My guess is that, as soon as they could, they changed straight back into their SS-uniforms."

"But there is no record of nine SS-men going through the Brenner Pass that night."

"There are other ways to get from Spinnental to Udine. Did you check with the border guards on the other routes?"

There was no response.

"My guess is that the enemy agents were parachuted into the Spinnental area, and blew up the dam."

"How did they do that?" Kupfer snarled.

"You said that the explosives went off at the base of the penstocks. All they had to do was drop the explosives down the penstocks, and that was that."

"But the openings of the penstock are under water."

"The dam wall was only about 40 meters high. A team of frogmen could easily swim down to the penstock openings."

"And where are the two teams of *Volkssturm* now?" Kupfer asked.

"One team was killed in the explosion. My guess is that what's left of their bodies is well downstream by now, perhaps even in the ocean, together with the bodies of the two technicians. And the enemy agents probably ambushed the other team so that they could steal their truck. The saboteurs could have weighted the bodies and dumped them in the lake. No, that's not right, the lake no longer exists. But they could have dumped the bodies anywhere in the vicinity of the dam. Has the area been searched?"

Again there was silence.

"Next, they stole the truck and drove it to Spinnentaldorf, where they filled it with gasoline. That indicates that they were going to drive it a considerable distance. When Eberhard Schweinfuss approached the truck, the SS-Sergeant told him a cock-and-bull story to distract him, so that he wouldn't realize that the soldiers weren't SS-men at all.

"Then they drove to the next village and acquired the *Tracht*. I have no idea why they did that. Perhaps it was to confuse us. After all, what enemy agent would parade around in the Austrian national costume at a time like that? They then changed back into their SS-uniforms and crossed into Italy. They left the truck near Udine—"

"Just a minute," Kupfer said. "When did the frogmen dry their uniforms?"

"What on earth do you mean?" SS-General Schellenberg asked.

"Well, Krassheim said the enemy agents were frogmen who dropped explosives into the penstock openings. But we know that when they got to Spinnentaldorf in the truck they were wearing SS-uniforms. So, when did they dry their uniforms?"

Schellenberg tried hard not to roll his eyes, but his usual steely self-control failed him on this occasion.

"Kupfer, the men landed by parachute wearing frogman suits. They brought with them their SS-uniforms. They must have paddled down the lake in inflatable boats. They put all their supplies, including their uniforms, in the boats. When they reached the dam wall, they jumped into the water. After they dropped the explosives into the openings of the penstocks they swam up to their boats, climbed in, took off their frogman suits and put on their SS-uniforms."

"So where are the frogman suits, then?"

"The same place as the boats and the *Volkssturm* guards—when the dam burst, the water stored in the lake swept over the ruins of the dam wall, taking with it everything in the vicinity, including the guards, the technicians, the boats and the frogman suits."

Schellenberg paused for a second to make sure that Kupfer had understood the explanation, and then he went on.

"Lieutenant Colonel, you were saying that the enemy agents left their truck at Udine. Please continue."

"Thank you, SS-General. Yes, they left their truck at Udine and met up with the local partisans who assisted them to get to the coast, where a boat took them to southern Italy."

"But why should the partisans help them?" Kupfer asked.

"The enemy agents brought with them the American products and the forged correspondence and ledgers that were used to convict and execute the Italian civilians who were leading the fight against the partisans. My guess (and it's only a guess) is that the agents were Americans. After all, they brought American products."

Kupfer could not tolerate being humiliated for one instant longer. "Krassheim, are you trying to tell me that Italian partisans helped men wearing SS-uniforms? The moment they saw the Americans they'd have killed them."

Schellenberg answered him smoothly. "Kupfer, they weren't wearing SS-uniforms when they met the partisans—they'd changed into their *Tracht*."

Once again there was silence. Then Schellenberg spoke again.

"What am I to tell the *Führer* about all this?"

A precise, educated voice spoke softly from the end of the table. It was SS-Captain Claus Klopper, Schellenberg's adjutant.

"With respect, SS-General, before we can answer that question, there's another issue that I suggest we need to discuss first: What was the enemy's objective in demolishing the Spinnental Dam?"

"Go ahead, Klopper," Schellenberg said.

"The Spinnental hydroelectric power station generated a minimal amount of power, certainly less than 100 Megawatts. The commandos killed about 25 elderly Volkssturm soldiers, plus two technicians. In short, the results of the raid won't change the outcome of the war in any way. But in order to achieve this meager result, a major operation was put together.

"If our conclusions are correct, and I think they are, the American saboteurs flew in by air and left by sea, so the United States Air Force was involved, as well as the United States Navy if a submarine picked them up. Forgers played a role in the operation, men who were sufficiently skilled to create materials, written in Italian, that were sophisticated enough to fool the court. In order to produce those papers, the planners must have been in close contact with the partisans in northern Italy. Several messages must have gone back and forth, as well as samples of del Monte's handwriting, but we detected none of this activity.

"The attackers spoke fluent German. They wore SS-uniforms and carried the weapons that SS-personnel use, such as MP 43 assault rifles. In my opinion, the wide range of extraordinary skills they exhibited almost certainly means that they were Special Forces soldiers of some kind.

"The question is: Why? Why would the Allies pour time, money, effort and men into this operation? If they wanted to blow up a dam, why not choose one with a large, critically important power station? Or a spectacularly large dam? Or a dam situated near a major population center? Why carry out their dramatic feats of valor on an insignificant dam situated in the middle of nowhere? In short, what's so special about the Spinnental Dam?"

"And what's the answer?" Schellenberg asked.

"The sole distinguishing feature I can find is that Spinnental is the only Austrian hydroelectric dam on the southern side of the Alps," Klopper answered, and leaned back in his seat.

Von Krassheim spoke up. "And another way of putting that is: It's the dam closest to the American air bases in Italy."

"Krassheim, what are you saying?" Schellenberg asked.

"SS-General, I've just realized that I've been wrong, completely wrong. For months we've been receiving reports from PICKFORD crammed with information from his Dickens subagents. The reports have included copious details of an Allied invasion plan to attack us in force in three different locations simultaneously, and for months I've doubted the veracity of those reports. An attack on Pas-de-Calais makes perfect sense—it's the shortest distance across the English Channel, a notoriously stormy and dangerous crossing. An attack on Norway makes good sense, given the huge Allied build-up in Scotland. Furthermore, a simultaneous Allied invasion of Norway would prevent our sending reinforcements to France. In passing, the reports we've been receiving from a wide variety of sources other than PICKFORD indicate, to me at least, that a major build-up of men, weapons and supplies is indeed taking place for invasions in both locations."

Lieutenant Colonel von Krassheim waited for a few moments and gathered his thoughts.

"The problem for me has been the concept of an invasion of Austria. We first learned about the attack in January 1944, when most of the Italian mainland was in our hands. That would mean that before they could attack Austria, the Allies would have to successfully carry out a full-scale invasion of northern Italy, hundreds of miles behind our lines.

That made no sense to me militarily, and I repeatedly insisted that we were being fed disinformation.

"It's now nearly the end of April 1944. There've been at least four major Allied offensives in Italy since then, but Rome is still in our hands, as well as the whole of Italy to the north of Rome. So I considered it impossible for northern Italy to be in Allied hands in time for the invasion of Austria that PICKFORD has described to us in some detail. Nevertheless, we've continued to receive reports from the Dickens subagents stating that the Allies are planning three simultaneous invasions, one of them in Austria.

"What I've learned from the attack on Spinnental is that the Allies are planning an *airborne* invasion of Austria, effectively bypassing northern Italy, which we continue to control."

As von Krassheim concluded his remarks, heads started to nod all round the table.

"Everything makes sense now," Klopper said. "The objective of the raid wasn't specifically to destroy the Spinnental Dam, but rather to evaluate the feasibility of an airborne assault in the Alps. Hannibal used elephants, the Allies want to use planes."

"There's something else that we've learned," added Kupfer, who seemed to have recovered from the assault on his intelligence. "We now know beyond all doubt that we can unconditionally rely on information that the Dickens subagents have gathered and PICKFORD has radioed to us. Krassheim, your continual nitpicking of information in the PICKFORD reports must stop, right now. We have a spy network in place in Britain that's going to win the war for us.

Reichssicherheitshauptamt Headquarters, Berlin
Wednesday, April 26th, 1944

"Come in, Krassheim, and take a seat," Schellenberg said. "I've just flown back from a meeting with the *Führer* at the *Wolfsschanze*. First I answered all his questions regarding the Spinnental raid."

"Yes, SS-General."

"Next, Colonel General Jodl, deputy head of the Supreme Command of the Armed Forces, expressed the view that no invasion of Austria is possible, airborne or otherwise. His superior, Field Marshal Keitel, then pointed out that almost all the intelligence we've received via PICKFORD since 1937 has proven to be correct in almost all respects. Yes, there've been a few discrepancies, but that was to be expected. Also, two of the Dickens subagents proved to be disappointments, and after several of their reports were viewed as unsatisfactory, we ordered PICKFORD to terminate their links with the *Abwehr*. But there haven't been any negative issues of significance.

"Keitel then pointed out that the intelligence regarding the invasion of Austria had come via a number of different Dickens subagents, each of whom had slowly acquired new informants and contacts over time. Furthermore, the overall information we've received regarding the invasion of Austria has been reasonably consistent over the past three and half months. In fact, bearing in mind that all plans continually change, the Field Marshal pointed out that it would've been suspicious if successive reports hadn't reflected modifications of the plan and improvements of various kinds. Keitel then suggested that I ask PICKFORD to instruct his subagents to concentrate on the Austrian invasion, even if it meant skimping on intelligence on the other two sites. Hitler refused to sanction this. He stated that he needed the maximum possible information on all three invasion sites so that he could adequately defend against the relevant threats.

"*Herr* Hitler then issued an order to move a significant number of anti-aircraft weapons to Austria to repel the coming airborne invasion; our engineers would need to construct concrete gun emplacements for them at sites where airborne landings are possible. His adjutant wrote down the order.

"Jodl then asked where the additional air defense weapons were coming from. The *Führer* said that Flak 37 cannons, our top-of-the-line 88 mm anti-aircraft guns, would be moved to Austria from German cities other than Berlin. Both generals seemed unhappy with this response, though neither man said anything. I gathered that we just don't have enough Flak guns, especially Flak 37s, to adequately defend both the home front and the mountains of Austria. It soon became clear that the *Führer* was prepared to defend his homeland, Austria, at all costs, even if it meant that Allied bombing would reduce several German cities to piles of rubble as a result.

"At that point, Colonel General Jodl spoke again. Taking great care to avoid posing the question to *Herr* Hitler, he turned toward me and in a low voice asked, 'How are the paratroopers who are about to jump into Austria going to link up with the rest of the Allies?'

"There was absolute silence. At that instant it became crystal clear to every single person seated around the large table that the Allies are about to commit a blunder of momentous proportions, one so major that it will almost certainly result in their losing the war. No matter where in Austria they choose to land or what damage they cause, superior numbers of our forces will sooner or later surround their airborne troops and wipe them out.

"I said nothing, of course, and waited for Hitler to respond to Jodl. 'Under no circumstances,' the *Führer* thundered, while small white flecks of saliva accumulated in the corners of his mouth, 'under no circumstances whatsoever will we do anything at all to discourage the invasion of Austria. In particular, we will not move a single Flak cannon, just in case the Allies learn of it and cancel the invasion of Austria. We will move nothing, I repeat, nothing to Austria from northern France or from Germany or from Norway or from anywhere else in the Third Reich—not a soldier, not a gun, not a tank, not a plane. The forces we already have in Austria will easily be able to eradicate every single Allied paratrooper who dares to land in Austria.'

"The meeting came to a close straight after that, and I flew back here.

"There's one final item I wanted to mention. For some reason, the *Führer* and his large staff kept referring to the forthcoming airborne invasion of Austria as Operation KANGAROO. Have you any idea why?"

CHAPTER FIVE
The Princess and the Bomb
1945

Los Alamos, New Mexico
Thursday, June 28th, 1945

The sergeant ushered Dr. Ulrich zu Westerheimer into General Comptine's office in Los Alamos. They greeted one another the way old friends do even if they have not seen one another for years. Comptine indicated that they should sit on the two visitor's chairs on the far side of his desk.

"Silas, where have you been for the last two years," Ulrich asked, "or can't you tell me?"

"Well, soon after we all returned from Siberia I was sent to London to work on Operation FORTITUDE, the deception plan for the invasion of Normandy. And after the German surrender in May, I was sent back here to Los Alamos."

"You were over in Europe, so can you tell me: Has there been any news about my brother?" Ulrich asked.

"Nothing yet. We believe that, after Carl Friedrich met with Hitler in the *Wolfsschanze,* he returned to his work for von Ardenne. Von Ardenne's laboratory was in Berlin-Lichterfelde. As you obviously know, Berlin is in ruins. After the Battle of Berlin, the Soviet conquerors indulged in mass rape, pillage, arson and murder. If someone in the Red Army spotted your brother wearing a German officer's uniform, I regret to say that he was in all probability killed. But if he was in civilian clothes, the Russkies may well have spared him. One possibility is that they took him to the Soviet Union to work for them. I've sent a message to our mutual friend General Dmitri Gribowski to ask him if he knows anything. I'll certainly let you know the moment he gets back to me with any information.

"I understand your concern, but that's not why I asked you to come here today. I need your help in a vital project, and possibly in another equally vital project. I'm not exaggerating in any way when I say that, if we succeed, it'll save hundreds of thousands of lives, maybe millions."

Comptine could tell from the look in Ulrich zu Westerheimer's eyes that he was still thinking about his brother, Carl Friedrich. The general needed to get Ulrich's undivided attention.

"What was your reaction to TRINITY?" he asked. "Were you there at Alamogordo when we detonated the first atomic bomb?"

"Yes, I was there. I assume that you were watching with the VIPs from the South Bunker, six miles from the TRINITY site. I was with the scientists

292

in the base camp, 10 miles away. And my reaction was the same as that of many of my colleagues. First, we were speechless with awe when we saw the fireball, then we rejoiced that our years of work had succeeded. But our final emotion was just sadness."

"You mean sadness at the consequences of unleashing the power of the atom?"

"Precisely. We built the bomb to win the war against the Nazis; the Nazis have been defeated so we're presumably going to use it now to end the war against the Japanese. The key issue is: What happens after that?"

Comptine decided that it would be safer to just ignore the question. "Ulrich, I need your help to bring the war against Japan to a swift end. We have a problem. As you know, the Japanese are on the brink of defeat. We've recaptured almost every Pacific island. The only territory Japan still controls on the Asian mainland is Manchukuo, their puppet state in Manchuria. The Imperial Japanese Navy has effectively ceased to exist.

"The economy of Japan is in ruins. Our submarines and the mines that we've laid around Japan have destroyed their merchant fleet, so the Japanese are fast running out of oil, coal, iron, steel, rubber—in fact, just about everything they need to continue the war. It's reached the point where they're using fragments of our bombs to make shovels. And, no, that last statement isn't United States propaganda; it's a direct quote from the Japanese Emperor relayed to an envoy of a neutral nation.

"Our bombers roam the skies of Japan essentially unhindered, raining down destruction from above. The Japanese government is well aware that the Allied invasion of the Japanese Home Islands is imminent and that they can do nothing to prevent it ending in the ignominious defeat of the Japanese people. And yet they refuse to surrender."

"Why?"

"One simplistic answer is that the Japanese are a proud people, and surrender would mean 'loss of face.' Another is that six months ago, Emperor Hirohito sent out an imperial order encouraging Japanese civilians to commit suicide rather than be taken prisoner. But I think that the real answer is *kokutai*."

"What's *kokutai*?" Dr. zu Westerheimer asked.

General Comptine noticed that Ulrich finally seemed interested. He decided that the way to keep zu Westerheimer's attention was to concentrate on Japanese culture, rather than military issues that might cause him to recall their previous collaboration and, therefore, to think about his brother again.

"A reasonable translation of *kokutai* might be 'national identity.' It incorporates the official state teaching on every aspect of Japanese culture and civilization. Indoctrination in *kokutai* began in 1868 and has intensified over the years. In particular, the people of Japan have been taught to put nation before self. In short, as a consequence of nearly 80 years of *kokutai*, the 100 million people of Japan believe unquestioningly that it is an honor for them to die for Japan and their Emperor.

"And now let me tell you the irony of the situation. Japan has been making peace overtures via neutral nations like Sweden, Switzerland and the Vatican City. And the person behind all this is the Emperor himself. Can you believe it? Out of respect to their Emperor, the Japanese people are expected to die rather than surrender, but it's the Emperor who realizes that the war is lost and is trying to do something about it."

General Comptine saw that Ulrich was still listening to what he was saying about Japan, so he continued. "The problem is that the Japanese leadership have painted themselves into a corner. The members of the Supreme Council for the Direction of the War, the 'Big Six,' dare not say anything publicly, because overzealous army officers immediately assassinate anyone who even mentions the word 'surrender.' And if the militarists were to hear about settlement overtures, there'll be a military coup.

"And right now the situation is getting even worse. The leaders of the United States, the United Kingdom and the Soviet Union are meeting in Potsdam, just outside Berlin. They're calling for unconditional surrender of Japan followed by occupation, disarmament, punishment of war criminals and the removal of the Emperor. Obviously, all of this is unacceptable to almost one hundred percent of the people of Japan, who've been ceaselessly indoctrinated in *kokutai*.

"As a human being, I'm concerned that millions of innocent Japanese civilians are going to be slaughtered in vain as they give up their lives for their Emperor. And as an American and an American general, I'm extremely concerned that at least half a million of our troops are going to be killed and millions injured in the coming unnecessary invasion."

"Silas, why are you asking me to help you? Two years ago you brought me into one of your cloak-and-dagger schemes because of my brother. Obviously, Carl Friedrich has nothing to do with the situation in Japan. So, why me?"

"The problem is security. The atomic bomb is top secret. If we can persuade Japan to surrender before the first bomb is dropped then it can stay top secret. So I cannot involve anyone who doesn't know all about the bomb."

"But Silas, what do you want me to do? As you've explained, the Allies want nothing less than unconditional surrender; the Japanese top leadership is looking for some sort of negotiated peace treaty; and the militarists in Japan are calling for nothing short of victory or death to every Japanese man, woman and child. I'm afraid that there's nothing that I or anyone else can do. I simply cannot think of any way we can avoid detonating the atomic bomb somewhere in Japan."

"I understand your position, Ulrich, but I'm not prepared to give up. I think we need to meet on a regular basis until the matter is resolved, one way or the other. Meanwhile, there's a separate but related issue."

General Comptine shifted in his chair, and then continued. "Ulrich, let's assume that you're right, and that we're forced to drop an atomic bomb on Japan. And let's further assume that nothing changes, even though a hundred thousand people are killed. So we drop a second atomic bomb on Japan. Another hundred thousand are killed. What then?"

"I'm not quite sure where this is going. Have I missed a key point?"

"Well, you know that there are two types of atomic bombs. You can build a bomb from plutonium, or using highly enriched uranium. We successfully exploded a plutonium bomb nearly two weeks ago at Alamogordo. Unless we can persuade the Japanese to surrender, we're going to drop a uranium bomb on Japan. If they don't give up, we're going to drop a plutonium bomb a few days later. And after that—"

"Yes?"

"And after that, nothing."

"*What?*"

"Well, all we've got left is two bombs."

"But that's not possible," Dr. zu Westerheimer said. "Our team did the calculations. We're enriching uranium at a huge plant, the Clinton Engineering Works at Oak Ridge, Tennessee. At Hanford, Washington, we've built nuclear reactors to transmute uranium into plutonium. We continuously measure the output of every part of both plants so we know exactly how much enriched uranium and how much plutonium we're turning out. What I'm saying, Silas, is that we know how much nuclear fuel of each kind we're producing, and I'm sure that there should be at least nine remaining bombs, including the two you talked about."

"Yes and no. The figures that you mentioned certainly show that we're capable of producing three bombs a month. So, over the next three months, if all goes according to plan, we'll have nine bombs, as you said. But after we've dropped the two that we have, there's going to be a delay before we can get another bomb ready, and then further delays in the coming months."

"I understand the situation now. So, Silas, what do you want me to do?"

"Ideally, after dropping the second bomb, we'd want to threaten the Japanese government with a third bomb, this one over Tokyo. We'll drop leaflets telling the local inhabitants what's going to happen, in the hope that there'll be a mass exodus out of the city that would put pressure on the government. But the Japanese people are amazingly disciplined, so when they're ordered to stay put they'll probably obey."

"So what you're saying is that they'll probably ignore the threat and, since we won't yet have another bomb to drop, we're going to look extremely foolish."

"Exactly. In short, I have two tasks for you. The first is to convince the Japanese people to surrender because we have a weapon of incredible destructive power. And if that fails, you must persuade the Japanese people into surrendering after we've used both our weapons of incredible destructive power, even though it's going to be a while before we get another one. Anyhow, please come and see me as soon as you get some ideas for either task."

"No."

"What do you mean, no?"

"No."

"And why not?"

"Because there's nothing whatsoever that can be done about the first problem, and I've got the answer to the second problem right now."

Comptine stared at zu Westerheimer. "Are you telling me that you've solved the second problem just like that?"

"Yes."

"You don't have to go away and think about it?"

"No. I can tell you how to do it right now," zu Westerheimer said.

"So tell me!"

"We drop leaflets on Japan right away. We tell them that we have a superweapon of incredible destructive power. And if they don't surrender right away, we're going to use it."

"And what will that achieve?" Comptine asked, trying extremely hard to hide any hint of skepticism in his voice.

"On the surface, nothing. After all, the late Adolf Hitler boasted ad nauseam to the German people about his innumerable superweapons, his *Wunderwaffen*. Occasionally the *Wuwa* actually existed—I'm thinking about the V1 and V2 rockets. But they didn't significantly change the course of the war. Also, the Japanese people are mindless slaves of the regime, mechanical robots obeying the orders of their masters. As I just told you, I'm convinced that nothing can be done to solve your first problem, that is, persuading the Japanese to surrender before we drop the bomb. So it really doesn't matter what you put in the leaflet, just as long as it mentions that we have a superweapon."

"But why would we do that?"

"Because I need a copy of that leaflet to take with me to Stockholm, Geneva or Rome."

"Now you've lost me." General Comptine shook his head.

"You've just told me that the Emperor of Japan has been making peace overtures through three neutral nations: Sweden, Switzerland and the Vatican City. I need to meet with the Japanese envoy in one of those places, taking with me a copy of the leaflet. I also need to take with me a report that states how many bombs we're producing each month, but scaled up. For example, I can multiply all the figures by a factor of 10. I can modify the report in such a way that the Japanese will be unable to detect the changes. After all, they don't have any nuclear physicists who've been working on building atomic bombs, so there's no one in Japan who could point out any inconsistencies. Also, I'll move all dates back by a month, so my report will reflect the fact that we have at least 30 bombs, with 30 more being built each month."

"That sounds good, but what if someone in Japan consults with a German nuclear physicist? We think we've rounded them all up, but with the chaos in Germany, less than two months after the Nazis surrendered, anything is possible. In fact, someone in Japan may even be in contact with your brother. Would Carl Friedrich be able to detect that your figures are just too large?"

"Possibly. He has no idea of the actual size of the plants at Oak Ridge and Hanford, but he's clever enough to realize that no nation, not even the United States, has enough electricity to run plants that would have the output claimed in my report and still be able to light people's houses. And he might work out that we don't have the raw materials to construct plants that big and still turn out all the planes and ships and bombs and jeeps we've built that enabled us to win the war in Europe. In fact, I'm pretty sure he would. So, just in case someone in Japan catches on, or if they show it to someone abroad like my brother, maybe my report should just double our actual output. Also, all dates should be moved back two months. That will mean that someone reading the falsified report will immediately deduce that we have about 12 bombs, and that we're turning out another six every month."

"Would you say that, other than the people working on the Manhattan Project, no one would be able to flag the fact that you've doubled the actual figures?"

"In fact, I'd be prepared to go further than that. I'd say that no more than ten people in the whole world could detect the change, and all of them are working here in Los Alamos."

"You're sure about that?"

"Positive. To detect the change, you'd need to be a nuclear physicist with intimate knowledge of the inner workings of both the Hanford and the Oak Ridge plants."

"What if there's a spy who's smuggled details of one or both plants to Japan? Or, for that matter, to Germany?"

"Well, suppose that someone somewhere has somehow managed to obtain the plans of, say, the Oak Ridge plant. They're enriching uranium there using three different techniques: gaseous, electromagnetic and thermal. No one outside Los Alamos could possibly understand all three techniques in sufficient depth to be able to determine that I've doubled the numbers. After all, the only place in the whole world where scientists and engineers are enriching uranium is Oak Ridge, and the techniques they're using there were developed here at Los Alamos. So, someone examining the plans of the Clinton Engineering Works couldn't possibly even begin to estimate how much enriched uranium we're producing there each week."

"But what if they've seen the actual original report?"

Zu Westerheimer's mouth dropped open. "Are you saying that there's a spy here in Los Alamos?"

"I'm simply asking: What if there's a spy here?"

"Well, if someone has seen the original document, then they can see that I've doubled the numbers and backdated everything by two months. But unless someone has actually seen the original, they'll never realize that my version of the report has been falsified."

"You're sure about that?"

"Positive."

"Fine. So let's go back to where we were. You were saying that you're going to give a copy of the leaflet we're going to drop over Japan to their envoy."

"Yes."

"And then you want to give him your report."

"After we've dropped the first bomb, the Japanese envoy will get a copy of my report."

"But why should he believe any document you give him?"

"Who said anything about my *giving* him any document? He's going to beg me to hand the report to him. And here's how it's going to work."

Los Alamos, New Mexico
Monday, July 30th, 1945

"Ulrich," Comptine said, "here's your passport. It's in every way a genuine passport that the United States Department of State has issued. It has your photograph in it. It correctly states your date of birth and that you were born in Germany. But one aspect of the passport is false."

"Yes?"

"Look here. It shows your name as Gottfried von Engelhardt. You'll be using that name for the duration of the mission; if anything gets out, we certainly don't want Dr. Ulrich zu Westerheimer to be branded as a traitor to the United States who passed secret papers to the enemy, let alone consorted with the Japanese. Yes, I know, nothing is going to go wrong, but it certainly does no harm to take precautions. Also, it maintains reciprocity."

"Reciprocity?"

"Call it symmetry, if you prefer. The fact is that the Japanese envoy is also masquerading under a false name."

"Why?"

"Just think about it. Suppose you want to fly an envoy from Japan to Sweden. The problem, of course, is that it's impossible to fly out of Japan without someone in the Japanese government knowing about it. The militarists have infiltrated everywhere, so there's a grave risk that anyone to be sent out of Japan will be assassinated before he can board the plane, merely on suspicion that he's on a peace mission."

"And what was the solution?"

"Well, the Emperor announced that his sister, Princess Yura, was being flown to Zurich for treatment for tuberculosis. The only possible air route from Tokyo is via the Soviet Union to Sweden, and from there to Switzerland. After all, Western Europe is enemy territory, but the Soviet Union hasn't yet declared war on Japan, for some reason.

So, it's not too hard for someone to get permission from the Russkies to fly from Tokyo to Leningrad, and from there it's an easy hop to Stockholm. And there's a plane every day from Stockholm to Zurich.

"So, Princess Yura, looking extremely frail, was put on a plane, accompanied by a doctor. They arrived at Stockholm Airport. A car took them to a private clinic in Stockholm where she could rest for two days before resuming her trip. Unfortunately, she collapsed, perhaps due to the strain of the journey, and she has to stay in the Swedish clinic until she's strong enough to fly to Switzerland. But that's never going to happen."

"Is she that ill?"

"Not only is she perfectly well, she's also not Princess Yura."

"What?"

"The Emperor sent a diplomat disguised as a woman to Stockholm. The 'doctor' is a bodyguard. The diplomat is traveling under the name of Minoru Nishimura. The people at the clinic smuggled him out of a side door of the clinic and into a waiting taxi that took him to a small but luxurious hotel in the countryside just outside Stockholm. It's actually a completely refurbished 15th century castle. They've installed an elevator but they left the fortifications."

"But surely there's little or no resemblance between Princess Yura and Minoru Nishimura disguised as a woman?"

"That's true, of course, but members of the Royal Family are rarely photographed. In fact, it's strictly forbidden for ordinary people to photograph the Emperor. Also, they swathed 'Princess Yura' in numerous blankets and quilts because she's so desperately ill. Up to now they've gotten away with it."

Dr. zu Westerheimer smiled at the deception.

"Here's your itinerary," General Comptine continued. "Again, it's in the name of Gottfried von Engelhardt, as are your State Department credentials and everything else you're carrying. As I'm sure you know, there are almost no civilian flights yet, so you'll have to fly on military planes from here to La Guardia Field in New York, and from there to RAF Northolt, just outside London. A car will take you from RAF Northolt to Croydon Airport. The car will pick you up at the foot of the stairs as you get off the plane, drive you to Croydon Airport, and drop you off there at the foot of the stairs for boarding the plane from Croydon to Gothenburg."

"Gothenburg? Why Gothenburg? I thought you said I was going to Stockholm."

"You are, but not directly. When you land at Gothenburg, another car will take you straight to the Gothenburg Central Station. The driver will have your train ticket, he'll give it to you when you arrive at the station, and you'll board the next train to Stockholm. Consequently, when you step off the train at Stockholm Central Station, it's unlikely that anyone will realize that the United States government flew you there. You should be indistinguishable from the thousands of other train travelers at the station. Like all neutral capitals, Stockholm is brimming with spies from all countries, and the less attention we draw to you the greater the chance that the Japanese envoy won't be connected to the United States government, which would probably prove fatal, not only to him but also to any chance of our saving lives.

"When you get to Stockholm, tell the cab driver to take you to the Niedermeyer Hotel. A suite has been reserved for you there. Check in, go to your room and wait. You will receive a phone call from the envoy."

"And how will he know when I've arrived?" Ulrich enquired.

"The front desk clerk will tell the manager who will tell Minoru Nishimura, the Japanese envoy."

"But I thought Sweden was neutral?"

"During the war, officially, yes. In practice, the government made a few concessions to both sides. When Germany invaded the Soviet Union in 1941, the Swedes allowed the Germans to use the Swedish railways to transport men and weapons from Norway to Finland. They sold iron ore to Germany all through the war. In both cases, they had no choice, of course; if they hadn't agreed, Germany would have invaded and conquered Sweden. But the Swedes also voluntarily shared military intelligence with the Allies, and they provided refuge for nearly all of Denmark's Jews and those Norwegian Jews who managed to flee over the Scandes Mountains into Sweden.

"But the war in Europe is over now," Silas continued. "Sweden is doing everything it can to help bring the war with Japan to a close, including allowing us to use the Niedermeyer Hotel as a base for secret peace talks. This means that soon after you check in you should receive a phone call from Minoru Nishimura or someone acting for him."

"Does Minoru Nishimura have to stay inside the hotel all the time?"

"Yes, for his own safety. If he were to venture out, someone might recognize him. As I mentioned, the militarists have no hesitation in assassinating anyone whom they even suspect is on a peace mission. As a further protection, they've emptied the hotel; you and Nishimura will be the only guests staying there."

"But surely there's a risk that someone working at the hotel, a chambermaid, say, might tell her husband about the Japanese visitor staying in the otherwise deserted hotel? Shouldn't you arrange for soldiers to patrol the area day and night to protect Nishimura?"

"Your chambermaid is still going to tell her husband about the Japanese guest, but now she'll add that Swedish army personnel are guarding the hotel. When that information reaches the ears of the militarists in the embassy, they'll undoubtedly send a suicide squad to assassinate Nishimura. Surrounding Nishimura with guards will only draw undue attention to him. You're right. His life is in danger. But there's not much anyone can do against fanatical killers who are willing to throw their lives away for a cause they believe in."

"Does he at least have a good cover story?"

"Yes, indeed. The Emperor's people have informed the Swedish government that Nishimura is in Stockholm to buy iron ore for Japan. After all, as I just told you, Sweden sold iron ore to Germany during the European War. Now Germany is in ruins and urgently needs food, not iron. The Allies have bombed her factories out of existence, particularly those that use iron. Sweden now has huge stocks of iron ore that Germany doesn't want, while Japan desperately needs all the raw materials it can get, especially iron, so the cover story is solid.

"Just how much does the Japanese embassy in Stockholm know about all this?" Ulrich asked.

"There's no way that the arrival in Stockholm of someone with Japanese facial features could be kept secret from the embassy. For that reason, the Japanese Ambassador to Sweden has been informed that 'Minoru Nishimura' is in Stockholm on a delicate trade mission involving iron ore, and that all embassy personnel are to stay away from the Niedermeyer Hotel until the trade deal has been signed. The militarists at the embassy are delighted, of course. They believe that Minoru Nishimura is here to buy the iron ore that Japan so urgently needs to continue fighting. So, far from killing him, they're obeying the order to stay away from the hotel in the hope that Nishimura can pull off the trade deal. And if he were to call on the embassy for any sort of help in closing the deal, they'd rush to his assistance.

"The funny part about all this is that mining experts who've met with Minoru Nishimura have reported that he seems to be really knowledgeable.

He's definitely involved in iron ore, though we haven't yet been able to find out whether he's a government official of some kind or if he's an industrialist who produces iron and steel from ore."

"Isn't there anyone here in the States who can identify him for us?"

"We've interned everyone who could help us. There are about 110,000 people of Japanese ancestry in our 'War Relocation Camps.' More than half of them are United States citizens. I'm convinced that almost all of them, whether citizens or not, are loyal to our country in every respect and would help us in any way they could, despite spending the last three years essentially in prison. But the powers that be here in the United States are concerned that we might show a photograph of Nishimura to one of the handful of people who are our enemies, and that could destroy the whole scheme. They're just not prepared to take the risk. The stakes here are too high; hundreds of thousands of lives are in the balance, perhaps millions. So the bottom line is: We don't know anything about Nishimura, other than that he's the envoy of the Emperor himself, and that he's an expert on iron ore. And that last fact is of no use to us.

"Officials of the Emperor have provided Nishimura with appropriate documentation. As I told you, the militarists have infiltrated all the ministries, so it would have been disastrous if anyone outside the Palace had learned about the mission. All it would have taken was one person innocently questioning the purpose of Nishimura's trip, and that would have been that. There are two vital secrets. The first is Nishimura's real identity, which no one outside Japan seems to know. The second secret, of course, is the fact that Princess Yura was actually Nishimura. You need to keep that second secret intact if Nishimura is to stay alive.

"And expanding on my answer to your earlier question, Nishimura is not permitted to leave the hotel. Instead, officials from the Swedish government and the iron mines come to the Niedermeyer to meet with him. And when he's with those people, he talks about buying iron ore. His cover story is excellent. But when he's not discussing iron ore, he's involved in peace negotiations through intermediaries such as you. No American official has been anywhere near him. In fact, all the Allied embassies have instructed their personnel to keep away from the Niedermeyer Hotel until further notice.

"A word of warning: All the reports we've received indicate that Nishimura is highly intelligent and an excellent negotiator. He listens far more than he talks, and his manner is always diplomatic and polite. Yes, he's the Emperor's representative in Sweden. But he may also be a spy, sent to Sweden to obtain as much information as possible regarding the forthcoming invasion. So be careful at all times. One of the reasons we're sending you to Sweden is that, while you know all about the atomic bomb, you know nothing about Operation DOWNFALL."

"What's that?"

"I rest my case."

"Can't you at least tell me what it is?"
"No, I can't. Good luck and Godspeed!"

Stockholm
Friday, August 3rd, 1945

Every effort had been made to ensure that Dr. Gottfried von Engelhardt would have as easy a trip as possible from Los Alamos to Stockholm, but at 3 p.m. when he finally found himself ensconced in his luxurious suite at the Niedermeyer Hotel, he felt drained. He was not sleepy; he had slept most of the journey, which never seemed to end. But he was enervated, and he hoped that there would be some sort of mix-up that would cause a delay in his being summoned to meet with Minoru Nishimura.

He took a hot bath, put on clean clothes and lay down on the comfortable bed to rest. Hardly had he settled himself when there was a knock. With a groan he dragged himself to his feet and staggered to answer it. He looked through the peephole. Standing outside was a uniformed bellboy. Gottfried opened the door. The bellboy politely proffered a small silver tray in the middle of which lay an envelope. Gottfried took the envelope. The bellboy left at once, making it obvious he expected no tip.

Gottfried closed the door and examined the envelope. He turned it over. It was sealed. He turned it back. The envelope was clearly Niedermeyer Hotel stationery; the name and address of the hotel were embossed on the top left-hand corner. Written in the middle of the envelope were the words "Room 9," Gottfried's room. That was all.

He tore the sealed envelope open with some difficulty; it was made of thick, high-quality paper. Inside was a single sheet of Niedermeyer Hotel stationery; the name and address were again embossed, but now centered across the top of the page. On the paper was written "Room 14" in the same handwriting as before.

Gottfried put on his shoes and his suit jacket, checked his appearance in the full-length mirror and headed for the elevator. The elevator operator took him up one floor; Gottfried was too exhausted to climb even one flight of stairs. Finding Room 14 was easy, because it was opposite the elevator. Gottfried knocked. A smartly dressed Japanese man opened the door. He was shorter than the American envoy, but had much wider shoulders and a bigger chest, so he appeared to be stronger than Gottfried. His thick bowed eyebrows gave him a perpetual expression of surprise.

He invited Gottfried into the suite. When he had firmly closed the door, he asked politely, "Dr. von Engelhardt?" His English was excellent, with only a slight foreign accent.

"Yes. Mr. Nishimura?"

"Yes."

"Please come in and sit down. May I offer you some refreshments? Tea, perhaps?"

"Yes, that would be nice."

Nishimura picked up the telephone and asked for room service. He ordered tea for two, with sandwiches and scones. While they waited for the tea to arrive, he enquired politely whether Gottfried had had a good trip. Nishimura was careful not to ask about the route Gottfried had taken or even whether he had flown in from the United States. Then came a few minutes more of pleasant small talk—it was clear that, as General Comptine had advised him, Minoru Nishimura had finely honed diplomatic skills.

A room-service waiter soon arrived with their order. Minoru was a solicitous host, and soon Gottfried was enjoying his afternoon tea. The small talk continued.

When they had finished their tea, Minoru took the initiative. "I understand that you have come to see me with a proposal of some sort."

"Not exactly a proposal," Gottfried said. "My mission is twofold. I want to inform you about an American superweapon. And I want to give you a document that you can use to save your country from total destruction and your people, particularly your civilians, from being butchered by the millions.

"I'm faced with an extremely difficult task," Gottfried continued. "When I tell you about the superweapon, I'm sure that you won't believe me. In all frankness, if someone told me about it, I wouldn't believe it either. And you may or may not accept that the report I have for you is genuine.

"With your permission, I'll tell you about the superweapon. I'll then propose a way of convincing you that what I'm saying is true. Once you are satisfied regarding my veracity, I'll give you the report."

Throughout this monologue, Minoru Nishimura listened attentively without moving a facial muscle. Even when Gottfried had finished speaking, Minoru sat completely motionless. Finally he spoke.

"Please tell me about this superweapon."

"Yes, certainly. The United States of America has developed a weapon of destruction more than two thousand times more powerful than all the bombs that can be dropped from a fully loaded B-29 Superfortress bomber. This weapon can be delivered at little or no risk to American troops. Each time this weapon is used, we estimate that about 100,000 Japanese will die, and no American will be harmed.

"Here is an actual leaflet that our air force has dropped on Japan using our so-called Monroe Bombs. We load each bomb with about 70,000 leaflets. At a predetermined time after release, the two halves of the bomb separate and the leaflets flutter down to earth. I regret that I cannot read your language, but I'm told that this particular leaflet warns civilians that they face destruction from a superweapon, and that they need to overthrow their government or face obliteration."

Nishimura put on a pair of round horn-rimmed glasses with a wide frame, scanned the leaflet and then nodded. He removed his spectacles. Again he said nothing.

Gottfried continued. "I realize that most people cannot conceptualize a weapon of this power. I also appreciate that your reaction may well be that this is some sort of deception, that I have come here to trick the Japanese nation into surrendering. I assure you that this is not the case; I have seen the weapon in action. Nevertheless, it would be most surprising if you were to believe anything that I've been telling you today. To convince you, I would like to provide you with evidence that I know what I'm talking about, and that what I'm saying is true.

"I have here a sealed envelope containing information regarding the name of the first city in Japan that this superweapon will annihilate. I'm about to sign my name here across one side of the flap of the envelope. You will be able to detect if the envelope has been opened and resealed."

And Gottfried took out his fountain pen from inside his jacket and signed his name across the left-hand side of the envelope flap.

"I ask you to sign your name, in Japanese characters, across the right-hand side of the flap. You and I will then take the envelope downstairs, and I will put it in the safe keeping of the hotel manager. I will then return to my room, where I will stay until you contact me. You may telephone my room at any hour of the day or night; I'm at your disposal at all times. As soon as I hear from you, we will go to the manager together and retrieve the envelope. We will both examine it to be certain that no one has tampered with it. Then you will open the envelope. The contents should convince you that I'm telling the truth."

"But why should I contact you?" Minoru asked in a calm, quiet, dignified voice.

"When you hear that the superweapon has been used," Gottfried replied, "I have no doubt that you will want to contact me. As I said, I'm at your disposal 24 hours of every day."

Minoru Nishimura continued to keep his face motionless, but it was clear from his eyes that he was thinking hard. Eventually he spoke.

"I agree to this arrangement. I have nothing to lose by signing my name on the back of this envelope. In the best case, your visit will save many millions of Japanese lives."

Gottfried noticed that Minoru had said nothing about the worst case. He handed his pen to Minoru who turned the envelope around and signed his name downward across the other flap. He handed the fountain pen back to Gottfried and, for the first time, smiled.

"Would you please be so kind as to come with me to the hotel manager?" Gottfried asked.

"Of course."

The two men left the suite and took the elevator down to the lobby. Gottfried led the way to the reception desk. "Could we please see Mr. Jönsson?" he asked.

"Certainly. Please step this way," the clerk said, leading the two men into the manager's office.

Magnus Jönsson turned out to be tall and slender, dressed in an exquisitely cut suit. His long blond hair was brushed to the side, but kept falling over his dark brown eyes. Whenever this happened, he would flick it away with a twitch of his neck muscles.

Jönsson invited the two men to sit down. "How can I help you?"

"I would like to place this envelope in your safe custody," Gottfried von Engelhardt said. "I understand that it will be available to me 24 hours a day."

"Of course. If I'm not here, the duty manager will give it to you on production of the receipt that I'm about to give you."

The transaction was soon completed. Gottfried escorted the Japanese envoy to the elevator. When the elevator reached the second floor and the operator had opened the doors, Gottfried politely said goodbye to his companion and went straight to his room.

Shidoma, Japan
Monday, August 6th, 1945

At 6:29 a.m., Corporal Yuuta Murakami, the operator on duty at the early warning radar station in Shidoma, detected an incoming enemy plane heading for the southern region of Honshu, the largest Home Island. Following orders as always, he alerted the officer on duty, Captain Harada.

The captain checked the radar screen, noting that there appeared to be just the one plane that Murakami had observed.

"It's probably only a reconnaissance flight," he told Murakami. "Log it and report it to all relevant stations."

Three quarters of an hour later, at 7:14 a.m., Corporal Murakami detected a small flight of incoming planes. Again he alerted Captain Harada. On the one hand, Japan was desperately short of both aircraft and fuel, so a decision had been taken at the highest levels not to intercept small formations. On the other hand, even a handful of American B-29 bombers could cause huge damage, especially because many of the materials used to construct Japanese houses were inflammable. In particular, the wooden frames, the tatami floor mats made of rice straw, and the translucent paper used for doors, windows and room dividers were susceptible to firebombs dropped in an air raid. Accordingly, the order was given to alert the people living in the region of the apparent intended flight path that enemy planes were approaching.

At 7:31 a.m., Sergeant Saburo Ishii, a radar operator at Hiroshima, picked up a lone B-29 Superfortress heading for the city. He sent out the standard radio broadcast to warn the citizens of Hiroshima to go to their air-raid shelters.

Meanwhile, the B-29 bomber, nicknamed *Straight Flush,* continued to cruise steadily toward Hiroshima at an altitude of 32,000 feet. The mission of the pilot, Major Claude Eatherly, was to determine if the weather over the target was clear so that another plane could make a subsequent bombing run. There were no clouds, so the radio operator sent out an encrypted message in Morse code advising the pilot of an incoming B-29, *Enola Gay*, that the skies were clear. Soon *Straight Flush* turned around and headed out to sea in a south-easterly direction, back to the Northern Mariana Islands from where it had started its journey.

It was now nearly 8:00 a.m. in Hiroshima. Some six hours earlier, three other B-29 bombers had taken off from North Field Air Base, Tinian, in the Northern Mariana Islands, and climbed slowly into the still dark Pacific sky. The third plane carried a variety of different instruments to measure the force of the anticipated blast. The second plane carried a number of scientific observers and was loaded with photographic equipment. The lead plane was named *Enola Gay* after the mother of the pilot, Colonel Paul Tibbets. It carried a large bomb in its specially modified bomb bay. The weapon, nicknamed "Little Boy," was an atomic bomb weighing about 9,700 pounds that contained about 140 pounds of enriched uranium.

At 7:58 a.m., Sergeant Ishii saw on his radar screen that no more than three planes were approaching Hiroshima. In view of the fact that the previous plane had headed back out to sea without dropping any bombs, he assumed that this was just another component of some sort of reconnaissance mission, and he sounded the all clear.

At 8:09 a.m., with the plane at a height of 30,700 feet, Colonel Tibbets started his bombing run. He handed over control to his bombardier, Major Thomas Ferebee. The other two B-29 Superfortresses slowed and dropped back.

At 8:15 a.m. Ferebee saw the Aioi Bridge in the cross hairs of his Norden bombsight and released the bomb. Instantly, Tibbets retook control of the aircraft, turned it sharply through 155 degrees to the right and dived away. His escape maneuver lasted 43 seconds, during which time he was able to fly the plane more than 11 miles from the detonation point. Meantime, the bomb dropped to an altitude of 1,890 feet.

Suddenly the sky was filled with a searing white light, many times more intense than the brightest midday sun, like a vast sea of giant flashbulbs all going off simultaneously. Two shock waves struck the plane. The first came directly from the fireball; the second, reflected from the ground, was somewhat weaker.

Some of the crew looked back. A purple mushroom cloud bubbling upward shrouded the city. The cloud rose to a height of 45,000 feet as Tibbets piloted the *Enola Gay* away from Hiroshima as fast as the plane could fly. Six hours later he landed back at Tinian to a hero's welcome.

On the ground at Hiroshima, those closest to the fireball died instantly. An overpowering wave of heat killed almost everyone within half a mile of the explosion. Buildings within a radius of a mile from the detonation point were reduced to rubble. And then came the firestorm. Hiroshima as a city ceased to exist.

Radio and telephone communications had ended suddenly at 8:15 a.m., so it was hours before the Japanese high command knew what had happened. They dispatched an observer, a young officer on the general staff, in a plane to Hiroshima. He was able to report a huge pall of smoke from more than 100 miles away. When he landed in Hiroshima, he described the complete devastation.

At 5 p.m. in Stockholm, nearly 16 hours after the attack, Minoru Nishimura was in his suite. As always when he was alone, he had the radio tuned to the Voice of America. He was completely stunned to hear a prepared statement from President Harry Truman informing the American public that the United States had dropped a new type of bomb onto the city of Hiroshima, an atomic bomb with more power than 15,000 tons of TNT. Truman went on:

> *If they do not now accept our terms, they may expect a rain of ruin from the air, the like of which has never been seen on this earth.*

Without waiting to hear any more, Minoru rushed to the stairs, ran down one flight, and knocked on the door of Dr. Gottfried von Engelhardt's suite. His perennial equanimity, practiced throughout his life, had escaped him. For the first time ever, Minoru Nishimura was in a state of panic that he could not control.

Gottfried came to the door. He took one look at Minoru's face and escorted the Japanese envoy to the manager's office. He showed Magnus Jönsson his receipt and was given the envelope in return. Thanking the manager of the hotel, he took Minoru by the elbow and propelled him back to the elevator and from there to Room 9. He helped Minoru into a chair in the sitting room of the suite.

Standing next to Minoru, Gottfried showed him that the signatures on the flap were untouched.

Minoru nodded, the first time that day that he had reacted to anything that Gottfried had said or done. Gottfried handed him the envelope and pressed a paper knife into his hand.

With shaking hands, Minoru somehow managed to slit the envelope open. He extracted a plain piece of paper. On the paper was typed the following:

Primary target: Hiroshima

Alternative targets: Kokura and Nagasaki

Minoru Nishimura started to gasp. He seemed to be having difficulty breathing. His eyes rolled upward. Gottfried thought that his companion was about to faint, but he somehow managed to regain control. He stared at Gottfried, who rushed over to a side table, grabbed the cut-glass decanter and quickly poured him a glass of whisky. Nishimura downed the drink in almost a single gulp, gasped, shuddered and then spoke for the first time.

"You were telling the truth."

"I was."

"When we first met, you spoke of a document that would save my country from total destruction and my people from senseless annihilation. May I see that report now?"

"Yes, of course. Would you please excuse me for a minute?"

Gottfried went into the bedroom, closed the door and retrieved the report from under the mattress where he had hidden it, just in case Minoru had somehow managed to arrange for the suite to be searched while Gottfried was sleeping. He returned to the sitting room and handed Minoru a large sealed envelope. Then he retrieved the paper knife from the floor where Minoru had let it drop when he read the list of targets. He handed the knife back to the Japanese envoy.

Minoru slit open the envelope with a firm stroke and withdrew the contents. The report was only three pages long. He read the executive summary on the top third of the first page. It stated that the United States currently had 12 atomic bombs, and that the current production rate was six more bombs every month. Minoru then read the remainder of the report. Sitting opposite the Japanese envoy and watching him study the report, Gottfried realized that Minoru was an engineer or a scientist; without training of that kind, the tables of data would have been incomprehensible.

Gottfried leaned back and forced himself to relax, while giving Minoru the opportunity to think about what he had just perused.

"Are you familiar with the contents of the document you have brought me?" Minoru asked.

"I am."

"There's no question that the United States of America has accomplished the greatest scientific and engineering feats the world has ever known. I cannot begin to comprehend the time, money and effort that have gone into this mammoth undertaking. How truly stupid of the Nazis to expel their Jewish scientists!"

And Gottfried suddenly realized who Minoru was.

"I know who you are. You're Professor Katsu Umenosuke. You worked with Werner Heisenberg in Leipzig, where you wrote a paper with Isaac Levy on the elastic scattering of photons. In fact, you're one of the two co-authors of the Umenosuke–Levy formula. After that, I believe you returned to Japan where you've led their research in physics. I've heard you referred to as the father of modern physics in Japan. It is an honor and a privilege for me to finally meet you."

There was a long pause while Minoru tried to decide how to respond. Then he smiled.

"Yes, I am Umenosuke."

"But why were you sent here? You're not a professional diplomat. And whoever ordered you to Sweden to negotiate with the Allies couldn't have known that I would be sent to Stockholm with nuclear information to hand to you."

Katsu Umenosuke just smiled again.

"You mean, you knew you were going to meet a fellow nuclear physicist?"

"It can do no harm now to tell you the full story. About two months ago, it became clear that Japan wouldn't be able to wage war beyond the end of 1945, and that civil unrest would be sure to follow. The situation was becoming desperate. So the Emperor decided to ask the Soviet Union to assist in making peace with the United States, to try to save what was left of the Japanese nation."

"Why the Soviet Union?"

"Other neutral countries were willing to help us, but they're too small and powerless to do much more than just ferry documents back and forth. Discussions with the Soviet Union began, both in Tokyo and in Moscow. As part of the negotiations, we received a message that the Americans wanted the Emperor to send an envoy to Stockholm who had a deep understanding of nuclear physics. No one could understand this request. It made absolutely no sense to anyone. But we complied, as the Americans had known we would. The Emperor's staff chose me, perhaps for obvious reasons. The Soviets facilitated my travel in every way. I think that they assumed that the Japanese nuclear physicist to be sent to Stockholm was about to play a major role in whatever it was that the Americans were planning."

A thought began to course through Gottfried's brain.

"Just when did this American request come through?"

"Oh, we received it in mid June. I arrived here in Stockholm on June 24th, after spending two days learning everything that there is to know about iron ore."

And General Comptine summoned me on June 28th, Gottfried said to himself. There's definitely more to this mission than meets the eye.

Aloud he said, "It looks to me as if the Allies have brought you and me together as part of a scheme to convince the powers that be in Japan that, unless they surrender unconditionally, the Allies are going to destroy Japan with an unending hail of atomic bombs. Do you agree?"

"I do. That's the only conclusion that makes any sense at all."

"What's the next step?"

"I have to contact my government and communicate the contents of this report."

"Of course. Please get back to me if there is anything more I can do."

Afterwards, Gottfried wondered why Katsu had believed the Voice of America broadcast. After all, Hitler had repeatedly made claims for superweapons that did not yet exist, so Truman could have done the same thing. The radio announcement might have been a hoax, designed to trick Japan into surrendering. Until the Japanese government officially announced the destruction of Hiroshima, Katsu had every right to withhold judgment. In fact, it was two days later before Radio Tokyo started to broadcast descriptions of the almost total annihilation of the city of Hiroshima.

Stockholm
Tuesday, August 7th, 1945

Katsu Umenosuke knocked on Gottfried's door. There was no reply. Katsu waited for nearly a minute then knocked again. This time he heard Gottfried hastening to the door.

"Did I keep you waiting? I'm so sorry. Please come in and sit down. Would you like some morning tea?"

"No, thank you. I just came to tell you that I have to fly back to Japan. The Soviets are finalizing the arrangements but, as things now stand, I'm on a flight tomorrow morning from Stockholm to Leningrad, en route to Tokyo."

"I think I understand. Your leaders received your telegram but now they want to see the document for themselves. Can't you just send it by radiofax?"

"There are security issues here. I can't take it to our embassy for obvious reasons, and I can't let the hotel operator here see it, either. And when it arrives in Japan, who knows who'll be standing next to the receiver. No, I have to go back in person with the report."

"That's quite a coincidence. The reason that I kept you waiting at the door was that I was on a phone call. They also want me to leave Stockholm as soon as possible."

Taking care not to mention any of the details of his trip, and in particular that his final destination was Los Alamos, Gottfried continued, "I've also been instructed to take a flight tomorrow morning."

"Is there any reason why we can't share a taxi to the airport?" Katsu asked.

"I understand that you're here to buy iron ore. I'm not connected to iron in any way. Bearing in mind that our two countries are at war, with the greatest respect, I think it would be better if we took separate cabs."

"I understand. In fact, I think it probably would be safer for both of us if we said goodbye now."

"Yes."

"Goodbye, Dr. zu Westerheimer."

Ulrich gasped. "You knew all the time?"

"Certainly."

"How? Have we met before? If we had, I'd remember for sure."

"No, our paths have never crossed. But I suspected that the Americans would send a nuclear physicist, so I brought with me all the photographs from nuclear physics conferences that my Japanese staff had. You were at the Zurich conference in 1936, weren't you?"

"Yes, I was."

"I hope that you won't hold it against me that I didn't let on until now, but I didn't want to do anything that might impede negotiations. Now that I know you as a person, I realize that I'd taken an unnecessary precaution, but once I'd pretended that I didn't know who you were, I couldn't act as if I'd suddenly worked it out. Please forgive me."

"Of course. I understand. We're both over here for one purpose and one purpose only, to bring this war to an end with minimal loss of life. I hope and pray that our journeys have been fruitful. Goodbye Dr. Umenosuke, and good luck."

Stockholm
Wednesday, August 8th, 1945

The Aeroflot Lisunov Li-2, the Soviet licensed version of the Douglas DC-3, took off from Arlanda Airport in Stockholm at 9:05 a.m., precisely on schedule. Almost immediately, the pilot made an announcement in Russian. Minoru Nishimura thought that he heard the word "Moskva." At first he wondered if the pilot had said that the plane would fly to Moscow after Leningrad, but he soon rejected that possibility. So, when the grim-faced overweight air hostess next walked past him, he stopped her.

"Did the pilot say we're flying to Moscow? My ticket says 'Leningrad.'"

"Comrade, if the pilot says that we're flying to Frunze Central Aerodrome, that's where we're going."

"Frunze?"

"You may know it as Khodynka Aerodrome or Moscow Central Airport. It was the only airport in Moscow until the opening of Vnukovo in 1941."

"But why aren't we flying to Leningrad?"

"Comrade, I just told you. The pilot says we're flying to Frunze Central Aerodrome."

And there the matter rested until six hours later when the plane landed. Umenosuke took his briefcase from the overhead rack and followed the other passengers out of the aircraft. As he walked toward the terminal a Red Army officer approached him, with a Russian–English translator in tow.

"Mr. Minoru Nishimura?"

"Yes?"

"I'm General Dmitri Gribowski. You're probably surprised to be landing in Moscow instead of Leningrad."

"Yes, I am."

"You were scheduled to change planes in Leningrad for your flight to Tokyo. I'm afraid that that particular Tupolev ANT-35bis had to be used for another flight. So just after take-off we sent a radio message to the pilot to bring you to Moscow, where we have another ANT-35bis waiting to fly you to Tokyo. In the meantime, please allow me to escort you to the VIP lounge. There you can relax, read, have something to eat and something to drink, and just take it easy until your plane is ready to take off. And don't worry about your suitcase; it'll be transferred for you to the Tokyo plane."

General Gribowski accompanied Nishimura to the VIP lounge. It contained a few elderly armchairs, a rickety table with a tea samovar and three bottles of vodka, and the grim-faced overweight air hostess from his flight from Stockholm.

"Please make yourself comfortable," General Gribowski said. "I'm sure it won't be too long before your flight is ready to depart for Japan."

Nishimura helped himself to a cup of tea and sat in one of the armchairs. It proved to be as uncomfortable as it looked. He glanced at the clock on the wall and saw that it was just after 1 p.m. Moscow time. He adjusted his own watch and then took a book out of his briefcase and started reading.

An hour later nothing had happened. He got up and approached the air hostess. "When is the flight to Tokyo leaving?" he asked politely.

"I do not have that information, Comrade," she replied, "but you will certainly be called when the flight is ready to depart."

Nishimura settled down to read again, trying to find a comfortable spot in the armchair. He was still sitting there just after 5 p.m. when General Gribowski returned, this time wearing the uniform of a general in the NKGB. The interpreter and three soldiers with automatic weapons accompanied him.

"You are under arrest as an enemy agent. Give me your briefcase and come with us."

"Enemy agent? I'm not an enemy agent. There's a Neutrality Pact. Japan and the Soviet Union aren't at war."

"Oh yes, they are. We declared war on Japan an hour ago, at 11 p.m. Trans-Baikal time. It's now a few minutes after midnight there, and we've just invaded Manchuria on three fronts."

"You kept me here for four hours just so that you could arrest me. In fact, that's why you flew me to Moscow, so you could arrest me here."

"Shut up. You are under arrest. You will keep silent."

Two of the soldiers shouldered their weapons. One violently grabbed Nishimura's briefcase out of his hand and gave it to Gribowski. The two soldiers then each took one of Nishimura's arms and marched him out of the terminal building into a waiting black ZIS-101 limousine. General Gribowski climbed in front, next to the driver. Nishimura was bundled into the back of the seven-seater vehicle, with a soldier seated on either side of him. The third soldier and the interpreter sat on the middle seats.

The driver drove them straight into Lubyanka Prison. Guards opened the doors of the car and motioned Nishimura out. General Gribowski led the way to an interrogation room. He put the briefcase on a table, sat down on a chair on one side of the table, and ordered Nishimura to sit opposite him. Two armed guards stood behind Nishimura. The third soldier left the room, closing the door behind them. The interpreter looked inquiringly at the general.

"What is your name?" Gribowski barked.

"Here is my passport. It shows that I am a Japanese citizen. I demand to see the Japanese consul."

Gribowski laughed. "What Japanese consul? We're at war with Japan. Once we declared war, all Japanese envoys with diplomatic immunity were sent back to Japan, and every other Jap was thrown into an internment camp. There's no Japanese consul in the Soviet Union. Now, answer my question. What is your name?"

"Minoru Nishimura."

"No, I mean your real name."

"Minoru Nishimura."

"You traveled from Japan to Stockholm masquerading as Princess Yura. When you arrived in Stockholm you became Minoru Nishimura. What's your real name?"

"As I told you, Minoru Nishimura."

General Gribowski opened the briefcase. There were only two items inside: a book and a three-page report in English.

"Well, well, well, what have we here? A report on the production of atomic weapons in the United

States? How very interesting. Pray tell me, Minoru Nishimura, how did you come to acquire this top-secret document?"

Nishimura was silent.

"Watch him carefully," ordered General Gribowski. He left the room, carrying the report. He went straight to his office and ordered his secretary to get Professor Gordin on the phone.

After a few minutes, a voice said, "Gordin speaking."

"Comrade Professor, it's Gribowski. I've just obtained a secret report that I think will be of the most tremendous assistance to the project that you lead. I need you to do two things for me, if you will."

"I am always at the disposal of the Motherland, Comrade General." The NKGB listeners who routinely monitored all the telephone calls of key Soviet personnel like Professor Gordin noted the patriotic pride in his voice.

"Good. I'm sending a car to bring you to meet with me at the Lubyanka. When you get here, I want you to tell me if the document is genuine, and I need you to try to identify the person who was carrying it. The car will be at your laboratory in about 20 minutes."

"Please tell the driver that I'll be waiting downstairs for him, Comrade General. I look forward to seeing you again."

It was nearly an hour later when a stoop-shouldered, bespectacled middle-aged man with a few remaining strands of gray hair carefully brushed over his otherwise bald head was ushered most respectfully into Gribowski's office. "Yakov, what a pleasure to see you again. Please come in and take a seat. Can I offer you a glass of Georgian brandy? I received this bottle from Comrade Stalin himself— it's the same kind that he always drinks."

"That's very kind of you, Dimitri, but could I please see the document first?"

"Of course, of course, I understand. Here it is."

Professor Gordin scanned the three pages, and then reread the report line by line, occasionally pausing in deep thought. After about ten minutes he asked the general for pencil and paper, and proceeded to perform some calculations. After another 30 minutes he turned to the general.

"I think that this report is genuine. I also believe that this document is one of the most important finds imaginable. And I'd like that glass of that brandy now, please."

"It will be my pleasure. Let's drink to the health of Comrade Stalin and to the Soviet atomic program that you lead."

"Most willingly, Dimitri, most willingly."

After a few minutes of pleasantries, General Gribowski turned to Professor Gordin. "I don't want to interfere with or curtail your enjoyment of the brandy, but I would be most grateful if you could try to identify the man who was carrying the document. I noted that you said that you 'think' that the document is genuine. The identity of the man we arrested may help to strengthen your conclusion."

Professor Gordin drained his glass and wiped his lips meticulously with a snow-white handkerchief that he took from an inside pocket of his suit. Then Gribowski led Gordin from his third floor office to the interrogation room on the first floor.

"Would you please stand here, right in front of this one-way mirror? I'll order the prisoner to face you, and you can tell me who he is."

"As you well know, I'll do my best to identify him, Dimitri."

General Gribowski re-entered the room. "Nishimura, stand up and face that mirror. Now turn round slowly, and keep turning until you are facing the mirror again."

Minoru Nishimura did as he was instructed, then sat down again. General Gribowski left the interrogation room, closing the door carefully behind him.

"Do you recognize that man, Yakov?"

"Yes, I certainly do. It's Dr. Katsu Umenosuke. He's Japan's leading nuclear physicist. I met him before the war at a conference at Oxford University."

"You're quite sure?"

"Yes, I'm certain."

"Yakov, I don't mean to insult you in any way, especially in view of our many years of close friendship and in the light of the fact that you are one of a handful of scientists who have been awarded both the Stalin Prize and the Lenin Prize, but I do have to ask you this: Is it in any way possible that you think that this man is a nuclear physicist because you know that he was carrying a secret report from the American atomic program?"

"Dimitri, the man in there is undoubtedly Dr. Katsu Umenosuke. I would have recognized him no matter what document he was carrying."

"Thank you, Yakov Moisevich. Thank you very much. Would you like my driver to take you back to your laboratory now? It's always good to see you. And please give my warmest regards to Sara Abramovna."

Gribowski returned to the interrogation room.

"Dr. Katsu Umenosuke, I asked you how you obtained this document. And I am waiting for your answer."

The General could see that he had severely shaken Umenosuke by addressing him by his real name. But he could also see that the Japanese nuclear physicist was not prepared to divulge any information. So he decided to frighten Umenosuke by showing him how much he knew about the situation.

"You traveled to Stockholm at the behest of your Emperor; I know that because you were pretending to be his sister. He sent you there to try to arrange a peace agreement short of total surrender; I know that because for months your government has been asking my government for help in achieving precisely that aim. That was what they told you to do, but that wasn't the real aim of your mission; I know that because you're not a diplomat, and yet your Emperor sent you to Stockholm ostensibly to arrange a peace agreement or an armistice, something that has eluded even your finest diplomats.

"The real reason they sent you to Stockholm because the Americans asked your government to send a nuclear physicist to receive the document that I found in your briefcase; I know that because there can be no other reason for your traveling to Sweden. They ordered you to return to Japan with the report you were carrying; I know that because you were on your way home without any sort of peace agreement but with a briefcase containing nothing but a book and a three-page secret document.

"The person who gave you that report must have been an American nuclear physicist sent to Stockholm to give it to you, rather than a spy who stole it from America; I know that because there's no possible way that a spy could have arranged for you to travel from Japan to Sweden; only the American government could have done that. And the person who gave it to you must have been an American nuclear physicist, in case you had any questions about the report.

"So, the person who gave you that report in Sweden was an American nuclear physicist sent there for the specific purpose of handing over to you a copy of a secret document to convince your government to surrender unconditionally. I want to know his name."

Umenosuke stayed silent.

"You have two choices. You can either tell me the name right now, or we will extract the name from you. Either way, we'll find out. It's up to you whether we obtain the name in a friendly and dignified manner or an exceedingly painful one."

Katsu thought quickly. He realized that he had a way out. He would give the false name that zu Westerheimer had assumed. The Soviets could investigate further and discover that Dr. Gottfried von Engelhardt had indeed stayed at the hotel. There had to be some sort of travel trail in and out of Sweden that they could follow. But the important thing was that Gottfried had left the hotel that morning and presumably was on his way back to America. There was no way that the Soviets could kidnap him in Sweden and interrogate him, too. Katsu made up his mind.

"General, you are right on all counts. They instructed me to travel to Sweden ostensibly to negotiate an armistice of some sort, but while I was there Dr. Gottfried von Engelhardt gave me the document you found. Like me, he was staying at the Niedermeyer Hotel. I was in Room 14, he was in Room 9. It is my understanding that this morning he left Sweden for the United States."

"Thank you," the general replied. "We will now investigate further and see if your story can be corroborated. For your sake, I hope it can."

Turning to the guards, General Gribowski gave the order: "Take him to a cell."

Tinian, Northern Mariana Islands
Thursday, August 9th, 1945

At 2:49 a.m., the two B-29 weather planes took off for Japan. One was headed for Kokura, the primary target. The other flew toward Nagasaki, the secondary target.

From the very start, things seemed to go wrong with the attempt to drop the second atomic bomb. It had been scheduled for August 11th. Then the meteorologists predicted that there would be five days of bad weather starting on August 10th, so the date was moved back to August 9th.

An hour after the weather planes left, three more B-29s took off. As before, one ferried the instrumentation for measuring the magnitude of the blast, the second was for the observers and the photographic equipment, and the third plane, *Bockscar*, with Major Charles Sweeney as pilot, carried the atomic bomb. However, this time the weapon, nicknamed "Fat Man," was a plutonium bomb weighing about 10,200 pounds.

The weather planes arrived at their destinations and reported that both targets were clear. Accordingly, Sweeney proceeded to the assembly point for flying on to Kokura. When he arrived there, the instrument plane was where it should have been, but there was no sign of the plane with the observers and the photographic equipment. The other two B-29s circled for 40 minutes. Now half an hour behind schedule, they decided to proceed with the mission on their own.

When they reached Kokura, they found that 70 percent cloud cover obscured the city. In addition, the city was enveloped in heavy ground haze and smoke. Their orders were to make a visual attack, so they made three futile runs over the city, unable to see the target despite their best efforts. Fuel was now running low because a transfer pump on a reserve tank had failed. Sweeney decided to head for their secondary target, Nagasaki, some 700 miles away.

Earlier that day, at about 7:50 a.m., there had been an air raid alert in Nagasaki. The authorities gave the all-clear signal at 8:30 a.m. When only two B-29 Superfortresses were detected at 10:53 a.m., the Japanese assumed that the planes were on a reconnaissance mission, and no further alarm was given.

When the planes reached the city, they found that Nagasaki was also shrouded in cloud. Should they drop the bomb by radar, contrary to orders? Should they return to Tinian, jettisoning the priceless bomb into the depths of the sea for safety? And what were they going to do about the shortage of fuel on *Bockscar?* Landing the plane at Kadena Air Base on Okinawa now seemed to be the only alternative.

At 11:01 a.m., with Sweeney on the point of calling off the mission, a sudden break in the clouds appeared. This enabled the bombardier, Captain Kermit Beahan, to see the target, the industrial area of Nagasaki. He released the bomb.

Forty-three seconds later the bomb exploded near the Mitsubishi-Urakami Ordnance Works, the factory that had manufactured the torpedoes used in the attack on Pearl Harbor that had started the Pacific war. The wheel had turned full circle.

Tokyo
Thursday, August 9th, 1945

It took two days after the destruction of Hiroshima before the Supreme Council met to assess the new situation. At 4 a.m. on August 9th, the Japanese government received the news that the Soviet Union had broken the Neutrality Pact and declared war on Japan; the Soviets immediately followed this proclamation by invading Manchuria.

In the light of the double disaster, the Prime Minister and Foreign Minister both called for an end to the war without delay, but the Army leadership strongly disagreed. They started to prepare for imposing martial law in order to prevent any attempts at peace.

The Supreme Council met at 10:30 a.m. In the middle of their deliberations, they received news of the detonation of the Nagasaki atomic bomb. Even this was insufficient to persuade the three military leaders on the Supreme Council to agree to make peace. Finally, the Emperor insisted that Japan accept the terms of the Potsdam agreement.

Negotiations with the Allies now commenced, culminating in the Japanese government agreeing to the Allied terms of surrender. The decision was received in Washington, D.C., on August 14th at 02:49 a.m.

That night, the militarists attempted the anticipated *coup d'état*. Major Kenji Hatanaka led a group of hundreds of Japanese officers who tried to prevent the surrender. They managed to occupy the Imperial Palace where they spent hours vainly searching for the recording of the speech announcing the surrender of Japan that the Emperor had made for broadcasting to the Japanese public the next day. Fearing a possible military takeover, the Emperor's staff had hidden the phonograph recording in a pile of documents; the next day a loyal servant smuggled it out of the palace concealed in a laundry basket of women's underwear and took it to the radio station.

The plotters finally abandoned their coup attempt under orders from Army Headquarters. Hatanaka then shot himself an hour before the broadcast of the Emperor's recorded speech, which went out, on schedule, at noon on August 15th.

Many of the listeners in the streets had difficulty understanding what the Emperor was saying because the phonograph recording was of low quality. Also, the Emperor spoke in an archaic court Japanese that was unfamiliar to almost all of his listeners. Finally, the noise of gunshots interrupted the sound of the Emperor's voice as military officers committed suicide listening to their Emperor. To ensure that all listeners fully understood the Emperor's message, at the end of his speech a radio announcer stated categorically that the message indeed meant that Japan had surrendered.

Steve Schach

NKGB Headquarters, Moscow
Thursday, August 30th, 1945

"So, Major Pleshkov, what have you found out about this Dr. Gottfried von Engelhardt?" General Gribowski asked. The General sat at the head of the table in a conference room in the Lubyanka Building. The afternoon sun slanted in through the three windows. There were four uniformed NKGB officers ranged on each side of him.

"Comrade General, he arrived in Stockholm on the afternoon of August 3rd, and left on the morning of August 8th, the same time that Dr. Katsu Umenosuke left. Like Dr. Umenosuke, he stayed at the Niedermeyer Hotel. He arrived in Stockholm by train, but we haven't been able to find out from where—he doesn't seem to have bought a ticket. He left Stockholm by air for Croydon Airport in London. When he got off the plane, a car was there waiting for him. After that, he seems to have disappeared."

"So, Pleshkov," General Gribowski responded, "von Engelhardt arrives in Stockholm by train from nowhere. And he disappears when he arrives in London. What does that tell you?"

Major Pleshkov was silent.

"Let me ask you something else. Dr. Umenosuke told us that von Engelhardt is an American physicist. Where did he get his doctorate? Who was his doctoral advisor? Who are his doctoral students? What research papers has he published and in which journals?"

344

Pleshkov stayed silent, then blurted out, "Comrade General, von Engelhardt speaks English with a pronounced German accent. I assume that he was educated in Germany. As we all know, it's impossible to get any information out of Germany at the moment—the country is in chaos, records have been destroyed. All I can tell you is that Dr. von Engelhardt is a nuclear physicist born and educated in Germany, and I assume that he's now working in America and—"

"Pleshkov, I've had enough of your assumptions. Here in the NKGB we deal with facts. Have you spoken with our Soviet nuclear physicists and, if so, can they tell us anything about von Engelhardt? We've arrested dozens of German scientists—have you tried to ask them? And what about our Soviet agents in America? Have you asked any of them to try to find information on von Engelhardt?"

Again there was no response.

"Pleshkov, there's a village called Meynypilgyno in the Chukotka Autonomous Region in the northeast corner of Siberia. The population is about 500, most of them indigenous, mainly Maritime Chukchis but also a few Koryaks, Yukaghirs, and Siberian Yupiks. I'm transferring you to Meynypilgyno with immediate effect. As of now, you are the head of the about-to-be-established NKGB Bureau in Meynypilgyno. Crime is almost unknown there. Which is good, because your crime-solving ability is zero. The village is on the shores of the Bering Sea, so I'm sure you're going to take up fishing in the almost unlimited free time your new position will afford you. Now get out!"

Gribowski looked around the table. "Lieutenant Lutikov, would you like to be appointed Major Pleshkov's assistant in Meynypilgyno? No? Then I hope that you have some better answers than he had. What, if anything, have you found out about Dr. von Engelhardt?"

"Comrade General, like Major Pleshkov, I found out quite quickly that von Engelhardt arrived by train from parts unknown, stayed in Stockholm, flew to London, and disappeared. I spent two days trying to obtain information about him, but I couldn't find any trace of a nuclear physicist by that name. It therefore seemed likely that the name 'von Engelhardt' is a pseudonym, a *nom de guerre* if you wish. So I went to Stockholm by train and tried to obtain as many descriptions of von Engelhardt as I possibly could. Then I put together a facial composite picture of Dr. von Engelhardt and showed it to Professor Gordin and those members of his staff who have traveled abroad. I obtained three positive identifications. They all said that the picture looked exactly like Dr. Ulrich zu Westerheimer and—"

"What did you say? Did you say Dr. Ulrich zu Westerheimer?"

"Yes, Comrade General. Is something wrong?" In the light of what had just happened to Major Pleshkov, Lieutenant Lutikov was understandably concerned that he, too, might have angered General Gribowski.

"Maybe. Maybe not. Go and get Dr. Katsu Umenosuke and bring him here, together with someone who can translate from English into Russian."

About five minutes later two warders escorted Katsu into the conference room and took him round the table to sit in the chair that Major Pleshkov had recently vacated. The interpreter stood behind the nuclear physicist.

"Gentlemen, this is Dr. Katsu Umenosuke," General Gribowski said. "You all know who he is. I have some questions to ask him. The interpreter will translate for us.

"Dr. Umenosuke, I believe that you have been treated well. In particular, we have given you access to English language newspapers. We have no quarrel with you now—the war is over. So I would be most appreciative if you would assist us in our deliberations."

Katsu thought for a moment, then nodded.

"Dr. Umenosuke, when we last met, why didn't you tell me that the person you met in Stockholm was actually Dr. Ulrich zu Westerheimer?"

There was a short pause as Umenosuke collected his thoughts. Then he started speaking softly, but enunciating every word clearly.

"At that time there was no reason for me to cooperate with you—we were at war. You asked for his name, and I gave it to you. Furthermore, your staff could easily verify that the person was Dr. Gottfried von Engelhardt. There was no way you could verify the name Ulrich zu Westerheimer."

"I understand. Do you think that the report he gave you is genuine?"

"I do. I've analyzed the figures. I'm not familiar with all the items included in the report—only a top American nuclear physicist could possibly have a sufficiently comprehensive knowledge of all the many processes mentioned in the document—but the pieces within my range of expertise all checked out correctly.

"Moving from science to politics," Umenosuke continued, "I doubt that the Americans would have taken the risk of handing over a fictional document. They desperately wanted to avoid having to invade the Home Islands, because American casualties would have been frightful. Also, there are some Americans who were truly concerned about millions of innocent men, women and children losing their lives senselessly, irrespective of nationality. They, too, wanted Japan to surrender unconditionally. And they, too, would never have taken a chance with a falsified report."

"In retrospect, do you think that if you'd been able to deliver the document it would have made any difference?"

"I'd sent my government an encrypted telegram describing the contents of the report. The only reason they called me back to Tokyo was so that others, more qualified than I am in certain areas, could see the actual report and check those aspects of its authenticity. My personal belief is that everyone already knew that the document was genuine, but no one was prepared to act on it. It took the detonation of the second atomic bomb to bring sanity to the government. The report was essentially irrelevant."

"I see. Thank you for being so cooperative. The war is over. You're free to return to Japan. My staff will assist you in organizing travel arrangements."

As a bewildered Katsu Umenosuke left the room, General Gribowski turned to Lieutenant Lutikov.

"Please give General Fomarenko my compliments, and ask him how soon we can meet in my office. I'm on my way there now."

And General Gribowski marched out of the conference room and returned to his office where he greeted his friend and colleague when he arrived a few minutes later.

"Vladimir! Thank you for coming to see me so promptly this late in the afternoon. I know how busy you are dealing with the current situation in Germany."

"My dear Dimitri, that keen young Lieutenant made it perfectly clear, without saying a single word or making the slightest facial gesture, that you needed my undoubted brilliance to solve your current problem. How could I not rush over to your office at once?"

Both men laughed heartily. Gribowski fetched two glasses and the bottle of Georgian brandy and poured a generous amount into each glass.

"Is that still the same bottle that the General Secretary personally gave you more than three years ago?"

"Of course! Like all things Georgian, it improves with time and lasts forever."

Again the old friends laughed, secure in the knowledge that there were no bugs in the room.

"Now, Dimitri, tell me your problem."

"I don't believe in coincidences and I know that you don't believe in coincidences."

"Correct."

"Two years ago, a German-American nuclear physicist named Ulrich zu Westerheimer came to the Soviet Union on a mission to send a copy of the Chadwick report to Adolf Hitler. The Americans had hidden it in the lining of a briefcase."

"I remember. The report ended up in our hands, not the Nazis."

"Quite right. And there was no doubt at all that the secret report was genuine."

"I agree."

"And the experts have assured us that the Chadwick paper is most important and extremely useful to us."

"Yes."

"Well," General Dimitri Gribowski said, "about three weeks ago, the Americans sent the same man to Stockholm to deliver a secret report to a Japanese nuclear physicist. Again the report appears to be genuine, again the document appears to be most important and extremely useful to us, and again the report has ended up in our hands, not the enemy's."

"Are you suggesting that the Americans are deliberately feeding most important and extremely useful genuine reports to us?"

"I'm not suggesting anything. I'm simply mystified."

"Could the Americans have constructed this new document to mislead us?"

"Our experts say no. Just about everyone who has seen it is certain that the document is genuine in all respects. What I found particularly convincing was the wide variety of different reasons that they gave to support their opinions."

"Are you prepared to put all these similarities down to coincidence?"

"We agreed up front that neither of us believes in coincidences."

"Yes, we did, didn't we?"

"Let's assume that General Comptine is behind all this. What would that tell us?"

"He's no friend of the Soviet Union, that's for sure."

"I fully agree. So why is he sending us documents that are so important and so useful?"

"I've no idea. No idea at all."

"More brandy?"

"I'd love some more. Thank you!"

The two men sipped their drinks in companionable silence. Suddenly General Fomarenko shouted, "Dimitri, I've got it!"

"So tell me."

"The solution came to me because I was drinking this wonderful brandy. Like all things Georgian, it's all wise and all knowing."

"What did the brandy tell you, Vladimir?" General Gribowski groaned as he clenched his teeth in frustration.

"It's not coincidence. It's our brilliance."

"What?"

"The answer," General Fomarenko said, "is that we've outsmarted Comptine twice. The first time we weren't supposed to find the Chadwick report in the lining of the briefcase. But you had the bright idea of switching briefcases, and we found the report. That wasn't Comptine sending a document to us, that was you using your brains to find the document.

"Now look at this latest incident with the Japanese nuclear physicist," Vladimir Fomarenko continued. "Suppose that we'd declared war on Japan three days later. The document would then have traveled the full length of the Soviet Union and on to Tokyo in Dr. Umenosuke's briefcase without our knowing a thing about it. And if we'd declared war one day earlier, we'd never have allowed Dr. Umenosuke to fly from Stockholm to the Soviet Union—as an enemy alien, he'd have had to find some other way to get back to Japan. It was only because the Soviet Union declared war within that specific four-day time interval that we were able to acquire the document. In other words, it was the genius of Comrade Stalin, our revered General Secretary, in choosing precisely the correct period of time in which to declare war on Japan that resulted in our laying our hands on that document."

"You're saying that Comptine isn't sending the finest quality material to us in briefcases—we're just serendipitously laying our hands on it," General Gribowski suggested.

"That's not exactly what I'm saying. In the case of the first briefcase, it wasn't luck or good fortune that led to us finding the Chadwick report, it was your cleverness. There's no way Comptine could've imagined that we'd switch briefcases after we'd sealed the first one as he asked. And in the case of the second briefcase, there's one thing I know for certain. There's absolutely no way on earth that General Comptine or anyone else could possibly have known that far ahead the exact day on which the Secretary General would repudiate the Neutrality Pact and declare war on Japan. No, my old friend, Comptine isn't sending us anything—we're taking it."

"Yes, I think you're quite right. It's the only way to explain the facts. More brandy?" Dmitri Gribowski offered.

"Of course."

"I'm so glad that I sent that keen young Lieutenant to tap your undoubted brilliance."

"If you're going to be sarcastic, I'm not going to help you in the future. And we both know you can't possibly do your job without my continual assistance."

And the two comrades laughed heartily again.

Los Alamos, New Mexico
Thursday, September 6th, 1945

"How's Ulrich zu Westerheimer doing?" General Groves asked General Comptine.

"I saw him two days ago, and he's happy as a clam at high tide. He seems to have fully recovered from his understandable tiredness after traveling halfway round the world and back at breakneck speed. Thank heavens he did what I firmly ordered him to do and fled Sweden before Dr. Umenosuke could tell the Russians about him. By the way, Dr. zu Westerheimer still thinks that we sent him to Stockholm to deliver that report to the Japanese—I've no intention of telling him what really happened, of course."

"When are you going to tell him that his brother died under Gestapo torture soon after Hitler ordered him to be sent to Berlin?"

"I don't know," General Comptine said. "I was careful to say nothing to him before his trip, for obvious reasons. But he's going to have to be told the truth some time. I just hope he'll never find out that, pretty soon after the fall of Berlin, we learned what happened to Carl Friedrich."

"Agreed. By the way, I meant to ask you: How did you know that the Soviet Union would declare war on Japan on August 9th?"

"Well, I had two bites of the cherry," General Comptine admitted. "The first was that, at both the Teheran Conference in November 1943 and the Yalta Conference in February 1945, the Soviet

Union promised to declare war on Japan within three months of the end of the European War. August 9th was exactly three months after the German surrender, which took place on May 9th at 43 minutes after midnight, Moscow time."

"And the second bite of the cherry?" General Groves asked.

"At the Potsdam conference last month, President Truman briefed Uncle Joe Stalin about the atomic bomb. Observers reported afterwards that it was obvious from his manner that Stalin not only knew all about the bomb, but that he wanted us to know that he knew. In practical terms what that means is that there's at least one Soviet agent here at Los Alamos, probably a whole spy ring. I'll come back to that a little later.

"Returning to your question about my second bite of the cherry, ever since we defeated Germany, Stalin has known that we were going to drop atomic weapons on Japan. He readied his troops on the border of Manchuria, or Manchukuo as the Japanese referred to their puppet state there, and he waited for us to drop the first bomb, knowing full well that that would have the effect of paralyzing the Japanese high command. And so it was. After that it took Marshal Vasilevsky only a week to crush the Kwantung Army of over a million men and conquer an area the size of Western Europe. I knew when we were going to drop the bomb, and that told me when Stalin would declare war."

"So your purpose in sending zu Westerheimer to Stockholm was to get the falsified report to the Soviets, not the Japanese?"

"Precisely," General Comptine said. "There was no way whatsoever to persuade the Japs to surrender without our dropping the two atomic bombs. And even after we'd done that, it was still up to the Japanese themselves—there was nothing anyone outside of Japan could possibly have done to persuade them to agree to unconditional surrender, the only option that the Allies offered. For the past five years we've been reading every important message sent between Tokyo and Japanese embassies all over the world. The Japanese sent them in encrypted form using their cipher machines that we call Purple, the one that their Foreign Office used for all high-level diplomatic messages. We cracked the Purple Code a year before the attack on Pearl Harbor on December 7th, 1941, so we've known all along exactly what the Japs were considering in the way of peace proposals, including the fact that they were not prepared to consider unconditional surrender under any circumstances. So, there was no way that sending zu Westerheimer or anyone else to Stockholm or anywhere else in the world could have made the slightest difference to the outcome of the war against Japan. What changed their minds was our dropping those two atomic bombs—earlier discussions with the Japanese were nothing but a big waste of everyone's time.

"So, instead of trying to engage in diplomacy with the Japs, my actual concern was to make the

Russkies believe that we had enough nuclear weapons to deter any military action on their part after the Japanese had surrendered. And we were keen to dissuade the Soviets from trying anything in Germany. I knew the date on which we were scheduled to drop the first bomb, and I sent zu Westerheimer to Stockholm at that time. The idea was that he'd pass that altered report on to Katsu Umenosuke who would have to take it to Japan via the Soviet Union. If I had the timetable right, the Soviets would arrest him as an enemy alien and find the report. Which is precisely what happened."

General Groves smiled. "And the brilliance of your plan is that if one of the Red spies here at Los Alamos had sent the falsified document to Moscow, there's no question that the Soviet leadership would've treated it with the gravest suspicion and probably viewed it as a forgery. But because the Russkies confiscated the report from a Japanese nuclear scientist who was in transit through the Soviet Union, it fell into their hands with unimpeachable provenance. Highly satisfactory!"

AFTERWORD

Highly Satisfactory is fiction embedded within historical fact. For example, Operation KANGAROO is my fictional plan for invading Austria, but I have presented it in Chapter Four within the context of Operation FORTITUDE, the actual plan the Allies carried out to deceive Hitler into believing that the June 1944 landings of the invasion of Europe would not take place in Normandy, but rather in Pas-de-Calais and Norway. That is to say, I have built fiction inside a factual framework, which is the best form of deception.

The scientific explanations I have presented in this book, including the workings of the *Knickebein* beam and the atomic bomb, are factual, as are the historical-scientific documents such as the Einstein–Szilárd letter and the Frisch–Peierls memorandum. Also, in late 1942, Dr. James Chadwick had indeed concluded that impurities in plutonium might cause pre-detonation, and that plutonium might therefore be unsuitable for nuclear weapons.

The characters in this book are all figments of my imagination, including Helga Ziegler, Johnson and Carlyle, "D," Otto Trumbauer, Sir Percival, the zu Westerheimer brothers, Dr. Katsu Umenosuke, Captain Reginald Wallstead, Major Georg Strauss, Colonels Siegfried Kupfer and Warren Foxglove, Air Commodore Archibald Pankhurst, and Generals Silas Comptine, Vladimir Fomarenko and Dmitri Gribowski. Where I have given characters the names of historical figures, such as Adolf Hitler and Dwight D. Eisenhower, the statements attributed to them are all fictional.

Meynypilgyno is an actual village, situated in the Anadyrsky District of the Chukotka Autonomous Region in Russia. However, it was founded in 1957, well after the end of the Second World War.

The idea of writing this book came to me as a result of my reading *The Deceivers: Allied Military Deception in the Second World War* by Thaddeus Holt (Scribner, 2004). Holt's book, which is more than 1,100 pages in length, is encyclopedic. For example, in his appendices he lists all the Allied deceptive operations, the agents and sources the Allies used, and even the numerous fictional fighting units that the Allied deceivers created.

In the prologue of his book, Holt describes General Edmund Allenby's many acts of deception in his campaign to capture Beersheba in 1917. I decided not to mention Richard Meinertzhagen's role in the famous Haversack Ruse in Chapter Three of *Highly Satisfactory*, notwithstanding what Holt wrote (or the 1987 Australian movie *The Lighthorsemen*), because newer research seems to indicate that it may not have been Meinertzhagen who planned the deception, let alone who carried it out.

R. V. Jones's extensive autobiography, *Most Secret War: British Scientific Intelligence 1939–1945* (Coronet Books, 1979) is a mine of first-hand information on the countermeasures the British took in response to the *Knickebein* beams. A useful source on *Abwehr* and MI5 activities during World War II is *The Game of the Foxes: British and German Intelligence Operations and Personalities Which Changed the Course of the Second World War* by Ladislas Farago (Pan Books, 1971). Both Farago and Holt describe the many spectacular successes of MI5's Double Cross System.

ACKNOWLEDGEMENTS

I would like to thank Howard Aksen, Rosalind Fischl OAM, John Gallo, Johan Koeslag, and Jane Wolfers for their careful reading of the manuscript and for their helpful suggestions. I greatly appreciate the time and the trouble they have taken.

For the third time, it has been a real pleasure to work with my publisher, Jennifer Chesak, of Wandering in the Words Press. As before, it was most instructive to interact with an editor with her skills. And for third time, she has designed a striking cover.

Finally, I would like to thank my wife Sharon for her invaluable ideas and support throughout the writing of this book. We co-authored *Coopers Island*; I look forward to our writing our next thriller once again as a team.

www.ingramcontent.com/pod-product-compliance
Lightning Source LLC
Chambersburg PA
CBHW061313170626
46817CB00001B/165